W9-AHC-201

**Praise for Hannah March's
Robert Fairfax mysteries**

"[March] is adept at delineating characters with just a few telling phrases. . . . A well-paced, exciting book."
—The Charlotte Austin Review

"A gloriously rich tale of London at its grandest and seamiest, well told, at a cracking pace."
—The *Evening Chronicle* (Newcastle upon Tyne)

"A clever and accomplished first novel . . . witty and convincing; for fans of period dramas such as *Moll Flanders* and *Tom Jones*, this will slip down like a cup of sherbet."
—*Scotland on Sunday*

"Well written with a great deal of self-assurance. I liked the period detail and the characterizations of the large cast of suspects."
—Deryn Lake, *Shots*

Also by Hannah March

The Complaint of the Dove

The Devil's Highway

A MYSTERY OF GEORGIAN ENGLAND

Hannah March

Ⓢ
A SIGNET BOOK

SIGNET
Published by New American Library, a division of
Penguin Group (USA) Inc., 375 Hudson Street,
New York, New York 10014, U.S.A.
Penguin Books Ltd, 80 Strand,
London WC2R 0RL, England
Penguin Books Australia Ltd, 250 Camberwell Road,
Camberwell, Victoria 3124, Australia
Penguin Books Canada Ltd, 10 Alcorn Avenue,
Toronto, Ontario, Canada M4V 3B2
Penguin Books (N.Z.) Ltd, Cnr Rosedale and Airborne Roads,
Albany, Auckland 1310, New Zealand

Penguin Books Ltd, Registered Offices:
80 Strand, London WC2R 0RL, England

Published by Signet, an imprint of New American Library, a division of Penguin Group (USA) Inc. Originally published in Great Britain by Headline Book Publishing.

First Signet Printing, November 2003
10 9 8 7 6 5 4 3 2 1

Copyright © Hannah March, 1999
Excerpt from *A Distinction of Blood* copyright © Hannah March, 2000
All rights reserved

  REGISTERED TRADEMARK—MARCA REGISTRADA

Printed in the United States of America

Without limiting the rights under copyright reserved above, no part of this publication may be reproduced, stored in or introduced into a retrieval system, or transmitted, in any form, or by any means (electronic, mechanical, photocopying, recording, or otherwise), without the prior written permission of both the copyright owner and the above publisher of this book.

PUBLISHER'S NOTE
This is a work of fiction. Names, characters, places, and incidents either are the product of the author's imagination or are used fictitiously, and any resemblance to actual persons, living or dead, business establishments, events, or locales is entirely coincidental.

BOOKS ARE AVAILABLE AT QUANTITY DISCOUNTS WHEN USED TO PROMOTE PRODUCTS OR SERVICES. FOR INFORMATION PLEASE WRITE TO PREMIUM MARKETING DIVISION, PENGUIN GROUP (USA) INC., 375 HUDSON STREET, NEW YORK, NEW YORK 10014.

If you purchased this book without a cover you should be aware that this book is stolen property. It was reported as "unsold and destroyed" to the publisher and neither the author nor the publisher has received any payment for this "stripped book."

The scanning, uploading, and distribution of this book via the internet or via any other means without the permission of the publisher is illegal and punishable by law. Please purchase only authorized electronic editions, and do not participate in or encourage electronic piracy of copyrighted materials. Your support of the author's rights is appreciated.

For Bill and Angela

One

The body of the man was suspended some twenty feet in the air. It swung with a slight pendulum motion in the east wind that came tumbling across the bare black fields, here on the lonely reaches of the Great North Road.

The clothes in which he had been hanged, and then brought here to be gibbeted, still clung to him in strips and tatters. Indeed, they had lasted better than he. As the carriage rattled past, Robert Fairfax gazed from the window and saw a crow alight on the crossbar of the gibbet; but the bird was only spying out the land. It did not bother with the corpse dangling below it. Meager pickings, now.

Hard to believe, Fairfax thought, that this blackened horror had ever been a human being—a man who had been nursed by a mother, had known the pleasure of food and drink and fire, had had his loves and fears and hopes. And yet . . . and yet in the way the body lazily twisted in its iron bands as the carriage trundled below it, Fairfax could almost fancy a kind of greeting; a ghastly good day to the passing travelers from a fellow who was going nowhere.

Sir Edward Nugent, who had been half dozing in the opposite seat of the post chaise, roused himself and looked out.

"Hm. Been there since the Lent assizes, I fancy." He grunted and settled himself again. "Supposed to set an example, though I misdoubt it does."

"A highway robber?" Fairfax watched the grim shape re-

cede into the distance. The gibbet post was set about with
iron spikes to prevent the criminal's relatives from climbing
up to retrieve the body for a decent burial. Against the
lemon-white October sky they gave the gibbet the look of
some bristling nightmare tree.

"Likely enough in these parts. Don't be sentimental, Fairfax. There's one such rogue who's been plaguing the roads
about my country since late last year, and I'd gladly see him
swinging. The highway between Huntingdon and Stamford
is his favorite hunting ground. A dozen robberies to my
knowledge; some quiet folk are too feared to stir abroad. A
good friend of mine was held up by the knave at pistol point
in broad daylight. One doughty old fellow, a farmer in his
cart, refused to pay up and was used very roughly. 'Twas
after that the justices put a hundred-pound price on the fellow's head. One hundred pounds' reward for the apprehension, or information leading to it. Usually these villains are
known to other reprobates, at least. But this fellow has the
devil's own elusiveness. Plies his damnable trade alone, and
disappears into the wilds leaving nary a clue."

"Has he killed?" Fairfax asked.

"Not yet. But what's to prevent him? Highway robbery's
a hanging offense, and he knows he'll dangle, blood or no.
That's why I want the fellow caught."

"Between Huntingdon and Stamford . . . Isn't that the
road that lies ahead of us?"

Sir Edward gave a deep bay of laughter. "Of course. Best
hide your pocket watch in your boot, Fairfax, and say your
prayers. Nay, nay, I warrant we'll get to Cheyney Hall safe
and sound. I was born with a caul, you know; I'm generally
lucky."

Well, I am lucky too, Fairfax thought—lately at least.
The profession of private tutoring, which he had never intended for himself, had turned out moderately well. Having
to extricate his first young gentleman pupil from a charge of
murder, as he had had to do last year, was not a part of the
job he had bargained for, but somehow he had crowned that

with success, and won golden opinions from his pupil's father. The trouble with tutoring young gentlemen—bear-leading, as it was disrespectfully called—was that they very soon reached an age when the bear-leader was no longer required, and they could be turned loose. And so it had happened this summer. Robert Fairfax, with no home, family, or fortune of his own, had shaken hands with his pupil for the last time, and turned to face the unfriendly world again.

But he did have a warm recommendation from his former employer—and a wealthy family was prepared to engage him as tutor for their two young boys on the strength of it. They were set to return to their Surrey seat from Ireland at the end of the summer. Relief turned to dismay. The return was postponed until Christmas, perhaps the new year, depending on the weather for the sea crossing. The family was in the process of marrying off an elder daughter to an Irish peer with estates all over Kerry and Cork—maybe there *were* Kerry and Cork—and such important business naturally had the first claim. Fairfax must shift for himself until then—which was easier said than done.

Into the choppy sea of his perplexity swam the figure of Sir Edward Nugent, baronet, of Cheyney Hall, Northamptonshire.

Sir Edward had no dull sons in need of polishing. He was a widower with two daughters. But he had heard of Fairfax's scholarly accomplishments, and sought him out because of them. (Which put Fairfax to the blush a little, thinking of his years as a Grub Street hack, often translating dirty French and Italian books into dirty English ones.) Sir Edward wanted someone to catalogue and put in order a vast and eclectic collection that he had inherited from his recently deceased father—several thousand volumes, as well as maps, prints, coins, curios, papers, and correspondence. The someone would receive a secretary's salary and live with the family while the task was in progress. An accessible antiquarian, a biddable bookworm, was needed.

And so, it seemed Fairfax's luck had held after all! A

short interview with the baronet at his London apartments—
Sir Edward was in town for a few weeks on legal business—
and the bargain was struck. Fairfax, who had been living in
an attic lodging by St. Paul's in hopes of picking up some
hack work from the booksellers thereabout, paid his last
week's rent with his last shillings, packed his life-containing
trunk, and joined Sir Edward at the Bull in Bishopsgate
Street. They were to travel in easy stages by hired post
chaise, up the Great North Road to Stamford; Cheyney Hall
lay within a few miles of that elegant market town. They had
broken the journey overnight at Royston, and now were
bowling along in good time in the windy autumn morning,
brittle torrents of leaves swirling and racing about their red-
rimmed wheels, and hoping to reach their destination before
dinner.

"Ah, it'll be sweet to see my little chicks again," Sir Edward said. "Not so little now, mind—I fear I'll find them
grown again after a mere month. Letitia is just turned seventeen, Amelia fifteen. Aye me, they'll be taking wing all
too soon. They've plagued me, in every letter, to be allowed
to go to the Assembly in Stamford this week. 'Tis a genteel
occasion, right enough, and I daresay fitting for their first
out. But I see it as—well, the stage from which there is no
turning back." He shrugged ruefully. "A fond father's folly.
Well, they are excellent girls, pretty as paint, and with good
heads on their shoulders. I don't believe in women being
brought up to nothing but ignorance and coquetry."

Fairfax was finding the baronet an interesting mixture.
Sir Edward was vigorous and straightforward and thoroughly conventional in many of his ways—yet he was no
boor. His ruddy English face, with strong nose and pugna-
cious jaw, was enlivened by gray, intelligent, faintly melancholy eyes.

"The young ladies have had instruction?"

"Aye, they've been well taught—they have French and
music and so forth; and then they have instructed themselves—what with their grandfather's library, and his in-

quiring spirit too. They were sore grieved when he died—always lived at Cheyney with him, you see. As did I, from the day I was wed. By the time he died, my father was elderly, and wrapped up in his books, and I was pretty much the master in all but name. A common enough arrangement in the old families. And, of course, I was sore grieved too . . . but I think you are sufficiently a man of the world, Fairfax, to understand that I was also a mite relieved. I was proud to be old Sir Jemmy's son—but not that alone, forever. At two-and-forty, the title 'young master' doesn't sit too well on your shoulders, you know; to be plain, it itches like a drover's blanket. Mind, I've no thought of breaking up my father's collection, nor selling any part. 'Tis only that I'm no scholar, and don't know my way about it—nor did anyone but he, in truth. We used to say he lived in it like a badger in his sett, and not even the housekeeper dared disturb the diggings."

"I hope I shall do justice to it," Fairfax said, very humble—and fascinated. He had actually had dreams of being let loose in such a library, and woken full of disappointed longing. God's life, he thought, what does *that* say about me . . . ? "And the Assembly, Sir Edward—shall you relent?"

"Ha! They know full well I will, little minxes," Sir Edward said with a smile of great tenderness. "Ah, excellent, we're coming to Huntingdon. I've the devil's own thirst, and my guts are yawning. We'll get good victualing at the Bridge. Then fresh horses, and on"—he slapped his great knee—"to home and hearth. God saving, of course, that we don't find ourselves staring into a highwayman's pistols at the foot of Alconbury Hill." He gave his great trumpeting laugh again.

Fairfax laughed too; then wondered why he should think of the old proverb, He laughs ill who laughs himself to death . . .

                    *   *   *

The yard of the Bridge at Huntingdon was as busy as befitted a coaching house on the Great North Road: sleek horses being led out to exercise from the stables; lathered horses being taken from the shafts of post chaises; farmers chewing the fat and doing a little business over the backboards of their carts; grooms and postboys hurrying across the cobbles with clomping boots on their feet, leather tackle festooned about their necks, and loud horsy argon on their lips. "Wisp her over, Sam—gently, she's a miller." "This drag's took a scrape—that lame hand over there feather-edged it on the bridge." "Sharp on the ribbons, that's why."

Then, more comprehensible, the innkeeper welcoming Sir Edward and adding, as he wiped his hands on his apron, "You drove up from the South road, sir?"

"Aye, Royston was our last stage. Why?"

"Oh, I was wondering, if you'd come from the north, whether you'd seen aught of the *Stamford Flyer* on the way. The public coach, you know, sir, and regular as a coach may be; we expected it here twenty minutes ago."

"The *Flyer*, eh? Usually keeps good time," Sir Edward said, surprised. "Mind, we found some heavy going in the hollows this morning, even driving post."

"Aye, just what I thought, sir—this late rain—it must be the state of the road." The innkeeper glanced with a frown at the inn-yard gate. "Not like the *Flyer*, though . . . Well, sirs, how can I serve you?"

Sir Edward bespoke a private eating room, ordering wine, veal and ham pie, and beef patties.

"It will stay our stomachs till dinner," he said, clapping his hands with relish. "I keep a good table at Cheyney, Fairfax, and you must take advantage of it—you're as thin as a rasher of wind."

A man of erratic appetite, Fairfax wondered how he would keep up. He felt like a frail-stemmed glass beside the sturdy Toby jug of Sir Edward.

Crossing the yard, they passed a man holding a saddle horse by the bridle, and talking to a groom.

"She seems to favor that foot—something amiss with the shoeing, perhaps," the man was saying tentatively.

Sir Edward, who Fairfax already knew was a passionate expert on the subject of horseflesh, turned at once and deftly lifted the horse's foot onto his knee, examining the shoe with keen eyes. "By your leave . . . Why , man, it's the most mob-handed shoeing I ever saw in my life! The nails are half out, don't you see?"

"I had not observed it." The man was plainly, soberly dressed, the broadcloth coat and worsted stockings suggesting a small tradesman or farmer: spare, square-shouldered, a little gaunt, he wore his own grizzled hair tied severely back and had the most intensely blue and penetrating eyes Fairfax had ever seen.

"I don't know how you could miss it," Sir Edward said in his bluff way, releasing the horse's foot. "But you'd do best to change your blacksmith, for whoever did this isn't worth his hire."

The baronet was plainly a man accustomed to a certain deference. Just as plainly, the stranger was a man who did not readily give it.

"I seldom visit the same smith twice," he said. "I am about the country a good deal, traveling on the Lord's business. The shoeing of my horse is a small matter."

"Not to the horse it ain't." Sir Edward gave the man a thorough look. "What, you're a parson, sir, are you?"

"I have not been ordained," the man said in the same pale, informative, unaccommodating tone. "I have been called by my God to carry the bread of His Word to those famished for it, wherever they may be."

Sir Edward's great head went up—very like a shying horse, Fairfax thought. "A Methody." The baronet's tone said everything, and he was about to stump past into the inn when the man spoke again.

"I find no disgrace in the term, sir."

"Oh, plainly, my good fellow, plainly. Come, Fairfax,"

Sir Edward said, shaking his head and chuckling, "else we'll be preached to death before we get our victuals."

Fairfax followed, feeling—as his employer did not seem to feel—the uncompromising stare of the homespun man following them into the inn.

"You do not approve of Mr. Wesley and his works?" Fairfax said, as a cloth was laid for them in a snug paneled supper room with low beams and a sulky fire.

"I do not. And neither can any rational, sensible man who wishes to preserve the property, integrity, and peace of the country." Sir Edward took a deep draft of his pint of wine. "What is this Methodism, after all? A set of wild preachers, constituted as such only by the say-so of fanatics and not by any established church, roaming among the poor and the impressionable and turning their wits with raving enthusiasm, till they think in their absurd pride they are the first and only creatures ever to be Christian. 'Tis a very ill meddling, sir, very ill."

"Yet Mr. Wesley is quite a Tory, they say—enjoins strict submission to the social order, humility, industry. The things of the next world concern him, not this . . . And often his people are bringing religion to places, in remote spots and mines and seaports, where there simply are no churches."

Sir Edward studied Fairfax with a shrewd look. "Ho, now *you* are trying to convert me."

"Not at all," Fairfax said, smiling. "I count myself upon the rational side. And much of Methodism repels me, as overheated superstition and emotionalism . . . Yet there must be some need for it. The poorer people, especially, seem to thirst for what it offers."

"There you have it precisely—the essential germ of danger and sedition in it. For what is it planting in these folks' minds? The notion that the Church has failed them. Duly established society—parish and parson—has nothing for them. So they reject them. What next? Landlord, government, king? I wonder. I say, Fairfax, stand the door ajar, will you? This fire's smoking like the devil's dunghill."

As Fairfax did so, in the common dining room beyond he noticed the Methodist preacher sitting down at a plain board close by, and quietly asking for bread and cheese.

"By the by, Fairfax," Sir Edward said, refilling his glass, "I can't swear to this, but I fancy there may be some rather broad material among my father's collections. He really did take all knowledge for his province, as Bacon has it, and there may well be engravings or volumes of a rather, hum, pagan character. I thought I'd mention it, while we're on the subject of morality . . . Ah, here comes our provender. Leave the door, man, this fire's smeeching. Not that I see you as a prig, Fairfax, in the least. After all, weren't you telling me your mother was a Frenchwoman?" Sir Edward chuckled.

"She was indeed. And the very fact was sufficient to make people think her like to be immoral, when she first came to England. After all, to anything dubious or indecent we tag on the word *French*—yet in France they do the same with us. You have doubtless heard of the 'English vice,' and of *copotes anglaises . . .*"

Sir Edward was rumbling with laughter as he ate. "So, sin is always what the other fellow is up to, eh?"

At the word *sin* Fairfax saw the preacher in the next room lift his head from his frugal meal like a dog alerted by its name.

"Well," Fairfax said, "some would say sin is absolute."

"Both—such as yon fellow with the half-lame horse, you mean? Oh, but 'tis a ranting tinker's faith they preach, and a damned intrusive one, poking into the privacy of men's souls. The state of my soul is a matter for me and my Maker. And I hope when the time comes we may settle the account like gentlemen, without bawling the business out in a farm-yard prayerfest with hysterical women fainting on all sides. All I ask of religion is that it should not be *vulgar*."

It was a rational, worldly, aristocratic attitude often met with in people of Sir Edward's class. Fairfax had even known eminent divines who shared it. As an admirer of

Voltaire and a freethinker, Fairfax himself privately took enlightenment a step further . . . And yet there was a dark and
melancholic side to him that saw the allure in the hellfire
conviction, the black-and-white fervor, of men like the
Methodist preacher—who was now standing in the doorway
of the supper room, regarding the occupants with his com-
pellingly pale eyes.

" 'What is truth? said jesting Pilate; and would not stay
for an answer,' " he said. He had a singularly beautiful and
musical voice, deep and resonant with a slight edge of sadness. Fairfax could imagine its effect at an outdoor field
preaching.

"Ah!" Sir Edward sat back good-humoredly, glass to his
lips, regarding the neat slight figure much as his ancestors
might have regarded a motleyed jester capering up to divert
them. "Bacon again. Our minds run parallel, my friend, even
if they cannot meet. Will you drink a glass with us?"

The preacher shook his head minutely. "I don't touch it,
sir."

"No. Scripture, I suppose. But then doesn't Scripture say
something about taking a little wine for thy stomach's
sake?"

"I cannot be provoked, sir, by such trifling. My feet are
set too firm upon the rock of salvation for that. I mean no
disrespect, but I cannot sit by and hear a man speak jestingly
of holy things." The preacher pointed a steady finger at the
baronet. "Out of very concern for *your* immortal soul, I cannot."

Sir Edward's bushy eyebrows rose. "My eternal soul
ain't your business, my good man. But this rock, now, with
your feet so firmly set upon it, and so forth—how do you
know this, might I ask? This is what perplexes me about
your sort, Mr. Preacher. You sincerely believe that you are
utterly in the right of it—always, world without end? Such
assurance! Almost like pride, is it not? And after all, what is
to separate you from any mountebank at the fair who says

that his miraculous elixir will cure everything from toothache to the pox?"

Sir Edward was amusing himself; that the preacher knew it was plainly written on his face, but he spoke temperately. "All men's souls are my concern, sir. And just now I tremble for yours. I see the flames licking about it."

"I'm conscious of no heat, Mr. Preacher." But there was vexation in Sir Edward's laugh.

"I have a name, sir; it is Henry Griggs."

"Well, Henry Griggs, mine is Sir Edward Nugent, of Cheyney Hall, Northamptonshire. I don't know where you intend pitching your next prayerfest, but let me advise you I will not allow it on my land, and as a magistrate I shall not look kindly on such gatherings either."

Henry Griggs barely inclined his head, and said composedly, "I have a standing invitation from the Methodist society here at Huntingdon to speak, and to wreak a revival of the Spirit here, if the Lord wills. We meet only in peace and brotherhood, sir, to be washed in the blood of the Lamb. None come to harm; many come to good, You might come to good yourself, Sir Edward Nugent."

"An entertaining impudence. But one can have enough of it." Sir Edward looked suddenly bored, and helped himself to the last pie. "Good day, Mr. Preacher."

Henry Griggs seemed about to correct him again, but with another passionless, penetrating stare, went away.

"You meant it?" Fairfax said.

"Certainly. And I know that Lord Burghley of Burghley House, who is the most considerable man in the district, and chairman of the justices, is no friend to our Mr. Griggs and his like either. Why, man, never tell me he's won you over?"

"No, but I should be interested to hear such a man preach, as an experience."

"You're like my father," Sir Edward grunted, "interested, in everything. A man should cultivate a little dull indifference, Fairfax, to give him ballast. Well, let the good burghers of Huntingdon endure the fellow's ravings." Sir

Edward tossed a handful of coins down. "Come, Fairfax—why, man, you've hardly ate a morsel—we'll go see if the horses have been changed."

The post chaise, elegant in yellow and black, with a pair of fresh-groomed horses stamping in the shafts, stood ready in the yard. There too was the innkeeper, still fretting over the lateness of the *Stamford Flyer*.

"'Tis mighty unlike it. Dear me. Here's a gentleman booked an inside seat, and needs to be in Baldock this evening."

He pointed to a testy old clergyman leaning on a silver-topped stick, who patted his vast powdered wig pettishly and grumbled: "I am to officiate at a funeral. Two children, of *very* good family. If I do not appear, 'twill likely be conducted by some wretch of a curate with dirt under his nails: hardly fitting. I shall take this up with the coach proprietors, upon my word I shall, and my bishop shall hear of it."

"Coach must have foundered," Sir Edward said as the yellow-jacketed postilion mounted the lead horse, and he and Fairfax stepped into the post chaise. "Let's hope there's no one hurt."

The horses were very fresh, and as most postilions drove at a gallop, they were soon rattling along at a speed that made Fairfax wish he had eaten even more sparingly of the rich pie than he had. But a check soon came to their progress in the shape of Alconbury Hill, a notoriously hard climb for wheeled traffic of all kinds. As the coach strained and lurched up the ascent, Fairfax commented on the singularity of such a considerable hill occurring in such an expanse of flatness.

"'Twas a little provoking of Providence," agreed Sir Edward. "We are on the edge of the fen country here, which is no more hilly than a bowling green. And there are surprising dense woods down about Stangate Hole, before we get to Stilton, which have always been mighty convenient for our friends of the mask-and-pistol persuasion . . . Whoa, down we go. Don't looks so green, Fairfax, we'll soon be on level going again."

The coach bucketed down the descent with an almighty rattling of the axles and swingle bars, the glasses and the coach lamps; only the rattling of Fairfax's teeth in his head seemed louder. A long queasy swaying of the whole vehicle from one side to the other, like the lashing of a great tail, indicated that they had reached the bottom. Fairfax settled his hat on his head and swallowed down something unpleasant in his throat. Level going, thank heaven.

They had about five minutes of it before the coach lurched again—but this time because the postilion had pulled up the horses sharp, with a curious shout audible over the noise of hoofs and wheels. Swearing, Sir Edward pulled down the glass and started to bellow out to him.

"What the devil are we stopping for—"

Fairfax silenced him with a hand on his arm. Through the other window, over at the right-hand side of the empty road, he had seen what the postilion had seen. And even before the details had imprinted themselves on his mind, he hoped that he would never see a worse sight.

Two

The stretch of straight level road on which they had been traveling was lined on the left side by oak trees, outposts of the woods that lay in smoke-colored folds all about the near distance. On the right, the verge of the road fell away among gorse and bramble into a shallow ditch, with a steeper bank rising on the other side to a strip of plowed field and then more woods, close and dark.

There, with its far side wheels in the ditch so that the whole coach lay at a forty-five-degree angle, was the *Stamford Flyer*. The name of the coach was visible, painted in curlicue on the door panel that stood open on the near side. The horses were still in the traces, the front pair standing square on the verge, with the leader even calm enough to be nibbling grass, the rear pair half in the ditch, lathered and agitated and whinnying shrilly at the sight of the post chaise and the two men hurrying over.

But it was not the plight of the horses that chiefly concerned Fairfax and his employer. It was the bodies.

One lay on the edge of the ditch directly behind the tilted roof of the coach, with one booted foot still on the roof rail; an outside passenger, Fairfax thought. The other was the coachman, slumped across the driving seat and practically upside down, though the reins were still gathered up under his lifeless arms.

Fairfax stared down at the man sprawled by the ditch. His head spun and he felt sick.

"Does he live?" breathed Sir Edward beside him. "Oh—dear God."

Fairfax turned away. The man had been shot in the face, the ball entering the cheek and making havoc. The dark hair was matted to the roots with blood. With his arms spread wide and his smashed face he was more like a scarecrow than a human being.

"Devilish," Sir Edward grunted, turning away too. "Devilish work . . . Don't look, boy," he said to the postilion who had joined them, whey-faced. "Free those poor beasts from the traces—I doubt they'll bolt. Great God, are there any inside . . . ?"

Fairfax was already scrambling up the tilted step of the coach to look in the interior. He saw the dashes of blood on the glass in the open door first. Then the figure slumped across the horsehair seat, its head lolling at an impossible angle in the corner of the bodywork. No featureless mess this time: the man's face—white, pinched, and astonished—was unmarked beneath a powdered bagwig, with steel spectacles perched a little askew on the nose. Just below was the bloody horror—he had been shot in the throat. On the seat beside him was a carved wooden ear trumpet, and at his feet a small iron-clasped strongbox, open and empty.

There was no need to touch him: only death had that frozen stillness.

"Fairfax"!" Sir Edward's voice. "Help me—the coachman, I think he still lives . . ."

With trembling difficulty, the two of them clambered up on the footboard and lifted the coachman from the seat. The postilion, who had swiftly cut the coach horses from the traces with a sharp penknife, reached up from below and took his feet. The coachman was a big man, dressed in heavy boots and a cumbrous greatcoat. Fairfax felt the muscles in his arms would snap in the struggle to get the man down gently. But they managed it, and laid him on the grass.

The coachman's eyelids were fluttering. Sir Edward took off the man's broad hat, put a hesitant hand toward the bloodied lock of grizzled hair that covered his left temple, then withdrew it. Shot in the head, Fairfax thought. But might the ball have merely winged him, not completed its killing flight?

"We should send for a surgeon," Fairfax said. "The man inside is dead, but there may be hope here . . . What's the nearest town? Huntingdon?"

"Yes—yes, that would be best." Sir Edward addressed the postilion. "'Fas as you can back to Huntingdon, my boy. Tell them at the inn what's happened, and have them find a surgeon for this man. Then there's these other poor wretches . . . they cannot lie here . . . Bespeak a cart or a wagon of some sort too, boy; tell them Sir Edward Nugent will bear the change. Ride the lead horse from the chaise, that will be quickest. Off, now."

As the postilion galloped away, Fairfax bent close to the weathered face of the coachman, whose lips were faintly moving.

"Hod up, my friend. Help's coming. Can you speak?"

The coachman's chest rose laboriously. He gave a long, faint groan.

"Here . . ." Sir Edward fumbled in his pocket and brought out his brandy flask. "Put a little to his lips."

Before Fairfax could do so the coachman's eyes opened fully. They moved with a terrible snaillike slowness from one face to the other. A sigh came from his throat, becoming a word.

"High . . . wayman . . ." He could only give it the faintest articulation. Fairfax bent closer.

"We'll have the rogue," Sir Edward said. "Never fear, friend, he'll swing."

Forgetting himself, Fairfax made an impatient hushing motion. The coachman was speaking again.

"Tried . . . drive straight on . . . tried . . ." With sudden agitation he made an effort to turn his head in the direction of the crashed coach. "Never upset before . . . never . . . all my years . . ."

"Rest easy. You're not to blame." Fairfax unstoppered the flask and trickled a little brandy onto the coachman's lips. It ran down his chin. No response from the lips. Nor, Fairfax saw now, from the eyes, which in turning toward the coach had stilled, glazed, died.

Fairfax sat back on his haunches. A time for a prayer. But it should have come unbidden; instead the doubt and skepticism of his nature entangled and silenced him. It was Sir Edward who supplied it, simply.

"God have mercy on his soul." With a swift unsentimental motion the baronet closed the empty eyes and stood up. "Three innocent lives. Snuffed out for gain. Our man has excelled himself this time. Well, well."

"You think this is the work of the man you spoke of earlier?"

"No doubt of it. This is his haunt. Not for long, though. He shall be caught and dispatched to hell where he belongs. I shall personally double the price on his head."

"Yet he has never used such brutality before."

"He has now. Unless you think these poor creatures are dressmakers' dummies, hey, Fairfax?"

Fairfax glanced up; occupied with his thoughts, he had not realized quite how angry and disgusted Sir Edward was.

"The crime is unspeakable," Fairfax said. "I was just wondering at the manner of it. It would seem the coachman tried to drive on when accosted by the robber—perhaps to ride him down. Brave if foolhardy. And the robber stopped the coach in the directest manner—shot the coachman in his seat. Lacking direction, the coach tipped into the ditch. And then . . ."

"Then the brute murdered the passengers. One outside, one in. Simple and beastly enough."

"Yes . . . yet I wonder if there was more than one brute. Such a man would usually be armed with a brace of pistols,

I understand, primed and loaded so that he would get one shot from each if needed. Yet here are three people shot."

"An accomplice, think you? Or a gang? But this fellow's known for plying his trade quite alone."

Fairfax nodded. "Of course he might have had more than a brace of pistols about him, though it's unlikely."

"More probable that he primed and reloaded after the first two shots. Killed the coachman and the outside passenger—the poor fellow probably tried to make a bolt for it when the coach was upset—then proceeded to deal with the man inside at his leisure. Ecod, 'tis all as fish-blooded and efficient as you like."

Sir Edward's summary was very much how Fairfax saw these events, yet still something about the utter ruthless violence of the scene perplexed him.

"The gentleman inside carried a strongbox, which has been emptied," he said. "Perhaps he was the highwayman's main quarry."

"Which means the villain knew that gentleman would be riding the *Flyer* today. No great mystery there; these fellows make it their business to get such information from the inns and posting houses. They skulk about on their own account, or they pump ostlers and chambermaids and such. 'Tis not unheard of for innkeepers themselves to be in league with these fellows, taking a share of the profits. Ah, but the *FLyer* starts from the George at Stamford, one of the principal establishments of the country. The innkeeper there is a man of substance and unimpeachable character—indeed, I fancy he is part proprietor of the *Flyer*." Sir Edward put out a peremptory hand for the brandy flask and took a swig. "Good God, what a horror. Those poor beasts hardly know where they are."

With great address the postilion had managed to tether the coach horses by their cut traces to a fence post, but they showed no sign of wanting to go anywhere. They huddled together, shivering, stamping, scenting death. The now solitary horse in the shafts of the post chaise scented it too: it tossed its head and rolled its eyes at its brethren across the road.

"It is hard to tell what he meant," Fairfax said, still pondering. "He said 'highwayman'—or it might have been 'highwaymen.' The sound is much alike, even when clearly spoken. A puzzle . . . Well, I suppose these woods would provide cover for a dozen such, at any rate."

"Monks Wood, to the east there, covers scores of acres alone. Whose the land, I don't know: maybe Fitzwilliam. A thorough combing, by a great many armed men, might flush out a gallows bird or two—if such a body could ever be raised, and if they gave absolutely no hint of their approach. Unlikely at best."

"Perhaps whatever was taken from that strongbox will furnish the best clue," Fairfax said, accepting the proffered brandy flask. "The culprit will have to spend or dispose of it at some time."

"Aye, there's that—not that these villains don't have their own set of fences and brokers. Well, there may be something that's identifiable. Depends who these poor souls are. Their names will be recorded at the inn booking office in Stamford."

"The *Flyer*'s destination is London?"

"Aye—it takes in Huntingdon, but then goes byway of Biggleswade and Hatfield—the true Great North Road, rather than the old North Road we came by. More towns, so more fares to be had that way, I suppose. I've ridden the *Flyer* myself, with my girls . . ." Sir Edward visibly shuddered. "There are families awaiting the arrival of these murdered wretches even now: wives, children . . . I mean to make this my business, Fairfax, as a magistrate and as a fellow mortal. There is no forgetting such a sight."

"Amen to that," Fairfax said soberly. He had seen death before, but the bleak and grisly end that these people had met, on an empty high road of scuttering leaves and staring sky, was uniquely chilling.

There came hoofbeats from the road to the south, but it

was not the help they awaited: instead, a string of three packhorse riders, who pulled up at the site with all the shock and dismay of the first discoverers. But they were on their way to Stamford, so Sir Edward charged them with taking the news of the disaster to the George Inn there, the *Flyer*'s home port.

"The bodies had best be carried to Stamford for now," Sir Edward said when the riders had gone. "That's where they set out from. We can find out their names there, and identify them. There will have to be an inquest, of course. Though 'tis a plain and simple case enough: murder, no less."

Plain enough, Fairfax thought, but simple? He wasn't sure. He began studying the ground round about the crashed coach, trying to reconstruct the incident in his mind.

The assailant, or assailants, must have known the time when the coach would be due here—common knowledge enough—and waited among the trees for its approach. Then, out into the road—mounted, of course, for highway robbers always were, as opposed to the footpads who lurked about the outskirts of towns—a shouted challenge, pistols at the ready. The coachman's last words suggested that he had tried to drive on, courageously or stubbornly. Looking at the south road ahead, with its steep ascent to Alconbury Hill in the distance, Fairfax saw that that had been more foolish than either. His progress would soon have been slowed by the incline, certainly enough for a determined mounted man to have swiftly caught up.

It was a purely theoretical point, anyhow, because the coachman had met a very determined adversary indeed— one who had shot him without hesitation.

Fairfax conned the surface of the road, which was quite soft and muddy a this low point. But it was just a confusion of wheel ruts and hoofprints, including no doubt those of their own post chaise. He had heard tales from men who had been in the American colonies of Red Indians who could read the ground at their feet like a book, but the gift was beyond him.

So, with the coachman shot, and the coach horses no doubt in a panic, the vehicle itself had swerved and tipped into the ditch, its far-side wheels wedging there, the horses unable to go on . . . And the outside passengers? It would seem there was only one: the fellow who lay at the edge of the ditch. A youngish man, dressed in a long greatcoat and muffler, apt enough for outside traveling, which was a notoriously cold business. Dangerous too, as one had simply to cling on to the coach roof as best one could throughout the jolting, pitching journey. Not that the traveler could have anticipated such mortal danger as this . . . So, had he been thrown from the roof as the coach tipped into the ditch, and been shot where he fell? Or had he clung on, and then tried to make an escape, as Sir Edward suggested? Certainly it seemed likely that he and the coachman had been dispatched first, and then the robber or robbers had approached the coach door. If there was only one, that must have been when he primed and reloaded his pistols—cool and levelheaded indeed. After all, there were plenty of travelers who went armed themselves, as a precaution against just such an attack, and who knew what might await the criminal inside the coach? Unless, of course, he had precise knowledge of that very fact. And as for cool and levelheaded, the whole undertaking merited those words. Cool, levelheaded—and pitiless.

Taking a deep breath, Fairfax climbed up again to look in at the coach door. With the far-side window pressed against the bank of the ditch, it was quite dim inside, which would explain why, the first time, he had not spotted the object tucked into the dead man's right palm.

It was a flintlock pistol, of the sort called a "manstopper": small enough to be carried in the pocket, and in fact ideal for a man traveling with valuables. Fairfax himself had carried a pair like this on his Grand Tour of the Continent as a young man, though he had never had to use them. But what of this man? Had he perhaps managed a shot . . . ?

"Sir Edward—look here, if you will."

The baronet thrust his great head into the coach. "God in heaven, the poor fellow . . . I've seen enough blood, Fairfax—let us leave it until these bodies can be carried away decently."

"But look at this. He was armed." Fairfax lifted the pistol from the stiff curled hand.

"Think you he winged our man? God, I hope so. He'll be injured if so, losing blood; he'll have to seek out a doctor. 'Tis our best hope."

Fairfax, holding the pistol up to the light, shook his head. "This has not been fired. See? Primed and loaded—powder in the pan. But he did not fire." He laid the pistol down on the seat, then reached for the dead man's left hand, which was tucked at an angle in his breast. "And here, within the pocket, I believe we will find the other . . . Just so." The handle of the companion pistol protruded from the breast pocket of the man's snuff brown coat. Drawing it out was difficult . . . "Yes," said Fairfax finally.

"Yes what, damn it?"

"I once carried such a pair of pistols myself. Mighty convenient except for this—the exposed lock and trigger. Liable to snag in the lining of your pocket when you draw them out. No great matter, except—"

"Except when someone is pointing a pistol at you, and every instant is vital," said Sir Edward, shaking his head. "Poor fellow. I trust it was over quick. Come, Fairfax. The matter is plain enough."

Fairfax climbed out. But there was something more he wanted to examine: the rumble, at the rear of the coach, where the passengers' luggage was stored. It was empty.

"Probably stolen too, if there was any," Sir Edward said. "And the gentleman inside would no doubt wish to keep that strongbox close by him."

Fairfax nodded thoughtfully. "It would be curious for a man of substance, as he appears to have been, to have no baggage at all. Of course, it depends where he was going— which we can find out at the Stamford coach office. Probably a record of luggage too . . ." He raised his head: the sound of wheels on the south road.

Their postilion was returning, riding alongside a light cart driven by a groom. Behind them came a man on horseback.

The groom swept off his hat, very hushed and respectful, solemnly presenting the compliments of the innkeeper at Huntingdon, and saying that his master had placed him entirely at their disposal for this terrible occasion. "Terrible," he repeated, his eyes ghoulishly straying to the wrecked coach, "terrible . . ." Probably the whole staff of the inn were eagerly depending on him for the scarifying details.

"Dr. Tuplin," Sir Edward said to the mounted man, who had already got down and was hurrying over to the coachman, "I fear it's too late—we find no signs of life. All three slaughtered . . ."

Without comment the doctor, a fair, stooping man past thirty, with his own hair tied in a simple queue, bent to examine the coachman then passed swiftly to the man by the ditch. Finally he leaped up into the coach. He soon emerged, wiping his hands on a handkerchief, a kind of pained abstraction on his lined face.

"Dr. Tuplin," Sir Edward said in introduction to Fairfax. "A Stamford man—fine physician."

"I might deserve your tribute if I could revive these poor souls," Dr. Tuplin said with a wan smile. "But I am afraid that is beyond any man's power. It was quite by chance I was in Huntingdon today, and had stabled my horse at the inn there. I am surgeon to all the jails, lockups, and workhouses hereabout, and this week Huntingdon was the scene of my delightful duty." In Tuplin's words and his expression Fairfax caught a familiar echo—the hollowness of a disappointed man. "Well, the best I can tell you is that these people can have suffered but little. The execution was swift and sure."

"The coachman lived a few minutes after we found him,"

Sir Edward said. "Long enough to tell us it was that villain we all seek."

"Our predatory friend has certainly excelled himself," Dr. Tuplin said, shaking his head at Sir Edward's proffered flask. "I'm no army surgeon, and have little experience of these matters, but it would seem that whoever wielded the pistols meant quite earnestly to kill." He frowned. "The man in the coach I believe I know vaguely . . . yet I am not certain. Death soon transforms. I can examine them more closely and certify the deaths if they are conveyed to a better place. Their bodies, I mean," he said with that same hollow look, meeting Fairfax's eye. "Their souls, naturally, have already made the journey."

"I thought to have them brought to Stamford, where they set out," Sir Edward said. "There can be no objection, I suppose? I am a magistrate for the borough, if not for this forsaken spot of ground."

"I can think of no better direction," the doctor agreed. Again he glanced over at the coach. "Strange, I swear there is something familiar about that gentleman . . . Well, no matter. I'm ready to bear a hand in lifting them into the cart. I have quite as much to do with the dead as the living—as do most of us sawbones, if we would but admit it."

It was soon done, the bodies being laid in the bed of the cart as decently as their condition allowed, and covered with some sacking the groom had brought for the purpose. The empty strongbox was placed there too. The resourceful postilion hitched the coach horses to the back of the post chaise; and thus the strange procession—cart, post chaise, and the doctor on horseback—made its way up the Great North Road. The packhorse men must have passed the news at Stilton, the next posting stage, for people came crowding out of the famous Bell Inn to stare at the impromptu cortege; likewise at Wansford, the next stop; and when at last they came in the darkening afternoon to St. Martin's, the outlying parish of the town of Stamford, people were standing expectantly outside cottage doors, many bareheaded. A pack of ragged boys came running alongside the cart, trying to peep in, undeterred by the groom's cutting about him with his whip.

Fairfax had never been to Stamford, but had heard much of its architectural and social elegance, which made it a favorite town residence for the gentry of the region. The prospect as they came down High Street St. Martin's, with ahead the bridge arching the river and leading to a graceful sweep of gray stone gables and soaring spires, was a handsome one—quite as fine as Oxford, he thought. Another time he would have given it close attention.

But any impression could only be faint compared with that made by the bodies in the cart. Somehow they seemed even more pathetic, laid and covered thus, than they had looked at the scene of the killings. There, something of themselves remained; now they were enlisted in the anonymous ranks of the dead.

The George at Stamford was one of the great inns of England. It announced itself with a great timber sign that stretched right across the street from roof to roof like an arch—or a gallows. Another crowd of people was gathered at the wide coach gate of the inn. This was the place from which the *Flyer* had set out on its doomed journey.

The procession turned into the yard. Almost at once a plump, pug-nosed, bustling man, his eyes round with alarm, was at the post chaise window.

"Sir Edward," he stammered, opening the carriage door, "I hardly know what to think. Some fellows came riding in with the most dreadful intelligence, but I cannot believe—"

"'Tis true enough, I'm afraid, Quigley. The *Flyer* has been held up, and is foundered." Sir Edward stepped down and addressed the fluttering man sternly. "You must compose yourself, my friend. The passengers are killed, and the coachman. 'Tis done. But we shall have this brute at last, Quigley, my word on it. This will be his last outrage."

Mr. Quigley, whom Fairfax guessed to be the innkeeper of the George, stared and swallowed and took a deep breath.

Then he nodded and walked slowly over to the cart and looked in.

When he returned his round comfortable face was ashen.

"Never in my worst dreams," he said huskily. "Safe and convenient traveling—that's how we have always advertised the *Flyer*. My partner in London once spoke of placing a guard on the coach, but it's an extravagance for a modest country operation . . . My poor coachman! A sterling fellow—I cannot believe it . . ."

"Has he been long in your service?"

"Ten years. He boards here at the George. Crabbe is his name, Charles Crabbe. Such a sturdy fellow, some other coach proprietors have tried to poach him away from me. Poor Crabbe . . ."

"Has he family?"

"No—no, thank heaven, a bachelor. Coaching was all his life. It was his boast that he had never had an upset, and true enough."

"He lived long enough to speak to us," Fairfax said, "and mentioned a highwayman, or men. Also something about trying to drive on . . . ?"

Mr. Quigley plucked at his lip. "That's likely enough. He used to be mighty fierce on the subject of this rogue who's plaguing the roads—said that if ever he saw him he would ply his whip and drive the scoundrel down in the road."

Sir Edward nodded. "The scoundrel, alas, was too sharp for him. I'm afraid your coach lies in a ditch, Quigley, down by Stangate Hole, and there must be some damage."

With an anguished shrug, and evident sincerity, the innkeeper said, "What's that beside innocent lives?"

Dr. Tuplin was there. "A place for laying-out is needed," he said, "and I doubt, Mr. Quigley, your patrons would relish such guests under your roof. I would suggest the Cross Keys—it is just round the corner in Church Street, and the publican there does undertaking; he has a room for the purpose." The publican-undertaker was not an uncommon figure in country towns. "I shall examine the bodies, and make an inventory of their clothes and possessions for submission to the coroner."

"Very well, Tuplin," Sir Edward said. "I leave it in your hands. Quigley, we shall need to know who these poor wretches were. You don't recollect who boarded the *Flyer* this morning?"

"I wasn't on hand when she loaded," the innkeeper said. "And I don't generally take down the bookings myself. Old Jacob has the charge of that. Used to be my head ostler till he got the screws in the back. We'll go see him. He writes a fair hand, and he's as honest a man as ever trod leather, so I find him some light work that way . . ."

Talking agitatedly, Mr. Quigley led them inside. Fairfax noticed twin coffee rooms for coach passengers, one with "York" inscribed above the door, the other "London." In each there was an urgent babble of talk, and pale expectant faces swiveled as they passed.

Old Jacob turned out to be a very old man indeed, so bent that the line of his shoulders came above his head, and the seat of his breeches below his knees. The snug office in which they found him, with a brass-railed counter and a high-backed chair, and a good fire burning, reflected well on Mr. Quigley's kindness as an employer, Fairfax thought. Old Jacob was also a little deaf, but his mind and his handwriting were clear enough.

"I have it to hand, sir—all as plain as you like." He opened the large ledger on the counter by tottering to one end of it and with both hands heaving at it like the hatch of a cellar. "Entered for the *Flyer*, departing for London at seven o'clock in the morning, Tuesday, the sixth of October 1761: outside passengers one, inside passengers two . . ."

"Two?" Fairfax said.

"One was a short stage, mebbe, and got down earlier," Mr. Quigley said, drawing the ledger toward him and reading his servant's careful script. "Inside, Mr. Twelvetree, for Huntingdon, paid fifteen shillings, to board the coach at the

Haycock, Wansford . . ." The innkeeper's voice grew faint.
"Twelvetree . . ."

"What's amiss, sir?" Old Jacob, who had evidently not
heard about the murders, quavered. "Not upset, is she? I
heard the grooms making a to-do outside.

"Aye, upset," Sir Edward said, "a bad business. Twelvetree, eh? That would explain the strongbox. My Lord,
Nicholas Twelvetree . . ."

"He is known to you?" Fairfax said

"I know of him. Most folk around here do, at least by
name: keeps himself to himself in the main. Kept, I should
say. Poor wretch." Sir Edward's look, though, was as much
wry as sorrowful. "He is a banker—damn it, was. One of the
warmest men in the town. When I say warm, I mean only in
the sense of wealthy. No one ever called him warm in the
other way, I think. Well, his people had better be told at
once."

"He has family?" Fairfax said.

"Not to speak of. I was thinking of the bank people. But
what's this about boarding at Wansford?"

"Sir, the fare was paid at this office," Jacob said, running
a proprietary finger down the columns, "on the fourth of the
month. 'Twas a clerk came in to book it, I seem to think. But
the gentleman was to board at Wansford, the next stop
down."

"That's rum," Sir Edward said. "Twelvetree hardly
stirred abroad from his house, seemingly, let alone from
Stamford."

"And with a strongbox," Fairfax said, "if that is the gentleman who was inside."

"Aye," Sir Edward said, "a close buttoned-up fellow,
with spectacles and an ear trumpet—that's how I know him,
though I misdoubt I ever said more than good day to him in
m'life. Nor did most folk. He had a reputation for—Well,
'tis no time to speak ill of the man."

"The strongbox . . ." Fairfax mused. "Is it not the case,
Mr. Quigley, that most coach proprietors demand an extra

premium on luggage, goods, and so on, above a certain value?"

"Oh, surely. If a passenger carries goods with him above the value of five pounds, we make a register of it, and ask for a small consideration. In case of loss or damage, you know. But there's nothing entered here," the innkeeper said, gesturing at the ledger.

"Devilish odd," Sir Edward said. "I'd have thought Twelvetree the last man in the world to be careless of such things."

"He certainly took care to go armed," Fairfax said.

"Mercy on us," Mr. Quigley said, mopping his brow. "Mr. Twelvetree—meeting such an end, on the *Flyer*! I'm dreaming in my bed—I must be . . ."

"No help for it, Quigley," Sir Edward said briskly. "You ain't responsible; that gallows bird of a highwayman is. Come, what are the other names?"

Mr. Quigley consulted the ledger. "Mrs. Parry, inside, to St. Neots. Paid, sixteen shillings, on the fifth of October."

"Now that lady I recall," old Jacob said eagerly. "Came in yesterday to book it herself. A young sort of lady, I think." He put an unsteady hand to his lips. "Leastways, a lady; and she paid from her purse."

"But this makes no sense, " Sir Edward said, frowning. "She was going to St. Neots? But that lies farther than the place the coach was found—past Huntingdon. She . . ." He shrugged in bafflement. "She must have been on the coach when it was attacked."

"Attacked!" murmured old Jacob piteously, and made a stagger to his stool. He was actually taller sitting down than standing up.

"But not a sign of her," Fairfax said. "Unless she never boarded the coach."

"No, she's marked," the innkeeper said, "see here—a tick. The coachman always gives the number of his load before he sets off—it's a thing I insist on at the George, anyhow. I've known some dishonest coachmen who'll accept a fare privately, and pocket the money—taking a bit of fish, they call it. No, the *Flyer* set out from here this morning with two inside and one out, that's certain."

"Then where's this woman?" Sir Edward said. "Could it be she escaped harm, and ran away for help when the coach foundered? It seems unlikely. No doubt she'll turn up, if so. Quigley, have you servants you can spare here? It might be as well to send along the road, to Stilton, Alconbury—anywhere there might be news of her. Also to discover any more passengers who were to join the coach at those places. 'Tis curious indeed. I don't know any Parrys, do you Quigley?"

The innkeeper shook his head. "You recollect anything more of this lady, Jacob?"

The old man looked lugubrious. "Ah, dear! I wish I could. I don't take a deal of notice of faces as a rule. I'm always so careful with my ciphering, and reckoning the money, y'see, sir—'tis a great trust, and so I keep my head bent over it. A lady—and she paid from a purse—and I'd say pretty. Only at my time of life"—he gave a vague rattle of humor—"there aren't many as *don't* look pretty. Mind you," he muttered, "there's old Nan Digglin who does the linen—she's ugly enough to wean a foal, even to me—"

"Well," Sir Edward said impatiently, "whoever and wherever this Mrs. Parry is, at least she escaped the fate of the others, thank God."

"Unless," Fairfax said, "she was on the coach when it was held up, and did not escape. It is an awful thought, but this highwayman may have considered her as part of his spoils."

"What?" Sir Edward stared at him. Then his mouth went tight. "I was going to say he cannot be such a beast—but who knows what he is not capable of? Quigley, send your servants as soon as may be. We must alert the local constables too—everyone. Cock's life, this grows darker."

Another notion occurred to Fairfax just then, though he decided to keep it to himself. It involved the mysterious Mrs. Parry going, not forcibly, but willingly, away with the attacker. An accomplice? Mere irresponsible speculation, of course; and he felt faintly disgusted with himself at the way his mind was eagerly fingering the pieces of this bloody puzzle.

"What of the outside passenger?" he said.

"Mr. Griggs," the innkeeper read out, "for Eaton Socon, paid seven shillings on the fifth of October."

"I remember a man yesterday," old Jacob said. "Not a gentleman, I think, just a quiet, decent sort of man, paid for an outside place . . . I''d remember more if I could," he said in a tone of anxious explanation, "only I can't."

"Wait a moment—Griggs—wasn't that the name of that damned preacher we met?" Sir Edward asked, echoing Fairfax's thought.

"Henry Griggs," he said. "Odd. Not that the surname is so very uncommon."

"Not so common neither," Sir Edward said. "We'd better see what the preacher knows too. Quigley, you must send to Huntingdon also, to the Bridge there. A man named Griggs was about the place, preachifying on all sides. With luck he'll not have gone far, for his horse was near lamed. Well, there's nothing more you can tell us, I daresay, my good man?"

"I would if I could," old Jacob said, seeming to have taken a liking to this formula, "only I can't, sir."

"So, we have Crabbe, the coachman, deceased, poor fellow. We have an outside passenger called Griggs, likewise; Twelvetree, inside, one of our most prominent citizens, likewise, and robbed; and a Mrs. Parry, who was supposed to be inside, but has disappeared into thin air." Sir Edward raised an eyebrow at Fairfax. "A pretty kettle of fish, eh, Fairfax?"

It was, Fairfax thought; and the fish had a mighty odd smell about them too.

While Mr. Quigley sent his servants on their various errands on the fastest mounts the George's huge stabling could offer, Sir Edward sought out the postilion of their post chaise. He dispatched the lad the few miles to Cheyney Hall with a written message, saying that he had been delayed on the road, and telling the steward to send his carriage over to Stamford.

"After that, back to Huntingdon with you, and my compliments to your master," Sir Edward concluded, giving him a heavy tip. The lad looked as if he had aged ten years today. "Now, Fairfax, I think we've earned a mug of ale."

They drank it in a quiet corner of the dim stone-floored taproom. Sir Edward placed a shilling on the tabletop and spun it idly.

"What think you of this business, Fairfax?" His voice was unusually tentative.

"As you say, Sir Edward, there is a most ruthless and stone-hearted killer abroad."

"But you do not think it a simple matter of a highway robber stepping out and taking his chance with the first coach that came along. Come, man," Sir Edward said as Fairfax hesitated, "it's written all over your face. Now, as it happens I'd heard of your exploit with your last pupil, when I sought you out. Young whelp found himself accused of a most appalling crime, ain't that so? And you tracked down the real culprit yourself. Rather remarkable."

"Well, I was terrified of my pupil's father," Fairfax said awkwardly. "Self-preservation can be a great spur."

"Nonsense. You must have a feeling for these things. Your father was a famous judge, wasn't he?"

"More notorious than famous," Fairfax said. "He was disgraced, and took his own life." Blurting it out crudely, he found, was as good a way as any: the pain was got over quickly, though it was no less intense.

"Ah? Well, well. No reflection on you. You know, one of my ancestors in the Tudor days was born on the wrong side of the blanket. Sired a dozen bastards himself, and was the most rascally pirate and adventurer."

Fairfax smiled. Though it was not the same thing, Sir Edward meant well.

"Anyhow, you can't deny you're a man with a nose for

such things. Now, I mean what I say: I shan't rest till I have whoever did this standing before me on the Bench, so that I can send him to the assize, and the appointment with Jack Ketch he deserves. But in the matter of finding him, two heads are better than one—especially if there is more to this man than initially appears."

"And that is what you believe?"

"At first I did not. But now that we know a little of the passengers on that coach . . . This business of the missing woman perplexes me .And as for that poor wretch Twelvetree—that surprises me greatly. At least, to find him traveling so—alone, and armed with pistols, of all things, and apparently carrying something of particular value."

"It is not his habit?"

"I don't know much of his habits, beyond the fact that the man's practically a recluse. Oh, not that he ain't a figure in the town—far from it. Some might say he has altogether too much influence—a finger in every pie, at least as far as his financial interests go."

"Would you say that yourself, Sir Edward?"

The baronet scowled at him. "You needn't cross-examine me, damn it. I don't bank with him, but I've nothing against him. Nothing beyond my usual feeling for these burghers who go shooting up into wealth. They think everything can be bought with money—gentility, respect, position, even men's souls—just a matter of cash over the counter. Of course there's always a sniff of antagonism between the landed interest and the townspeople in a place like this. Take a man like Twelvetree, with bottomless coffers and endless ambition, and he soon starts trying to carve out his own kingdom. Investing in property, even in land—and buying out men with a longer pedigree than he. They say he drives a sharp bargain. I don't say I've heard of anything actually underhanded on his part, but he's never been popular."

"So he was a man with enemies?"

"Show me the man without. But I don't think he will be much mourned."

"Well, it's entirely probable that a highway robber, gathering intelligence on potential travelers in the way they do, should decide on the *Flyer* as his target; a well-known banker on board, and likely to offer rich pickings, even if our man didn't know about the strongbox. Of course, it may be that the strongbox, and whatever was in it, was the attacker's whole and single aim. Mr. Twelvetree's people can perhaps enlighten us there. But why should he kill this man Griggs also? An attempt on Griggs's part to escape is certainly possible . . . yet it seems more unlikely as I think of it. Griggs, perched on the roof, had seen the coachman shot in the head. Wouldn't a rational man seek to put up his hands and surrender rather than risk a scramble to nowhere with an armed assailant behind him?"

"True indeed. Unless the first shot hit Griggs, though aimed at the coachman. Griggs, on the roof, would be directly behind the coachman's seat."

"That's a possibility," Fairfax said thoughtfully. "But then the question of this Mrs. Parry, as you remark, is a curious one. Either she was on the coach when it was attacked, or she was not—it would certainly seem she boarded it here—and both alternatives are mysterious. I suppose there would be nothing to prevent her leaving the coach at an earlier stage?"

"Nothing, except for the fact that she had herself booked and paid for a seat to St. Neots, a good way on. Why get down earlier? Unless an indisposition, perhaps—women don't greatly thrive in the jostle of a public coach. I remember my poor wife was always as sick as a cushion on the road, no matter how gently we went. Well, if that's the shape of it, we should soon know. The lady will surely come forward when she hears she's being sought all over the country. As for this Griggs, if our preacher friend can't enlighten us, someone must know him. Which leaves Twelvetree. I wonder if rumor has reached his house yet. Not a fitting way for a man's death to be announced, I fear, even for a solitary fish like him."

"Is it near at hand? I could carry the news of what has happened, if you like. Sir Edward Nugent's secretary would surely be credited."

"A good notion. Lord knows what tales will be started otherwise. I'd best wait here in case there's news. But it's only a step to Broad Street. I'll point you on the way. And perhaps once there, you might smoke out a few things: what was in the strongbox, and why Twelvetree got on at Wansford instead of here—pertinent things, you know. That is, of course"—Sir Edward stopped spinning the coin and looked dryly at Fairfax—"if you have a fancy to join me in delving into this matter. It was no part of your commission when I hired you, of course, and you may not relish it."

Fairfax smiled. "I think you already know me better."

Following Sir Edward's directions, Fairfax crossed the river bridge into the town, a busy, prosperous place: small wharfs and warehouses visible on the river, much foot and horse traffic, brewers' drays, water carts, private carriages, even one of two sedan chairs. A medley of bow-fronted stone houses, with plenty of crowded shop windows and cellar workrooms; some buildings of venerable age, with tiny casements and bulging walls; and a medieval almshouse, handsome as an Oxford college. Among these, fine tall town houses of a more recent date, evidently residences of gentry. Quite an inviting piece of civilization, this place, with its spires pricking the dark satin blue of the autumn afternoon, yet a place of contrasts too, quite as much as the grand and grim metropolis from which he had come.

In an alleyway off Broad Street, a couple of prentice boys were enjoying the torment of a cat and a dog that they had tied together by their tails. Whooping, grinning, button-eyed, their faces looked both empty and full of purpose. The small incidental cruelty gave Fairfax pause, in spite of, or perhaps because of, the more shocking sights he had seen today. Was this mankind, truly revealed? Sir Edward Nugent, in his cool aristocratic way, would no doubt grunt tolerantly, say that idle and untaught youth were always prone

to such things, and box their ears. Someone like the
Methodist preacher they had met earlier, though, would
draw a more strenuous moral: that nothing we did was
unimportant, that the state of our souls appeared in our every
action—that here, in fact, was evil. Perhaps that was why
such men were unpopular: they made you choose.

Fairfax soon found the place he sought: it bore the name
"N. Twelvetree" on a brass plate by the front door. It was a
large five-bayed town house fronted by garden walls and a
gate with ball-topped piers; there was an older side wing attached, with a great stone gable. An imposing place, though
there was something severe and frigid about its aspect too.

Fairfax mounted the steps and rapped on the door, wondering greatly at the position he found himself in—bringing
the news of the death of a man he did not know to a house
where there were apparently no loved ones to mourn him.

A manservant opened the door to him, and ushered him
into a spartan gray counting house, more like a tank than a
room. There was a row of pigeonholes, a bureau, and two
high desks occupied by two clerks on spindly stools, quill
pens wagging. One was a beardless boy; the other, an elderly man all in snuff brown with a scratch wig and an ingratiating tilt to his birdlike head, got down and softly
inquired of Fairfax how he might serve him.

"My name is Fairfax. I am secretary to Sir Edward Nugent, of Cheyney Hall. Traveling up to Stamford today, Sir
Edward and I—came upon some unfortunate news which
must be urgently conveyed to Mr. Nicholas Twelvetree's
household. I would say his nearest kin—though I understand
there are none."

The clerk inclined his head to an even meeker angle. "I
am Mr. Twelvetree's chief clerk, sir. Claymount by name. If
I can be of any assistance, sir? Or perhaps, if it is a matter of
urgency, I might step up and find out if Mr. Twelvetree will
see you himself?"

"Dear me, I'm afraid there is some mistake. The news
concerns Mr. Twelvetree himself, you see. The coach in

which he set out this morning met with an accident, a most tragic accident . . ." Fairfax found himself in some bewilderment as the little man's mild face assumed an almost disdainful look, but he plunged on. "I have to inform you—Sir Edward has charged me with informing you—that Mr. Twelvetree was killed as a result."

The clerk blinked, pursed his lips, and said, "Is that all?"

Was that all? What did the man mean?

"Perhaps, Mr. Claymount, I have not made myself plain."

"Oh, you have, sir, you have. We have not the honor of counting Sir Edward Nugent among our clients, but I cannot conceive that he would be party to such a poor jest, and can only conclude that it is of your own invention. If so, then you must forgive me—I am quite out of the fashion, sir, no doubt, but I think it a poor jest, a poor jest indeed."

"Why on earth," Fairfax said almost wildly, "should you suppose I would say such a thing in jest?"

"Why? I hardly think I owe you an answer, sir, but if you insist, I will say, because Mr. Twelvetree is this very moment upstairs in his drawing room, quite well but for a little tisick, and I know this because I spoke to him but fifteen minutes ago."

Three

Fairfax's utter surprise and bewilderment must have been plain on his face, so much so that the clerk relented somewhat.

"Sir," he said, "really there must be some species of misunderstanding here. I mean no disrespect to you, or indeed Sir Edward Nugent, but I must ask you, is it not possible that you have been gravely misinformed?"

"Something is certainly amiss." Fairfax said, recovering himself. "That fact is, we came upon the wreck of the *Stamford Flyer* ourselves. A passenger had been killed, and the booking office at the George identifies him as Mr. Twelvetree. The body of the dead man is this moment being laid out at the Cross Keys—a black-clad man of about middle height, slender, wearing a full wig and spectacles."

The clerk's eyes grew large.

"Dear, dear. Perhaps," he said, bobbing his little head in agitation, "it would be best if you spoke to Mr. Twelvetree yourself. I'll just step up, sir, if you would be good enough to wait . . ."

After a short interval, which the boy clerk occupied by staring full at Fairfax with no more self-consciousness than a baby, Mr. Claymount came tripping back. Mr. Twelvetree, he announced, would see him in his private apartments upstairs. His tone suggested that this was a favor rarely granted.

A provincial banker was often a merchant or other man of business. Trading in large amounts of goods and sums of cash, and possessing a highly credit-worthy name, he could become almost by default a clearinghouse for the financial transactions of a district. With enough weight and confidence he could become, as was plainly the case with Mr. Twelvetree, a banker proper, looking after the deposits of customers and even issuing banknotes, though these were seldom accepted far afield from the town he lived in. A greater measure of wealth and social eminence might result, and many men, of course, wanted these. Another result of banking was power. Following the clerk upstairs, Fairfax wondered what Mr. Twelvetree's chief motive was.

The room into which Fairfax was shown was plain rather than sumptuous. More striking was the fact that it was approached via an anteroom, with the clerk having to unlock both doors with keys; and the fact, which only dawned on Fairfax after the first few minutes, that it was the cleanest room he had ever been in. He was a fastidious man himself, but he had never known floorboards so scoured and polished, such a glare of whitewash, such a hygienic neatness in everything from the fire irons in the cold marble grate to the platoon of pens, wafers, penknife, and sandbox ranged along the top of the walnut desk that stood in the exact center of the room; and he did not think he could have lived with it.

"This it the—the *gentleman*, sir," the clerk said with a kind of impressive quaver, as if in ushering in Fairfax he was introducing the very devil himself. He left them, with a rattle of locks. Fairfax saw that there were bolts on the inside of the door too.

A thin, high-shouldered man dressed in black was standing by the window, his long hands clasped before him. He was starring at Fairfax just as voraciously as had the boy downstairs, but in this man's eyes there was alarm.

"I have the honor of addressing Mr. Nicholas Twelvetree?"

"You do."

"Sir, forgive me for troubling you with this strange errand. I confess myself somewhat perplexed also. My name is Fairfax, and I came here on behalf of my employer, Sir Edward Nugent, as the bearer of news which—which I see cannot be true."

"My clerk has told me of it." Mr. Twelvetree stepped forward, his eyes still riveted on Fairfax. Just as the room suggested an indifference to luxury, the banker's appearance was not that of a man who wished to dazzle socially. His coat and tight-wound stock were drab, and there was a certain gracelessness about his grasshopper frame and lean, whey-colored, sharp-nosed face. So power's his motive, then, thought Fairfax; then reproved himself for such hasty judging.

What was more notable about Twelvetree's appearance, though, was its resemblance to the dead man in the coach. The same full, old-fashioned frizzed wig; the same small spectacles. And as Fairfax opened his mouth to speak again, Mr. Twelvetree reached in his pocket and drew out an ivory ear trumpet.

"A moment, sir. I have an infirmity in my left ear. I must hear you plain." The cocked ear trumpet, the clipped parsimonious speech with a faint lisp, added to the impression of an elderly man. But a closer view convinced Fairfax that Nicholas Twelvetree was at most forty-five, and not without vigor. "If I understand aright, you claim that my name was entered as a passenger on the *Stamford Flyer.*"

"I have seen it in the booking-office ledger," Fairfax said, not liking the tone of that *claim.* "Sir Edward Nugent and I came upon the *FLyer* at Stangate Hole. It was half in the ditch; the coachman and the passengers had been shot to death, presumably by a highwayman. On reaching the George, we consulted the booking office. Your name was there." He hesitated. "Indeed, the passenger inside the coach appeared . . . he bore a resemblance to yourself. Sir Edward, knowing you but slightly, took him as such, and as a stranger here I could not know otherwise. The man was also in possession of a strongbox, which had been broken open."

He certainly had Mr. Twelvetree's attention. The banker's eyes bulged fishlike behind the spectacles, and his mouth dropped open. Fairfax felt quite at a loss himself. What could it all mean?

"And so," he concluded, "I came here as the bearer of dreadful news, as I thought. Yet . . . I suppose there is no one else bearing your name, sire, who this might be?"

"Hardly." The hand holding the ear trumpet had begun to tremble violently. Mr. Twelvetree stalked over to a side table, poured himself a glassful of something from a decanter—some sort of watery cordial—then sat down by the cold fireplace, leaving Fairfax standing. "I have no family. Besides, my name is known . . . You saw this with your own eyes?"

"Assuredly. You—or your name—had been booked two days since as an inside passenger on this morning's coach to Huntingdon, though to join the coach at Wansford, the next stop, rather than here in Stamford."

Again that thorough-going stare. Well, Fairfax thought, it must be the devil of a shock to find yourself apparently shot dead by a highwayman.

Or by anyone, come to that. And now Fairfax mentally framed the question that, he guessed, was revolving in Mr. Nicholas Twelvetree's mind: Was this a simple matter of a highwayman and his casual victims? Or something altogether more sinister, pointed?

Certainly the banker was not taking this strange news in any philosophical spirit. There were beads of sweat on his narrow brow that were not called forth by any heart in this cheerless room. With a jerk he pulled out a large snowy handkerchief and held it to his nose, adding a camphor smell to that of the scented pastilles burning on the mantelshelf and the bunch of medicinal herbs on the desk.

"I made no such booking," he said. "Nor did any of my servants. I can answer for that."

"The man at the coach office was not sure, but he thought it was a clerk who—"

"Also impossible. I know my staff. What is more, sir, I seldom travel abroad, being vulnerable in health. This whole business is a mistake . . . though what manner of mistake I cannot conceive." The banker gave Fairfax a sharp, suspicious glance. "What did you mean by this man's resemblance to me?"

"The dead man was dressed much like you. He wore spectacles and had an ear trumpet about him."

No wonder that the clerk had viewed him as some sick hoaxer. This was rather horrible. Just as Fairfax found himself pitying Mr. Twelvetree, his eye strayed to a painting above the mantelshelf. It was a portrait in oils of the banker himself, done by a journeyman artist, judging by the rather stiff technique and unsophisticated color. And yet that unknown painter, used no doubt to turning out likenesses of provincial gentry by the dozen, had responded to and caught something highly individual in his sitter. Fairfax sensed the heat of a tremendous will in Nicholas Twelvetree, and the painter had found the spark of it in that awkward, intent face. The portrait was of a man about to make a bargain— forever, instinctively, always about to make a bargain—perhaps even with his namesake, Old Nick himself.

Then Fairfax noticed a much smaller portrait, of a woman, hanging to one side; but Mr. Twelvetree spoke before he could give attention to it.

"Then this booking was made in my name by someone else—for who knows what purpose, what imposture . . ." In a self-communing way Twelvetree wrapped his coat around his thin frame, tapped his lips with intelligent fingers. "Some jest? A very elaborate one. I have no acquaintance of a jesting turn of mind. I am little disposed to society . . . A highwayman, you say, sir? Stangate Hole is a notorious bad spot, and I hear has been much plagued by one of these criminals of late."

"A highwayman, it would appear," Fairfax said. "Unless,

Mr. Twelvetree, you can think of any other explanation for this shocking event."

"I? It has naught to do with me, sir. I was ignorant of this whole matter until"—he actually consulted his watch—"twelve minutes ago. You have no reason to think otherwise, sir."

"Well," Fairfax said placatingly, "doubtless there is some explanation, which will appear in due course. Sir Edward, as a magistrate, is resolved to have the matter fully investigated, and the culprit brought to book."

Again the banker studied him. Then he tucked away the handkerchief and was brisk. "Most naturally. And though, I repeat, I have absolutely no knowledge of this matter, I shall exert all influence in my power to assist. This person must indeed be caught quickly." Pacing, he turned on Fairfax. "But what is being done? The constables alerted? The magistrates? Are we all to be murdered in our beds?"

"I think this particular malefactor confines his attention to travelers," Fairfax said. "But as I said, Sir Edward is determined on his capture. There is already a price on the man's head, and Sir Edward speaks of adding to the sum."

"Really? Then," Mr. Twelvetree said after a thoughtful moment, "I shall too. Dear, dear. To think . . . And others killed too." Very much an afterthought. "Stangate Hole. And Wansford was the place, you say, where this—person presumed to be me boarded the coach? Extraordinary. This person—I shall need to know, sir, who has been making free with my name. Very regrettable no doubt if the person is deceased, but you must consider my position. I need to know what has been going on."

"Dr. Tuplin is examining the remains now. I daresay some identification will be made soon enough. There is sure to be a coroner's inquest tomorrow, if you wish to—"

"I cannot attend." The banker was curt, gnawing his lip. "I do not stir abroad—almost never. I must take care of myself. I cannot expose my health at such a—public place." He went to the window again and ran his long questing fingers along the sill, as if testing it for security.

A frightened man, thought Fairfax. But then, it was alarming news. He tried to put himself in the banker's position. Someone turning up at his door, informing him that a person called Robert Fairfax, answering very much to his description, had been killed in an attack on a stagecoach . . . It would feel strange beyond words: a cheese nightmare, an opium dream.

It would be a matter of utter disbelief, in fact—in a way that it did not seem, quite, for this man.

"Well, Mr. Twelvetree, I'm sorry to intrude so unpleasantly on your time. I'm sure you may easily come by any information that you require, by applying to the George. I may tell Sir Edward you intend to add to the reward?"

"You may. Fifty guineas. Pounds, call it, rather. Fifty pounds," Mr. Twelvetree said, nodding in his self-communing way.

"And there is no information I may offer on your behalf to the magistrates?" Fairfax trod delicately. "You have no notion of who or what might be behind this curious deception—if deception it is?"

Nicholas Twelvetree, over his scented handkerchief, gave Fairfax a last transfixing stare, as if to commit his image to memory.

"None." He let it drop, a clipped halfpence of a word.

Fairfax went to the door, glad enough to get out: the medicinal smells were making him feel a little queasy. As he reached for the handle, however, Mr. Twelvetree spoke again.

"You cannot get out."

Of course, it was locked; he knew it, and the banker knew he knew it. Yet still Fairfax had an odd feeling that Nicholas Twelvetree enjoyed, even relished, saying it.

He waited while Mr. Twelvetree first rang the bell, then unlocked this door and then the door of the anteroom with a great bunch of shining keys. Another manservant had appeared in answer to the bell, hulking and beetle-browed and warty as a toad. Fairfax wondered if there was a half decent-looking person in the whole house.

"Starkey, return here when you have shown Mr. Fairfax out. I would speak with you urgently."

With a rapid jangle of keys, Nicholas Twelvetree locked himself in again.

An odd fish indeed, Fairfax thought as he made his way back to the George. More spider than fish, though—spinning his financial webs from the comfortless nest . . . Then he ruefully acknowledged his own prejudice. He had seen not a single book in that room, and though he had seen so little of the house apart from closed doors, he imagined the same throughout. Now if he was as wealthy as Twelvetree obviously was, he would line his walls with books, and pay homage to them from the comfort of a great wing chair with a full decanter of the choicest Madeira at his elbow . . . But he was not wealthy; he was not Nicholas Twelvetree; and people were various, Fairfax reminded himself. Anyhow, there was no reason to suspect that the banker was telling anything but the truth when he claimed to know nothing of this coach booking made in his name. Indeed, the more he thought about it, the more unlikely it seemed that a wealthy man of retiring habits would travel alone on an unguarded coach, carrying a conspicuous strongbox. With the road to Huntingdon known to be haunted by a notorious highway-man, it would be foolhardy.

In fact, it was almost an invitation.

Fairfax thought about that, and about the pistols in the dead man's hands, as he passed beneath the great gallows-sign of the George. A voice suddenly stirred him from reflection.

"Sir. Sir, I am wanted, I believe."

It was preacher, Henry Griggs, calling out to him. He was mounted now, his horse reshod, though the animal was coming up the south road at a weary plod. Patting its neck, Griggs got down and let it by the bridle.

"I came as fast as I could. A message from your master reached me at Huntingdon."

"My . . . ?" After a bitter moment Fairfax swallowed it. The consciousness of what he was and what he had been, the pricking reminder of his dark fortune, was always liable to come upon him like this. "Ah, yes, Sir Edward."

"It was lucky. I was still at the inn awaiting the shoeing of my horse."

"You know what has happened Mr. Griggs?"

"I have the drift of the tale: naught else is talked of in Huntingdon just now. I passed the wreck of the coach on my way here. There are people gathering on the road like carrion crows, to look. I tremble for them." He shook his head, austere, pale-eyed. "I came, because I understand there is a belief I might know something of one of the victims, though I do not see how this can be."

They went into the inn yard.

"It appears, from the register at the booking office," Fairfax said, "that one of the dead passengers bears the same surname as yourself. I hope . . ." He did not know how to go on. Griggs had stopped dead. The grave pallor of the preacher's face had turned to chalk. Fairfax had never seen a living man so utterly white. "I hope, indeed, that your errand is a futile one."

The preacher put a hand momentarily to his side, with a faint grunt, as if he had been struck. "Pray God it is so," he said with an effort. "But—whatever He wills."

"You have a relation who . . . ?" Again Fairfax couldn't go on. He had not expected this; and Griggs was a hard man to offer sympathy to.

"I have a relation." Griggs closed his lips tightly, glanced around him as if just coming out of a daze, then signaled to an ostler. "I must stable my horse . . . Sir, are the remains laid here? I must see of course. I must see with my own eyes."

"The . . . the dead were taken to the Cross Keys, a little way from here. A doctor was with them." As he spoke Fairfax saw, in the diamond-pained window of the coffee room, the leonine head of Sir Edward, and with him, Dr. Tuplin. "I see the doctor now. If you will follow me . . ."

"Ah, Fairfax." Sir Edward was polishing off a plate of cold meats. "Here's the damnedest thing. Tuplin tells me that poor butchered fellow in the coach *wasn't* Twelvetree at all. I says to him, but we've looked at the register. But no, turns out Tuplin's doctored Twelvetree in his time and knows his looks well."

"The deceased was a younger man," said Dr. Tuplin, who was taking brandy, "and local, I fancy. I think I know him by sight, though not as a patient. But he was certainly dressed much in the manner of Mr. Twelvetree."

"Yes," said Fairfax, "I have just seen that gentleman. I have never brought a man such odd news before."

"Seen him, eh? There's not many as gets an audience. The fellow's as close as an oyster," Sir Edward said. "Well, what had he to say to this diabolical business? Grows rummer all the time."

"He was—concerned, as one might expect. As is Mr. Griggs here." Fairfax presented the preacher, whose face was now stony. "He has come in answer to your request, and is under some apprehension, finding that Griggs is the name of the other victim, that—"

"I must see the body." Griggs addressed the doctor; he had not even glanced at Sir Edward. "Will you show me?"

"Certainly," Dr. Tuplin said, rising. "I should warn you, sir, if you think to make an identification, that the sight may be somewhat distressing."

Fairfax remembered the shattered face of the outside passenger, staring at the sky. Then he remembered the gibbet, and the crow—and quickly banished the thought of what horrors there might have been if the dead had lain there longer.

"I must see the body," Griggs repeated.

"You have kin in these parts, my friend?" Sir Edward said, softening his tone.

"All men are kin," Griggs said, with a bare glance, and turned to the doctor again. "I am ready, sir."

Fairfax and Sir Edward went with them to the Cross Keys, an old low-eaved tavern of stone and thatch with a capacious yard. There, among the barrels, stood the unmistakable form of a bier; there was a hammering in an outhouse. Let us eat and drink; for tomorrow we shall die, thought Fairfax grimly.

The laying-out room was at the rear, down a short flight of brick steps. Fairfax had seen enough, and was glad he did not have to go in. For an instant, it seemed that Henry Griggs would not go in either. He hesitated at the top of the steps, and swayed a little.

"Steady, friend," said Sir Edward, and offered his flask. "Take a nip to strengthen you."

"That is weakness, not strength," Griggs said. His face was still entirely without color. He took a deep breath and followed the doctor in.

"Bah, there's no doing anything with the fellow," Sir Edward said, shrugging and taking a nip himself. "Well, if it is some kin of his lying there, then that's one conundrum solved."

"Yes," said Fairfax uncertainly. "But again, it's curious. He said he could hardly see how it could be anyone he knew, then it was as if some thought came upon him. As if he concluded something . . . Yet Griggs is after all not that uncommon a name. And if he were expecting a relative to be traveling on the *Flyer*, he would surely say so."

"Well, perhaps—though he's too damnably stiff-necked to say anything much. But what's this hare you're starting, Fairfax? Some preacherly plot? Perhaps good Mr. Griggs doing a little highway robbery in between the prayerfests? In which case what has he done with this Mrs. Parry? Nay, man, you're overfinicking."

Fairfax smiled. "I daresay. But as you remarked, Sir Edward, it grows rummer all the time. I was most curiously struck by Mr. Twelvetree. He seemed horribly frightened—

and yet not greatly astonished by his own death, as it were. Tell me, was Mr. Twelvetree ever married?"

Before Sir Edward could reply the door opened.

Henry Griggs walked past them, across the wainscoted passage, into the dingy little taproom. He sat down heavily on a stool and it seemed, from his whole attitude, that he must bury his head in his hands. And yet he arrested the movement, as if with a flexing of will. He placed his hands on his knees—square, roughened, yet not coarse hands—and stared ahead of him. The preternaturally blue eyes were, Fairfax saw, filmed each with a tear precise and translucent as the cover of a watch.

Dr. Tuplin, somber, said, "Mr. Griggs had identified the body of the outside passenger as that of his brother."

"Jonathan," Griggs said, and for the first time Fairfax heard tenderness in that sternly musical voice. "His journey was not long. Well—well. Released, after all, from a world of sin. Praise God. The Lord gave, and the Lord hath taken away; blessed be the name of the Lord."

"A bad business," Sir Edward said, frowning. "A shocking business, my friend. Never fear, we will find that murderous dog, and he will be punished, my word on it. Now pray can you shed any light on this matter? Was your brother robbed too?"

Griggs put the back of his hand to his eyes, delicately, composedly. "The things of this world do not concern him now." The publican-undertaker, a little, greasy, eager man, was hovering near; Griggs waved him away.

"There is nothing in the dead man's pockets," put in Dr. Tuplin. "Nothing at all."

"Well, had your brother baggage with him, d'you know?" Sir Edward asked. "If there is anything identifiable taken, we may trace the culprit through it, when he tries to sell it."

"I can't answer such questions about my brother," Griggs said stonily.

"Perhaps when you have collected yourself a little. It was

a bad shock," said Dr. Tuplin, who seemed one of those men born to moderate and mediate.

"The shock is over," Griggs said, "and as you assure me, sir, that my brother's passing must have been swift, then as a Christian I must rejoice, for now he is happier than we can be." With his habitual mild truculence, he gazed at each in turn, then went on, "I cannot give you the information you seek, because I had no notion that my brother would be on that coach. I can tell you about him, if you wish. His name was Jonathan Griggs, and he was thirty-two years old, seven years my junior. Our parents died young, and we were much together till recent years. We lived and labored together, in sober and godly content; Jonathan did not join the connection, but he was always . . . full of God's grace." Again it seemed he would cover his face; again the gesture was suppressed, though with a visible shudder. "I am the last man to question any dispensation of Providence; but still, what happened seemed—seemed hard. Some two and half years ago, my brother lost his reason. He had always been a man of tender and impressible feeling—a child's sweetness—the gentlest creature ever born. There was an unhappy attachment to a girl. What seemed a melancholy fit became . . . a malady of the mind, with no hope of a cure. I would have kept him by me. I resisted what had to be done. But there was no help for it. When he was at his worst, he was not fit to be free. So he was taken into an asylum for lunatics—Mr. Rowe's asylum, at Ryhall, a few miles north of here."

"I know the place," Dr. Tuplin said, nodding. "I am sorry indeed. But your brother recovered, to be released?"

"He was not released. He never got any better," Griggs said bleakly. "He wasn't violent, and he had times when his mind was clear. But he didn't get better. My brother escaped from Mr. Rowe's house three days ago. Mr. Rowe sent a servant over to my house at Eaton Socon directly, to tell me what had happened. He thought—as I did—that poor Jonathan might try to make his way to me. I believe now"— he licked his dry lips—"that it was so."

"Mr. Griggs, outside passenger to Eaton Socon," Fairfax said, remembering the booking-office register.

"Good God," murmured Sir Edward. "But how the devil came he to escape? Was he not properly confined? And how did he come by the money for the coach fare?"

"I chose Mr. Rowe's house because 'tis known for kind usage of its inmates," Griggs said, his brows lowered at the baronet's language. "I have stinted myself to pay for his keep there, rather than see him chained in some parish mad-house. Such poor souls as live at Mr. Rowe's long, and who are not dangerous, have a measure of freedom. They take a turn in the garden; they are encouraged to occupy themselves. Some may walk down to the village, accompanied, of course. Jonathan was always furnished with some money, and with decent clothes. And as I said, his mind would clear sometimes—it was so the last time I visited him, a fortnight ago. 'Twas like a cloud lifting from the sun. Though the cloud always fell again." Something of this same effect was visible on Henry Griggs's face as he talked of his brother. "It would be a simple enough matter to get away, if the fancy came upon him. So, that is why I am abroad this week. I couldn't journey on the Sabbath, of course, so yesterday I rode up to Ryhall to see Mr. Rowe and discover what I could. It was as I thought: Jonathan had been in good case, it seemed, and had been enjoying the garden by himself. And then, over the wall and away. If it was one of his clear times, he may even have wondered why he was there at all. Mr. Rowe was good enough to point me to a cottage in the village where I could have a bed for the night. I was up betimes this morning, and set out to ride southward, taking in Huntingdon on my way to see my brethren in the connection there, and lead them in prayer. I confess too that I—I held a little hope that I might hear word of Jonathan along the road. Perhaps even find him, if God willed it." His eyes fixed almost dreamily on the sanded floor, Griggs added, "He did not."

"It is a grim end to your hope, Mr. Griggs," Dr .Tuplin said quietly.

Griggs's head went up. "I am content. How can I not be? Jonathan is happy."

Fairfax saw a twitch of irritation in Sir Edward's burly shoulders. "But cold-blooded murder must be punished, my friend. And when one of the victims is, begging your pardon, a harmless lunatic, then it sticks in my craw all the worse. He *was* harmless, Griggs?"

"To everyone but himself," Griggs said. "You may ask Mr. Rowe all about it; he will confirm what I say."

Fairfax intercepted a glance from Sir Edward: *your job.*

"I daresay you saw the other poor creatures in there," Sir Edward went on, nodding his head at the laying-out room. "The coachman, and a gentleman who was riding inside the coach. You don't happen to recognize him?"

Griggs shook his head. "I never saw him before. But I am not much in these parts, except when I would visit Jonathan—once a month, twice if I could shift for it. I have my bread to earn. I am a seedsman in a small way, and have a little market garden; my life is simple." He seemed to throw this statement of fact at the bewigged and beruffled baronet like a challenge.

Sighing, sticking out his jaw, Sir Edward said, "Well, I suppose you know no one of the name of Parry? Mrs. Parry. Apparently she was on the coach with your unfortunate brother—yet the deuce knows where she's gone to."

"No. I know no one of that name."

"Might Jonathan, perhaps, have known this lady, Mr. Griggs?" Fairfax put in.

"He knew no ladies. He lived in his own world." All at once Griggs was on his feet. "I think I have told you all I can. Now there are things for me to do. Jonathan must have a burying. The person of this house makes such arrangements, I think . . . ?"

"Nothing of that sort may be arranged till after the coroner's inquest, my friend," Sir Edward said, "which is to be tomorrow. You had best be on hand to testify, as his kin."

Griggs inclined his head. "And then I may have him buried? Because I must soon be on my way. I have promised the brethren at Huntingdon a preaching. I have the Lord's work as well as my own."

"Well, as long as you are here tomorrow," Sir Edward said. "The George, I would suggest, offers comfortable accommodation and a good table."

"For a man of my means and wants," Griggs said austerely, "this place will do, if the man can give me a bed overnight." The publican had popped up again, nodding eagerly.

"Well," Sir Edward said, stumping to the door with barely concealed annoyance, "I thank you for your help, Griggs, and I'm sorry for your brother . . . Insufferable fellow!" he burst out as soon as they were outside. "Like he's swallowed a poker! If these are the godly, give me the devil's party any day of the week."

"He was much affected, I think, by the sight of his poor brother," Dr. Tuplin said temperately.

"The brother I pity. But there's no pitying such a man as that—he'll throw it back in your face. And as for affected— why, I think it's pretty cold, the way he wants to get the poor fellow buried so he can be off to his preaching."

"I think Mr. Griggs's faith is sincere," Fairfax said, "and so he sincerely believes that his brother has gone to a better place—is to be envied, even; and thus his mortal clay is of very little account. All the things of this world are corrupt, and not to be valued a jot. 'Tis a severe sort of belief, difficult for rational men to penetrate." Also, he thought, a repulsive one; but he felt his own touch of envy for it. Such utter certainty must be a great resource. It helped this man view the murdered corpse of his brother without once crying to the skies or swearing vengeance.

Sir Edward grunted, unconvinced. "So, on the coach we have a disappearing woman, a man who seems to be

Nicholas Twelvetree but isn't, and a lunatic from a local madhouse. What do you know of that place, Tuplin?"

"Nothing bad—which, as asylums go, is as good a recommendation as any. I hear the regimen is enlightened, though I have never visited it, and I know of no medical man who has. The asylum-keeper, Mr. Samson Rowe, was, I believe, a physician in the North Country. He took a special interest in diseases of the mind, and opened the asylum with a legacy."

"I have seen Bedlam, of course," Sir Edward said. "A barbarous place. My girls were all a-dangle to go and see it last time we were in London, but I had to be pretty firm. None but a brute could find entertainment in goggling at those poor tormented creatures. I would have the practice forbidden."

"It sounds as if Mr. Rowe's establishment is much more humane," Fairfax said. "One wonders why, indeed, Mr. Griggs's brother should suddenly choose this time, after two and a half years, to make an escape."

"Oh, there's no knowing how the mind of such a poor afflicted soul works," Sir Edward said. "Still, it will be worth our while to talk to this Mr. Rowe."

"You don't trust Griggs's account?"

"My dear fellow, I've served as Justice of the Peace for nigh on fifteen years. I never trust anybody's account of anything."

Evening was descending as they came once more to the inn yard of the George. Lights glowed in the many latticed windows and there was a genial smell of roasting beef. Dr. Tuplin said he would have to leave them now, and while he spoke with Sir Edward on arrangements for the inquest tomorrow, Fairfax found himself gazing at the York coffee-room window with a wistful sense of being chilled, tired, and hungry.

As he looked, a woman stepped into view, right in the center of the window. She stood there quite still, looking out—at him?—perfectly framed, like a three-quarter-length portrait. She was young, dark-haired and dark-eyed, oval-faced, not very tall though with a well-rounded figure, and she was dressed simply and fetchingly—straw hat, flowered gown with laced stomacher and a crossed white handkerchief over her shoulders. A genre painting, then, stressing nature and light and simplicity, rather than the grand flourish of a society portrait.

This fanciful notion so absorbed him that it was startling to see her suddenly move, her hand going up to her face. There was distress in the gesture, perhaps also a sort of comfort—as if she found reassurance in cupping the lovely shape of her cheek in the palm of her hand. Then, more startling, another figure appeared in the frame. A dark stocky young man approached from behind her and tentatively reached out to touch her arm.

She gave such a convulsive jump, turning, that Fairfax jumped in sympathy.

"Handsome creature," Sir Edward said at his elbow. "Now, let's find Quigley. Ah! Here he comes. Well, Quigley, my carriage has arrived, I hope? I think we've done all we can for now, and I'd like to see my home."

"It's here, sir." Mr. Quigley, who was very agitated—almost dancing on his toes, with the oddly poised delicacy of fat men. "And so is a young woman, come asking after her husband. Lord bless me, in quite a taking she is. I told her you were in charge of the matter and that you'd be here soon. The fact is"—he lowered his voice—"she says her husband took the coach to Huntingdon this morning—the *Flyer*—and hasn't returned."

Four

Quite a taking, Mr. Quigley had said, but when they entered the coffee room, what struck Fairfax about the young woman was her composure. She turned from the window to face them, her hands folded in front of her, and fixed Sir Edward, Mr. Quigley, and Fairfax in turn with a luminous, unblinking gaze. And then Fairfax saw that the composure was more like a gathering in of vast energy. Her breathing was as rapid as a kitten's; her nails shone whiter against the white-pressed skin of her elegant hands.

"My dear, won't you sit down? I am Sir Edward Nugent; my secretary, Fairfax." All courtly gentleness, the baronet steered the young woman into a seat by the fireplace. "As Justice of the Peace, I am looking into this unfortunate affair of the *Stamford Flyer*. You have heard, perhaps, that the coach suffered an accident."

"Molly came to me with some news, or gossip," the young woman said. "My servant girl, that is. It was all round the town. About the *Flyer* being held up by highwaymen . . ." Her voice, light and musical, lost its firmness very suddenly, her hands writhed, yet her gaze did not falter. "And everyone killed."

"We came to find out the truth of it. These things get twisted, don't they? It was the stocky young man whom Fairfax had seen with her in the window; he was hovering at a kind of tenderly respectful distance. "Tom should have been home by now—but there may be any number of reasons why he mightn't, you know . . ."

Sir Edward said, "And you are, sir?"

"This is Mr. Joseph Fox," the young woman said, her voice steady again. "He is a friend and partner to my husband, Tom. I am Barbara Honeyman. My husband is a timber merchant at Water Street. It was with regard to his business that he set out early this morning to go to Huntingdon. He said—last night, that is—he said that he would take the coach."

"The *Flyer*?" asked Sir Edward.

"I believe so—though I cannot recall him saying the name."

"I thought it must be the *Flyer*," Joseph Fox said. "It's the only one I know of. There's the *Daylight* from Grantham, Tuesdays and Thursdays, but that doesn't come to Stamford until about half past ten, and Tom went early. That I can engage for, because I saw him go. 'Twas before six—not even full light. I'd come to the yard early because we were expecting a load of timber by lighters from Spalding. They sail by night when there's a moon. Tom was up and about, said he was coaching it to Huntingdon today. I had my morning draft with him in the kitchen, and off he went. It was mighty early. It's only a step from Water Street to here, and I thought he would have time and to spare before the coach; but he said something about getting breakfast at the George first."

"Did he take anything with him?" Fairfax said.

"He had a small bundle, wrapped in sacking," said the young man. "I don't know what 'twas."

Mrs. Honeyman, at Sir Edward's inquiring glance, said, "I know nothing about that. I wasn't astir when my husband left. He had merely told me last night that he was coaching to Huntingdon on the morrow, and to expect him back by the early evening. I might have felt no anxiety yet, if it were not for these reports—these tales . . ."

"I was at the yard all day, dealing with the timber,"

Joseph Fox put in. "I was just getting ready to go home when Mrs. Honeyman comes out to me with this dreadful tale she'd heard from Molly. The wench is always full of gossip, mind; so I said we'd go round to the coach office and find out the truth of it."

"Mr. Quigley," Sir Edward said, "will you bring a glass of brandy? My dear Mrs. Honeyman, we must look at the facts carefully. I have to tell you that the reports are true: the *Flyer* was attacked, and both coachman and passengers, I regret to say—"

"He's shot—he's shot!" The cry she let out was loud, agonized—yet musical still: the notes, Fairfax's ear discerned, a perfect fifth and seventh.

"Hush, now, ma'am—don't take on," Fox said, looking pained. "We know nothing yet."

"Madam, the identity of one of the passengers is still unknown," Sir Edward said. "He booked his seat on the coach in the name of Mr. Twelvetree, the banker, whom you may know; but the man we found is not Mr. Twelvetree, though there was some superficial resemblance." He glanced at Fairfax a moment; both were thinking the same thought. "Perhaps, Mrs. Honeyman, you could describe your husband?"

"He is—he is a man of six-and-thirty." Barbara Honeyman, whom Fairfax guessed was no more than twenty-three, composed herself again, biting her lips. The biting could add nothing to their redness. "Quite tall, slenderly made, fair—he generally wears his own hair, curled; it sat quite gentlemanly upon him . . . oh I beg you, tell me if it is he. It is the most appalling torture—"

"Does he wear spectacles, ma'am?" Fairfax said.

A startled silence, almost as if he had asked something indecent. Barbara Honeyman stared at him, then at her knotted hands.

She said, "He does not. But last week—last week, Tom brought home a pair of spectacles that he had got at second-hand from the market. He said he fancied his eyes were growing weak and wanted to try if they would help. I did not much like them on him and he put them away . . ." Tears began to bead on her eyelashes. "What is going on? Please tell me . . ."

With another glance at Fairfax, Sir Edward said, "I was going to ask you, Mrs. Honeyman, whether you could think of any reason why your husband should pass himself off as Mr. Twelvetree. But I think what we had best do, if you feel strong enough, is walk over to the Cross Keys. Nothing is certain, I repeat, but equally, I think, nothing can be known until you have viewed the person lying there. It will not be pleasant; it may be the hardest thing you will ever have to do."

Sir Edward's making a dramatic challenge of the request, Fairfax noticed, seemed to have its effect. Mrs. Honeyman looked up, nodded, and rose. Her face was dewy with tears that she did not wipe.

"What about me? Perhaps I could do it. I'm Tom's best friend, and his partner," Fox said, keeping watchfully at Mrs. Honeyman's side.

"You also, perhaps, sir," Sir Edward said, "but Mrs. Honeyman, as next of kin, must make the identification. Or otherwise, my dear," he added gently.

But Barbara Honeyman seemed to need no comforting flannel now: ready, resolved, wanting it over and done. Her step was steady as they made their way back to the Cross Keys, though Joseph Fax still hovered near, as if fearing some collapse. He was a man in his late twenties, dressed in a blue brass-buttoned coat of faintly naval cut, dark and, for all his sturdiness, lithe with an animal vitality; his own black curly hair tied in a queue, large strong restless hands. There was an open obligingness about him, a directness of accent and look. Fairfax had a feeling that he had been at sea.

It was Fox who kept talking nervously as they walked, trying almost desperately to make the best of things. "I keep thinking perhaps he didn't go by the *Flyer* after all. He might have gone by the carrier's wagon—half a dozen of them a day plying that road. What business he had in Huntingdon I don't know. I leave that side of things to him. Some builder perhaps. Tom started up the house, you see, and does the managing and accounting. I put in my little nest egg, a third share really, and I do the day-to-day business in the yard. Seasoning and dressing and cutting. Good with my hands, you see, not so much with my brain. That's Tom. So I keep thinking the carrier but I don't know . . . He was dressed rather—well, I can't imagine him sitting in a wagon among a lot of straw and farmer's chickens. He had on a suit of a kind of rusty black—very sober-looking, I'd never seen it before. I joked with him before he went, said he looked as respectable as a parson, but he just smiled."

"His father's."

Barbara Honeyman, walking just ahead of them, stopped dead as she spoke these words. Now Fairfax saw how slight she was, how young. They were just about to cross the street to the Cross Keys, and a dray was turning in, lumbering, tilting. It was entirely loaded with the carcasses of ducks and other wildfowl, plentiful in the nearby fen, and for a moment that whole deathly load—limp necks, daintily stiffened feet—overshadowed and seemed on the point of toppling onto her.

"It was an old suit of his late father's. He took it from a trunk the other day, where it had been laid up in mothballs. He said it was a pity it should go to waste."

Fairfax met her eyes. In the lamplit evening they were unfathomable, as befitted the situation.

For this part he had very little doubt now that the unknown man lying in the stone-flagged room at the Cross Keys was Barbara Honeyman's husband. What curious deception the man had been involved in. Why had he made a booking in the name of Mr. Twelvetree? Why had he taken pains to imitate that gentleman's appearance? Why had he gone to join the coach at the next stage at Wansford? What had his errand been with a now-empty strongbox? A way to the answers must be through Barbara Honeyman and Joseph Fox. But first there must be confirmation.

It came, soon enough. Sir Edward gently ushered the lady into the back room of the Cross Keys. There was a single, hollow sob, almost owlish in its tone. Joseph Fox, waiting in the taproom with Fairfax and the ever-eager publican, went white.

Barbara Honeyman came out, supported by Sir Edward. "Brave in you, my dear," he said, helping her to a seat, "damned brave I call it. There, over now . . . Mr. Fox, if you are ready . . ."

Joseph Fox looked far from ready. But he went in, and emerged very soon, trembling.

"Bring me a glass of something strong, will you?" he said to the publican. "Blast my eyes before I see such a sight again. Poor old Tom. God rest him."

"Ma'am, it is your husband, Mr. Thomas Honeyman?" Sir Edward pressed gently.

Weeping silently, the young widow nodded.

"It's Tom," Fox said, swiftly draining the brandy that was brought him, "though I never saw him in such a rum old wig before. My God, I can't believe it. My God." He waggled his glass for more, sweating.

"We shall have the devil who is responsible, ma'am, never fear," Sir Edward said, seating himself near Mrs. Honeyman. "But I think we shall need help. And anything you can tell us that may furnish that help . . . All we know, ma'am, is that the coach was attacked at Stangate Hole sometime before noon. The coachman, name of Crabbe, was killed too, and also a man named Jonathan Griggs; and it seems there was a third passenger called Mrs. Parry—of her fate we know nothing. Are any of those names familiar to you?"

"I don't think so . . . but I can't think . . ." In her distress Fairfax noted that she had reverted to that earlier gesture of self-comfort—holding the shape of her cheek in her hand.

"I never heard of them," Fox said. Brandy had turned his

pallor to a flush. "Why would a highwayman slaughter so? What need was there?"

The pertinent question. Fairfax said, "When we discovered Mr. Honeyman, he had about him a brace of pistols. They had not been fired. Also he had with him a small strongbox, about the size of a jewel box, emptied, presumably by his attacker. You knew your husband possessed such things, ma'am?"

"Yes. Or—no . . . I don't know of any strongbox . . . He bought a brace of pistols, I know, some months ago. I did not like to see them about. But he said it was as well for a man of property to have such things. I don't know why he had them, or why he was dressed so . . . I only know I have lost the best of husbands, and I cannot—I cannot support it . . . I don't know what I shall do . . ." Weeping bitterly, she covered her face.

Fairfax mouthed to Joseph Fox the word *Children*? Fox, after a moment of puzzlement, shook his head.

"I'm greatly sorry, my dear. There is no mitigating such a loss," Sir Edward said feelingly, patting her hand. "I have known it myself. All I can offer is the assurance of Dr. Tuplin, who examined the victims, that the end was entirely swift. Little enough, I know." He nodded at Fairfax, adding, "I think we should trouble you no more with questions. And I think you should go home and take care of yourself. Is there someone who can be with you?"

"Me," said Joseph Fox promptly. "I'll take Mrs. Honeyman home, and stay by her. I'm much about the place anyhow. I thought of poor Tom like a brother if anything."

"You are very good, sir; but I was thinking perhaps a lady to bear you company, Mrs. Honeyman."

"I want no one," she said. "I can be alone. I *am* alone, now"—drawing herself up—"from this moment. It must be faced. Alone—that is me."

It was affecting. Was it also, Fairfax wondered, too readily, consciously tragic? He recalled those melodic cries, *He's shot—he's shot!* And now it occurred to him that no one had said anything about shooting at that point. But of course, news of the *Flyer*'s fate had already got round the town, garbled or not: that was how it had reached her. And at moments of high emotion, one tended to fall into dramatic postures. That was where drama came from, after all.

"There's old Mrs. Raimey next door," Fox said. "She can come in and sit with you, you know."

Mrs. Honeyman seemed not to hear him. She turned the white oval of her face, not to the benignly bending Sir Edward, but to Fairfax. She was utterly charming, he thought randomly. Charming not in the sense of the polite drawing room, where the word was applied to an insincere compliment or a frock with bows, but in its true meaning. In his younger years as a Grub Street hack Fairfax had labored as one of Johnson's assistants, compiling the great *Dictionary*, and words were the furniture of his mind. To charm was to enchant as by a song—which, of course, was where the word *enchant* came from likewise. Chant, canto, cantata. He was willing to bet, suddenly, that Barbara Honeyman was skilled in music. "What about . . . my husband?" she said. "Must I leave him in this place?"

"I think it might be as well," Fairfax said. "The landlord here undertakes such work. And the—other matters must wait until after tomorrow, when the coroner and jury will sit in inquest on the death of your husband and his fellow travelers."

"What does it mean?" Still she turned her intensity on him. "Tom is dead, and murdered, and bloody." Said with a sort of defiance, as if, Fairfax thought, everyone else had pusillanimously shirked these words. "Do they have to take his poor wounds and parade them publicly? And—a jury: 'tis as if he murdered himself—"

"It's to decide the cause of death, and when they've done that, they can look for the villain in earnest," said Fox—rather shortly and irritably, it seemed to Fairfax. "You must see that, Mrs. Honeyman. But I know, it's hard . . ." He shuffled his feet, awkward as a schoolboy.

"Yes, Joseph. It is hard."

"You've not doubt heard, ma'am, of this rogue who's been plaguing the north road in our parts," Sir Edward said. "We have good reason to believe now that he has added murder to his crimes. But he'll suffer for what he's done, ma'am, never fear."

"Hang him," the widow said, in an undertone of chilling conviction. "Hang him up and let people see . . . But what is being done? Isn't this murderer being sought, hunted down? He took my husband—does no one care?"

"Come, Mrs. Honeyman, I'll take you home," Fox said. "You'll do yourself no good here."

Tragically, Barbara Honeyman stood facing the closed door of the beery morgue. A glow of sickly candlelight leaked through the crack beneath, as if it were some last spectral emanation from the dead within. "I have lost the best of husbands," she pronounced tonelessly. "I am alone . . . I must go away. Yes, that is what I shall do. I can't stay in Stamford, with all the memories about me . . ."

"Time is enough to think of that." Again Fox was faintly impatient. "Come."

"Did no one survive?" She addressed Fairfax. "Did no one see this monster?"

"Our task would be easier if so. But no matter," Fairfax said. "Every beast leaves a trail. He will be caught, and justice will be done."

She gave him a challenging look. "And will justice bring back Tom?"

"No."

"Then it's no justice."

A woman always ready to fight her corner, he thought: emotional truth versus male facts.

"Come, Mrs. Honeyman," Fox pressed her, "let's get home with you. It's a raw damp sort of evening. You'll catch cold."

"Why, what could that possibly matter?" she said. A reasonable enough question, Fairfax thought; though again it had the effect of making others, in this case her anxious attendant Joseph Fox, seem clumsy, obtuse, heavy-footed. Watching them go at last, Fairfax thought of another question, and was sure that one of them or both, must know the answer to it: why on earth was Tom Honeyman passing himself off as Mr. Nicholas Twelvetree?

They had done, as Sir Edward said, all they could for now; he was eager to be at Cheyney. At the George his carriage was ready, their luggage in the rumble, so after a few last words with Mr. Quigley they were off on the final leg of their interrupted journey. The carriage took them at a clip out of Stamford, through a pleasant well-settled country of limestone villages, sheep meadows, fields neat as strips of corduroy. The counties of Lincolnshire, Northamptonshire, and Huntingdonshire met here, as did the clay midlands and the eastern fens; the place was like a distilled essence of Shire England. Cheyney Hall stood on the edge of a robust little village called Barnack. Limestone deposits here had led to its being quarried, six hundred years ago, for the building of the cathedral at Peterborough. This explained a curious stretch of landscape that Sir Edward pointed out to Fairfax between the lights of the cottages, a miniature range of heathery hills and hollows, as if a piece of moorland fell had crept down from the north.

The same Barnack stone, Sir Edward told Fairfax proudly, had gone into the building of Cheyney Hall a hundred years ago, with slate for the roof from nearby Colleyweston.

The house presented its face at the end of a long straight avenue of lime trees, like an architectural reflection of its owner, Fairfax thought at first sight: handsome, square, civilized, approachable yet absolutely assured. Rambling wings and Gothic turrets would never have done for Sir Edward. As the carriage drew up on well-raked gravel, Fairfax saw that the house was commodious but not overlarge: two stories, a flat central pediment, three rows of scroll-finished

windows on either side of it, rusticated base and a short
flight of steps to the front door, steep hipped roof with dormers. Outbuildings in pavilion style, low and retiring. A very
English compromise between classical and domestic.

"Papa! You are here at last, and what a perfect pig you
were not to come before!"

"You're so late, Papa. We were fancying all sorts—at
least Amelia was, being a goose, and she would not heed me
when I said—"

"Goose to you. Letitia was worried too, Papa; she lies—
and did you bring me the shawl that you promised? Only—"

"There is filial duty for you, Papa. The little miss would
rather have a shawl than you—"

"Oh, boh to you, that is the most monstrous—you know
I have been missing him prodigiously, and I only mentioned
the shawl but once, and . . ."

Like an explosion, Sir Edward's daughters had burst
from the house. Laughing, hugely happy, Sir Edward
hugged and kissed them.

"Well, my dears, I am safe, and so is the shawl, and so are
one or two other things that you shall see by and by. And so
is Mr. Robert Fairfax, who is come to work on your grandfather's library. Fairfax, my daughters: Letitia and Amelia."

Shyness utterly extinguished the two girls for a few moments, as they murmured red-faced greetings. Then they
were off again, bearing their father up the steps. At the top,
in a proscenium of candlelight, servants waited; at their
head, a plain woman whom Sir Edward introduced as Mrs.
Hargrave. She was, Fairfax gathered, governess-companion
and general female presence to the girls in the motherless
household. She had the faintly acid skeptical look of one
who spends much time in the company of those who know
everything, in other words: the young. I shall have that look
myself sooner or later, Fairfax thought. And had the little
minxes been good, Sir Edward inquired, his arms affection-
ately round their shoulders? Only one answer, of course.

But then, the girls or young ladies did seem agreeable,

delightful, not much spoiled. Listening to the teasing and counterteasing that went on between them and Sir Edward—"The blue silk, Papa—we ordered it before you went away." "Whatever for, my dear?" "Why, for the Assembly, Papa—you ordered the gown, so we must be allowed to go." "No, no, I know nothing of this, my dears—" Fairfax was conscious of not fitting in. This was family life, foreign country to him now. He felt regret, also comprehension; this was how people harmlessly and productively used up the restless energy that in a solitary being like him was a continual inward ferment. He was glad to be away for a space, shown by a manservant to his room where he could unpack and wash and dress before joining the family for supper. Well, he had certainly been worse accommodated than this in his time: an ample country-house bedchamber, snugly wainscoted and smelling of beeswax, with a wood fire burning. He parted the brocade curtains to look out over the stable yard. Grooms were unharnessing the carriage horses by lantern light; a maid called out a ribald pleasantry from the back door. Beyond, the soft symmetrical shapes of a formal walled garden; then black folds of country, a cold sea around the warm domestic island. Impossible not to think of the bleak high road where three people had met death, sudden and stark. And impossible not to think of that someone—out there somewhere, walking or resting or drinking, certainly living—who had killed today. Fairfax conjured a notional diary entry: *Tuesday, the sixth of October 1761. Today I, whoever I might be, shot to death three people.* It must be graven thus on the mind, if not on a physical page. How did it feel?

Dark thoughts. Going down to supper he dismissed them, or had them dismissed for him; Cheyney Hall, well lit, comfortably gracious, was an Augustan riposte to morbid imaginings. Reason ruled. There was a touch of grandeur about the hall, with busts in niches either side of the great carved staircase, but in the dining room the chill of aristocratic marble extended only to a monumental chimneypiece. The ceil-

ing was molded with restrained festoons, the walls were
hung with crimson damasks and tapestries, the high-backed
chairs were upholstered, and supper was served on a walnut
dining table large enough for ease but not so vast as to make
conversation a matter of hallooing across the empty spaces.
Though Fairfax had lost count of the number of times Sir
Edward had eaten today, he was not surprised to find the
supper substantial and the baronet's appetite undiminished.

Inevitably, the journey's adventure was spoken of. Sir
Edward tried to play it down, said it was no fit subject for
the table. His daughters were having none of that: London,
clothes, the Assembly, the wrongs of Mrs. Hargrave, were
forgotten; this was excitement. We are all ghouls, thought
Fairfax, but the young are not hypocritical about it.

"And you absolutely saw the coach in the ditch, and the
people lying murdered! How vastly awful and thrilling! I
declare I shouldn't be able to sleep for a week for nightmares!" That was Amelia, the younger, who even as she
spoke was eating as heartily as her father.

"That's no wonder. You had nightmares after that foolish
play we were at, with a ghost who was nothing but a man all
chalked, and a handkerchief round his head." Letitia was,
Fairfax remembered, seventeen. The two years' seniority expressed itself in a selective decorum: she ate little and fas-
tidiously; she kept her back straight; and where her sister
had quite lost her shyness of the stranger, she could not address Fairfax without a pink tinge and a curious arching of
the neck. Her talk, though, was uninhibited. "Papa, do you
suppose the highwayman was watching you from the woods
even then? With his pockets full of his spoils, and his pistols
smoking?"

"My Lord, a highwayman—how monstrous romantic!"
cried Amelia. "With a mask, and pistols and everything, just
like Macheath or Dick Turpin!"

"Macheath was a pretend fellow in a play, my dear," Sir
Edward said. "And Dick Turpin, no matter what the broadsheets say, was a cowardly brute."

"Or Claude Duval," Amelia went on, unperturbed, "who asked the lady to dance a galliard with him, and spared her jewels!"

"A Frenchman," Fairfax could not resist saying, "and so, of course, a more mannerly species of robber."

"You would not find it romantic if you had seen what we have seen, my dears," Sir Edward said. "Nor, indeed, did Mr. Devereaux when he was robbed in broad daylight. The friend I told you of, Fairfax; I must have a talk with him and see if he remembers anything useful."

"Then you are going to catch this man, Papa?" Amelia asked.

"A dreadful crime has been committed. As a magistrate, I shall see to it that everything is done to bring the malefactor to justice. Mr. Fairfax shall be my right arm in this, before I turn him loose in Grandfather's library."

"What about the Assembly ball on Saturday, Papa?" Letitia said. "Just think—there will be any number of people coming in to Stamford by carriage. Rich pickings for your villain. Will people hazard it, do you suppose?"

"Well, now, would you, my dears?"

The girls chorused their determination: fir and flood would not stop them, let alone a highwayman . . .

It was fascinating to observe them. In many ways they were very different. Letitia, at a ball, would be no less than a beautiful young woman. Amelia, scarcely less tall, had a child's unmoderated voice and the square-bodiced dress hung flatly on her, as on the jointed dolls that were used by dressmakers. And yet one could see that the elder had looked like the younger only very recently, and that Amelia would very soon resemble Letitia. The effect was as if they were growing and changing visibly, right before one's eyes. It must make a man philosophical, Fairfax thought, to live with it: the hourglass ever running.

Sir Edward did not insist that the men stay at the table with the port when dinner was over, a custom Fairfax always disliked. Instead he proposed that they look over old Sir

Jemmy's library. "Let us see if Mr. Fairfax is daunted, eh, my dears?" He chuckled, an arm about each of his daughters.

The library was actually two rooms, one formerly a music room, with double doors connecting them. A gentleman's library was often a quiet room with some books locked in glass cases, where the gentleman came to get away from his family, perhaps tope or snore. The late baronet of Cheyney Hall had turned his into a Byzantine extravagance of learning, a Babel of books. The deep coving had been removed so that the bookshelves could mount to the very cornice. Like the miser's hoard, it was grand, secretive, illogical. Many volumes were shelved spine inward, the edges of their pages worn shiny and smooth as from fond fingers that had known them by touch. Tables were stacked with slablike folios. Fairfax's hesitant fingers touched incunabula or early books, beautiful monsters from Caxton's day. Codices, horn-bound, the ink seeming as fresh as when it poured from the monastic pen. A treatise on medicines in medieval Latin, together with what was surely the Arabic manuscript from which it had been translated.

"But this is remarkable," Fairfax devoutly murmured. "This, surely, is a first printing of *Le Morte D'Arthur*. And this—this must be a Tyndale New Testament; I thought they were all burned . . ."

Through the double doors, more books, but also many paintings and prints—some, Fairfax judged, mere rubbish, some precious; and seafaring maps, beautiful specimens of Portuguese and Turkish cartography, though surely fanciful in some of their details—landmasses to the south of the Indies, for example. Cabinets of coins, medals, relics. It was overwhelming, almost intimidating; he was glad to find some homely touches here—old maps of the Cheyney estate covered with earthy English place names, and drawings in chalks and pencil by the young Misses Nugent, fondly preserved by Grandpapa. The most recent were very accomplished—the girls had talent and had been well taught—but the older ones started off a lot of mutual teasing, and remarks about squint eyes and six-fingered hands.

They were a close family. Fairfax could not help but feel a touch of melancholy exclusion, perhaps more so when Letitia said to him before retiring, with mingled awkwardness and grace, "I hope you'll enjoy your stay with us, Mr. Fairfax." Always a stay, and then a going!—on to some other illusion of home.

Even the prospect of being let loose in that fantastical library, enticing as it was, could not quite hold off gloom as Fairfax blew out his candle and turned in. "Cerebration, young Robbie," his old mentor, Sam Johnson, used to advise him when in these dark moods. "Exercise the sickly mind as you would a limb." So he set himself to thinking, not of the highwayman whom Sir Edward had resolved they would catch, but of highwaymen in general. What did he know of them? He had never had the misfortune to be held up by one himself, though in London he had had his pocket picked several times, and once had been knocked over the head by footpads in a dark byway. The work of a moment; he had found himself on the ground, without hat or purse, while heavy feet trotted swiftly into the darkness. Not even a glimpse of his assailants.

The robbers who plied the high roads were of a different stamp. They were of necessity mounted and armed. Not for them the casual pickings of a teeming city. Their trade entailed a degree of forethought and also of risk; though commonly masked, they had in a way to go before their public like actors. Main roads, well traveled but not overbusy, were their favorite haunt, and in recent years the number of depredations on the main roads out of London—Hounslow Heath, Gadshill, and Shooter's Hill were particularly notorious—had become something of a scandal. Such places offered, of course, the other necessity for the highway robber, a hideout. Sometimes one heard of cases where the criminal had lived a normal life among unsuspecting neighbors—Fairfax remembered one who had been a respectable farmer—but

more usual was the thieves' den, the lonely tumbledown cottage, the drover's hut or lean-to in the deep woods, ready to
be abandoned at a moment's notice.

And then, of course, there were the legends that gathered
around these mysterious rogues. There was no doubt that the
tales of chivalrous larceny, of courtly plundering, came from
the time of Cromwell, when dispossessed Royalists had
taken to the road because their estates were gone and they
knew, or chose to know, no other way to get their living. And
one still heard of scapegrace sons who ran through their inheritance and chose a short life of crime with style rather
than a long one of dull hardship. Yet most, Fairfax thought,
must be of the Dick Turpin type of professional criminal—
and Turpin, as Sir Edward said, had been, for all the mythol-
ogizing, a hardened, calculating brute. He had tortured an
old woman over a fire, among other atrocities, before his
eventual appointment with the gallows at York twenty-two
years ago.

And what of the faceless scourge of the Stamford to
Huntingdon road? His act today had surely made him
among the worst of his kind, though the case would not be
really exceptional in itself were it not for the curious elements that were accreting round it like barnacles: the missing woman, Mrs. Parry; the apparently harmless lunatic,
Griggs; the man who had appeared to be but was not Mr.
Nicholas Twelvetree.

As he dozed at last, Fairfax tried to picture the killer riding out of the trees, masked, pistol uplifted. The thought
came to him just before sleep took hold: what if he did not
mean to kill, but recognized and was recognized by someone on the coach? Then he was in the coach himself,
squeezed in between Barbara Honeyman and Joseph Fox,
who seemed to resent his being there. Opposite him Henry
Griggs the preacher looked on in granite disapproval; beside
him, Mr. Twelvetree and the impostor Tom Honeyman, both
in spectacles and bagwigs, squabbled over a strongbox, tug-
ging it this way and that. *Where is Mrs. Parry?* his dream-

self asked. But no one answered: all looked to the coach window, where a masked figure had appeared. *Mr. Fairfax*, it said, *you must come back to the asylum at once. I shall have to shoot you else.* The muzzle of a pistol flashed, and Fairfax saw, as the ball hit him, that they were all wearing masks . . . He jerked in the bed, then turned over and found other dreams.

Five

The vast carnivorous breakfast served the next morning at Cheyney Hall was a hunter's spread, suitable for a morning in the saddle. But Sir Edward Nugent was not going after hare or fox today: his quarry was the highwayman of Stangate Hole—"my rogue" as he had begun proprietorially to call him. So Stamford must be their destination, first to attend the inquest on the dead passengers before setting in train their inquiries.

For Sir Edward, these concerned a highwayman and no other; but that "something smelt odd" he willingly agreed, and Fairfax, as his agent, was to pursue any track he chose. Sir Edward was very much the country justice this morning, determined to set his corner of England in order, brisk about business. The briskness extended to their means of travel into Stamford, to Fairfax's dismay.

"Why, of course you can ride, Fairfax. Any man can ride. Never fear, you shall have the gentlest nag in my stable. 'Tis the sensible thing, man. After we've heard the coroner, you must be off about your sniffing, and you'll need a mount to get around." So Fairfax rode beside Sir Edward, who sat a horse as if he had done so straight from the cradle, as he probably had. Of course, as Sir Edward said, Fairfax could ride. He just hated doing it, feeling as uncomfortable as a fairground dog walking on its hind legs. The horse, he could tell, hated him instinctively. It seemed to make its back deliberately stiff, and kept rolling its eyes evilly, as if debating whether to bolt.

At the George, where they stabled, Mr. Quigley met them with news of a sort. He had had the damaged *Flyer* brought back, and it was being refitted at the coachmaker's in St. Martin's. He had had reports from his fellow innkeepers on the posting route, including details of the passengers who were to have joined the ill-fated coach later, but there was nothing of note here: there was the elderly clergyman whom Fairfax remembered impatiently waiting at the Bridge in Huntingdon, and much farther on, at Royston, a seamstress had been booked for an outside place. Neither knew any of the other passengers, nor had any information to offer. No one at the inns could recall any suspicious characters hanging about the yards and making inquiries about the expected traffic on the road—though, as Mr. Quigley said, these rogues were sure to be subtle about it anyhow. But the inside passenger going under the name of Twelvetree *had* been remembered, both by the innkeeper at Wansford, where he had joined the coach, and at the next posting stage at Stilton; because "Mr. Twelvetree" had been very noticeable, making a great fuss about safety of the box he was carrying, insisting on having a glass of small beer brought out to the coach, and generally being a demanding customer.

"Well, whatever this Honeyman was up to, he wasn't secretive," Sir Edward commented.

"Quite the reverse," said Fairfax thoughtfully. " 'Twas rather as if he wanted to be noticed."

Nothing was known, however, of the mysterious Mrs. Parry. The innkeepers at Wansford and Stilton thought perhaps they remembered a lady traveling on the coach, but couldn't be sure. In the busy concourse of a coaching inn it was only someone who made a great nuisance of themselves, like the man with the box, who attracted attention. Neither Mrs. Parry nor anyone who knew her had yet come forward. Plainly more publicity was needed, and Mr. Quigley had made a start. He showed them a hand-lettered notice—old Jacob's work, he said—pasted to the inner arch of the George's great gateway. It announced:

> *WICKED & FELONIOUS ATTACK on the Stamford FLYER, upon the road about STANGATE HOLE, Tuesday, 6th October 1761 in which divers person were ROBBED and MURDERED. Wherefore any person with information leading to the capture of the perpetrator or perpetrators of this Horrid Deed, apply to MR. QUIGLEY, Prop., at the George; or to the Magistrates of Stamford. A REWARD is offered. Also, information is sought as to the whereabouts of a MRS. PARRY, missing from the said Flyer, and feared a victim of the same Lamentable CRIME.*

"Excellent," Sir Edward said. "We must have more of these. Posters, handbills. Linton at the *Mercury* office does printing, don't he, Quigley? There's a task for you, Fairfax, when we're done with the inquest. Get a hundred bills printed, matter much as here, at the offices of the *Stamford Mercury*. Quigley can have some fellows post 'em about the town. Have some sent on to the other posting houses too. I'll bear the expense of the printing."

In the yard a coach was preparing to depart for Lincoln. Baggage was being stowed, passengers climbing up; life resiliently going on. Amazingly, Sir Edward still had an appetite, and wolfed a pasty in the coffee room before they set out for the inquest. Fairfax wondered at his own faint distaste. The sin of gluttony? Why should that offend him, the self-confessed freethinker and admirer of M. Voltaire, coolly refusing to tremble at the thunder of Moses? It was perturbing to think that there was some puritanical part of him—something that linked him with the preacher, Henry Griggs, whose stern handsome face was to be seen outside the town hall where the inquest was to be held, patiently awaiting the dignitaries.

Coroners often conducted inquests in inns and public

houses, but it seemed the gravity of this case demanded the use of the town hall, an ancient building housed in the gateway that straddled the river bridge. In its murky mullioned chamber the mayor of the town presided as coroner, seated at a desk piled with fragrant herbs. His name was Ambrose Plum, though there was more of prune about him: a pouchy dyspeptic man with pursed lips that gave him a look of counting up figures under his breath. The jurymen were awkwardly squeezed in on benches beneath the grimy windows; witnesses likewise on the other side. Various gaping and gawking townsfolk also crowded in, gossiping and chewing and spitting, though quietly, in deference to the solemnity of the occasion. Its theme was death, the great drawer of crowds.

And Mr. Plum conducted the proceedings with his own prim relish; dramatic occurrences of this kind, after all, must be few. He heard first from Sir Edward, who, easy as at his own fireside, told of the discovery of the wrecked *Flyer* in ringing tones, concluding with a strong pinch of snuff. Fairfax, and the postilion of their post chaise who was so nervous he could hardly speak, needed to do little more than corroborate the baronet. Dr. Tuplin was called to give the medical evidence. The gawkers murmured in anticipation of gore.

"I examined the victims in situ, and later more fully in the morgue room at the Cross Keys. Each had died as a result of wounds from a single pistol ball shot at quite close range into their vital organs. Charles Crabbe, the coach driver, had received a ball in the right temple, which entered the brain. The outside passenger, who has been identified as Jonathan Griggs, had been shot between the eyes, the ball carrying away much of the nose, both bone and cartilage, and smashing part of the cheek." A woman in the standing crowd gave a deep groan as if about to faint—perhaps indeed did: there was no room to fall down. "The inside passenger, identified as Thomas Honeyman, had been shot in the throat, the ball smashing the larynx and severing the carotid artery. For all, death was swift and inevitable."

"And these wounds, Dr. Tuplin, are, I take it, definitely of outside provenance?" the coroner said, and consulted his own notes. "I mention this only because one of the deceased—Mr. Honeyman I believe—was found with a pistol in his right hand and another in his breast. 'Tis an unlikely turn, I know, but as we are here to determine the cause of death, we must be sure."

"Certainly. No, sir, Mr. Honeyman could not have shot himself in such a way. The trajectory of the ball, and the impact on the flesh, would have been quite different. More devastating, as it were." As the surgeon spoke there was another groan: the woman either fainting again or coming to. "Also, as I believe Sir Edward and Mr. Fairfax determined, the pistols carried by Mr. Honeyman had not been fired; they were each ready primed and loaded with a ball and powder. I also examined them when making an inventory of the deceased's possessions."

"Indeed—the deceased's possessions—we must come to that anon," Mr. Plum said. "But I am afraid first we had better hear from the kin of the deceased. I regret the circumstance, of course. We will be swift."

Mr. Quigley stepped up to the desk to speak for Charles Crabbe, who had no family. Crabbe had been in his employ for ten years, he said. As well as his weekly wage he got lodging at the George, and when in London at the Blue Boar in Holborn, owned by Mr. Quigley's partner in the coach run; and all short-stage fares of less than two shillings went to Crabbe as well as tips from passengers. He had been an excellent coachman, not drinking overmuch as was common in his trade, nor racing to outdo competitors ditto, and never once a crash or upset; a sturdy old fellow. But he had spoken of his determination never to be held up—to ride down any highwayman that dared challenge him. Sad shakings of the head from the coroner, the jurymen, the gawkers.

Henry Griggs, called next, gave his evidence simply and

pithily. His musical voice carried well. But still, Fairfax
noted, he could not keep that intolerant stare from his eye—
as if even at a sympathetic coroner's inquest into his
brother's death he was ready to be martyred at a moment's
notice. Sympathetic the atmosphere certainly was, though
when Griggs spoke of the lunatic asylum there was a general
stir, and Mr. Plum grew more prunelike.

"You will appreciate, sir," the coroner said as Griggs
turned to deliver a stare at the murmurous crowd behind
him, "that this matter is of some concern to the public. I
mean that your unfortunate brother was, as it were, let
loose."

"My brother would never hurt a soul," came the answer.

"But he *was* confined, sir, which suggests . . . You must
consider that we are dealing with a horrid and bloody oc-
currence. Is it possible that your brother might have had,
perhaps not any direct involvement, but anything to do with
the criminal or violent sort?"

"Jonathan was confined in Mr. Rowe's house at Ryhall
these past two and half years. All that time he was good.
Turned in his wits, and not safe to shift for himself, but
good. If my word as a Christian who hopes to be saved is not
good enough for you, then you must consult Mr. Rowe the
asylum-keeper yourself. He will answer for what I say. I
went to him straight this morning, to give him the news that
his late charge was a dead man, and to see to my brother's
effects. One secondhand coat, a shirt and some stockings, a
pipe, and a Bible. I asked that they be given to the poor. Mr.
Rowe is a man of plain dealing, and will confirm all: you
must ask him."

The coroner did not like that *you must*. The preacher had
a talent, it seemed, for raising people's hackles. But Mr.
Plum did not pursue the matter; really, Fairfax thought, there
was nothing to pursue. The pompous little man had too
many ideas. The way to learn was not to have any. Fairfax
felt irritable. The chamber was a stuffy stew of bad smells,
and he was aching from that damnable horse ride. But what

had really put him in a bad humor, he realized, was the coroner's innocently referring to him in his preamble as Sir Edward's "clerk." He would be down to "footman" before the week was out.

"What do you suppose, Mr. Griggs," the coroner said, with an attempt at authority, "your brother was doing on that coach?"

"I can't answer for what went on in poor Jonathan's brain. Maybe, when he slipped away from Mr. Rowe's house, he had some thought of coming to me at Eaton Socon; Mr. Rowe thinks it likely. I was all he had."

"It would not seem, then, that the late Mr. Jonathan Griggs can have been in any way responsible for these events," the coroner said, nodding half regretfully.

"Only a very foolish man could think so," the preacher said.

The coroner was clearly glad to be rid of Henry Griggs. With solemn gallantry, he called Mrs. Barbara Honeyman.

Fairfax had not spotted her before. She had been obscured by the solid form of Joseph Fox, who avidly watched her making her dignified way to the desk. How unfair life was, Fairfax thought. An old widow, careworn and wretched, deprived of her prop and stay, would have made a pitiful spectacle at such a time—a spectacle of a sort to make one turn one's eyes away. But grief, pallor, black velvet, did much for Barbara Honeyman, shedding a new sidelight on her beauty. The eye was engaged as well as the sympathy.

"Madam, I thank you for attending today. It must, I fear, be a sore trial to you," Mr. Plum said. "I knew your husband a little, as did many in the trades and professions of the borough, I think. It is a great shock, a man so young dying so horribly; a husband especially."

"Sir, you are all goodness," Barbara Honeyman said. Sincere, or stagy? Or even a touch of contemptuous irony? It was hard to tell with this woman; any number of feelings seemed to glow beneath her exquisite skin. Mr. Plum, at any rate, seemed delighted to have his opinion of himself confirmed.

"You see, my dear madam, why we must intrude on your grief thus. The jury must come to a decision regarding the circumstances of your husband's death. And there are certain elements that require—elucidation." The coroner smiled at the word he had brought out; was instantly grave again. "Now, you identified the inside passenger as your husband, Mr. Thomas Honeyman, as did his trading partner, Mr. Fox."

Joseph Fox, the ever-willing, looked ready to acknowledge his name with a bow, or a huzzah, or something; then looked very awkward.

"Yes, sir," Barbara said. "I knew my Tom. Beneath the blood."

"Ahem, quite so. And you came to the George last evening, as your husband had set out on the *Flyer* that day and not returned; and your servant had heard some gossip about the accident. Now the curious fact is that your husband's place on the coach was booked in the name of Mr. Twelvetree, who is a prominent citizen of the town. Mr. Twelvetree is, of course, alive and well, and has sent a note"—the coroner touched a sheet of paper with a sort of disdainful reverence—"stating that he knows nothing of the matter, and regretting he cannot attend in person. His chief clerk is here, I think?"

Little birdlike Mr. Claymount made a timid gesture from among the onlookers. His head was inclined at such an ingratiating angle he might have been carrying it under his arm.

"Not only was Mr. Twelvetree's name used," the coroner went on, " but it seems your husband was not dressed in his usual habit. Indeed, he seemed to have made some effort to imitate Mr. Twelvetree's, ahem, distinctive appearance. It was not, I think, Mr. Honeyman's custom to wear the bagwig or the spectacles in which he was found? I may add that in my private capacity I knew Mr. Honeyman well by sight, and never saw him thus attired."

"I know nothing of it, sir. My husband left home very early yesterday morning. I did not see him." The widow was very calm now. "He bought a pair of cheap spectacles, to try them out as he said, quite lately. The bagwig I know nothing of."

"And the—let me see—the ear trumpet?"

Barbara Honeyman's face, a nobly sculpted grief mask, repudiated the faintly ridiculous term. "I know nothing of that."

"But all this suggests nothing to you? Because, my dear madam, Mr. Thomas Honeyman, if my memory serves, was once an employee of Mr. Twelvetree's, was he not?"

Something new. Fairfax intercepted a glance from Sir Edward, then returned his attention to the young widow. The mask did not slip.

"Yes, sir, he was. He left Mr. Twelvetree's employ about a year ago." She shrugged; it would have looked petulant on a less graceful figure. "What of it, sir? Tom is no less dead and bloody for that."

Mr. Plum looked deferential. "I merely raise it, as possibly relating to the reason why Mr. Honeyman made his last journey so disguised. Obviously, this aspect of the tragic matter is of some concern to Mr. Twelvetree himself."

"Again I say I know nothing of it. Perhaps in that case you wish to suggest that I did not know my Tom. I was only his loving wife, and am now his widow, after all. What should I know?"

Mr. Plum coughed, pink-cheeked, as if sensible of appearing rather a brute. "Of course not, Mrs. Honeyman— please do not distress yourself. We are just trying to shed light on a perplexing business. Perhaps we might pass on to the pistols your husband was carrying. We have the deceased's effects to hand there?" The town clerk, with a ceremonious gesture, opened a linen bundle on the desk. "These will, of course, be returned to you after the inquest,

Mrs. Honeyman. You knew that your husband carried these?" Gingerly Mr. Plum lifted one of the pistols. Necks craned.

"I knew that he had bought them, from Mr. Whitaker the gunsmith in High Street, some months since. That's all I know, sir." All at once she was crying. No dramatic collapse; she wept as simply and desolately as a child. "I wish I could tell you more."

"All right, my dear. Take a little time . . ." Embarrassed, the coroner peered at the incised barrel of the pistol. "Yes, there it is: Whitaker and Son, Stamford. Dear me. It would appear that your husband carried these on his journey, mindful of the danger besetting the road lately, but was . . . unable to use them. Mr. er, Fairfax has given it as his opinion that the first may have snagged on the lining of the deceased's pocket, in his attempt to draw it and defend himself . . . Dear me."

Fairfax received a full, unreadable look from the young widow.

"There is also the matter of the box which Mr. Honeyman carried with him. Do you know of it?"

She wiped her face with a handkerchief. "No."

The coroner addressed the jury. "This box was found, opened and empty, beside the deceased. It was not broke open; presumably the key was taken from Mr. Honeyman and used on the lock." He peered inside the lid, which was lined with red baize. "There is here a small label—it reads 'N. Twelvetree, Broad St., Stamford' "

Mr. Claymount's piping voice carried over the mutter of interest. "Sir—sir—Mr. Twelvetree will most certainly wish to know of any property of his being made the subject of these investigations—and to recover it, sir, as soon—"

"Certainly, certainly." The coroner stared the little clerk down—with a certain pleasure, Fairfax thought. As if he wished he could do the same to Mr. Twelvetree himself, or dared to. "But the purpose of this court is only to determine the cause of death. Mrs. Honeyman, you have no notion of the probably contents of this box?"

"None."

"Nor of Mr. Honeyman's errand to Huntingdon?"

"A business errand, he said. Mr. Honeyman, you may know, was in timber."

"He soon will be again," came a sniggering voice from the back. Barbara Honeyman gave no sign that she had heard the cruel joke; but Fairfax fancied that the air around her quivered as round a candle flame. The coroner's lips went thinner; then he inclined his head gallantly to the widow.

"Madam, I thank you. We need trouble you no more. Is Mr. Joseph Fox here?"

Briskly, blinking as if in a strong light, Joseph Fox stepped forward, his big restless hands clenching, unclenching, tapping.

"Mr. Fox, perhaps you can tell us more about your partner's last journey."

"I wish I could, sir. All I know is, he had this jaunt to Huntingdon in mind. A sale, I supposed, or one in the offing. He always dealt with such things: had the way for it, you see, genteel-like. I saw him go, right at cockcrow it was. He seemed normal enough, as I told the gentlemen yesterday, except rather sober-suited; and he had a bundle with him."

"Was it has habit to travel armed?"

"Not as I know of. Tom was a good friend to me—aye, a rare friend. But he was his own man, you know, with his own thoughts. He thought too deep for me sometimes. I stuck to the timber yard, and the business I knew best. That's where I was all day yesterday—at the yard."

And so you keep saying, Fairfax thought. Very hail-fellow-well-met, that was Mr. Fox. The shaggy hair, the carelessly tied neckcloth, the broad out-thrust chest all gave him the look of permanently standing in the open air in a bracing breeze. There were two sharp lines between his brows, though, that gave a strained effect as of an overtightened muscle.

"And you have no notion why Mr. Honeyman should seek to pass himself off as Mr. Twelvetree?"

"No, sir. Unless 'twas a jest of some shape. Tom was a rare clever joker sometimes. But he wasn't a deceiving man, sir, that I'll warrant. There'd be no harm to anyone in it, whatever it was."

The coroner gave a forensic shrug and dismissed Fox.

"Well, now, gentleman of the jury. You have heard the story of the passengers and their ill-fated journey, and how these three persons met their lamentable end. You have heard that Charles Crabbe, in his last expiring moments, spoke of a highwayman or men, and it seems reasonable in the circumstances that we consider the question of robbery of the deceased. This inventory lists their effects, as the victims were found. Mr. Jonathan Griggs, dressed in a serge greatcoat and muffler, plain cocked hat, boots. No money or personal possessions at all. Mr. Griggs? That accords with what you know of your brother?"

"My brother had little or nothing to be stolen," the preacher said from his seat. "What money he had must have secured him his place on the coach."

"Very well. Mr. Honeyman, black stuff suit, bagwig, spectacles, ear trumpet; the box and the pistols as we have seen. Also, in the pockets of his coat, a flask of powder and a pouch of shot—for the pistols, presumably. A cambric handkerchief, embroidered with the initials T. H. This snuffbox of tortoiseshell"—he took a small round object from the bundle—"engraved, I see, with the initials B. C. . . . Mrs. Honeyman?"

"That was Tom's." She was tearless now, dry and almost detached. "A gift."

"And a leather purse, containing one shilling and twopence coin. The jury must make of that what they can. My feeling is that that the perpetrator of this deed was satisfied with, or made as his prime object, the strongbox carried by Mr. Honeyman—or rather whatever it contained. Charles Crabbe, greatcoat, broad felt hat, top boots: in his pockets a small brandy flask and threepence coin. Well. The jury has heard all the relevant facts, I think. We are here to decide what caused the death of the coachman and passengers on the *Flyer*, and there are no witnesses to the act itself—that is, as far as we know. But it has been ascertained from the booking records that a third passenger was, or should have been, on the *Flyer* when it met its mishap at Stangate Hole. This was a woman about whom nothing is known but her name—Mrs. Parry—and that she was to travel to St. Neots. There is as yet no trace of her, though I know that the magistrature is anxious to find her, both out of concern for safety and in case she may shed light on the particulars of this dreadful case. The jury may feel, however, competent to record a verdict now, if it seems sufficiently clear to them that these persons, Charles Crabbe, Jonathan Griggs, and Thomas Honeyman, were unlawfully killed. I may add, *obiter dictum*, that this is not the first outrage committed upon innocent travelers on the Great North Road, though it is the most unspeakable; and that every citizen here, including the jury, must have a strong suspicion that the same nameless villain is behind them. But if anyone here present has anything to ask or add . . ."

This came out distractedly, as there was a hubbub at the back of the chamber, where the staircase was. Out of the confusion emerged a parish officer trying to stop a gentleman coming in and then, finding the gentleman determined, ushering him forward instead.

This was a man with a presence, very tall, quite young, and remarkably handsome: skin as fair as a lady's, a high brow, and the kind of profile called aquiline but, Fairfax thought, more properly Roman. He was well though not showily dressed, with a curled pigtail wig, frogged velvet coat, and riding boots; and swift and graceful in his apologies.

"Gentlemen—I am properly speaking an intruder here—

but I made inquiries at the George, and heard the purpose of this meeting. It seemed best to present myself. I am William Parry, attorney at St. Neots. My wife—Margaret." A gentle cultured voice, a buzz of high emotion in it. "She was to come home yesterday on the *Stamford Flyer.* She did not come home." He glanced around him, breathless. "I pray God that she is not—that you are not met to inquire into her death too—"

"No, no. Sir, you are distressed—a seat," the coroner said. Fairfax yielded his. William Parry looked ready to drop. Introducing himself, the coroner said, "We were just considering the curious question of Mrs. Parry, in relation to the accident of the *Flyer.* What do you know, sir?"

"I know nothing. Margaret was due to come home yesterday, as I said. It was a settled thing. She had been on a week's visit to my sister here in Stamford—Mrs. Bland, at St. George's Square."

"Widow of the Reverend James Bland, late vicar of St. George's. I know her," Mr. Plum said with a certain self-congratulation.

"Well, Margaret did not return. I was away from home myself till a very late hour last night. An old friend was on his deathbed. I stayed till the end, then came home in the small hours. Margaret was not there . . . It was too late to inquire at the coaching house in St. Neots. I stayed up all night, wondering—thinking perhaps her return had been put off, that perhaps she had been taken suddenly sick . . . All the manner of thoughts. This morning at first light I went to the post house at St. Neots, and there learned that the *Flyer* had—had never come. Some sort of accident on the road, they said. So I at once took horse, and came here—went straightaway to my sister's. She had just heard the news that the *Flyer* had been—attacked on the road. She was on the point of sending to me to ask after Margaret. My wife had definitely taken the coach yesterday—my sister had seen her to the yard of the George with her bag before parting . . . So I applied at the George, and a groom told me that the *Flyer* had been held up by highway robbers—all the passengers shot to death." He passed an unsteady hand over his eyes; a woman gave a motherly cluck. "But the groom said he could swear there were no women killed. He swore to it, but I thought he must be sparing me—"

"Sir, your wife is missing, it appears." It was Sir Edward who spoke. "But count on it, no woman's body was found. I can vouch for that: 'twas I came upon the wrecked coach by the road. There was not a sign of her—though the other passengers were indeed killed, alas. The booking records show that Mrs. Parry had paid for an inside place, and took it, as it seems. But she was not on that coach when it was found. I am Justice of the Peace for Stamford: Sir Edward Nugent. You may readily understand, Mr. Parry, that finding your wife has been a first concern with us."

Mr. Parry gazed in wonder, his curved lips parted, looking more than ever like some classical hero. "This—this is impossible."

"But it would seem to be the case, sir," put in the coroner. "Perhaps there is something you can tell us, relevant to our inquiry. It would seem, certainly, that the *Flyer* and its passengers fell victim to a ruthless robber. Was Mrs. Parry carrying any valuables?"

Mr. Parry shook himself, and gave a thoughtful attention to the question; he was, after all, a lawyer himself. "She had some small items of jewelry—her wedding ring, a locket on a chain about her neck, I think . . . besides that only a small carpetbag with such a few necessaries as she took with her . . . Why, have any of these things been found?"

"No, sir. It is indeed a mystery," Sir Edward said. "So, think now, Mr. Parry. Does anything suggest itself? If, as we devoutly hope, Mrs. Parry made some manner of escape, is there anywhere she might have gone to?"

William Parry was already shaking his head vehemently. "No. She . . ." He made a face of pained apology. "She would have come to me. We are very much—all in all to one another. It sounds affected and sentimental perhaps, but it is the simple truth. Margaret and I have not been married above two years. Even the separation of a week, when she was at my sister's, played hard with me. I am afraid even at my poor friend's bedside I was thinking of her return . . . Pray, what is being done? Is this—this villain, this robber being sought? She may be—she may be anywhere—"

"Please, sir, consider," said Mr. Plum, who was having a kind of tug-of-war with Sir Edward for authority, "as an attorney, you will know that all due processes of the law must be carried out. First, of course, our inquest on the unfortunate victims—of whom your wife is not one, sir. That at least would seem to be the hopeful case."

Mr. Parry glanced round, and his mild liquid eyes fell on the black-clad figure of Barbara Honeyman. He bowed his head. "Forgive me, I—I am quite unmanned. I'm sorry I can offer you no other information. I am quite in the dark."

"As chairman of the justices, I can assure you that we shall do everything in our power to catch this rogue, and to find your wife," Sir Edward said. "Perhaps, sir, we might speak with you to that end when you are better composed. A description of Mrs. Parry, for example, would be helpful. All in good time."

"Yes, certainly." Mr. Parry got up. "You will find me at my sister's. Anything—anything I can do . . . As for a description, I am partial, of course. A fair woman, slenderly made, of the middle height, blue eyes—it can say nothing of what she truly is." He gave a broken laugh, went hurriedly to the stairs. "My apologies again . . ."

The spectators had certainly had a free show today, Fairfax thought. They waited until Mr. Parry was gone before swapping loud conjectures. "Took into the woods—took away to be the rogue's doxy." "Took her away, then knocked her on the head when he'd done with her." "What if she wasn't took? Mebbe his doxy afore." "Mebbe 'twas all her doing—robbing and killing, like Moll Cutpurse . . ."

A fair compendium of Fairfax's own wondering thoughts—though the notion of Mrs. Parry, wife of a young

country-town attorney, returning from a visit to her sister-in-
law, as a daring triple murderess and thief was one he had to
reject. Besides, there was the shooting of the coachman on
his box—that had to be the work of an outside assailant,
surely . . .

But the sudden appearance of Mr. Parry, and the tale of
the missing, beloved young wife, with its darkly mysterious
associations, had created a new sensation in the chamber.
The inquest itself lost its novelty. A formality: the dead were
dead. The jury were swift in agreeing to record a verdict of
unlawful killing, and when the coroner discharged them,
they made a trampling exit down the stairs, off to do what
everyone else was doing—talk about it with a thrill.

There remained the relatives of the deceased. Henry
Griggs stepped up and demanded, self-possessed and even
impatient: "I may proceed with arrangements for my
brother's burial?" Yes, and he was off without another word.
Barbara Honeyman moved like a sleepwalker, her arm rigidly
looped through that of Joseph Fox, who had to speak for her.

"Poor old Tom—he can be buried decent now, can he?
Well, that's something."

"And there is, of course, his property," the coroner said,
indicating the pathetic bundle on the desk. Pathetic, and
very interesting, Fairfax thought. He hoped for another look
at those pistols, and that snuffbox engraved with the initials
B. C.—why B. C?

Mrs. Honeyman looked as if she had been offered a meal
of worms. "What good," she said distinctly but tonelessly,
"are these things to me?"

"Well, we'd best take 'em, mistress, anyhow," Fox said.

Watching, Fairfax thought: She habitually dissociates
herself from mundane things; her soul is too fine for them.
Yes, and thus those close to her take on the dull business of
life, the working and worrying, to please her. And in turn she
can reproach them for being so earthbound and petty.

Unfair—she was grieving. And he was still crotchety. He
felt he knew why now: vanity, Robert, he reproached him-

self, mere vanity. The fact is, you think that your great mind must seize on some key to the mystery that eludes these well-meaning burghers, mayor-coroners, and wearers of two hats . . . and yet you have no firm idea at all.

Yet . . . his vanity replied.

Mr. Claymount was questioning the matter of the strong-box, which Mr. Fox was making ready to take. "Sir, really, as that is marked the property of Mr. Twelvetree, quite clearly, then—"

"But it was in Tom's possession when it was found. Isn't that so? Simple enough. Why, my coat has my tailor's mark in the collar, but that doesn't mean it belongs to my tailor," Fox said, smiling, keeping a firm grip. His voice was always pitched slightly above normal volume; as if, Fairfax thought, deliberately to contradict the subtle and cunning connotations of his name.

Sir Edward stepped in. "If it has Mr. Twelvetree's mark, then let Mr. Twelvetree claim it if he wants. 'Tis no matter. We shall be talking to everyone this sorry business touches, so naught will escape the attention of the law. We have a murderer to find now."

That seemed to chasten both the clerk and Joseph Fox, who shrugged and urged Mrs. Honeyman away.

But first she stopped, right in front of Fairfax, looking him full in the face.

"I want to see the man hang," she said.

All he could do was bow his head.

"I want to see it. You—think me bloodthirsty, perhaps?" She said with a kind of wild gasp, her breast heaving.

"Madam, I think nothing," Fairfax said. "Such a grief as you must be feeling is . . . beyond reason.

"Come your ways, mistress," Fox said, soothing. "Rest up at home. You know I can see to everything—the under-taking and such."

Lucky he was around, Fairfax thought. What, indeed, would the pretty widow do without him?

*   *   *

"Well, Fairfax, 'tis quite a tangle, eh?" Sir Edward said. They had left the town hall, and stood awhile in one of the bays of the bridge, looking upriver. A chain of lighters trailed their green reflections in the slow water. The warm bready smell of a maltings came on the wind from the wharfside. "Aye, quite a tangle." He was fishing.

"Well, the matter is plain enough, but for some curiosities: Mr. Honeyman's peculiar disguise and the whereabouts of Mrs. Parry."

"Mrs. Margaret Parry, of St Neots. At least we have some substance to that wraith now. But we must put more flesh on the bones. Talk to the young attorney when you can, Fairfax. He seems straight enough, but then he *is* a lawyer."

"Very well. And also this Mr. Rowe, the asylum-keeper."

"We must have his story too. Ryhall's but a few miles north of the town, on the Bourne road. Nothing for a rider." Sir Edward's eyes twinkled, shrewd and gemlike. "Unless, of course, this is too much for you. You might prefer the quiet of the library at Cheyney. I didn't engage you to be my bloodhound, as you would be quite within your rights to say."

"As you remark, sir, I was not engaged for this. But I have just as much interest in it, as a free man, as if I were the baronet instead of the secretary. And though I dislike the leash as much as most dogs, I am on the scent now, and will not be shaken off. I won't say I will give you your killer, but if I do not, I will take my hat off to the man who can."

"When I first inquired after you, Fairfax, I heard many good things. But I also heard that you were proud." Sir Edward stared at the river." "It was partly why I hired you." A faint dry smile. "Well, before anything else we must have our publicity. You'll find the *Mercury* offices in High Street. Linton, the proprietor, is a clever fellow—used to run a London journal; but he topes, they say, and sometimes don't attend to his business, so take no nonsense. Make free with my name if he drags his feet. As for me, I shall seek out my friend Devereaux and pick his brains. He was on the Bench for years before his health gave way. I'm thinking that besides doubling the reward, we might offer pardon for any accomplices turning our rogue in, but I fancy that must be authorized by the Crown through the Lord Lieutenant . . . Also, Devereaux is someone who has met our rogue in the flesh. He may remember something of note. I shall see you at Cheyney for dinner."

Rain was spitting from a troubled sky as Fairfax walked up St. Mary's Hill. He was starting to get his bearings now in this surprisingly substantial town. No wonder that the gentry of the region chose it for their winter residence; he had not seen so many handsome town houses outside of London or Bath. And every street seemed to have at least two decent inns, often more. He was delighted to find one, in High Street, rejoicing in the name of the Naked Boy and Periwig. Nearby were the offices of the *Stamford Mercury*. The name was familiar to him, for though many provincial newspapers had sprung up in recent years, this was reputably the oldest in the country. Suitably it was housed in an ancient timber-framed building with a jettied street-front. Going in at the low studded door was like entering a dark cool cave.

"Oh, sir, for shame, you have brought it with you."

The woman who spoke was standing at a lectern desk, pencil in hand, poring over a great sheaf of galley proofs. More of these hung on pegs like laundry from the low ceiling beams, and the wainscoted walls were covered with handwritten notices and advertisements. A brass-railed counter was slightly visible beneath heaps of newsprint. The light was dim enough to warrant the candles burning on either side of the desk, though it was alarming to see how the flames flickered and lurched at the draft from the door, with what must have been a ton of paper near at hand.

"The rain," the woman said in explanation. She was not looking at him; she must have heard the patter of drops from his coat on the floorboards. "We have had naught but rain lately—only yesterday did it turn fine. And now you have brought it again." She gave him a quick bare smile, as if to show she meant no harm, then bent to the proofs again. Her thin fingers were inky to the knuckle, and there was a blob of ink on one curl of the bronzy hair that fell untidily over her shoulder.

"I am an inconsiderate visitor," he said and felt perplexed.

"How did I know you are a visitor?" The bare smile again. "Well, I fancy I know most people hereabouts, by sight at least. This is after all the newspaper office. It is our business to know—and I am besides incurably curious. Can one say that or is it a, you know, tautology? Cure and curious, they have a common root? Never mind." Energetically she whipped the crackling page over. "Also something about you proclaims you a stranger."

Fairfax had a sudden sense of this being all too true.

"Quite impertinent, you would say," she said with a little forced yawn, "and you would be right."

"No, I congratulate you on your percipience. I've come to the right place, at any rate. I am also incurably curious. Both from the Latin, *cura*, care. I am also someone who—needs to know."

He will her to look at him, not knowing why. She threw down the pencil and turned. Six-and-twenty, he guessed; rather shabbily dressed in a striped open robe gown, the stays not quite laced, and down-at-heel slippers. Tall, a little angular in figure; not a beauty, but this was a thought he found himself immediately revising. She had uncommonly dark and luminous eyes. (Dark and light eyes—could one say that? His lexicographical past was haunting him today.) Something vulnerable, uncertain, heartbreaking about the shape of her mouth, yet a decidedly jaunty chin, suggesting strong humor, also will or willfulness. He could not place her voice, which had some roughness or burr in it that was not rural.

"I wish to place an order for a hundred printed handbills," he said. "If you can—"

"I can oblige, certainly, I can serve though only a woman. No, of course you meant nothing like that. Some people presume, on seeing me here. A maid, they think. Or they demand to speak only with the gentleman of the establishment, who is my husband, by the way, Mr. George Linton, proprietor of the *Mercury* but indisposed at present."

"I hope not seriously."

"Oh, so do I," she murmured, reaching up to take some sheets from a drying rack, "but it is a poor climate here, you know, with the fens so close at hand, and George is forever . . . It does not suit him. But I like to lend a hand. Now, sir." She took up tablets and a pen. "The handbills?"

She seemed to doing much more than lending a hand. Fairfax repeated Mr. Quigley's sign verbatim. Her eyes widened as she wrote.

"Lord save us . . . I heard about it, of course. I shall be writing it up for this week's paper—that is if George is not recovered from his indisposition. Oh, I scribble, no more," she said with a self-deprecating gesture. "I have no style, certainly no talents like my husband, good heavens." Fairfax found it hard to tell, with Mrs. Linton, whether irony was intended or not; there was a kind of continual twist in her speech, as if everything was equally wry to her. "Very well, sir, they shall be printed at once. I shall take this to old Mr. Wimbling who works the presses, a wonderful name, is it not? Oh—have you any directions as to type and so on?"

"Say fifty folio and fifty quarto, roman type, bold double pica for the heading, left justified, italic for proper names."

She gave him a look. "You know the trade."

"Only from the unprofitable end. I scribbled in Grub Street for some years, to no effect. Now I seek some more reliable means of nearly starving, and go tutoring where I can. But I am presently engaged to Sir Edward Nugent at Cheyney Hall—to catalogue the collections of his late father."

She gave a whistle, which he had scarcely ever heard a woman do. "Sir Jemmy's collection—a trove of wonders

they say. Is it to be sold? I would dearly love to see it. I
might afford *one* volume."

"It is not to be sold. I shall have the privilege of delving
in it, at any rate. That is, after I have set this business in
train. Sir Edward is resolved on catching this marauder, and
I am on the hunt for his spoor."

"It is a horror indeed, and the dreadful thing is I am a
hypocrite to say so; because whenever he strikes, people buy
more newspapers, so that they may read and terrify themselves. The invoice?"

"To Sir Edward Nugent. Delivery to Mr. Quigley at the
George." He watched with indefinable pleasure her rapid
hand. She jabbed and stabbed her signature down as if in
contempt for her own name: *Cordelia Linton*. A thought
came to him, pushing out another that he should not have
had. "Mrs. Linton, I wonder, do you keep back copies of the
Mercury?"

"There are specimens going back fifty years, to its foun-
dation, though I confess I have never much investigated
them. Since my husband bought the concern three years ago
we have kept up the practice."

"It is the more recent numbers that interest me. Any that
report antics of our highwayman, which I believe date from
the beginning of this year. Not of vital importance, but they
may help give a pattern of his activities."

Cordelia Linton was shaking her head. "There you have
me at a disadvantage, I fear. You are not the first person to
make such a request. A gentleman came in, oh, about three
months since, asking for the very same copies. I was here
with my husband, I recall. There was the smallest of disagreements between us on the matter, because George let the
gentleman take away what turned out to be the only copies,
George having contented himself with filing only one spec-
imen of each number instead of two or three as his prede-
cessor did. But there, the gentleman was prepared to pay
twice the cover price to have them, so I daresay George was
in the right. As a woman I cannot pretend to understand

business." Again the glinting smile, the indecipherable irony.

"Well, it is no matter. But I wonder—"

"Who the gentleman was? That I can tell you. It was Mr. Fox, who had an interest in the timber yard at Water Street. Him I know because he was dealing in pulp paper at one time, and tried to get us to buy, though we always deal with the papermills at Wansford. I fancy the timber business had not thrived."

"Joseph Fox . . ." Fairfax said. "That is curious."

"It is? You know him?" She surprised him by tapping him skittishly with her pen. "You said you were a stranger."

"Well, I have met him. I have just come from the inquest upon the bodies. One of the victims was Fox's partner, Mr. Tom Honeyman."

"No! God save him . . . Poor man, he could not have been above six-and-thirty. And he has a pretty young wife, or had, I should say. George will be sorry."

"You husband was a friend of his?"

"Not precisely. We procure books from London for some customers, of whom Mr. Honeyman was one. Quite a reader."

"Ah . . . What sort of a man was he, would you say?"

"Oh, always polite, quite a gentleman-like man. A little abstracted. He seemed rather older than his years."

"Yes . . ." Fairfax remembered the dead man in the coach. In death he had worn a double disguise, but still one saw a man of gaunt, rather worn looks.

"Mr. Honeyman dead, I can scarce believe it. But then there have been a thousand rumors about the town today—killing off half the population I think. The name that's mentioned most is Mr. Twelvetree the banker, though I suspicion that may be wishful thinking."

"He is definitely alive, for I have seen him. But it seems he is not much loved. I wonder why."

"Oh, sir—"

"My name is Robert Fairfax."

"Well, Mr. Fairfax, I grow a little afraid of you. You are *investigating* and relying on the indiscretion of a woman's tongue. But you know, whatever I may privately think of Mr. Twelvetree is merely incidental. *Gedanken sing zollfrei*—thoughts pay no duty, you know."

Her German accent was perfect. "Certainly. I was going to say I sought your opinion as a typical person of the town; but I suspicion you are not typical."

"And now compliments," she said, "or at least, I assume—"

"You assume rightly."

She looked away, half smiling, her hands nervous. "Well, sir, Mr. Twelvetree is not much loved, and that is common knowledge. Perhaps a wealthy man who has risen from nothing, and got a good deal of influence and power into his hands, never is. But I can give you, for example, my husband's opinion of him: a dried-up unnatural grasping chill little tyrant of a moneylender who passes bills instead of stools."

"And your opinion?"

She answered his grin crookedly. "Oh, *ich bin Frau*: my opinion is my husband's, of course. And now *I* am curious, Mr. Fairfax, because you have been at the inquest, and would seem to know much that it should be my business to know. While George is indisposed, I mean."

He smiled. Consider me your source. I ought to be a good one, as it was I, along with Sir Edward, who found the *Flyer*."

She seized a pencil and tablets. "Do you mean it? Will you really . . . ?"

"Surely." He told her all he knew: none of it was secret, and he felt pleased to be able to oblige her, and save her some trouble. She seemed overworked and undervalued and already he had taken against the "indisposed" Mr. Linton. Quite without reason—none of his business, he told himself; but then, as she said, *Gedanken sind zollfrei.*

" 'Shocking intelligence of murder and robbery'—that

shall be the headline," she muttered, looking over her scribbled notes. "Or, no, ' . . . of robbery and murder.' I think folk hereabouts would fear the first more." She tapped her lips, reproving her own tartness, her dark eyes probing him. "I'm sorry I couldn't oblige in return—with the back copies I mean. But wait . . ."

She darted to the counter, pulled out with admirable strength a huge calf-bound ledger, shoving papers carelessly to the floor to make room.

"Now let's see. I call this my theme catalogue. I make a note of the substance of every article in every number of the paper. A musician's habit, adapted. My father kept one, with the leading themes of all his compositions."

"Ah, your father was German."

"You have me. Poor Papa, he had need to record his themes, they were not very memorable. His name was Johann Toller and you needn't pretend to have heard of him. He was *Kapellmeister* at the little court of Weissenburg, which is even smaller and sillier than most German courts, and then he came to England to try to emulate Mr. Handel. One or two of his operas were not booed very loudly, and he cut enough of a figure for the moonstruck Englishwoman who was my mother to marry him, and I am told Mr. Handel once dandled me on his knee when I was a baby, which I do not believe."

"Your father is no longer living?"

"Died ten years since, and my mother did not long survive him, though his debts did . . . Now, here we are." She had been turning the great pages as she spoke. "This, I think, was the first outrage ascribed to our unknown friend. The roads had been peaceful for some time. Then, a carrier's wagon held up at Alconbury, January the twentieth. A mounted and masked assailant, who presented a pistol to the driver's breast, escaped with ten pounds and sundry goods . . ."

"You are remarkable," he said.

She shook her head, almost irritably. "And just five days

later, another attempt on a wagon—emboldened by success, perhaps—but another vehicle appeared on the road, and he made off. Next . . . February the fifteenth, a private carriage held up near Monks Wood, the occupants robbed of sixty pounds and a quantity of jewelry. Quite a bag. Nothing more till April: a gentleman on horseback robbed on the very outskirts of Huntingdon. This was always our leading news, you see. Much of our matter is very dull—digests from the London papers, advertisements for sales and auctions, prices of corn and pigs, marriages. Sometimes it is deathly."

"Perhaps one has to be fully English to appreciate its charm."

"As you do?" Curtly.

"My mother was French. I can only stomach so much of *le rosbif.*"

She stared at him. For a strange moment she seemed about to weep. Then she equipped herself with that bare smile and said lightly, "So I am not the only two-headed monster. I exaggerate, of course. Now: May, a farmer's cart held up, and a string of packhorses robbed. June, the York *Daylight* coach: passengers robbed of twenty-six pounds cash, jewels, and luggage . . ."

"None hurt?"

"It appears not. Perhaps he has grown more desperate with time. July, nothing reported. August, Mr. Timothy Devereaux, notable local personage, held up in his private carriage near Stangate Hole."

"That would be sir Edward's friend."

"The reward for the highwayman's apprehension raised to a hundred pounds, and his description circulated, for what it is worth: a man between the ages of twenty-five and forty, of medium height and build, goes masked and wrapped in a greatcoat. September the second, a man driving a cart held up but suffered to go unmolested when he pleaded his poverty; two days after, a packhorse man carrying the lace and trinkets held up. The miscreant fired his pistol into the air when his victim at first refused to yield . . . And so to yesterday's exploit."

"You *are* remarkable," Fairfax said again; then, hastily, "And so is the violence of this latest attack, I cannot account for it. Why do you think Joseph Fox wanted these reports?"

"A taste of sensation, I supposed. He is a young man, and it's always young men who are after the criminal broadsheets from London—confessions of condemned men, true tales of notorious pirates, and whatnot."

"Yes, I daresay . . ." He became aware of a harsh peremptory knocking somewhere above. A twitch at the corner of Cordelia Linton's mouth showed that she had heard it too, though she kept her eyes fixed on his.

"That will be my husband. He needs something perhaps, poor dear, he is very poorly abed. Well, Mr. Fairfax, the handbills will be printed with the greatest dispatch. A thousand thanks for your information. We will be much ahead of the *Lincolnshire Chronicle*—a wretched rag, of course."

"Of course. And thank you for your information, Mrs. Linton. You have proved—"

"Invaluable, you are going to say, or some such nonsense . . ." She was already on her way to the door at the back of the office. The knocking grew more impatient. "But if I have really been of help, I hope you will not hesitate to—pick my addled brains again." With a nervous laugh she was gone.

Six

Fairfax had much to think of now. Mr. Joseph Fox, and what might be his peculiar interest in the local highwayman's activities . . . Those activities themselves—fairly regular, centered upon the Great North Road between here and Huntingdon, apparently increasing in their threat of violence if not its use . . . The villain's targets generally seeming well chosen, suggesting a careful reconnoitering of the traffic on the roads; though last month, it seemed, only meager pickings—a poor carter with nothing to give, a packhorse loaded with trinkets . . . So perhaps the attack on the *Flyer* was born out of desperation . . . Mrs. Cordelia Linton . . .

Ah, but that was not something he needed to be thinking about, or should be thinking about. Yes, she was remarkable; yes, strange indeed to come upon such a woman in the dusty newspaper offices of a provincial town. Yes, he had been struck by that inky, slatternly, sharp-minded, intensely human woman back there, but that was by the by. In his position all such things had to be by the by. And besides, she was *Mrs.* Linton.

The rain had eased off, and splashes of autumn sun fell on the busy street. It was market day, Fairfax saw, and for all its elegance the town was no less noisy. Indeed there was a mighty din: of sheep and cattle being driven, of hawkers' bells, of iron-rimmed wheels on cobbles, of human voices in every pitch. Drink, he noticed, fueled everything. Market traders had jugs of it brought out from the taverns, old wives sitting with baskets of eggs warmed themselves with it in the shape of glasses of gin, respectable farmers dining in the window booths of a timbered inn were red-faced with it. Pushed by the jostle into a little bay by a cellar workshop, Fairfax took a moment to study the faces passing by: a study indeed. Fat dropsical dewlapped faces framed in powdered wigs like vast dandelion heads; faces pitted with pox and narrow with perpetual hunger; women's faces, corpselike with paint, patched, plumped with cork in place of lost teeth, here and there a slit nose betokening a convicted prostitute; every expression from a fixed grimace at the stink of the gutter, to the pinch of avarice, to the wet grin of a dirty quip shouted across the street; laughter, bargaining, banter, dispute, all with a plentiful swearing of gamy oaths.

What would that fervent Methodist Henry Griggs, with his intense conception of sin and salvation, make of the scene? He would sigh, surely, Fairfax thought—but probably would not be repulsed. He would see souls to be saved: humankind, his life's work. Well, it was noble in a way, if altogether too officious for Fairfax's taste.

The cellar workshop below him had a sign, he saw, in its bottle-glass window: WHITAKER & SON, GUNSMITHS.

It was fiercely hot and close inside, and rather grim with guns in cases and bodies of guns and entrails of guns, and blackened files and vises like torture instruments, and a diabolic smell of saltpeter. Mr. Whitaker, or son, was at the counter eating oysters spread out on a newspaper, which he was reading at the same time. A big swollen warty man, with puffs of grizzled hair starting from his nose and ears as if he were as combustive as his trade, he stared and wiped his hands on his apron and then said in a surprisingly tiny, choked voice, "How can I serve, sir?"

In fact, Fairfax wasn't sure what he wanted to know. He began, "My name is Fairfax. I'm secretary to Sir Edward Nugent, chairman of the magistrates," and got a harder stare in return. This, he thought, was not a good introduction: folk immediately felt accused. "You may have heard, sir, of an attack made yesterday on the *Stamford Flyer*. One of the passengers who was killed was armed with a brace of pistols bearing your mark."

"What of it?"

"I was merely wondering, as part of our investigation into these events, what you could tell me about them. And about their owner, Mr. Tom Honeyman. His widow—"

"Eh? Killed, is he? My stars. That's a pity." The gunsmith shook his head, looked at his last oyster, regretfully deferred it.

"His widow says he bought the pistols here a few months ago."

Mr. Whitaker took out an iron toothpick and made free with it while he turned over the pages of a daybook. "Let's see. Aye, I recall. Flintlock pocket pistols, brass-butted and barreled, very neat . . . Why, you don't suggest there was aught amiss with them, I hope?"

"No, not that I could see. I don't believe Mr. Honeyman even got to fire a shot from them when he was attacked. I would guess that the exposed lock and trigger caught in the lining of his pocket, and hampered him."

The gunsmith shrugged. "It can happen. They're meant for ease and lightness of carrying—not a sportsman's gun by any means. You know I can't be held accountable."

"No, no, I do not suggest it. I seems he was up against a ruthless adversary in any case. Did Mr. Honeyman say what he wanted the pistols for?"

"Not as I recall. But I didn't wonder specially. He's in trade, isn't he? Was, was, I mean." It was interesting, Fairfax thought, how slow people were to use the past tense about a dead person. Life refusing to acknowledge death. "A merchant, going about on business—it makes sense to carry some protection in these times. And they'll get worse, you know." Mr. Whitaker tapped the greasy newspaper; it was the *Stamford Mecury*. "This Scotch dealer of the King's will push us headlong into peace. Aye, I know it's wanted, I know folk are sick of the war—but at what price? Come peace, there's always sailors and soldiers turned loose on the country with no work. Where there's no work, they'll thieve. Not," he added with a lowering look, "that they'll thieve from *me*."

"They would be very foolhardy," Fairfax agreed, glancing at the steely armory around him, and admitting the truth of what the gunsmith said. Indeed this was an aspect of the case he had tended to forget. Few stole and robbed out of vocational pleasure. It was the brutality of the murders that made one think only of justice, but he knew that the majority of crime was goaded by harsh necessity. And now he found himself examining the case from that angle, through the eyes, as it were, of the criminally desperate. The shooting of the coachman could be seen, from that side, as a "necessity": the loot was wanted and he was a barrier to it. And the inside passenger? Tom Honeyman, fumbling for his pocket pistols—again, perhaps, a "necessary" act on the part of the attacker. It was him or me. But why kill the harmless lunatic, Jonathan Griggs? Surely there could be no real threat there. Erase the witness to the deeds, perhaps. Or maybe a metaphysical indifference after so much killing, like Macbeth: "I am in blood stepped in so far . . ." But Fairfax just couldn't make this seem likely to his mind. And then what of the other passenger, Mrs. Parry?

"Well, as I said, 'twas no sportsman's gun, and Mr. Honeyman was no sportsman," the gunsmith said. "A clerkish sort of fellow, I recall, and knew nothing of arms. It was his partner who had an eye for such things, and knew what he was about. Tried to haggle the price down, as I recall, though it was as cheap a pistol as you'll get."

"You mean Joseph Fox?"

"That's the man, I reckon." Mr. Whitaker referred again to his daybook. "Aye, Mr. Fox. Bought an identical brace."

"Fox bought pistols too?"

"Aye, same time—they came in together. Same reason, I supposed. He's not killed too, I hope?"

"No . . . not he."

"Ah. Well, 'tis a shocking thing; but there, it comes to us all." The gunsmith seemed to feel he had paid sufficient respects to mortality now, and took up the last oyster.

Again Mr. Joseph Fox! Not only had the young man taken an uncommon interest in reports of the local highwayman, he also possessed a brace of pistols, and apparently knew how to use them.

But of course this did not necessarily mean anything, nor the fact that Fox had signally refrained from mentioning these matters—not when it was a notorious highwayman they were after. Unless of course Joseph Fox, respectable tradesman, *was* the highwayman, responsible for all those robberies that Cordelia—Mrs. Linton rather—had listed for him. Again that was not impossible, but difficult to swallow as a likely proposition.

Instead Fairfax allowed the *What if* . . . that had been at the back of his mind to come cringing into light. What if the bloody work at Stangate Hole had been an act of premeditated murder? Leaving the gunsmith's shop, he pondered.

To commit murder on the coach road was certainly an unusual way of going about it. But it had definite advantages in this case—the chief of which was that the authorities were likely to cry "Highwayman!" and look no further. A daring theory or an absurd one, depending how you looked at it; but Fairfax decided to follow it to its logical conclusion, which involved the nature of the intended victim. It was unlikely to be the coachman, a functionary with little life outside his job; his death was surely a means to an end. So was it Tom Honeyman, or Jonathan Griggs, or Margaret Parry? Or the one who had *seemed* to be on that coach but was not—Mr. Nicholas Twelvetree? Or, most bizarre idea yet, all of them?

He had started his hare, and what a wild and crazy creature it was—perhaps a mythical beast that it would be folly even to pursue. He didn't know. But his first steps were plain enough in any event. As he had agreed with Sir Edward, the asylum at Ryhall warranted a visit. He decided he would have a sustaining morsel at the George before mounting his dreaded horse. Coming to the inn, he found a commotion.

It was at the door of the cockpit, which was housed in an octagonal brick building adjoining the stables. A bill advertised six matches today, followed by a Battle Royal. At the center of a group of men, but very different from them, stood Henry Griggs. The men were sportsmen and gamesters, bowlegged, boozy, a couple attended by hideous dogs. One bore a basket containing a fighting cock, a creature with a mere ruff of dull feathers, more lizard than bird. Some of them were laughing, but one was all seriousness. Bullet-headed, he had his bristly face thrust close to that of Griggs. Even Fairfax, drawing near, could smell the liquor on him. But Griggs didn't flinch.

". . . I'm asking you again, you snot-nosed bastard, what concern is it of yourn? You hear me, shite-hawk?"

"You are men, and so you are all my concern," Griggs said, quite composed. "We are all brothers in Christ, if we can be brought to see it."

"I'm no brother of yourn." The bullet-headed man hawked and spat vilely.

"You are. That is why I beg and beseech you, just as if you were my own brother, not to go in to that shameful exhibition. Think of what you are doing. Gaming—drinking—crowing over a brutal slaughter."

"Well, you know, 'tis our own money to spend as we like," said another man, a prosperous farmer in a horsehair wig, long clay pipe in hand. He was amused, more temperate. "And if we wager it, and so very likely lose it, why then we've had our punishment at once. Probably the Almighty laughs to see me lose: I don't mind that."

"Friend," Griggs said, turning to him, "you are as deep in the pit as this man. To speak with such levity of holy things—"

"Never mind that, piss-emmet," growled the bullet-headed man, dancing round after Griggs like a boxer. "I want to know what business it is of yourn. You say to me don't go in there, but I say I'm going, and I want to see you stop me. Come on—how are you going to do it? I want to see it. I'm ready. You look like you need a man's fist in your eye, you do—"

"The laws of man would not take kindly to it," Fairfax said, stepping between them, "leaving aside the laws of God."

"You're another, are ye?" The bullet-headed man gave Fairfax the full blast of his breath: enough to flatten a cart horse.

"I need no help, sir," Griggs said. "I am doing only my duty—trying to dissuade these poor wretches from putting their souls in deeper peril. My concern?" He turned to the bullet-headed man. "How could it not be, when I heard you cursing and blaspheming in the common street?"

"Aye, Sam has a foul tongue sometimes," the farmer said, "and no one likes to hear that, true enough, preacher. But a cockfight, now: where do the laws of God come in there? Cocks will fight one another, willy-nilly: and surely it was God who made 'em so."

"You think *you* are talking, my friend. But I say to you, as I hope to be saved, that that is the devil's own voice coming from your lips. The Father of Lies is in you, I hear his rasp, and I tremble for you." Griggs said this as prosaically as if he were talking of the weather.

The farmer only chuckled; and just then a bell rang inside the cockpit to signal the first match. In a moment Griggs was forgotten, the men hurrying inside. No one hesitated or hung back. The preacher had done nothing to sway them. But he looked quite undaunted, even refreshed.

Fairfax, who had no taste for the barbarism of the pit, said, "A voice crying in the wilderness, I fear, Mr. Griggs."

The Methodist would not acknowledge even his sympathy. "Sir, you should not cite Scripture lightly," he said.

"And I am only a poor vessel of God's Word. I cannot compare myself with the prophets of old."

Oh? Fairfax thought. Perhaps he was prejudiced, but he thought there was such a thing as prideful humility. But he was glad, anyhow, to have found Griggs. There were some questions he wanted to ask. "Mr. Griggs, I thought of taking a meal here. Will you join me?"

The preacher considered. "Very well. I will break bread with you, sir. Then I must be brisk about burying poor Jonathan."

He made it sound gruesomely physical. They went into the dining room. It was busy, being market day, but a maid found them a quiet eating booth. Griggs asked for bread and cheese and water. Fairfax was going to follow suit, as a gesture of solidarity or pump-priming, then decided against it. Veal collops and a large brand-and-water for him. To thine own self be true, he thought.

"I may lay Jonathan in a parish plot tonight," Griggs said. "With luck and with, I find, a bribe to the sexton. What times."

"His life was unfortunate."

Griggs shrugged. "The world is as it is—a vale of tears."

"Yet this world has beauty, has it not, and goodness?" Fairfax said. It was the good French brandy warming his vitals that made him think so just then. "It must have, as God's creation. Believe me, I am not echoing those men: I mean no disrespect. It is a question that perplexes me."

"It is vain to place *any* hopes in the goodness of this world," Griggs said promptly. "Or of men, without Christ's grace. Without that, all is corrupt. This"—he waved his square hands at the table, the food, the glasses—"you must think of all of it as corrupt—defiled—pitchy." And he rubbed his thumb and fingers, as if he really felt the stickiness.

"And yet," Fairfax said, "all men fear leaving this world."

"If they are saved, they should welcome it, not fear it."

"Your brother Jonathan—was he saved? Or at least—"

He caught himself up; he had been about to say, innocently, "half saved" until he remembered that it was a contemptuous slang expression for "insane."

"He was always a good and naturally pious man," Griggs said, calmly eating. "When his wits turned, the purity of his soul was not besmirched."

"There are still some . . . religious authorities," Fairfax said tentatively, "which claim that insanity is the result of demonic possession."

"My religious authorities are my Bible, and the conscience in my breast," Griggs said, fixing Fairfax with his compelling blue eyes. "There was no devil in my brother."

Fairfax made a respectful nod before returning to the attack. "Why do you suppose Jonathan should choose this particular time to run away from Mr. Rowe's asylum? What can have prompted him?"

Griggs took a deep draft of water. "Perhaps he feared to die there. That is all I can think."

"To die there? Was he ill—in body, I mean?"

"Not strong. Few in his care are, for they do not care for themselves. But also there had been a death there recently— one of the inmates. He spoke of it the last time I saw him— on my last visit to him, a fortnight ago. I think it preyed on him. Perhaps dwelling on that made him decide to slip away. He always had a deep attachment to home and familiar things. I offer this merely as a conjecture. We shall never know . . . It is not given us to know everything, Mr. Fairfax."

Fairfax, as a good Voltairean rationalist, could not agree with this position, but he did not say so. "So, it was Saturday that Jonathan made his escape. Monday, you rode up to see Mr. Rowe at the asylum about the matter; and Tuesday, yesterday, Jonathan was found killed on the *Flyer*, heading presumably for your home at Eaton Socon. What, I wonder, did he do in the time between leaving the asylum and boarding the coach?"

"You are fond, sir, of questions that cannot be answered.

Who can say? Wandering as he was, he may have feared pursuit, and hidden up for a time. He found his way to Stamford, that much is certain. He may have got a penny lodging somewhere, or some charitable soul may have sheltered him. He cannot tell us now, and even in life he might not have been able. The light of reason would fade very quickly from him, poor creature, and he would quite forget what had passed just an hour before. Once, when visiting him, I sat with him awhile and then stepped outside a moment to speak to Mr. Rowe. When I went back into the room, Jonathan jumped for joy to see me. He thought he was seeing me for the first time in a month. I think, Mr. Fairfax," Griggs said, his voice at its most somberly musical, "that I need not try to describe the painful sensations such things excite in the breast, when that unfortunate person is the one you love best in all the world."

"Words are not equal to it. It is the most bitter irony that he ran away only to meet death."

Ever strenuous, Griggs would not have that. "There is no such thing as irony in this world, sir. That is a pagan notion. Everything that happens is God's will."

Fairfax finished his brandy, a little tired of standing corrected. "This death at the asylum," he said, "you have no reason to suspect it was other than—natural?"

"I don't know what you mean, sir. Mr. Rowe's establishment is of the best. That is why I entrusted my brother there."

"Of course . . . There is one more thing I feel I must ask you, Mr. Griggs. When Sir Edward and I first met you yesterday, at the Bridge in Huntingdon—you had just come there, is that not so? You had lain the night at Ryhall, and then ridden down to Huntingdon where you were to do a preaching?"

"That is so."

"Which means, surely, that you had just come by that very stretch of road where the *Flyer* was attacked. We were the first to come upon the wreck, going the other way. It cannot have been there long. Surely you must have either passed the coach, or—"

"If I had been riding the coach road," Griggs said, "then yes, I suppose so. But I seldom travel by those ways, sir. There are turnpikes where one must pay a toll, are there not? I am a man of limited means, and must husband my resources, especially when I am traveling about the Lord's business. There are country roads through the fen villages, unsuitable for a carriage but serviceable for a man on horseback; one goes by Holme and the Stukeleys into Huntingdon. That answers, I think, your question." He dabbed his mouth neatly, took up his hat. There was no outrage at what Fairfax might be suggesting, only a look of sad disdain. "Now I must be off. I shall probably lie at the Cross Keys again tonight, and go on to Huntingdon tomorrow for my preaching."

Well, Fairfax thought when he had gone, was it so outrageous? Griggs's alibi was weak; pistols were easily come by. And as for whether he had it in him to kill . . . well, from a theoretical point of view, the man had utter self-belief, a sheep-and-goats morality, and a view of death as a release from a fallen world. That certainly fitted. Unfortunately the wholesale slaughter of the *Flyer* made no sense in that light. And Fairfax found it impossible to doubt, for a single moment, that Henry Griggs had devotedly loved that tragic brother who was one of the victims. The man was nothing if not wrenchingly sincere.

A conundrum. Fairfax went to get his horse, which tossed its head in displeasure at the sight of him. From the cockpit close by came a profane chorus of whoops and yells. The birds in the sanded ring would be ripping and gouging with their steel spurs. Robert Fairfax mounted his horse and departed for the relative sanity of Mr. Rowe's asylum for lunatics.

Seven

The madhouse, as the hedger who directed him called it, was just beyond the little stone-built village of Ryhall. Screened from the road by a stand of fine chestnut trees, it might have been taken for a modest manor house or a comfortable rectory. It was a mellow stone building of two wings, with steep gables and long sloping dormers, set in an expansive walled garden with trim lawns and shrubberies sloping down to a stream. The gate leading in was unlocked, and a very civil manservant came from the main wing to take the horse's reins and ask how he might help the visitor.

"My name is Fairfax. I am secretary to Sir Edward Nugent, at Cheyney Hall. I wonder if I might speak to Mr. Rowe."

The servant took him into the main wing, and into a little wainscoted side parlor, neatly furnished with oak and polished to a luster. A bow window looked out on to a part of the garden, where Fairfax could see an old woman, well wrapped in a shawl, sitting on a wooden bench and looking mildly into space.

It was a long way from the bars and chains and echoing screams of Bedlam. Fairfax was impressed, also relieved. He had found himself faintly fearful as he came here. Not fearful of mad people—the fear was more to do with the depths of his own self. Moods of black melancholy came upon him still sometimes. In his younger years, when his

fortunes had been wrecked by his father's suicide and disgrace, they would swallow him up for days at a time; he
would treat them, or feed them, by vast doses of drink. At
such times his reason, which he valued so acutely, seemed a
frail butterfly, about to fly away or else be crushed . . .
Dread thought.

"Mr. Fairfax." A man had come in silently, though he was
big: six feet tall, upright, broad-chested, and muscular. He
was perhaps fifty, with his own white hair tied back, strong
black brows, a rich complexion, a sharp jutting jaw and
chin, rays of wrinkles surrounding shrewd eyes. "How
d'you do, sir? I regret there is no fire laid in here—I am so
little susceptible to cold myself."

"I will not detain you long, I hope. I am investigating, on
behalf of Sir Edward Nugent, the deaths of the passengers
on the *Stamfort Flyer*—of whom one was your former
charge, Jonathan Griggs."

"Poor Jonathan. A dreadful business. I hope he did not
suffer. Mr. Griggs, his brother, brought me the news this
morning." Mr. Samson Rowe sat down, rubbing his hands
briskly. His tones had a touch of North Country about them.
"Has the culprit been found?"

"Not yet. I am seeking to learn a little more about the victims, and the circumstances surrounding them."

"Mr. Rowe studied him a moment, then nodded; his de-
meanor had something of the firm kindly headmaster about
it. "Certainly. Since Jonathan came here, some two and a
half years ago, I think I have known him better than anyone.
He was suffering from an intermittent disorder of the brain,
and some such maladies, of course, can change the person-
ality of the patient, sometimes drastically; but this did not
seem to obtain in Jonathan's case. I understand he had always been a gentle, genial man, of a warm and frank disposition, with a tendency indeed to be the prey rather than a
master of his emotions, particularly melancholy: this was
the character of the patient throughout his illness—the form
that still showed, as it were, through the draperies of his dis-

ease. Extreme melancholia with sporadic manic symptoms is how I would diagnose it: a progressive condition manifesting in young adulthood. It was not syphilitic in origin, and it did not entail a degeneration in function. Jonathan could always dress himself as well as you or I, reckon a sum in figures, write his name. I am, by the by, a licentiate of the Royal College of Physicians, Mr. Fairfax, and I have made the afflictions of the mind my special study."

"Jonathan was a tractable patient?"

"Almost always. He did not rave, behave turbulently, or commit indecencies; he never offered violence except to himself, when his melancholia was at its worst. Those were the only occasions I had to use a measure of restraint—mild only. But perhaps you know I do not favor stringent treatment, whenever it can be avoided. We have locks here, and restraining chairs for use when needed, but in general I advocate as great a degree of liberty as possible, a strengthening diet, air, and such occupation as the patients are fit for. Some, for example, make baskets of cane and do other work. Jonathan did not, as he lacked the necessary concentration. As a general description of his condition, I would say that he had retreated into the fastnesses of his own mind, and chose to remain there." Mr. Rowe paused, fingers steepled; the headmaster again, making sure his pupil was attending. "Walking in the garden was his favorite occupation. He loved plants and growing things in general. And hence, of course, he was able to go over the wall and escape when the fit came upon him on Saturday. This is, of course, an inevitable risk of the regimen I run for those patients who are not dangerous, and I make no bones about it. Relatives fully accept it, as the price to be paid for enlightened treatment, and there is no threat to the public. It is tragic that Jonathan should find such a shocking end, but that could hardly be anticipated. Usually, on those occasions when an inmate has wandered, he has been soon brought back, or come back of his own accord."

It seemed, indeed, as humane an establishment as could

be imagined. While some private asylums were moving toward a more gentle treatment, one still mostly heard of cells, fetters, and plunge baths.

Fairfax said, looking out of the window, "I can well understand his partiality for that garden. And he had visits, I believe, from his brother?"

"Indeed. Mr. Griggs came as regularly as he could, and Jonathan was always immensely heartened when he did. Sorrowful, sometimes, after he had gone, but his erratic memory would blot out the cause of his sorrow. I remember more than once coming upon Jonathan weeping, and asking him what was amiss. 'I am sad for something,' he would say, smiling through his tears, 'but I can't think what, so it don't signify.'" Mr. Rowe gave a hard, frowning smile. "One must pity, but not take it to heart, any more than the woes of little children. In my profession I have seen a world of suffering. I recall a tailor who had an abscess under a tooth which poisoned the blood; his entire body swelled like a marrow until there was not an inch without agony, yet still he could not die, at least for some unimaginable months. A man's heart would bleed at it, if he let it . . . Will you take a glass of canary?"

"Thank you. Can you suggest, Mr. Rowe, what might have prompted Jonathan to slip away at this particular time?"

"I really cannot." Samson Rowe poured wine from a glass decanter with a chased top of silver. The scrubbed strong hand was fringed with a sleeve of fine Ghent lace. "But then if our inmates behaved according to predictable and rational courses, they would probably not be our inmates." He smiled that frowning, worldly smile.

"Of course . . . I had a suggestion, from his brother, that Jonathan perhaps got into his head a fear of dying here. On account of the death of another patient, some weeks ago."

Mr. Rowe sipped appreciatively. "I think you'll find this canary has a taking flavor . . . We have had no deaths here lately, sir."

"Oh . . . ? I was given to understand that Jonathan told his brother, on his last visit, that a fellow inmate had died. Apparently this troubled Jonathan."

"Jonathan may well have said that. Again, sir, you must remember the people we are dealing with. They are prey to fancies we cannot even imagine. There have been no deaths here this year, or last year. The last time a patient died in the house was in '59, the spring if I remember aright: a very old man who had been long bedrid. Poor Jonathan was given to black thoughts and fears. He would ask for a taper at night because he thought the darkness might physically consume him. From time to time one of the patients may not appear in the garden, or in their accustomed place at table, because a bad turn in their illness necessitates confining them. Jonathan may have mistook such an occasion. The sensitive morbidity of his temperament makes it quite likely."

"Yes. Yes, I see."

"But it is perhaps wrong to look for some external stimulus as a trigger for Jonathan's flight. In the condition of these poor creatures, the mind has its own landscape—its own geography and history and laws, one might say, whose strange dictates they must obey. I had a patient once who decided one day, quite abruptly, that he was his own father. He would not be shaken in this belief, and persisted in acting according to it right to his last breath."

Fairfax had a feeling of being gently bludgeoned with superior knowledge. He wondered if this was how his own pupils felt. "Mr. Griggs was Jonathan's only visitor?"

"Oh, yes. A most powerful family feeling there. You have met the elder Mr. Griggs? Ah yes. The, shall we say, biblical turn of phrase does not disguise the feeling heart. When he first brought his brother here, he demanded the firmest assurances of tender and humane usage, and could hardly bear to take his leave."

"Was there not some event that turned Jonathan's condition irrevocably to the worse—that unhinged his mind, in fact? I heard something about a broken love affair . . ."

"I understand there was such. Jonathan never spoke of it to me—but then his retreat from past reality was complete, and one would not expect it. Some misfortune of that kind, acting upon so sensitive a temperament as his, might indeed have turned the scales. But with a predisposition to mental disorder, the triggering event is not significant: the collapse is inevitable at some time. I have known patients lose their wits following some quite happy turn of fortune. It is the pressure upon the unhealthily strung nerves that is the important thing. You're sure you are comfortable without a fire, sir? I can have one laid directly, though I seldom feel cold myself."

"Thank you, I do very well. So, it was on Saturday that Jonathan slipped away, and the first person you informed was his brother."

"Saturday evening." Mr. Rowe admired the color of his wine. "Mrs. Heath, my housekeeper, was the first to miss him. The rain had started up again, and she went out to the garden to advise him to come in—a necessary precaution: he has sat happily in falling snow before now. Once we had established that he was nowhere on the premises, I sent a manservant down to the village to inform the vicar there— the village headman as it were—and to look about for him. In the morning I dispatched another servant by horse to Mr. Griggs at Eaton Socon to notify him, while the others made inquiries around the locality, and in Stamford. My belief was that either Jonathan would be spotted wandering nearby, and probably wishing to come back, poor fellow; or else he had taken it into his head to go to his brother. I really could think of no likelier destination. He had on his great-coat, and there was always some money in his pockets, and he was by no means helpless except in his worst fits. But still I felt considerable uneasiness as time wore on. When Mr. Griggs arrived here late on Monday, I think the two of us made a poignant spectacle—each hoping for good news from the other, and each disappointed. I recall him trudging up the drive to the house in the rain, his eyes meeting mine

with the most beseeching look. 'He has not come to me,' he
said. And I was obliged to tell him that there was no sign of
him here either. He was most stricken. I feared for his
health, as he was caked to the ankles in mud; I had Mrs.
Heath make a fire and pressed him to take a hot toddy, but
of course"—the worldly smile again—"Mr. Griggs's principles will not countenance liquor. The passage of time, you
see, made a happy issue less likely, but I endeavored to keep
his spirits up. He kept trying in vain to think of anywhere
else Jonathan might have gone. We settled at last on the
hopeful conclusion that he must still be on the road somewhere, making his way to Eaton Socon. I decided to notify
the local constable in the morning, though of course
Jonathan was no felon who could be pursued by the law."

"Mr. Griggs did not regret the gentleness of your regime,
which makes such escapes possible?"

"Not in the least. There was no hint of that. As I said, I
make this a condition of acceptance here. And you have perhaps seen, sir, the barbaric alternative in establishments such
as Bedlam. There was anxiety, but no regret."

"Yes . . . yes, I'm sure I would have felt the same."

"He did not speak of attempting to look after Jonathan
himself at his home, if it should turn out that he had gone
there—driven by an acute yearning for familiar things, for
example. I doubted such was the case, but if so, and Mr.
Griggs felt equal to the demands of nursing his relative, then
of course the decision was his. Well, Mr. Griggs found a bed
in the village for the night, and set out the next day. He was
philosophical, I think. He was engaged to do a preaching at
Huntingdon, and determined upon fulfilling it; and piously
hoped he might hear word of his brother on the way. Admirable, the resources of the religious mind! So he left, and
I waited in vain either for a result from my own inquiries,
which I extended to all the country round, or a word from
Mr. Griggs. It came, alas, this morning. Poor Jonathan! It
appears that he had been heading for Eaton Socon, and his
family home, after all. And rather than tramping the roads,

he had secured himself what should have been the safest and most expeditious way."

"Did it surprise you that he was able to do this?"

"It did not. I know your meaning. You think that Jonathan must have been freakish, incapable."

"Not at all, I—"

"These misunderstandings are common. Perhaps, Mr. Fairfax, your ideas would be clearer if I were to show you a little of the establishment." Mr. Rowe was on his feet. "You can even see Jonathan's lodging, if you like."

"Thank you." No time, Fairfax thought, to get irritated by that breezily condescending manner.

Samson Rowe led him through the hall, spacious and with a fine carved staircase. On the wall above it hung several guns—a fowling piece, a musket, two pistols. Mr. Rowe saw Fairfax looking, and gave a loud metallic laugh.

"Never fear, sir. The inmates do not and cannot enter my dwelling house. I will show you." At the end of a passage beyond the stairs there was a stout iron-clasped oak door, double-locked. "This communicates with the other wing— where the patients live. I am fond of country pursuits, coursing above all, though I have ridden to hounds. Indeed I am invited to join the Fitzwilliam Meet on Boxing Day. Pretty fair, I think, for a North Country physician." He turned as a man in a carpenter's paper cap came down stairs carrying a piece of old paneling. "Now, my good man, you will be careful of my wallpaper there, will you not? One scratch is enough, I thank ye."

The carpenter nodded, like a reprimanded schoolboy.

"I am refitting some of my private rooms," Mr. Rowe went on, unlocking the door, "for a rather urgent reason. I am soon to marry. My first wife died ten years ago, and since then I have dedicated myself chiefly to this place. But happy chance has opened a new chapter for me. My new bride is niece to the Bishop of Peterborough—well connected, as you may imagine. A man must be a hypocrite to say this does not gratify." He led Fairfax into a paneled passage.

"My congratulations."

"Thank you. I think one cannot live long alone without becoming dull in habit. And, of course, a man is made of flesh, and has needs." Mr. Rowe smiled, his strong yellow teeth showing like a dog's in the dimness of the passage. Fairfax found himself absently probing with his tongue the lower molar that had been troubling him of late. Sometimes when he bit on something sweet it gave him an excruciating twinge. Perhaps it was unfair of him to find this similar in its effect to the flashes of vulgarity that kept appearing in this apparently civilized and compassionate man. The good and true were not necessarily those who shared your tastes.

"Ah, Mrs. Heath. I was just showing this gentleman the house."

A large thickset nut brown young woman in starched apron and cap was emerging from the door at the end of the passage. Her bare arms, firm as apples, encircled a bundle of laundry. She faintly nodded a greeting.

"Dear me," Mr. Rowe said, "it looks as if Mrs. Berry has let us down again."

"She got agitated again last night," the housekeeper said, "and was frightened to go to stool. She's sorry for it." Behind her, before she closed the door, Fairfax saw into a bright, plainly furnished room, with a middle-aged woman sitting on the floor. She hugged her knees and her baleful eyes met Fairfax's, unseeing.

"She always sits so," Mr. Rowe said quietly. "Her conduct is docile, but childlike: she likes to dress dolls."

"Shall I lock it, sir?" Mrs. Heath said.

"I think not today, Mrs. Heath. She will do . . . Sad, aye, aye," Mr. Rowe said as they went on, past other doors, "but she does not much suffer, apart from night terrors. Her case might be much worse. One learns not to agonize. Such people cannot live in society, sir: they are happiest retired, their excesses restrained, their simple wants quietly met until the

sands of life run out. They are all a blink in the eye of nature, that great prodigal, who disposes of her creatures with
a rough hand. The wolf rends the lamb, fledglings hatch
only to fall from the nest, and men's brains and bodies are
beset by a thousand cunning maladies, but the world goes on
pretty well."

"A vale of tears, no less."

"Indeed—though I would not use such terms, as our
friend Mr. Griggs would. I see only the remorseless workings of nature."

Fairfax thought of the dull eyes of Mrs. Berry. "Mrs."—
so was there a husband somewhere, sorrowing—or forgetting? He had heard tales of inconvenient relatives being put
away to rot in such places, certified by ignorant or bribed
doctors, their deaths being hastened by neglect or ill treatment . . . Mr. Rowe, he found, was watching him, smiling,
and apparently reading his mind.

"Are these people deposited here, unwanted, for me to
make a profit from? That was the thought in your mind, Mr.
Fairfax, or something like it. I say this because it occurs to
everyone—and that is because so many private asylums are
shockingly conducted. Certainly I make a charge for their
maintenance, and profit by it. That is how I maintain myself.
It is not an excessive charge; Mr. Griggs, for example, a man
of modest station, has been able to bear it, though in his devotion he has, I know, always made it the first charge on his
purse, and was prepared for any personal sacrifice to pay it.
There are at present twelve inmates—dear me, I should say
eleven now—and all are mourned and loved by families and
friends, though some have not the fortitude of mind to visit
them . . . Ah, good day to you, Andrew."

A young man, painfully tall and thin, had opened the door
of his room. He stood gazing down at them both, licking his
pink lips, then gave a deep chuckle of pleasure and amusement.

"That's right," Mr. Rowe said, "that's right, my friend.

You are going to the garden, are you? Take care of your shoes, it is still wet."

The young man went gangling ahead of them to an outside door, craning over his shoulder and laughing hilariously.

"Andrew is delightful," Mr. Rowe said urbanely. "Nothing troubles him—except his own reflection, as we discovered: he becomes wild at the sight of it, and then he does have to be forcibly restrained. But we make shift to keep mirrors and such away from him." They had come to the foot of a plain floorboarded stairway, with two more doors on either side. "Six of the inmates live upstairs. The upper windows are lightly barred, as a precaution, but there are curtains and the effect is not intolerable. And here we have poor Jonathan's room."

It was light and airy, and had the same shipshape smell of sun on polished wood as all the house. There was an iron bed, a ewer and basin, a tin candlestick, a trunk beneath the window, which overlooked the lawns, a small table with a Windsor chair, a faded rug on the floor. On the table there was a pipe and a pouch of tobacco. Mr. Rowe touched them gently.

"Jonathan dearly liked a smoke. A curious thing: many do even when cold to other pleasures."

Fairfax was looking at the whitewashed wall above the narrow bed. Spidery, shaky, though not childlike drawings were there, of trees and flowers, a many-windowed house in reasonable perspective with two little figures at its gate, birds and dogs, and also some writing.

"You see why we do not run to wallpapers and brocades in this part of the house," Mr. Rowe said. "Often this kind of scribbling affords relief, and I do not discourage it unless indecent. Andrew inscribes a very neat calendar upon his wall."

Fairfax peered at the writing. It was distorted by the roughness of the plaster beneath the whitewash, but the capital letters were clear enough:

SWEET NELL.

"I wonder . . . Sweet Nell. There is no one of the name Nell here?"

Mr. Rowe shook his head absently. "Nor has been. Well, here you have it: this was Jonathan's little world. His brother, you may know, has asked that his few effects be given to the poor. I think Jonathan would have agreed, as far as he was able. He was of a tender disposition—the only person I have ever seen *genuinely* to coax wild birds to eat from his hand. They will miss him."

"The other inmates to, perhaps," Fairfax said. There was nothing more to see and he gladly followed Mr. Rowe out of that room.

"Perhaps. But they are self-absorbed, not much attached to one another. And Jonathan had no neighbor," Mr. Rowe said, indicating the other door beside the stairs. "Empty— we have not a full complement at present."

"If you did, it would be that unfortunate number, thirteen."

Mr. Rowe gave his loud clanging laugh. "Oh, sir, you divert me. I know you cannot be a man of benighted superstition. It is written all over you; you are a believer in reason and science as I am. That is why you are so fully examining and, I may say, cross-examining me." Mr. Rowe lowered his great strong head and grinned at him.

Fairfax made a noncommittal gesture, hoping he had not blushed. Damn man, he *did* make you feel like a schoolboy. "I am merely gathering facts," he said. "Murder must be investigated. The laws of man are not like the laws of nature, I hope. If the human wolf rends the human lamb, we hunt him down."

"Oh, surely." Mr. Rowe still smiled. "But he may be just obeying his wolfish nature, you know?"

"No. We can always subdue our natures, Mr. Rowe," Fairfax said. "Unless we have really lost our wits, like these poor people, we can always subdue our natures, if we will. My congratulations again on your marriage, sir, and thank you for your time."

Eight

Very civilly did Mr. Samson Rowe part with Fairfax, and very civilly the manservant brought round his horse; and as he rode out through the gate a ray of full sunshine broke through the troubled clouds, as if in tribute to the gentleness and reason of the spot.

Yet Fairfax could not escape a feeling of eyes watching his back, while his mount shook its head with a grunt, as if it were glad to get away from there. It was the first fellow feeling between him and the beast. Fairfax tentatively patted its neck—*her* neck, he told himself, he must think of the gray mare as *she*. As Sir Edward had said, saddle horses weren't dogs, faithful unto one man alone. If the rider was kind and assured, they responded at once. Fairfax patted her neck again.

"This doesn't mean we're going to start taking fences, though," he said aloud.

No dark secrets at Mr. Rowe's asylum, then: everything was open and aboveboard. But there was a discrepancy, and because he could not account for it, Fairfax questioned everything. According to his brother, Jonathan had said there had been a death among the inmates recently, which had unsettled him. Now either Henry Griggs had lied when he said that, which made no sense, or Jonathan had been mistaken, as Mr. Rowe had suggested. Yet that didn't add up. Jonathan's mental condition, as far as Fairfax could tell,

seemed not to include fixed delusions or habitual misper-
ceptions. Of course, he was no expert, but he could not quite
picture the man who had been described to him, who was
able to go about the normal business of living with some
freedom, suddenly imagining that one of his fellow inmates
had died, and persisting in the belief against all evidence to
the contrary.

The alternative was that Mr. Samson Rowe had been
lying. But he doubted whether he would get any more out of
that large, mildly patronizing gentleman, who seemed so utterly prepared for everything. (He pictured briefly Death
with a scythe coming for Mr. Rowe, and being briskly
greeted with: "Oh, there you are, my dear sir, just a little
late.") He would find out, though, somehow. He even had an
idea of the means.

But first he had a call to make on a widow. Not the relict
of Tom Honeyman, the dramatic and beautiful Barbara, but
someone whom he imagined as far more homely. Mrs.
Bland, the parson's widow, whose brother was Mr. William
Parry, and whose sister-in-law, the mysterious Margaret,
must, he felt, hold the key to the whole business.

In Stamford he parted with the mare at the George and
walked up to St. George's Square. Here was the triumph of
gentility: no taverns had squeezed in among the tall gray
town houses grouped around the church. Instead Fairfax noticed the well-bred facade of the Assembly Rooms on the
south side, and thought of Sir Edward's daughters and their
excitement about going there. The joys of youth, when
everything was untried, and romance awaited. Sweet Nell.
Who was that lost love of Jonathan Griggs's if such she
was? A childhood sweetheart, perhaps; or the one his brother
had spoken of, the broken affair that had darkened the poor
man's mind beyond lightening. Well, something of a blind
alley: Nell was a common enough name, and whoever and
wherever she was, and whether sweet or sour, Fairfax
doubted she could lead him any nearer to Jonathan's killer.

Rapping at the door that was pointed out to him as Mrs.

Bland's, Fairfax was surprised to find it opened by a girl in a flood of tears. A maid, plainly, though she had on her bonnet, and she could only sob at him and hold open the door. She had a very fair, snub, freckled face, which crying did not flatter at all. It fairly tore his heart to see her and he was about to ask her what was wrong when a woman appearing in the hall cut him off with a sharp voice.

"You needn't do that, Esther. Your duties are over here. Let's have none of your games now. You have your things, you needn't dawdle."

The girl was crying so hard she had given herself hiccups. In between them, she said, "I wouldn't stay—not if you begged me."

"Oh, ho, begged indeed! There'll be no begging, miss, not while I've breath in my body. You have your pay, the full quarter's, and lucky to get it after that behavior. Now pick up that basket and let's have no more of it."

The basket plainly contained all the maid's possessions, and it was not large. She picked it up meekly, then sobbed defiance. "Where am I to go? What am I do to? It's not fair—"

"Fair? My goodness, what has fair to do with it? Fair words don't make the pot boil, miss—and mighty pretty in *you* to talk of fair when it's a wonder that nasty poisonous tongue of yours doesn't drop off." The woman interrupted her diatribe to give a momentary smile to Fairfax, as if to say she would be with him shortly. "Such filthy lies as I never heard. Count yourself lucky you're not put in the stocks for them, you unnatural creature."

"You're the unnatural one," the girl said quietly, setting her jaw, "and you know it."

"Get out!" Her mistress bore down on the girl, would have struck her if Fairfax had not decided to stay where he was, in the way. "You ought to be whipped—"

"Selina." It was Mr. Parry, coming with heavy steps down the stairs. "Selina, please, compose yourself. We've had enough trouble now, I think." He looked wan and tired.

"My dear, don't think of me," the woman said. "It's no trouble to me. I can bear up under a good deal worse than this. It's the trouble to you that I cannot abide, William, and will not have."

"Esther, you'd better go," Mr. Parry said, frowning.

The maid stared, swallowed something back, and then was gone, leaving the front door open behind her.

"Time was when servants were content to serve," Mrs. Selina Bland said with a glassy brightness, closing the door, "but now, of course, they are our masters. I daresay you know it as well as I, sir, and will excuse your reception accordingly. Probably there are half a dozen spoons in her basket, but there, I am only the mistress of the house, and have no rights at all."

"I'm sorry to call at an inconvenient time," Fairfax said. "My name—"

"It's Fairfax," Mr. Parry said, "the gentleman I was telling you about, Selina. This is my sister, Mrs. Bland. You have news, sir? It's not in your face," he added with a sad wry smile, "but I can hope."

"No news of your wife, I'm afraid. But there are handbills being printed that will circulate widely. I'm sure they will bring some intelligence of her."

Mr. Parry nodded bleakly. "Dear God. Having to advertise for my wife like a lost pocketbook."

"I only hope Margaret is aware of the grief she has put you to, William," Mrs. Bland said, touching his arm. "Well, Mr. Fairfax, forgive me playing a maid's part, will you walk up?"

The drawing room was large and well appointed in the latest fashion, but rather too prim and precise for comfort. The spotless marble hearth, the military ranks of shining chinaware, suggested that Mrs. Bland was quite a martinet to those servants who did not run away from her tears. She was a smart, broad-hipped, buxom woman not much past thirty, with full red lips and buttery hair and the same chocolate brown eyes as her brother, though rather hard than melting. She began at once to primp about the room, adjusting a candlestick here and smoothing a fold there.

"Pretty in her to start her tricks on a day like today, with everything at sixes and sevens," she went on relentlessly. "Thought she could get away with it, no doubt. Unluckily for her, you have to stir mighty early in the morning to catch *me* napping. You'll wish your bread dough before I'm finished with you, miss, thinks I, and so she did, I fancy."

"Sit down, Selina," said Mr. Parry, who had already done so, and taken up a half-full glass of wine. "It isn't worth distressing yourself."

"It's of no account to me, William. I can take a harder knock than an ignorant little chit can deal out, believe me. My concern is all for you: it always has been, through all your troubles."

Fairfax said, "Mr. Parry, has anything further occurred to you that might help us in our quest?"

"I have thought until my head aches," Mr. Parry said, stretching out his long feline limbs and looking at the ceiling, "and have come to no conclusion. Margaret's picture, by the by, is there, if that is of any use. It is a good likeness."

He pointed with a smooth white hand at an oval miniature hanging by the mantel. Mrs. Bland at once snatched it from its hook.

"Here, sir. It is as my brother says a good likeness, though I fancy the painter has flattered somewhat. The firmness of the mouth is not something, I regret to say, I have ever observed in Margaret . . . William, I am concerned about your headache. You must let me prepare an infusion for you."

"It's of no account, Selina," he said. His sister's hovering attention did not seem to irk him; rather he appeared to take it as his due.

Fairfax studied the picture It was well executed, and showed a fair, slight, pretty woman, features small and delicate, something decidedly waiflike about her. To look up from it to Selina Bland was to return to the earth earthy.

"Thank you," he said, returning it. "If there are any other details about your wife, Mr. Parry, that—"

"What would you have? Her height? It is five feet two inches. She is twenty-seven years old; she was born at Grantham; she has no parents living and an elder sister married in Devon; her maiden name was Mortimer; we were married in St. Neots church . . ." He sighed and looked unhappily at Fairfax. "I'm sorry. I am simply at a loss. My world has turned upside down."

"I understand. It has been a great shock. But do not give up hope of a happy result."

"I'm sure that's what we all wish," Mrs. Bland said, with briskest skepticism. "Dear me, of course. But what *sort* of result is a different matter. You may call me a very partial prejudiced woman if you like, I don't mind a bit, but what concerns me is *your* happiness, William. I have a good deal of family feeling, Mr. Fairfax—very out of fashion, I know, but I can't help it. So you mustn't mind me if I think first of William's welfare rather than Margaret's. I am only speaking the truth when I say he deserves it more—but there, deserves and rewards never keep company. An old saw no doubt, but true, I'm afraid, oh, yes, and I wish it wasn't."

If she always had this dreary perkiness, Fairfax thought, this dreadful humorless jocularity, then the late Mr. Bland's life must have been a trial.

"Hush, Selina," Mr. Parry said, "it's better left. Let us just wait and see before . . . You are partial, as you said; you could not love Margaret as I did, that's quite natural."

"Certainly. I don't deny it. I loved her as much as she would let me, that I firmly believe, but it's in my character always to make an effort. I'm not a stickler: an effort is all I expect from others, and you'll agree, Mr. Fairfax, that to ask for more would be to cry for the moon in this world of ours. I am sure an effort is all I asked of Margaret, as the wife of my only brother, and a woman who could count herself really remarkably fortunate to be so. No, William, I only speak truth; 'tis not as if she brought a fortune, and no one could call her a wonderful housekeeper—they would be simply lying if they did. I told her so when she was here. I'm plain like that, I'm afraid, always have been."

"There was some disagreement between you and Mrs. Parry during her recent stay?"Fairfax said.

"Oh, that's no mystery, sir," she said. "You're very wide of the mark if you think I make a secret of that. I am as fond of Margaret as can be, because she is William's choice, and that's good enough for me, but I speak as I find. If I see a spot I clean it; if I detect a moping discontented spirit, I take it to task. But we made it up. I make it a rule never to let the sun go down on my wrath, and we parted friends." Seeing that her brother's wineglass was empty, she hastened to re-fill it. "I was not severe—though if what you have in your mind is true, William, then I wish I had been."

"Perhaps I spoke wildly. I—I have hardly slept, and my mind is a little disordered. Let it rest, Selina," Mr. Parry said, closing his hand over hers as it rested on his shoulder. "It's not really a thing to be spoken of before our visitor."

"I don't know about that, William. I'd never contradict you, but under the circumstances, perhaps it should be said."

"If you have something germane to our inquiry, sir," Fairfax said, "I must press you to be frank."

Lifting his head, Mr. Parry said, "Are you a married man, Mr. Fairfax?"

"No, I'm not."

"Just so. But you are about to say that you understand, whatever it is. Well, I don't think you really can." Fatigue and wine gave the lawyer the look of a handsome, flushed, slightly sulky boy. "No matter. I have a suspicion—or the suspicion has me—that Margaret has a lover."

"Indeed . . . Whence comes this suspicion, sir?"

Mr. Parry smiled, quite gently. "There, you see. If you were married, you would not need to ask. I do not speak of love notes dropping out of pockets. When you are closely tied to someone—someone you consumedly love—you become sensitive to small changes. You notice things. Subtle alterations, absences, little secretive tricks that make no sense. Enough to be certain? I don't know, because I cannot speak objectively. I love Margaret, and love is proverbially blind. Probably there is a mountain of evidence that some-one not in love would see at once, but in my position one re-sists, one refuses to acknowledge it until . . . until something like this happens." He was breathing hard. "I do not like talking of this, Mr. Fairfax."

Fairfax inclined his head. "I thank you for the confi-dence, and I do think it needed to made. It does indeed throw a different light on the matter, if you think she may have—"

"Gone to him—gone off with him," Mr. Parry said harshly, "whoever he may be. And of that I have no inkling. She always went about much as she liked during the day, when I was occupied with business: calling, sick visiting, helping with the church . . . She is devout."

"Excessively so, I would say," his sister put in. "There is a place for everything, and I think a woman should look to her home, not go listening to the spouting of divines and troubling about her soul."

"I don't understand it," Mr. Parry said, gazing away. "How she could . . . I gave her everything. I adored her and she, I believe, adored me . . ."

This was certainly something new—but not entirely hopeful or helpful, Fairfax thought. It all went swiftly through his mind. Suppose, then, Margaret Parry had a lover; suppose that she had never intended returning home to St. Neots, but had got off the coach at one of the earlier stages, Wansford or Stilton, and met him there, and so away into the blue illicit yonder . . . If that were the case, then it explained why she had not been on the coach when it was attacked. And probably she and her lover were miles away now. Yet even if she could be got hold of, it seemed likely she would have anything useful to tell them about the high-way robbery and murders. She had just by lucky chance escaped a different rendezvous, with death. Another blind alley.

And yes, and yet . . . How well founded were these suspicions? The serious-minded woman described by Mr. Parry did not seem the type to throw away marriage lightly. As for disagreeing with Mrs. Bland, he saw that as more of a recommendation than otherwise. And the possibility remained that Margaret Parry had been on the coach when it was attacked, and had gone away with the attacker—willingly, or otherwise . . .

"But you still have no notion, sir," Fairfax said, "of where she might be?"

William Parry drained his wine. "Do you think, Mr. Fairfax, I would be sitting here if I did?" With a motion at once athletic and pettish, he sprang upright and stalked to the window. The Roman profile brooded against the light, with a beating of soft lashes. "Forgive me. This exposure is— quite a torment to me. It's like having all that is most intimately precious thrown into the common gutter to be picked over."

"Well," Fairfax said, "I will not affront you by saying I understand. But I appreciate the distress, and I will guard your confidence—"

"My dear sir, I don't see how you can," Mr. Parry said, smiling with exquisite gentleness. "My wife's name is bandied abroad: she is sought in connection with an appalling crime. You are pursuing this matter on behalf of Sir Edward Nugent, and will surely report to him. There can be no question of confidence."

"As you say, sir. But of course your wife's safety outweighs such considerations. And I still hope to bring you a happy report of that. You will be remaining here?"

"I will stay till dinner. Then I must go home."

"Oh, no, William, you must stay here the night," Mrs. Bland said. "I can't bear to think of you going back there alone. I will have your room made up directly, and—"

"No, Selina. I will go home tonight. I have business to attend to. No doubt, sir, you can send word to St. Neots, if there is any news?"

"Certainly," Fairfax said. "On the subject, sir, there is something I am a little unsure of that you mentioned at the inquest this morning, to do with your whereabouts yesterday . . ."

"I stayed till a very late hour with a dying friend, as I said. I suppose you want his name. It is or was Mr. Daniel Poole, of St. Neots; and I know what you are about, Mr. Fairfax." William Parry was, of course, a lawyer, and it was with a wry forensic sniff that he went on. "And you are quite right to do so, of course. You must explore every avenue, very commendable. Well, Poole is no more, so it is of little use your checking with him. And before you say that a man on his deathbed would surely prefer spiritual comfort, I will tell you that Poole was a notorious miser, who lived alone with one servant, and had no use for religion. He reposed trust in me, I think, because I deal with worldly things, and he always greatly liked going to law against his neighbors." A twinkle of humor in William Parry's too-solemn eyes. "And so I kept his last watch. Those were my whereabouts, sir."

"It was good in you, William," his sister said going to him at the window, "and like you." Her voice now had a throaty quality, quite at odds with her chilly correctness. Faintly disturbing, as was the strong resemblance between the two of them, watching Fairfax with identical eyes as he took his leave. He was a stranger, of course, but he had never felt so utterly excluded.

He felt somehow out-maneuvered too, as he walked, deep in thought, down St. Mary's Hill. A lover . . . did Parry have a genuine reason for this startling suspicion? He had hardly provided one. But then, as he said, the signs and tokens were of their nature private and subtle. Margaret Parry was hardly likely to have written the name of her lover all over the walls, as poor Jonathan Griggs had apparently done. As for

Parry's alibi, there was no proving nor disproving it. In truth he could have been anywhere yesterday.

Fairfax felt the brush of secrets, teasing and evading him. He was more and more convinced that the dead of the *Flyer* had not fallen victim to a simple highway robbery; that something like an execution had been carried out on the Great North Road. Now for the first time he wondered if it could have been done by proxy: if, in fact, the deed had been done by the highwayman of Stangate Hole, but at the behest of someone else. Trying to imagine such a plot, he came up against a stiff obstacle. For someone to have paid or bribed or otherwise persuaded a highwayman to do this, they would first have to know his identity and where to find him—which made a nonsense of the highwayman's whole *raison d'être*. He would be completely in that person's power. Well, perhaps there lay the incentive—carry out these murders, or I will betray you to the law. And yet having done it, the criminal would have no guarantee that the person would not just turn him in anyway. Unless the highwayman in turn had some hold over his master. A quid pro quo . . . But here his imagination faltered again. A flight of such fancy needed stronger wings.

Just then he saw ahead of him a figure he recognized. It was the maid whom Mrs. Bland had so sharply dismissed. She had her basket over her arm, and she was still crying, scrubbing her hand across her eyes even as she stepped out to cross the street. A drayman tugged at the reins of his elephantine horses, cursing at her to get out of the road, and spitting. Mud from the lurching wheels spattered her plain frock, probably the only one she owned.

She flinched when Fairfax touched her arm.

"Don't be alarmed. You remember me."

"Has she sent you after me?"

"Who, Mrs. Bland? I don't take orders from her. You still have hiccups, I see, and now your dress is wet. Will you come into the George, and have a glass by the taproom fire? And I am not that sort of man, believe me." He smiled at her.

She could not smile back, but her sobs eased. "It's Esther, isn't it?"

"Yes, sir. Esther Fryatt."

"I'm Robert Fairfax. We're trying to find Mrs. Parry, as you may know. Perhaps you can help. If not, it doesn't matter. Let's just get rid of those hiccups."

In the taproom of the George she sat hugging her thin body and coughing over the brandy and hot water he gave her. The coughs at least interrupted the hiccups, and presently she gave him a weak smile.

"Thank you, sir. This is kind."

"Well, I don't know what your disgrace was, but I wouldn't care to be on the sharp end of Mrs. Bland's tongue myself."

"It weren't the first time."

"Unhappily for you it was the last. Or perhaps not so unhappily—but you've lost your position, and I'm concerned. Have you anywhere to go?"

She shook her head wretchedly, then nodded. "I can go to my mother's for now. In Huntingdon."

"Have you money?"

"A—little . . . I shall be all right. I'm not sorry to go. Folk might say I'm mad to lose a good place. But I'm made of flesh and blood and—and some people aren't."

"This trouble between you and your mistress—had it to do with Mrs. Parry?"

Esther Fryatt sniffed and hugged herself tighter, as if she would make herself as small as possible. "I can't really say . . ."

"You don't have to. But consider that you have nothing to fear now from Mrs. Bland. I'm afraid, from the look of things, that she may not give you a character for your next position anyway. But my employer, Sir Edward Nugent, is a kindly man. I think he can be persuaded to put in a word for you, especially if you have suffered an injustice. You see, we are very anxious to trace Mrs. Parry—and I am somewhat at a loss where to look."

"That I can't help you with, sir," Esther said cautiously. "But—the quarrel was to do with Mrs. Parry."

"You know the lady well?"

"Middling well. I mean, with her being married to Mrs. Bland's brother, and them often visiting and such. She'd been staying last week with Mrs. Bland, you know. Seemingly she'd been a bit mopish, and I think 'twas Mrs. Bland's notion to have her over and—put some life in her, as she says. A great one for that is Mrs. Bland." Another sip of brandy seemed to spark Esther to tart defiance. "Always knows what's best for everyone. Just be like her, and all'd be right with the world. Mrs. Parry wanted gingering up, she'd say. I thought Mrs. Parry was quite all right as she was. When she stayed she was very kind to me. A sweet lady—with a sort of misty look—not like Mrs. Bland at all. Mary says . . ." She stopped.

"Mary?"

"My sister. She's in service at the Parrys' house, in St. Neots. Our mother was nurse to Mr. Parry and Mrs. Bland when they were little 'uns, so 'tis a family thing. Mother taught us our letters; Mary's best at it, and she writes me pretty often. She says Mrs. Parry seems too good for this world, somehow, and she—feels sorry for her."

Fairfax nodded. "Mr. Parry, though, is surely a devoted husband, and I would guess that he is getting on in the world very nicely."

Esther would not look at him. "That's as may be. I don't want to speak out of turn because I don't know everything. Mrs. Parry wasn't my mistress. But what I do know is— well, she ain't what Mrs. Bland was saying today. A drag and a burden on her precious brother, she said, and lucky ever to get him—and if she was alive out there somewhere, and hadn't gone home of her own choosing, then she was a wicked foolish trollop who better deserved to get shot like the others. Then she turns on me and says I was very thick with her, did I know what she was up to? And I comes out with it and says that maybe Mrs. Parry was frightened to go home."

"Frightened?"

"Yes . . . I didn't mean to say it, it just came out. That's when Mrs. Bland went wild. Called me all manner of names. I thought she'd box my ears . . . but no, I didn't think she'd do that, 'twas a different sort of anger. Never mind turning me out of the house—I think she wanted to turn me off the edge of the world." Her lips grew thin. "I just hope Mary doesn't get into trouble on account of it. I didn't mention her. It was just me, and what I thought."

"Why do you think Mrs. Parry was frightened?"

Esther was uneasy. "Things I'd gathered. Things I'd heard from Mary. About how life went on behind closed doors. Mrs. Bland has to have things just so, you know, and in most ways her and her brother are alike—there was never brother and sister so alike, I think . . ." She began fidgeting agitatedly with her basket. "But I don't want to say more, sir. It was hearing those nasty things said about poor Mrs. Parry that made me break out, and now . . . I don't want Mary to have any trouble, sir. Two of us without a place would be too much. All I mean is that if Mrs. Parry is all right, which I pray God, and just didn't want to go home, then she has her reasons. Good reasons. That's all I can say and I don't think I can help you anymore."

"You cannot think of anywhere she might have gone to? Or any—person she might have gone to?"

Esther's pale, almost lashless eyes widened. "No sir."

And if she did, he thought, out of loyalty she would not say. It was a difficult position for the girl. He felt in his pocket.

"Well, thank you for speaking to me, Esther. Please accept my promise that what you've said will not go to the wrong quarters. Mrs. Bland or Mr. Parry will know nothing of it. No, please, take this money to help you. You are sorely beset, and I think you have not been justly treated. Only one thing I would ask. If you feel there is anything else you can tell me—anything at all—then you can find me here at noon tomorrow. No matter if not, but I shall be here, and will hear you in the same terms of confidence. Think on it, and good luck, Esther."

She thanked him almost inaudibly, and went away quickly. Some of the trustfulness, he felt, had gone from her look at the end, and he had doubts that he would see her again. But the food for thought she had given him was nourishing enough.

William Parry, when he had burst in on the inquest that morning, had evoked universal pangs of sympathy. All saw grief at the loss of a young wife. If there was instead a jealous fury that she should dare to leave him, he was surely clever enough to disguise it. Difficult to judge. Plainly Selina Bland doted on her brother, and would think no woman good enough for him. Dislike of Mrs. Bland might have distorted Esther Fryatt's attitude to both of them.

Mr. Quigley, the innkeeper, had been hovering near, and now he advanced with his usual mincing politeness.

"Beg pardon, Mr. Fairfax, but there was someone asking for you earlier—Mr. Twelvetree's clerk. Asked me to give you the message. Mr. Twelvetree, he says, wants you to wait on him as soon as may be."

"He does, eh? Thank you, Mr. Quigley. I suppose I had better go." He got up. "A summons from Mr. Twelvetree, I fancy, is not to be refused."

"I hope, sir, you don't owe him anything," said a crab-faced man sitting nearby. He had been drinking a mug of ale and going "tsk tsk" over a copy of the *Stamford Mercury*—at the matter not the style, Fairfax hoped.

"I do not, sir, but why?"

"Because," the crab-faced man said, "if you did and could not pay, you could expect him to skin you alive and sell your hide at the best price."

"Is Mr. Twelvetree so very—venal?"

" 'Tis reliably reported. I have never been in his clutches, thank heaven. But I've heard of his doings. He is more than a banker. His arm reaches everywhere. Property, now—he has got a good deal of that into his hands. But not just any old property. Not so long ago he took an interest in Market Pelling, over in Leicestershire. A poor moiling little place, you'd think. But he lent out money at a generous rate of interest to freeholders there—to plant a field, to set up a forge or a livery stable. On security of their property, of course. Then when they don't do well, he calls in the loans, takes possession when they can't pay, and becomes the landlord. The reason is, Market Pelling's a parliamentary borough. Not that Twelvetree wants to go into politicking himself, mind. Instead, the Member for Market Pelling has to court his favor, because he has the voters under his thumb. So he has power without responsibility. Then there was a young rakehell over Bourne way—expecting an inheritance through entail and living high on credit. Twelvetree's happy to advance him money. Meanwhile he encourages all the tradesmen he's got in his power to accept notes of hand from the young rakehell, and buys them up himself at a discount. When the young sprig comes into his property, Twelvetree presents 'em all for payment. Fellow's inheritance is half in hock when he comes into it, and Twelvetree's made a tidy profit. Nothing illegal, mind. What he does is look for the weak spots in human nature, and fasten on to 'em like a cur. Mr. Nicholas Twelvetree, supplier of enough rope." He chuckled harshly and drained his ale.

I have yet to hear a good word about Nicholas Twelvetree, Fairfax thought as he arrived at the banker's house in Broad Street. Going up the steps to the front door he found his way blocked by a large manservant in livery.

"I have to ask you your name and business, sir."

"Fairfax, and my business is with Mr. Twelvetree, I presume, as he asked me here."

The manservant stepped grudgingly aside. Once through the door, Fairfax had to face another—and this one, to his amazement, carried a blunderbuss at the slope.

"You are ready for a siege, it seems," he said to Mr. Claymount, who came scuttling to greet him.

"Not so bad as that, sir, I think, ha ha," the little clerk said, and kept tittering in an almost hysterical way as he led Fairfax upstairs. Another brawny servant was on sentry duty outside Mr. Twelvetree's rooms. It was like being ushered into the presence of the Grand Turk rather than a provincial banker. And for all his retinue, Nicholas Twelvetree was no more prepossessing than ever, pastily peering through his spectacles at Fairfax as if expecting him to—well, to pull out a gun.

"Mr. Fairfax," he said, snuffling into his scented handkerchief. "You could not come earlier?"

Singular charmlessness. "Mr. Twelvetree. What did you wish to speak of?"

"I should have thought it was obvious." The banker seated himself by his cold hearth, taking up a glass of that watery cordial. Hand not at all steady, Fairfax noted. "My clerk attended the inquest at the town hall this morning. A shocking business. An item of my property publicly displayed. And evidence of a most discreditable imposture. Someone was trying to impersonate me, Mr. Fairfax. For what purpose I know not—but it must have been mischievous, and probably criminal. If you know what that purpose was, Mr. Fairfax, I demand that you tell me."

"If I knew, I would tell you, sir, without the unpleasantness of *demands*," Fairfax said. "But I was hoping you might shed light on the matter. The impostor, as you must know now, was Mr. Thomas Honeyman—a former employee of yours, it seems."

"He was. And I rue the day I ever hired him. He was my chief clerk until about a year ago, when I had to dispense with his services. He had a genteel manner, and a good brain for ciphering, and might have done very well. But he had an insubordinate and impertinent spirit that would not be quelled. I do not expect my chief clerk to challenge my judgment on financial matters. I expect service and discre-

tion. I warned Honeyman more than once about this mulish
independence of his. At last he pushed it too far, and I dismissed him. I had no doubts about the rightness of this, and
still less now. The strongbox was obviously purloined from
me, and concealed. We missed one at the time, and Claymount looked high and low; but though I suspected and
questioned him, Honeyman flatly denied taking it. Had there
been money or valuables in it I would certainly have taken
the matter further, but it was an empty one from the strong-
room, and so I decided to let it go. I supposed he had taken
it in a mere spirit of mischief and malice."

"I see. And then Mr. Honeyman set up in the timber business, with Mr. Fox."

"What? What's that?" Agitation seemed to make Mr.
Twelvetree deafer; he flourished his ear trumpet. "Oh! Yes,
that. A poor pinchbeck affair by all accounts. Honeyman's
father died not long after I dismissed him. He was a bookseller in a small way, and Honeyman came in for what he
had, and took a fancy to be a merchant. He had not the capital or the temperament—I say this merely as a matter of
fact. He did not thrive. Hence, I presume, this scheme to
pass himself off as me. He must have sought to profit by
some imposture under my name, though what I cannot
think. I am most careful"—he wrapped his shiny old suit
closer around him, till it was like the skin of a peach—"*most*
careful in my business dealings. I would hardly leave myself
open to such an opportunity. But I shall want to know in
what other ways that rogue has been making free with my
name, sir; I shall need to know."

"If anything comes to light, you will. But that rogue, Mr.
Twelvetree, is dead, and I cannot see what harm can ensue."

"I can't help it if he's dead, sir; that's nothing to me." The
tone was not even frosty: it was the cold of November, dull
and gray.

"Perhaps, perhaps not. But I wonder if it has occurred to
you, as it has to me, that the reason the *Flyer* was attacked
may have been because you were on it." Fairfax watched the

banker closely. Out of the corner of his eye he noticed again that small unassuming portrait of a woman dwarfed by Twelvetree's own portrait. "Or seemed to be."

"Of course. Of course it has occurred to me. These ruffians keep a watch on the roads, do they not? My name as a banker and a man of substance is well known. And if it were observed that I"—he winced, and Fairfax sympathized, for it must have been horrible and dislocating to speak of this other "I" and its doings—"or at least the imposter, were carrying a strongbox, then there could be no greater provocation."

"Yes indeed," Fairfax said. A provocation . . . An idea that had been nagging at him spoke loud in his mind now. But he must consult someone else about that. "Yes, certainly. But I wonder whether you have more precise suspicions about this. I notice, for example, a change in your arrangements here. You are very closely guarded—far more than the security of a country bank would warrant. There are armed men on the premises. It suggests you are fearful of something, or rather someone."

"Wouldn't you be, sir?" A patina of sweat gave Mr. Twelvetree's skin the clammy look of a new mushroom. "Woulnd't you be alarmed after such an event?"

"Only if I though the attack of the *Flyer* was not an incidental act of highway robbery, but something more personal. If I thought, for example, that someone was out to kill me." Unbidden, Fairfax took a chair. "That someone was misled by Tom Honeyman's strange charade, and thought they had done the deed. But no: you live yet, sir, thank heaven. But must live under the fear that a second attempt may be made . . . I offer this, of course, as a mere hypothesis."

"A preposterous hypothesis," said Mr. Twelvetree—which considering his lisp was no mean feat.

"Certainly, if you say so. But if you do have in mind someone who might have done this, or might want to do it, then it would be of great assistance to us in our quest for the criminal—"

"Quest? I see no evidence of such a quest. Only a set of impertinent questions. The case appears to me, sir, that our roads are not safe for decent citizens, and for all I know our houses are not either. That is why I have had my menservants fetched here from my country place—yes, and armed them. There are two more at the back stairs, and I intend to have at least one always on the watch about my premises. If the law will not protect, then I must protect myself. I have a mind, indeed, to send my men out to the woods around Stangate Hole, where this villain seems to go to earth, and see if they cannot flush him out. That, I propose, would be a better means of solving the matter than prying and insinuations."

"I did not mean to insinuate, only to get at the truth. You are a man of wealth and influence, Mr. Twelvetree, and such a man is not unlikely to have enemies."

It was this remark that seemed to incense the banker. Fairfax saw the energy of the man beneath the hypochondriac fussiness as Mr. Twelvetree whipped out his keys, prowled over to the door and unlocked it, and stood pointing a peremptory finger to the anteroom beyond.

"This interview is at an end. You are a stranger, sir, and so may not know it—but no one deals with me in this offensive manner. No one. They learn not to. Consider this your lesson."

Meaning, Fairfax thought, count yourself lucky not to be kicked out. Though he felt very much as if he had been, as he emerged into the street shadowed by a glowering manservant.

Extraordinary creature! In Fairfax's experience, men generally liked to think of themselves as prone to have enemies. It made them fairly preen. Well, one thing had been proved: that dry stick of a man was prey to emotion after all.

That Twelvetree had lied, of course, went without saying. The fellow was frightened all right, and not of anonymous

highwaymen descending on his bank vault in the middle of
the night. The problem was narrowing down the many people who loathed him to the one, or ones, who loathed him
enough to kill him.

"A short acquaintance I know, but still to be cut dead in
the street like this, shocking."

The voice was Cordelia Linton's, and she was smiling
uncertainly at him, a straw hat on her unruly hair, handkerchief crossed over her shoulders, a basket on her arm.

"Good God, I'm so sorry, how'd you do? I was—thinking . . ."

"Perfectly legitimate human occupation, I reckon, though
not many people do. Thunderous you looked, though, very.
Cloud on the brow. A brown study as they say—strange
phrase. Your loan must have been refused," she said, nodding expressively at the bank.

"It certainly would have been," he said, "if that had been
my errand. Sent off with a flea in my ear, another strange
phrase."

"Well, I'm glad I saw you. That is, your handbills are
ready. Just this moment on the drying racks. They will be
dispatched to the George this afternoon—unless you have
already solved your mystery, of course."

He shook his head. "The pool is muddier if anything. Mr.
Twelvetree did not take kindly to questioning."

"Nicholas Twelvetree does not take kindly to anything
except money, so they say. Dead to all human feeling. A terrible reputation to bear, is it not? Even more terrible to experience, I would say. To know that of yourself."

"Yes . . ." Her eyes, he saw in the daylight, were full of
fascinating flecks of color, like agate. He did not like eyes
of pure color, or decided he did not. "I wonder if it is true of
that gentleman. Do you know, by the by, if he was ever married?"

"I do, and he was. Oh, yes, Mr. Twelvetree had a life outside of the counting house, though the tale is not an edifying
one, by all accounts."

"Really? Is she—But I beg our pardon, I interrupt your marketing."

She laughed. "You do not. I came out to buy some tongue, as George fancies that is just the thing to set him right again—curious how the most expensive things are always the best medicine—and I have it, and no money left. So I'll gladly tell you the tale, if you will go on a walk with me. Down by the river, away from all this racketing. People will talk, of course, but never mind—I shall look cross and distressed, as if you are bothering me, and that will preserve my reputation."

He laughed, though he didn't like the idea, even as a fiction, of bothering her. She led him by the sheep market and down to a place where there was a millrace and a wooden bridge crossing the river to a broad meadow. There were trees all around, fretted with autumn colors. Beauty, he thought again, lies more in mixture than in purity.

"Peaceful, isn't it? It won't be next month. Here is where they make the bullring for the annual bull-running, which is one of our delightful old customs. The bull is baited and set running around the streets and people chase it down with stones and sticks and dogs until it dies—having died a thousand deaths before, of course. What a piece of work is man!" Cordelia looked sidelong at him. "The custom has its opponents, of course. The shopkeepers do not like the damage to their shopfronts, the magistrates do not like the drinking and idleness; and the clergy do not like people enjoying themselves. So perhaps it is politeness that will finally stop us being torturers."

Fairfax thought of Henry Griggs outside the cockpit. "Some would say that only fear of God can make us good. My belief has always been that reason will do it—reason and enlightenment; and that there is no devil in man but ignorance. I hold to that belief . . . yet it is hard, sometimes, not to see damning evidence to the contrary."

"In others—or in yourself?"

He hesitated. "No one likes to see devil in themselves."

"Perhaps that proves that he is there ... Well now, Mr. Twelvetree: that is a man who has obeyed only the dictates of reason, you might say. Or perhaps not. It was certainly a surprise when he married. This would be a couple of years ago, perhaps three; it was after he had taken over the bank from Mr. Mortimer. He started out as a partner, you know, but very soon had the whole share. Still I believe he was building on slight foundations: he had nothing like the wealth and property he has now. Hence, some would say, the marriage. He took as his wife the widow of a rich brewer—Mrs. Jane Cornwell was the name. Several years older than he, and of good family, but rather a weak and dependent creature by all accounts, quite a mouse without a husband." Fairfax saw a cool distaste in her look. "Well, she sought advice from Mr. Twelvetree on what to do with her considerable fortune. 'Give it to me' you might say was his reaction; for he sought her hand in marriage, a man who had never shown the slightest amorous inclination before. But perhaps it was a love match. You wouldn't find one person in a hundred who would say so, but perhaps it was ... There was certainly no alteration in Mr. Twelvetree's manner of living. He shut her up with him in his tower of money, and they were never seen socially—though who knows, she may have been content with that. The money, of course, was now considerably more, and he began to put it to use. Then, about a year ago, she took sick and died. Perhaps Mr. Nicholas Twelvetree was inconsolable; again, who knows; but he was certainly very rich, which is always a comfort."

"He married money ... like a rational businessman."

"And the deal was all profit. There was one entry on the debit side, though—a son of Mrs. Cornwell's by her first marriage. Something of a scapegrace, it seems. He had gone young into an army regiment, and had spent his portion from his father in a very dissolute way of life, whatever that may be. I picture him in a red coat with a glass in one hand, a deck of cards in the other, a pipe in his mouth, and a hussy on his knee—I may be wrong. His mother, I believe, had indulged him—but his new stepfather would not. I think 'twas a case of chalk and cheese. Certainly Ensign Bennett Cornwell was seen around Stamford now and then—probably whenever he ran out of funds—but he never stayed long. Flea in the ear again. A coltish young fellow, six feet high and thin as a besom. Very silly girls sighed at him."

"Bennett Cornwell . . ."

"You know the name?"

"No—at least, I don't think so. So, his mother died, and he was left with Mr. Twelvetree for a stepfather."

"Precisely. But Mr. Twelvetree declined even to play a stepfather's part. He would do nothing for him—nothing. He had got the whole of the late Mrs. Cornwell's fortune into his hands. I think there was no legal redress for the young man—he had run through his own inheritance, as I said. But some might say that Mr. Twelvetree had a moral obligation to his stepson, at least. Well, he doesn't appear to have felt it. Bennett Cornwell was back in Stamford soon after his mother's death—he had left the army then, and I daresay had scarcely a penny to bless himself with. Certainly he got no warm reception from his stepfather. The gossip at the time was that Mr. Twelvetree turned him out of doors and told his servants never to give him admittance. Of course, you can imagine how gossip runs in a town like this—mountains out of molehills. But what happened next is a matter of record. The young man got mightily drunk one night, and took it into his head to go to his stepfather's house and throw bricks in at the windows. Even took a hammer to the door, they say; and all the while threatening the most ferocious violence against Mr. Twelvetree. A pretty commotion it must have made. Mr. Twelvetree's response was to send for the constables and have his stepson committed for trial at the next sessions. He actually ventured out for once, to attend the sessions and testify against him, and urged the magistrate to the most severity against the poor young pup. What do you think of that?"

Fairfax whistled. "I cannot help wondering what Mrs. Cornwell would have thought of it."

"Exactly. Mr. Twelvetree had a reputation as a cold fish, but this . . . Well, the magistrates had but little choice, and so Bennett Cornwell was sent to the House of Correction for a month. 'Twas over Christmas, that I remember, because folk talked of it—what sort of a man could send his wife's son to beat hemp in the Bridewell at the Christmas season, and so forth. What became of young Cornwell after his release I don't know. I never saw him about myself. It was rumored that he went up to Boston to be a shiphand. Certainly he must have been hard put to it, and desperate for any means of living . . . But there, Mr. Twelvetree acted rationally, and in prudent pursuit of his own interests, did he not?" she said, giving him a rueful look.

"A bitter story . . . The young man may well feel himself dreadfully wronged. Yet it was a wild and rash thing to do."

"Well, he was little over twenty, I think. The wildest and rashest age, supposedly." She laughed, a brittle sound. "We elders feel nothing of that, of course."

Fairfax was thinking of his own wild and rash time: the time after his father's suicide and disgrace, when Elizabeth, his intended, had drawn away from him, and all his world was in ruin. He had deliberately quarreled with Elizabeth's brother, and challenged him to a duel, and shot at him and wounded him, all in a red haze of bitterness and anger and hatred. Young and pained and purblind, he had hated enough to want to kill. Was that how Bennett Cornwell had felt?

"Well," he said, "Mr. Twelvetree certainly told me nothing of this. Whether that suggests an element of shame on his part, or whether he thinks it simply none of my affair, I don't know . . . But it is revealing." I must pay Mr. Nicholas Twelvetree another visit, he thought, not without relish.

"You think it important? Oh! My Lord, do you suppose Bennett Cornwell, and no highwayman, is behind the outrage? Let's see . . . there is no doubt he is violently affected toward Mr. Twelvetree. And if he was mistook about who was on the coach . . . my Lord!"

Fairfax's thoughts were along similar lines, but they went further. Was it possible that this Bennett Cornwell, after his release from the House of Correction, had taken to the road? That he *was* the highwayman of Stangate Hole—and, when he had heard of his hated stepfather traveling the road, had taken the opportunity to exact the ultimate vengeance? Tom Honeyman in his elaborate disguise had presented a fair enough resemblance to Twelvetree—enough for a desperate man, presenting his pistols at the coach window, to act upon. Perhaps he had realized his mistake straight after the deed was done; perhaps later, when news of the incident became general. Whichever, Mr. Twelvetree had reason to fear for his life . . .

And yet, why the killing of Jonathan Griggs? That surely didn't fit. Fairfax felt rather as he did when a megrim headache struck him: a segment of his field of vision on the right side would disappear, as if it had been cut out of paper. Much was likely in this case: nothing was completely likely.

"Have I spoke out of turn?" Cordelia said, studying him. "You have my word I will say nothing to anyone. These are vital matters, are they not? Law and justice and life and death." There was suppressed excitement in her voice.

"Oh, I can hold you to no such promise. But while all is speculation—"

"A word to the wise," she said, pressing his arm. "You may trust my discretion."

"I do."

"Even though I am a woman, and I write in a news-sheet?" she said, glinting.

"I would trust you with anything." He looked away. "But of course I—I cannot ask you to withhold confidences from your husband."

"Oh, never fear, Mr. Fairfax," she said brightly, looking away too, "George is a man much preoccupied, and it is a

long while since anything I have to say has held his interest."

He felt that a bridge had been crossed, and should not
have been; yet he could not wish it uncrossed. Damn, he
thought, damn everything.

"Well, your quest is a most diverting one anyhow, and I
hope you will let me know how it goes on," she said quickly,
and looked at the sky. A shadow crossed her face. "It must
be near five. I had better be going home." As she spoke,
bells began ringing the hour across the town.

Making out the tower of St. George's as they returned
across the meadow, Fairfax said, "Were you acquainted with
the late Reverend Mr. Bland?"

"He died not long after I came here. I saw him once or
twice. Lucky he was a Christian and not a Mohammedan,
because he was stinking drunk the whole time."

Fairfax let out a shout of laughter. "Now there is a revelation. I had the pleasure of meeting his widow today. I shall
look at her in a new light."

"I fancy it was rather a marriage of convenience,"
Cordelia said, laughing a little tensely. "Curious phrase, as
if marriages of the other kind are inconvenient."

"I sometimes wonder if there are any of the other kind,"
Fairfax said, and was shocked at himself as soon as he had
said it.

"Such skepticism, sir. No, the Reverent Mr. Bland did not
exactly shine—"

"Except for his nose, I take it."

"Don't be vexing. He left Mrs. Bland very well provided.
She is—what can I call it?—a very *busy* person, sick visiting, showing her poorer neighbors how to stretch a chicken,
not literally of course, and generally getting on very well
without her spouse. A skeptical person, which of course I am
not, would say she seemed happy enough to be rid of him."

Ah, but who after all could hold a candle to that beloved
brother of hers? Fairfax thought.

They had very soon come to the corner of High Street—too soon for him. But there must be a parting. Oh, yes.

"Well, sir." She was nervous and spiky again now, not meeting his eyes. "If you should need to pick my brains again, you know where to find me."

"You are a wonderful intelligencer, but the pleasure of your company does not stop there." Oh, fool, and worse, he told himself, get away. "However, I must not trespass. Thank you again, Mrs. Linton."

"I wish," she said, and then stopped with a crooked smile. "I wish I knew everything!" And very quickly she was gone.

A strange wish. He could not concur in it. If it included the future, for example, and all the secrets of one's own nature—how terrifying!

He turned his steps toward the river again. But not the mill side of the bridge; the other side where the modest wharfs and warehouses of the town's merchants huddled at the waterside under a canopy of smoke. It was time to intrude on the grief of Barbara Honeyman, and find out whether Bennett Cornwell took snuff.

Nine

A very young slatternly servant girl in a sackcloth apron answered the door to him.

"Shoo! Git away—git off with your nosing and sniffing!"

Not him, he realized after a not wholly surprised moment, but a stray dog that had followed him to the door and tried to slip in. The servant girl ejected it with a broom. It was not the only stray he had seen foraging about Water Street. The street was what might be called respectable, but it was old and catty-cornered and river-smelling; shabby children played here and there among the ash heaps and the dark entrances of mazy courts. Life with its rub and wear and awkwardness was closer here than in the airy gentility of the squares. The Honeyman house was very old, perhaps even thirteenth century, Fairfax thought; mellow stone that seemed to bulge out over the pavement, lancet windows that to his secular mind were inescapably churchy, and inside musty darkness and the creak of ancient paneling.

Pain too. He hit his head on the lintel of the door, following the girl into the parlor. One always forgot how shocking that pain was, and he stood for a few moments quite blinded with it, cursing the midgets of the Middle Ages.

There was music, a faint melancholy scrap of melody.

Barbara Honeyman was seated at a spinet. The instrument was not large, but prominent enough in that low-beamed parlor. Candles had already been lit, throwing huge shadows on the wainscoted wall and lending a waxiness to her white skin against the black gown. The dirgelike tune she played completed the deathliness of the scene. Fairfax felt as if he had wandered into an allegorical painting in which he was expected to hold an hourglass and a parchment inscribed *Here ye see, Death's selfe and mee, Yet as wee bee, So shall thee.* Or something. Wrong even to entertain such flippancy in the presence of the young widow, but somehow she brought it out in him, perhaps because he felt she was never, ever flippant herself.

"I should perish without my music," she said, stroking a last minor chord. She turned to face him. "You think me unfeeling."

"Not at all. Music is a great consolation, and you must have sore need of consolation just now."

But she wanted to explain more. "In my head are such thoughts," she said, pressing her white hands to her temples, "that I think they will torment me to madness. Only music, perhaps, can drive them out . . . except that it doesn't," she added, looking vaguely away.

"I'm sorry to intrude at such a time. I will not detain you long. I beg the indulgence of just a few questions."

She shrugged, and gestured him to a chair. "No matter. You can hardly, sir, make me feel worse."

"I wonder, have you seen a doctor?"

"What?" Her look startled him. "Why should I?"

"Well—it has been a deep shock. A sleeping draft perhaps, might benefit you." Certainly those great eyes looked terribly tireless.

"No. Though I thank you for the thought. But a doctor can hardly cure the pain at the heart," she said, putting her hand over her breast. He wondered if when she spoke of the foot of the stairs she pointed to her shoe. She got up and went to stir the fire, a strong blaze that made the room uncommonly, even uncomfortably warm. The comforts were solid if not extensive: a Turkey rug, slightly worn, an embroidered screen, some pewter on shelves, a good oak table, a glass-fronted bookcase well filled with volumes that looked well read. About to speak, he heard a tapping at the window, which was behind her. She went and pulled back the brocade curtain. The sturdy head and shoulders of Joseph Fox filled the latticed window. Peering in, his eyes met Fairfax's for a surprised moment.

Opening the window, Barbara said, "What is it Joseph?"

"Oh—just to see if there's aught you want, Mrs. Honeyman. I shall be at the yard for a while yet, there's kindling to stack. So just give me the word if you need—"

"Thank you, Joseph." She had closed the window before he finished speaking, and came back to the fire with a frown. "Your pardon, sir. Mr. Honeyman's business premises adjoin the house directly. A common enough arrangement in older days, but not overconvenient for genteel living. Then there is the damp from the wharf . . . I see you mark the books, sir. They were my husband's. He set great store by them."

Glancing along the spines, Fairfax got the impression of an eager magpie mind—rather like old Sir Jemmy with his collection, on a much smaller scale: mathematics, Shakespeare, some Latin and Greek, natural history . . . "Mr. Honeyman's father was a bookseller, I understand."

"Yes. His enthusiasms came from that source, I think; also perhaps his less-than-practical turn of mind." She gave him a solemn look. "Which I loved in him, of course. I cannot bear a grubbing vulgarity of soul."

"And I believe the means to set up the timber yard came from the same source."

"So they did. I wonder what questions you can have to ask me, Mr. Fairfax. You seem to know all the answers."

"Not at all. But I have talked to Mr. Twelvetree today— formerly your husband's employer, of course. Mr. Honeyman was chief clerk at the bank, it seems; a position of some promise, surely. A pity it was lost. Though I fancy Mr. Twelvetree may have been a demanding employer."

"Perhaps, though not excessively so. Tom had a measure of his confidence, and might have done very well there. Especially, you know, as Mr. Twelvetree had no son to take into partnership . . . But Tom would not bend, he would not accommodate himself. Of course I understand pride and independence of mind; I cherish it above all things. It is just a pity he could not be brought to see—just a little of the art of pleasing, just a few concessions, a little sacrifice of his own ideas, and he could have done so much better for himself. I mean this for Tom's sake. I hope I am the last person to care for mere worldly advancement, to covet money and trinkets"—she made a grandly dismissive gesture—"the last person in the *universe*."

The world would have done just as well, Fairfax thought. "Your husband's quarrel with Mr. Twelvetree ran too deep, though, I take it."

She nodded, raptly gazing into the fire. "I was sorry. I could not help but tell him I was sorry."

"Because Tom's talents deserved to be so employed?"

She glowed at him for his understanding, and for a moment her beauty made the fire seem a cool glimmer. "Exactly so. The most comfortable prospect was there, if only . . . You see, Tom was more a thinker than a doer. The quick spirit, the daring stroke, are needed if the life of trade, such as this, is not to degenerate into a mere monotonous scratching for subsistence, a narrow grinding of dullness. But he would not see it . . . and I was sorry."

"His disagreements with Mr. Twelvetree—they were personal?"

"They were—everything," she said with the little gasp of expression that characterized her. "Tom took it into his head to disapprove of Mr. Twelvetree's ways of going about business. He would actually say that if such men represented the future, he despaired of the world. Oh, everyone knows that Mr. Twelvetree is hard and shrewd. But I would have thought Tom's better course would have been to stay there—

to act as a moderating influence, perhaps. Well, no matter. Tom was a thinker, as I said, and went his own way."

Fairfax was beginning to like the late Tom Honeyman. Stubborn, a little cranky perhaps, but his own man.

"And when did he lose his position there?"

"A little over a year ago. He had been with the bank some ten years, back to when it was just Mortimer's Bank."

"And what about Mr. Twelvetree's wife? How did he get along with her?"

"She was not much seen about the bank, I believe— something of an invalid. She died not long after Tom was dismissed. But it was Mr. Twelvetree that he always talked of—Mr. Twelvetree and his endless wrongs," she said with a sigh.

"You mentioned that Mr. Twelvetree had no son. But there is a stepson, is there not? A Mr. Bennett Cornwell?"

"Yes," she said flatly, eyes half closed. She had a very emphatic way of letting you know when things were of no interest to her.

"Was your husband closely acquainted with him?"

"For a time. It was after he had lost his position. Bennett Cornwell came back to the town, though it was well known he was not welcome at his stepfather's. A rackety young man who had been a soldier—he was always on the carouse. I thought him a poor sort of companion, but Tom fell in with him for a time, I suppose because he also was at odds with Mr. Twelvetree. This absurd enmity quite overtook him. We even put Cornwell up here for a week or two, when he was quite out of funds and could get no other lodging. It was Tom's idea and I had to go along with it. Luckily it did not last long. Cornwell went too far with his antics and was sent to the Bridewell."

"The snuffbox that was in your husband's pocket, engraved *B. C.* That was Bennett Cornwell's?"

"Yes, he gave it to Tom as payment for his lodging—it was all he had, he said. That was when he was released from the Bridewell. He called round here, looking like the most shocking scarecrow. Tom liked it as a keepsake, though I can't think way."

"And after his release? Did Tom still associate with him?"

"No, for thankfully Cornwell went away, where I don't know. I was glad. He had been greatly spoilt by his mother, I think, and I dislike that sort of willful character extremely."

"Indeed," said Fairfax, who had a theory that what we most disliked in others were our own flaws.

"Tom used to say he looked on him as he would look on an erring younger brother," she said, and her mouth was full of distaste.

"Your husband was some years your senior."

She got up to trim the candles with a lofty look. "Oh, sir, such things are unimportant. It is the youth and vibrancy of the spirit that counts."

He wondered if one could ever truly relax in Barbara Honeyman's company. "And so you saw no more of Bennett Cornwell."

"Not for a long time. Then he turned up here quite unexpectedly a few weeks ago."

The human ears could not prick, of course, but Fairfax felt a vestigial twitch in his. "Really? How did he appear?"

"I saw him only briefly: he closeted himself with Tom. Gaunt, a little shabby: not so full of himself, anyhow. But he did not stay long. It sounded as if there were high words between him and Tom—quite a sharp quarrel. My guess was he had tried to touch Tom for money, and Tom had seen sense at last. We certainly did not have it to spare . . . And then off he went, and we saw no more of him."

So Bennett Cornwell was, or recently had been, in the district. "Your husband did not say what it was about?"

"No. He could be a close man. There was a want of openness in him—I can say this, sir, because I was his wife, and supremely loved him."

She stood very straight and proud with the taper in her

hand, as if challenging him to challenge her. He had a feeling that she would have liked nothing better.

Instead he said, "Would you say he was a man with more friends than enemies?"

She surprised him by breaking down in tears, desolate, uncontrollable. It was as if he had thrust all the tragedy of her situation in her face. It cut him to see her. He made her sit down, he spoke soothingly, but he could not console her. She came out of it at last, wiping her eyes with one hand, while with the other she squeezed his in a remarkably strong grip.

"You are very kind," she said. "You see, there is only so much I can bear."

He did not think he had been very kind. But he had heard enough. "Mrs. Honeyman, I thank you and I'll trouble you no longer. I would just like a word with Mr. Fox before I go." He had been getting a feel for the geography of the old house, and now he pointed to a recessed door at the other end of the parlor. "That connects to the yard, I think?"

"Yes—but I think it's locked."

He was already there, trying the handle: it was open. He smiled. "That's well. Don't stir, Mrs. Honeyman, keep by the fire. And thank you again."

Remembering himself in time, he stooped under the low lintel and out through a little leaded porch. An outhouse wall, with a stable and privy, was on his right. A horse stamped at his passing. Ahead a cinder path led across to a walled yard with a warehouse building, mossy and peeling and shored up with timber struts, giving right onto the river. HONEYMAN, TIMBER & MARINE STORES was painted on the outside. The large double doors stood open, and inside, among barrels and stacks of timber and lumber and snaky coils of rope and oakum, Joseph Fox was working by lamplight. He was sitting, lithe as a monkey, on a sawhorse, and making up bundles of kindling with twine. His bare forearms were like the stuff of his trade, taut and knotty and eminently practical.

"They sell for a song," he said, jumping down and stacking the last bundle, "but they do sell, which is something. How d'you do, sir? I keep a drop of something in here, if you'd care for it. Warms the vitals."

Fairfax had been offered nothing indoors, and was glad of the tot of brandy from a stone flask that Fox drew from a trunk in the corner. There was a brazier here to, and a couple of chairs and an old desk set about with the remains of a meal on brown paper. A high narrow window looked out onto the wharf, and a couple of ducks arrowed slowly across the dusk sky, heading upriver.

"Trade's poor?"

"Poorish. It shouldn't be: prices are healthy and there's plenty of demand still, though folk are cagey about the war ending. But the fact is we're not best situated here. There's only limited navigation, and it's a haul getting in goods. The place would do treble the business at Spalding or Boston. Tom knew it, but he'd only smile, bless him."

"I think you are more at home with these matters."

"Meat and drink to me. I used to work in a shipping house at Boston, and took a part share in a schooner that prospered pretty well. So I was looking for an investment, and came in with Tom."

"Though you must have had doubts about the venture?"

"Well, I did, but Tom was my old friend, and he had a persuading way about him. Once he had a gad-bee in his bonnet, he'd talk at you till you thought it was your own idea. I've sat up with him all night till my head was spinning, and he'd still be coming with fresh notions when the sun was a-sky."

"You were pretty confidential together, then?"

"Oh, aye. I don't think there's anything old Tom wouldn't tell me," Fox said with a misty look.

The man made something of a fetish of breezy openness, Fairfax thought, so it was probably best to approach him on that ground. "Well, plain speaking's best. But at a time like this you can't always think of everything, I understand that.

Like the matter of the reports in the *Mercury*, to do with our highwayman: you'd been collecting them. Following his exploits."

Fox's eyebrows went up. Then he took a deep breath. "Aye. That's so."

"And Tom's pistols—you bought a similar brace at the same time." Fairfax kept his tone easy. "Not important, perhaps. But as I have been looking into this matter, I have found things out, and I may as well tell you how it looks to me. There was a hundred pounds' price on the head of our highwayman: quite a bounty, if someone had the nerve and determination to go after it. And what was the best way? Why, study the habits and haunts of the rogue, and then make a journey, setting oneself up very conspicuously as a rich man carrying booty—but secretly armed, of course. Then if the highwayman, who has got wind of these rich pickings on the road, makes an appearance, you're ready for him. Shoot him, or apprehend him—the bounty is yours. A pretty scheme and a bold one, which would work best, perhaps, if there were two of you."

Fox stared fixedly, growing more swarthy and knotty in looks, until he might indeed have been carved out of wood. (A timber merchant, thought Fairfax; a merchant made of timber. Not a good joke, but it had been a long day.)

"Damn me!" Fox exploded at last, shaking his head. "Damn me from here to Candlemas . . . Well, I suppose 'twas likely to come out, after poor Tom's jaunt. Look here—nothing came of it, as I thought." He poured more brandy. "I didn't want to say anything of it earlier, with Mrs. Honeyman by. But of course it occurred to me that Tom must have took it into his head to try it alone after all . . . Aye, we hatched up this scheme—a few months ago it was, when the justices put a bounty on the fellow's head. The yard wasn't faring so well, and Tom says to me, there's a hundred pounds going a-begging. We'd sit up and talk of it—like I say, once Tom had a notion he wouldn't leave go of it; and I went to the newspaper offices, and got all the re-

ports to do with the rogue, and we conned them. That bounty
should be ours, says Tom. And we went so far as to get a
brace of pistols each from the gunsmith, and lay a sort of
plan. My notion was that we should travel by saddle horses.
That way we could ply up and down the road, over a couple
of days even; and if the fellow did come out of his hole, and
then decide to turn tail, we could always pursue him. But
Tom was against that, not being much of a rider."

Fairfax hailed a kindred spirit.

"Tom had a fancy that we should flig ourselves up in
some way—pass off as rich gents such as a highwayman just
couldn't resist. He even toyed with the idea of dressing as
women, in a lot of lace and jewels—defenseless, you know;
but I wouldn't entertain that, I thank you, sir." Fox swelled
out his barrel chest. "Well, so we talked around and around
it; and I think you've gathered that it was drifting pretty far
from likelihood—even supposing it was ever very near to it.
The more we went into it, the ore it seemed a fool's game,
to me at any rate. Aye, the sort of thing that looks marvelous
clever over a pipe and a glass or three, you know, when men
put the world to rights and fight the latest battle over with
pepper pots. But not real. Just damned foolhardy. A hundred
pounds is a deal of money—as much profit as we've turned
in a year of struggling—but this is the very devil of a risk
we're talking of. Mind, I think it was as much the dare and
the adventure that appealed to Tom. 'Not such a dull old
stick after all, eh, Joseph?' he'd say. Well, anyhow, we
dropped it at last. Tom knew I was having doubts; and
though he'd hold on to a thing stubbornly, he'd drop it flat
once he lost interest."

"And Tom was not used to handling guns?"

"That was another thing. I was country-born, and I'm
used to 'em, but I wasn't sure of Tom. He said not to mind
about that, though, and he'd show me diagrams in books,
angle of vision and angle of trajectory and whatnot, and say
'twas the same as any learning. Well, books are books, I

thought . . . And it looks as if I was in the right of it, after what happened." Fox sighed and drank deeply.

"You had no notion that Tom meant to try out this scheme alone, when he went off yesterday?"

"Not a bit of it. It was long since we'd spoke of it. I thought 'twas just put away and forgot. All he told me was, he was taking the *Flyer* to Huntingdon, to do business. I saw him go from here, and excepting the old stuff suit he looked normal enough."

"And he was carrying a bundle, you said. Which must have been the box, and the other items—bagwig and spectacles and so on. ready for him to put on when he joined the coach at Wansford, which is—what, a few miles from here? Hence the early departure. He walked to the next coach stop at Wansford because to leave from Stamford, where both he and Mr. Twelvetree were at least pretty well known, involved some risk of recognition, exposure . . . And there at the Wansford posting house he appeared in the guise of Mr. Twelvetree, wealthy banker, carrying a strongbox and making a deal of fuss about it. He was lighting a bright beacon for the highwayman."

"Damn me," Fox said, shaking his head. "I have to admire him for it. Though, poor fellow, it proved his undoing. I'd seen that box before, when we were turning out the lumber store here one time. He kept it hidden. It was a thing he'd took away from Twelvetree's when he got dismissed— just for the hell of it, I think. To show he was one up on Twelvetree, even in some small silly way. He was that fierce against the man. 'Twas like his hate possessed him; it would drive him to say the wildest things. And yet I'll bet it tickled him to be posing as Twelvetree, with the ear trumpet and all, and doing the voice too I shouldn't wonder—he was a prodigious mimic, old Tom. Aye, I'll bet it tickled him."

"Yes, I've heard how violently affected he was against Twelvetree, and he was not the only one, apparently. Do you know Twelvetree's stepson, Bennett Cornwell?"

"The young soldier fellow—aye, I've met him. Tom

made a friend of him, I recall, when he was about Stamford last winter, when Tom first set up here. Well, 'twas common cause, I suppose. Tom had been sacked, and young Cornwell got turned away from the old lickpenny's doors, they say. Tom gave him a bed here for a time—that was like Tom. And then the young fellow got put in clink for his wild ways, and that was the last I heard of him."

"You have not seen Cornwell since?"

"Not I. I didn't think him a good companion for Tom, in truth, for they would only go firing each other up against Twelvetree. The man's a grasper, no doubting, but that's the way of it in his line; and it's no use kicking against the pricks in this world." Brandy was making Fox cheerfully philosophical.

"You said Tom would say the wildest things against Twelvetree. What kind of things?"

"Oh! Well, every sin known to man, practically. Usually in his cups, which is why I took it with a pinch of salt. He would go on about how Twelvetree had married money, and how it was mighty peculiar the wife didn't live long, though of course the money did—shocking stuff really. I used to try and soothe him down. There was no call to come up with tales like that. And then he said Twelvetree had blocked his way when he applied for a new position. This was not long after he'd been sacked, and before he came into the bit of money for this place. He applied for a likely post over St. Neots way, clerk to a lawyer. He thought 'twas in the bag: the lawyer took a shine to him, all set fair. Then the lawyer turns about very smartly, and says no. Of course, Tom sees Twelvetree's hand behind it, though he couldn't prove it. But he did go ferreting about in records—which was like him again—and found out that this lawyer had done a lot of legal work for Twelvetree over a land enclosure or such. A big job, anyhow, and likely enough this lawyer wanted to keep on the right side of Twelvetree, knowing which side his bread's buttered. So 'twas possible Twelvetree gave him the nod, you know—don't give that scoundrel a job, sir—that's how Tom saw it, anyway. But like I said, he was a man possessed where Twelvetree was concerned."

"This lawyer at St. Neots," Fairfax said, "was his name Parry?"

"Why, so I believe it was. You mean the fellow who turned up at the inquest today? Damn me. I never saw him myself, but Tom would grumble about him."

"Did Tom ever see Mrs. Parry? I wonder."

"Couldn't tell you. I'd doubt it, as he only went to apply for a clerk's post in the fellow's office."

But Tom Honeyman certainly knew Mr. Parry, Fairfax thought, which was worth remembering.

"Poor Tom," Fox said, scuffing the wood shavings at his feet. "So he did it after all. but just wasn't quick enough . . . God, I wish it had never come into his head."

"Yes, he wasn't quick enough," Fairfax said, his mind elsewhere. "This scheme—it was never mentioned to Mrs. Honeyman?"

"No, no. Tom was determined on that. I don't know whether she'll have a suspicion of it now—I think she's pretty much like a sleepwalker, poor creature—but I don't see as it can help her to know, sir. Not really. She's been through enough. All she talks of is selling up and going away from this place, with all its memories, and maybe she'd do best that way."

"Yes . . . she will inherit, of course. Has she family she can go to?"

"Not as I know of. Her people were gentlefolk over Northampton way—decayed as you might say, with more pride than money, and she was left orphaned with no portion."

"So she took a step down in marrying Tom?"

"No, sir." The emphatic breath Fox let out, liquorish and steaming in the cold, gave him the look of breathing sudden fire. "No. I won't hear that said of Tom, never."

Fairfax nodded peaceably. "Tom was lucky in his friends. If not in his plans . . . Well, I thank you for your frankness,

Mr. Fox. Let us hope we shall soon bring Tom's killer to book. The funeral, I suppose, is arranged?"

"Tomorrow morning, at St. Martin's."

"I shall try to be there. By the by, do you still have your own brace of pistols?"

Fox put his glass to his lips, though it was empty. "Nay, I got rid of them once we'd laid the scheme to rest. I didn't like having them about. So I sold them to a traveling tinker."

Fairfax shook the young man's hand and left. He skirted the house by a brick passage, noticing the lights still glowing in the parlor, wondering whether that back door was locked now . . .

Wondering many things, in fact. Such as why a young man used to guns should dispose of a good pair to a tinker, probably for a fraction of their value. Why Bennett Cornwell should reappear in Tom Honeyman's life quite recently, and why there had been high words between them. And about Bennett's mother, the late Mrs. Twelvetree, and whether Tom Honeyman knew something about her life and death that was now lost to them . . . unless he had told someone else. Whether Joseph Fox ever used that convenient door into the Honeyman house, and whether he had anyone but Mrs. Honeyman's word that he had spent the whole of yesterday at the yard.

Most of all he wondered at Tom Honeyman's daring and foolhardy scheme. How must it have felt to board the coach in his disguise, clutching the strongbox—which Fairfax guessed now to have been empty, a mere lure—and feeling the weight of the pistols at his breast; looking out at the bleak leaf-strewn road, and wondering if or when a horseman might appear from the tress . . . He experienced the vicarious thrill, as well as the fear, as he pictured it. Yet why had Honeyman decided at last to put into action the bold plan, quite alone, after it had long been discarded? Why now?

And was it, after all, the highwayman of Stangate Hole that he had encountered on that strange journey? And was the highwayman none other than his friend, Bennett Cornwell? Or did some further and deeper secret lie behind these interlocking shadows? That was Fairfax's belief, though he still had more questions than answers.

But he had more knowledge now; and in knowledge was power. He had very much disliked his feeling of powerlessness at Mr. Twelvetree's house, where he had been curtly summoned and even more curtly dismissed. So, though it was late in the day and he was tired, he decided to return to Broad Street. He would seek an audience on his own terms.

Market wagons were rumbling out of the town, and poor wives in aprons and pattens were bargaining with the last traders for bruised and half-rotted remnants. At the bank Mr. Claymount was buttoning his coat as he came down the steps, and he gave Fairfax the uniquely spiteful look of a subservient person who sees no present advantage in subservience. At the door one of the slab-faced menservants grunted that there was no question of seeing Mr. Twelvetree, nohow, and seemed ready to throw Fairfax bodily down the steps.

"Tell him it's about Bennett Cornwell," he said. Instant effect. "And I'll wait inside, if you please. I'm not a milk-seller to dangle about cold doorsteps."

In a very short while he was being shown up to the banker's apartments—this time to a little dining room as spare and hygienic as the other. Mr. Twelvetree, seated in solitary state at a lustrous walnut table, had just been served by a manservant with hands like hams. The dinner looked pale and frugal, an invalid's mess, though there was at least a half bottle of wine—by Mr. Twelvetree's standards, a positive flourish of clubbable humanity.

Mr. Twelvetree was not pleased. "I hope you can justify this unwarrantable intrusion," he said.

"You did not have to see me, sir, but I presume my business has your interest. Shall I repeat my name?"

The banker glared, then gestured at the manservant. "Leave us."

"Mr. Twelvetree," Fairfax said, seating himself, "I think you have not been honest with me. I asked you earlier, in connection with the tragic incident on the *Flyer*, whether there was anyone you would consider as an enemy."

Chewing his pap, Nicholas Twelvetree watched him, with his old look of considering a bargain.

"Perhaps, in your agitation, you neglected to think of your stepson, Bennett Cornwell."

Mr. Twelvetree poured himself a glass of wine and drank. "You know nothing of Bennett," he said, his lips as thin as if the wine were vinegar. "You are a stranger here: you don't know what you're talking about."

"I know that there was a violent antipathy between you. That after his mother's death, you considered you had no obligations toward him. That you closed your doors to him, and at last pressed serious charges against him, and had him sent to the House of Correction." As Mr. Twelvetree sourly, silently regarded him Fairfax went on. "Yes, I am a stranger here, sir, but one charged with finding out the whole story of this business, so enlighten me, if you will."

"What you have said is true. Except that it omits Bennett Cornwell's character. But first I will ask you: have you ever been married?"

Again. Fairfax stirred restively. "No. But I—"

"Well, if you had, sir—if you had been united to a person whose well-being is precious, indeed sacred, to you alone— then you would know what I went through with that boy. As you have plainly been finding out about me, you will know that I married late: a widow lady of mature years, with a young son. That lady was a tenderhearted creature, not strong, and incapable by her very sweetness of nature of exerting a disciplining influence upon this very headstrong and self-willed boy. He had already dissipated his paternal inheritance, and was confirmed in the habit of expecting that the most outrageous requirements would be met by his mother's fond indulgence. Where wheedling persuasion would not answer, he resorted to threats and tantrums, accusing her in the coarsest terms of not caring for him, afflicting her shrinking sensibilities with the most violent language, and playing upon her fears for him with wild avowals that he would end his existence. In short, sir, Bennett Cornwell made his mother's life a very misery. And when I had the honor of taking her as my wife, and observed his behavior and its effect upon her, I resolved that there would be no more of it. He would not deal with me as he had with her. He knew it, and it confirmed his opposition to me, whom he was quick to libel with the name of fortune hunter." Mr. Twelvetree looked down at his plate suddenly as if he did not know what it was, then pushed it away. "He was a worthless hound, sir; and what is worse, a dangerous one. I made it my business to protect my wife from his outrages, and I sadly regret that her early death prevented my doing so for longer, and giving her a good measure of that peace she had never known since he had grown from a child. And after death . . . why, after her death I simply treated him as he fully deserved, and as I could not when her motherly partiality was there to speak on his behalf. An enemy? Yes, as he must be an enemy to all of decent society, settled habits, and property. After that last exhibition of his, I knew there was nothing he would not do: no lie or calumny he would not spread . . ."

In great agitation Mr. Twelvetree got up and darted to the window. He was some time peering out, then satisfying himself that it was firmly closed, before pulling the curtains to.

"I understand that he went away, after his spell in the House of Correction," Fairfax said. "Did you hear any more of him? Has he, to your knowledge, returned to the district at all?"

Mr. Twelvetree studied Fairfax for a long moment, fleshless jaws working. Then he took up a candle and said, "Follow me."

He led Fairfax into the next room—the chilly parlor-office he had been in before—and taking from his waistcoat a key on a great chain, which looked long enough to have gone three times round his meager body, he unlocked a drawer in the desk.

"Since that last time, when I was compelled to have the law on him, I have maintained a posture of alertness. A man in my position cannot be too mindful of his security in any case, but when such an extreme villain as Cornwell is at large, one must consider oneself in some degree under siege. I will show you that I do not exaggerate. See this. It was put through my door the day before he committed his final outrage."

It was a page torn from a Bible—from the Epistle of Paul to the Romans. Boldly circled in black ink were the words "Vengeance is mine; I will repay, saith the Lord."

"And the following day, this."

Another Bible page, this from Numbers, again boldly circled: "Be sure your sin will find you out."

"Of course I have no *proof* that this was his work," Twelvetree said. "And there it ceased. But you may draw your own conclusions." Suddenly his wiry hand was on Fairfax's arm: Fairfax tried not to jump. The mere fact of Nicholas Twelvetree having a fleshy presence at all was surprising, and the grip was very strong. "I have shown these to no one else, Mr. Fairfax. All I can do is humbly beg for your discretion—adding incidentally, that I would take a betrayal of my confidence very poorly, and have it in my power to make it exceeding hot for anyone who crosses me. And now *this* is the latest. It was pushed through the door last night, at some late hour when decent folk are abed."

It was a single sheet of notepaper, inscribed in ink with the words DO NOT REST, THE RECKONING WILL COME in large shaky capitals. Fairfax turned it over, held it up to the light. A common watermark: nothing out of the ordinary.

" 'Tis no use asking if I recognize the hand," the banker said, hustling all three sheets back into the drawer and locking it, as if there were danger even in their exposure to the air. "Such large block letters are a disguise in themselves."

"Yes, of course. It is rather alarming, sir—thought it may

not be what it seems. The pointless action of some fanatic . . ." He doubted it, though. What the biblical admonitions had first brought to his mind, curiously enough, was the figure of Henry Griggs the preacher. Yet even leaving aside the implausibility of Griggs, for whatever reason, persecuting the banker with veiled threats, Fairfax was certain of one thing: such a man would never desecrate a Bible in that way. It seemed, indeed, that Twelvetree had reason to fear the hatred of his stepson. "What do you think, sir? Do you see Bennett Cornwell's hand behind this?"

All at once Twelvetree's eyes seemed to shrink and retreat, as if the thick spectacles were working in reverse. He stowed away the great chain, his chin up. "I think nothing, sir. I think nothing, except that the law does not protect life and property as it should. It was far too lenient on Bennett Cornwell, who should never have been set at liberty to threaten the peace of his country. It is lax, shamefully lax, to allow our highways to be preyed upon, with such shocking results as we saw yesterday. I think nothing, except that, as things stand, an honest decent citizen such as myself is not safe in his bed unless something is done. And I shall see to it that something is done."

"The law is, or should be, impartial," Fairfax said sharply. "It cannot be called upon to aid citizens in a private vendetta."

Twelvetree sneered; and in a man so singularly lacking in charm or looks to start with, the effect was grim. "I expect nothing of the law, sir. I conclude it is an irrelevance, placed in the hands of amateurs and dilettantes. So you and your master need not trouble me anymore. Good evening."

The many locks and bolts and bars had rattled behind him, and Fairfax came down the steps of the bank feeling that if Bennett Cornwell had conceived a mortal loathing for Mr. Nicholas Twelvetree, then Bennett Cornwell was not such a bad fellow.

He glanced up at the darkened windows, and wondered

where the nuptial bedchamber of Twelvetree and his short-
lived bride had been. "Not strong," he had said. How not
strong—in poor health, in failing health, in mortal sickness?
Sickness that, perhaps, could be helped along? Had Tom
Honeyman had such suspicions, and passed them on to Bennett Cornwell?

Daring speculations—spurious and irresponsible, perhaps. Products of a tired brain. Having the measure of the
town now, Fairfax turned down a narrow street that would
lead him the quickest way to the bridge, the George, and his
horse. No doubt an ample dinner awaited him at Cheyney
Hall, and now he could welcome it. Threading another narrow ancient street of gables and timbered jetties, he found
to his surprise that he had come out at the west side of St.
George's Square.

The door of Mrs. Bland's house was open, he saw,
throwing a ribbon of light on to the cobbles, damp from another shower. Two figures were there, one on horseback. He
recognized the trimly voluptuous shape of Mrs. Selina
Bland, putting her hand up in farewell. Fairfax turned toward them, feeling he should make some greeting, also find
out if there was any news. He was within a few yards when
Mrs. Bland gripped the hand of the cloaked rider—her
brother, William Parry—and pulled it convulsively down so
that he was leaning at an acute angle out of the saddle.
Murmuring something Fairfax could not hear, she stretched
up and embraced her brother and gave him several feverish
kisses, on the cheeks and about the lips.

"There, my dear," he said. "All will be well—I shall see
to it. All will yet be well . . ."

The embrace was enough to pull an inexperienced horseman out of the saddle, but William Parry kept his seat ex-
pertly. He straightened up at last in a graceful arc, rapidly
squeezing Mrs. Bland's hand in a gesture part dismissive,
part reassuring.

Fairfax spoke. "Mrs. Bland, Mr. Parry, I hope—"

Both jumped visibly, Parry with such a jerk on the reins

that his horse snorted and danced its displeasure. For an instant, as Parry turned and glared, it seemed he was going to cut at Fairfax with his riding crop.

"Damn you, man," he hissed, "what do you mean by creeping about like that?"

"Extraordinary—extraordinary behavior . . ." Selina Bland drew back her skirts as if at defilement. Her eyes, flashing at him, seemed to reflect exactly like those of a cat. A feline pair, Fairfax thought.

"Well—hush, Selina, I'm sure Mr. Fairfax meant no harm. We're all a little on edge, I think, after such a day." William Parry, the mild-eyed and handsome, put a gloved finger to the tip of his three-cornered hat. "Your servant, sir. You do not bring news?"

"I'm sorry, no; I was about to ask the same of you. You are returning home, sir? You have a long ride."

"So I have. But I am a man of affairs, sir, and cannot be for ever from home. Besides . . ."

"You have some hope to find your wife there?"

Parry let out a slight cool laugh. "If it can be dignified with the name of hope. Let us be frank, Mr. Fairfax—for upon my soul I was frank with you earlier. Either Margaret is dead like the others, which is no hopeful prospect; or she is alive and well, and choosing to remain incognito. Which also is no hopeful prospect for a husband who has placed his whole happiness in the love and faith of a cherished wife. If you can find a measure of hope, then I salute you." He hitched his cloak and gathered up the reins. "Forgive me, I am indifferent company, and I have as you say a long ride ahead of me. You know where I am to be found."

Parry dug in his heels, and his flying cloak cracked like a whip near Fairfax's face as he went off at a canter.

"Your brother is an admirable horseman," he said to Mrs. Bland, whose catlike eyes followed Parry till he was out of sight.

"It is a family trait," she said, seeming to come reluctantly out of a daze. "A trait of the true Parrys, that is."

"Mrs. Margaret Parry is not so dexterous?"

"Oh, believe me, sir, nothing so ordinary would do for *her*."

She had turned to go in when Fairfax was transfixed by a thought, or two thoughts coming together.

"Mrs. Bland—pardon me—your brother said Margaret's maiden name was Mortimer, I think?"

"I daresay he did, because it is the case."

"I understand Mr. Twelvetree the banker was formerly in partnership with a Mr. Mortimer—"

"Mr. Arthur Mortimer. Yes, that was Margaret's father. A deceased gentleman." Her tone made it sound like *diseased*. Before Fairfax could speak again she said, with withering emphasis, "He left her without a bean, you know. Sent her to schools, and filled her head full of useless learning, and left her nothing. A chit with no money and soft hands. That's what William took on. And this is his thanks for it, if you please! A mad world, my masters!" And with her most knowing, can't-fool-me chuckle she shut the door in his face.

Again. Well, thought Fairfax, use is everything, as the man said when he fell off the cliff for the third time. He went to get his horse.

Cheyney Hall was a haven of warmth, light, and inviting smells.

"Is that Fairfax there?" came Sir Edward's voice from the parlor, as Fairfax gave his hat and riding crop to the servant in the hall. "Excellent. Come in, sir, come in, you must be fagged. Nay, never mind changing—Liberty Hall, sir. We were just resolving to have dinner without you. Cardew, dinner in ten minutes."

Seated in a place of honor by the fire, with a charcoal foot-warmer and a wine table at his side, was a guest whom Sir Edward introduced as his old friend Mr. Timothy Devereaux.

"I found Devereaux at his town place in Stamford, by

good luck, and we have been putting our heads together over our rogue. This, my friend, is my discovery, Robert Fairfax. And so, Devereaux, you are closing up Skellerby altogether for the winter? You will miss your gardens, I think. Skellerby is Devereaux's country place up near Bourne, Fairfax, and has the fairest park in the country."

"Well, I shall not miss the drips and drafts," Mr. Devereaux said. "I have spent but a day at my town house, and I have felt *warm* for the first time in weeks. There are other advantages. I hope, for example, that you and the young ladies will accept my hospitality after the Stamford Assembly on Saturday, and save yourselves a cold ride home. That is, my dears, if you are going. I know such things hold little attraction for young ladies."

Mr. Timothy Devereaux was a smallish, distinguished-looking man, elegant in a gold-frogged coat and silk breeches, with a delicate owl-like face and a smile of sweetness and reserve mixed. Though not much older than Sir Edward, his shoulders were painfully hunched, and his voice came laboring and whistling through thick breath: a congenital malady of the chest, Fairfax guessed.

"Will the town vapors not hurt your condition, my friend?" Sir Edward said.

"They cannot make it worse, I think. I do well enough. So, Mr. Fairfax, you have been on the hunt for our larcenous and now murderous celebrity. As I was just saying, I wish I could be more specific in my own recollections, as one of that gentleman's luckier victims. But all I can say is, at our brief meeting on the road he seemed almost as frightened as I. A masked figure about your height and build, gruff and quick, mounted on a chestnut horse—he was gone as soon as I handed over my purse."

"There, Mr. Fairfax," said Amelia to a general laugh, "now we have our suspicions of *you*."

"Dinner," said Sir Edward, clapping his hands, "and you shall tell us your discoveries, Fairfax, as long as they ain't nasty and won't spoil our appetites."

At the dinner table, where they were joined by Mrs. Hargrave, with her usual look of gloomy penance, Fairfax found it hard to know where to begin. "Well, I have now talked to almost everyone concerned. To Mr. Twelvetree, to the widow and the partner of Mr. Honeyman, to Mr. Parry, to the keeper of the asylum at Ryhall, to the elder Mr. Griggs—"

"You have been busy indeed. Does the fire smeech, Devereaux?" Sir Edward said, full of solicitude for his friend, who had fallen into a fit of coughing.

"No, no. Nothing. Your pardon, sir," Mr. Devereaux said, dabbing his eyes, "I interrupt you."

Really it was difficult to tell everything here, over the social dinner table. Much of it was intimate, and would come out like scandal—Mr. Parry's suspicions of his wife's fidelity, for example. Sir Edward seemed to see his difficulty. "I daresay your head quite swims with it. But you said *almost* everyone: is there someone new?"

"Well, I have heard much of a young man named Bennett Cornwell, Mr. Twelvetree's stepson—though not a fond relationship. He did a spell in the House of Correction at the end of last year, and has been little heard of since. I think Mr. Twelvetree entertains the greatest suspicion, and indeed fear, toward this Cornwell—a wild young sprig, it seems."

"Now that's interesting," Sir Edward said. "Sent to the House of Correction . . . aye, I remember some such talk, but I fancy I was in London then, and not serving on the Bench."

"I was," said Mr. Devereaux, recovered now, though hardly eating. "I recall the case. It caused a deal of tattle. Yes, the son of Twelvetree's late wife: a bold young fellow, very violent in his expressions. Criminal damage on Twelvetree's property. It was plain enough, and the Bench really had little choice. The young man had no one to speak for him; his nearest kin was his prosecutor. Dear . . . You are about to ask, could the man who held me up have been this

Cornwell? I could not say. One sees so many people brought before the Bench. It *could* have been; there's nothing to rule it out, that's all I can say. I do remember people being shocked at Twelvetree's apparent lack of feeling. For myself I was not. I had had a brush with him myself a couple of years before that. You may remember, Edward, the commotion when Twelvetree bought himself an estate near me."

"He did mention his country place today," Fairfax said. "He has had all his menservants brought over from there—and they surround him like the army of some little German prince."

"Well, they can have had little occupation at his country place," Mr. Devereaux said, with a gray smile of amusement. "He hardly ever goes there. He has no interest in the country itself, as a place of health, virtuous pleasure, and decent industry. He is rich, and therefore wanted an estate to confirm it, and the estate is not to be enjoyed, but turned to account, for profit and power. It did need a purchase, certainly. It had run out of the male line, and was decayed and mortgaged. Once he had it, he immediately set about enclosing it. Formerly the common-field system prevailed in those parishes. You have heard, Mr. Fairfax, of enclosure? It can be a great benefit, and also a great evil. The larger landowners of a district stand to gain. They can consolidate their various holdings, bringing them all together so that they can be farmed on a rational long-term system. And they can, of course, afford the cost of surveying and registering and fencing that an enclosure entails. But the smaller men, who have got by with their few scattered acres, and the use of the common to graze a few cows, are much harmed. They often find the expense of enclosure ruinous, and are left at the end with a small single allotment of land, not the best, which they cannot afford to drain or fertilize to make it worthwhile. 'Tis rather as if we at this table, instead of each partaking of every dish, were to parcel it out according to our size and strength. Thus Sir Edward would get most of

the meat, as the biggest—and you, Miss Amelia, would get
only the peas on your plate. Sir Edward would thrive, but
Miss Amelia would soon fade away. Which we would all re-
greting dear."

Fairfax said, "Is there no redress for the smaller farmers?"

"In theory. Enclosure is authorized by an Act of Parlia-
ment, which a rich and influential man like Twelvetree can
well afford to petition. Those against it may counterpeti-
tion—which is usually beyond the means and capabilities
of the smaller landholders; and if they do try it they are
likely to lose, and be even further out of pocket. Of course,
much also depends on the bigger proprietors—their character, the way they go about things. They may be reasonable,
or ruthless . . . like Twelvetree. A man with no feeling for
the country, no knowledge of its people or traditions; a man
who does everything through agents and clerks and bailiffs
while he sits in his private office like a . . ."

"Like a spider?" Fairfax said.

"A happy phrase, Mr. Fairfax," said Mr. Devereaux, with
a hitch of his owlish eyebrows. "Plainly you have got to
know Nicholas Twelvetree. I crossed swords with him, as it
were, over quite a small matter. Where my own estate bor-
ders his, there were certain paths and tracks that had always
been used as rights of way by my people and tenants. Country life is founded on such customs. But Twelvetree saw
only the letter of the law. Anyone setting foot on his land—
for example, where a footpath curved for a mere few yards
onto it—wouuld be prosecuted. But worse than this, he was
a stickler about grazing and gleaning rights, and about
drainage. In that country, bordering the fens, drainage is
lifeblood, and many farmers depend on cooperation. Twelvetree would not see it. To increase profits, he wanted sheep
pasture, and altered the drainage courses accordingly.
Farmers found streams on which they relied no longer
flowing, or ditch systems blocked. Oh, it was all within his

rights, as it seems. He had a very astute lawyer working on his behalf."

"William Parry," Fairfax said, nodding at Sir Edward.

"Curious," Sir Edward said, eating vigorously.

"And so Twelvetree examined every deed, called into question titles to corners of land, disputed boundaries . . . An abuse of power I call it—but there, I am old-fashioned. But more than one farmer in that district went to the wall completely, and was obliged to sell up cheaply; and you can guess to whom. Other small holders were reduced to laborers, hiring out for the day. The village of Westingfleet is all but deserted now, like some ruin of antiquity. It all left a very bad taste."

"Oh, the unfeeling monster!" said Miss Letitia, with shocked sincerity. She was always carrying a novel about her, and was strong on sentiment.

"Another thing I learn about Mr. Twelvetree," Fairfax said, "is that his bank was once a partnership."

"Aye, he was a partner, and not the chief one neither," said Sir Edward. "Old Arthur Mortimer was a decent man—almost a Quaker in his principles. Sound, but perhaps not so astute. He laid out money in philanthropic pursuits, you know, and rather overdid it, I fancy. Twelvetree bought him out—must be five years ago. I don't know as there was anything discreditable in it, though no doubt Twelvetree made a good bargain. The old man died not long after, and didn't leave much for a man who had once been so warm."

"The Mrs. Parry we seek is the late Mr. Mortimer's daughter," Fairfax said. And another person with a grudge against Nicholas Twelvetree, he wondered . . .

"Curious again!" Sir Edward said, motioning for more wine. "Even more of a tangle than I thought. Mind, links between folks are not uncommon in a district like this. We must be careful not to lose our quarry for sniffing at every fresh scent. For myself, I'd cry halloo for this Bennett Cornwell. He's a likely imp to go to the bad, by the sound of it, and these attacks started at the beginning of the year, which is about when he was set at liberty." Rain, borne on a gust of east wind, spattered at the window. "Hark, that's dismal. You will lie the night here, Devereaux? You shall have an excellent bed; and then we may go into Stamford together tomorrow."

Mr. Devereaux certainly seemed to bring out all the kindly side of Sir Edward's nature. Contrary to his usual habit, he stayed over the port after the ladies had left the table, to press several glasses on his friend and to inquire into his medical treatment. Quite soon Mr. Devereaux, drawn and tired, asked them to present his compliments to the ladies, and said he would take up the offer of that bed. Sir Edward sent a servant with strict instructions to tend to his friend's needs, and then poured more port.

"Poor fellow," he said, sitting back and easing the waist of his breeches. "He has suffered much . . . more than you can imagine. Well, Fairfax, now we are confidential, and you can tell me what you've found."

Fairfax recounted his day in full—more or less. He did not speak of Esther Fryatt, Mrs. Bland's maid. He had hopes that she might, after all, meet him at noon tomorrow, perhaps with important information, and if Sir Edward knew of that, he might want to be there himself—which could frighten her off.

"So we know why Tom Honeyman was so curiously disguised: he was bounty hunting," Fairfax concluded. "His partner, Fox, who was originally to have joined him in the enterprise, is a picture of manly sorrow . . . yet there is something about him, and his account of things, that does not ring true. I don't know what to make of Mr. Parry, or the missing wife; there is something we are not being told. And then there is the curious matter of why Jonathan Griggs was on that coach. According to his brother he was disturbed by a recent death at Mr. Rowe's asylum—yet Mr. Rowe denies there has been any such death."

Sir Edward frowned. "Why, you can't set any store by

the word of a madman, Fairfax. 'Tis some fancy of the poor creature's brain."

"Perhaps. Yet Jonathan Griggs's condition was not—"

"The fellow was a lunatic, and that's that. Drop that, Fairfax: you're on the wrong track there."

Fairfax was surprised, but he bowed his head in surface deference, having no intention of dropping it.

"Well, Sir Edward, my general conclusions are thus: either the *Flyer* was randomly attacked by an anonymous highwayman, who will turn out to be someone we have heard of; or the *Flyer* was not attacked by a highwayman at all, but stopped by someone who wanted one or all of the passengers dead—dead before they could reach their destination." Fairfax accepted the port. "There are so many curious features to the case that I now think the first alternative is wholly unlikely."

Sir Edward grunted. "Well, I go along with that . . . but you prefer the second alternative, I take it? I don't know, Fairfax. You're a scholar and a thinker, and used to having your head up in clouds of speculation, where the fancy can run riot, isn't that so?" He was trying hard not to be patronizing. A pity he wasn't succeeding, Fairfax thought. "Now I stay close to earth, and I measure what's likely. It's more likely, surely, that our man's a highway robber who's hiding out there in the woods somewhere—and now we've got a name that fits mighty well in all respects. If it is this Bennett Cornwell that's taken to the road, well, then we shall have him. And very sorry I shall be to oblige Nicholas Twelvetree in anything, for no doubt the old vulture will be mighty pleased if the young fellow's caught. But Cornwell will have to pay the price the same as anyone else."

"If it is Cornwell," Fairfax could not help saying.

"Not convinced, eh? Well, I doubt I have enough to issue a warrant for his arrest, though I'll consult the other justices tomorrow and see. But in the meanwhile, my dear sir, you have *carte blanche* to prove me wrong."

Sir Edward's port was very fine, and he was liberal with

it. When Fairfax went up to bed he felt quite fuddled. He opened his window, breathed rain-washed air, banished the image of Cordelia Linton's splendid light-dark eyes, and tried to put his thoughts in order. But they kept shuffling like a deck of cards: preacher Griggs, and Mr. Samson Rowe, and William Parry and his too-devoted sister and his apparently not-too-devoted wife, and Barbara Honeyman and Joseph Fox—devoted too?—and the great spider, Mr. Nicholas Twelvetree, with his scapegrace stepson, Bennett Cornwell . . . The cards would not form into any clear pattern, deal as he might. But he went to bed convinced that one of those names, at least, was that of a murderer.

Ten

Farifax's relationship with the mare from Sir Edward's stable had improved so much that he did not in the least mind
making the trip into Stamford the next morning on horseback, while the baronet rode in his carriage with Mr. Devereaux. He would, after all, be needing a saddle horse to take
him about today in pursuance of his inquires, as he said to
Sir Edward—which might be, his employer asked, precisely
what?

"It's a ticklish matter, sir," Fairfax said, prevaricating, for
he intended to seek out the truth about Mr. Rowe's asylum,
in spite of Sir Edward's proscription, and he still had hopes
of learning more from Esther Fryatt. But Sir Edward only
smiled indulgently, and said, "Very well, you know best."
Fairfax couldn't help wondering if Sir Edward was placing
more faith in him than before, or less.

He rode behind the carriage into the yard of the George,
and there found a gathering of men whom he recognized, if
not individually, then collectively by their hulking ugliness,
as Nicholas Twelvetree's servants. They were milling about
with a great parade of self-importance, some mounted, some
on foot, and all armed either with cudgels and staves or with
guns.

"Great God," said Sir Edward, stepping down from the
carriage, "what does this rabble do here?"

"Perhaps the Jacobites are upon us again," Mr. Devereaux said, leaning heavily on a stick.

"I think, Sir Edward, they are Mr. Twelvetree's people. He did speak yesterday of sending his men out to search the woods—not seriously, as I thought," Fairfax said. In the corner of the yard there was a closed carriage, unpainted and dull as a coffin, with a drawn blind that was pushed aside momentarily to receive from the hand of a serving maid what looked like a glass of cordial. Sir Edward had seen it too, and marched over there.

Nicholas Twelvetree opened the blind at his rap.

"Sir, are these your men?"

"I have the honor of addressing Sir Edward Nugent, I think," Twelvetree said, with a glance at Fairfax.

"You do. We ain't properly acquainted, Mr. Twelvetree, so perhaps I should remind you that I'm a Justice of the Peace, and being so I can't look happily on a scene like this. You mean to send these fellows off to flush out our highwayman, I take it?"

"Such is my intent," Twelvetree said. In the dark carriage he looked like an undernourished rabbit peeping from a hole. "My men are accustomed to patrolling my country estate, and are under the strict orders of my gamekeeper. It seems a good notion: this latest outrage has surely shown that the road between here and Huntingdon is a place of utter peril."

"Sir, this is a matter for the duly constituted authorities, not for some raggle-taggle private militia," Sir Edward said. "Sending out armed men—"

"Is more than the duly constituted authorities are doing," Twelvetree said crisply, "or are capable of doing. Whom are we to turn to, sir? The parish constables—a handful of old men unwilling to collar a stray dog? The magistrates? They are empowered only to issue warrants, and to commit a man once taken, and of this there has been no sign. Unless, sir, I am mistaken, and you and your fellow justices are about to surprise us all, and capture the rogue."

Sir Edward glared at him. "'Tis a rash proceeding, sir. If I cannot stop it, I shall watch it carefully. Any disorder or trespass arising from this business, and I shall be very severe."

"I'm sure no one doubts your zeal," Twelvetree said, closing the blind.

"Devil take the fellow!" Sir Edward said, coming away, swelling and reddening with indignation. Mr. Devereaux watched with quiet amusement. "Insufferable! And damn me—I can't help wondering if he ain't on the right track, after all! A thorough sweep of the rogue's haunts . . ."

"They do not look very expert," Mr. Devereaux said as the men began to stream out of the inn yard with much swaggering, waving of hats, and blowing of kisses to serving maids.

"Hm. But they're ahead of us, at any rate," Sir Edward said. The handbills they had ordered were pasted up around the inn yard, and he glowered at one, then shrugged. "Well, no matter: if they can bring him in, all to the good, I suppose."

"Come, my friend, and drink some chocolate with me," Mr. Devereaux said, smiling. "'Twill take away the unpleasant taste of Nicholas Twelvetree; and we'll look in my copy of Burns's *Justice of the Peace*, and see where the law stands."

Left to his own devices—a little grudgingly, he thought—Fairfax lost no time in making for the offices of the *Stamford Mercury*.

Cordelia Linton was there, taking down the details of an advertisement from an elderly gentlewoman who existed somewhere beneath a plethora of whalebone, lace, powder, frizzed wig, ribbons, rouge, and patches. While Cordelia did not look at him, her face registered his presence, first with pale constraint, then with a gleam of secret amusement as the lady spelled out her requirements.

"'Wanted by lady of quality, footman not above thirty

years, of good character and having had the smallpox,'"
Cordelia repeated.

"Sober, cleanly and honest, and must understand well
waiting at table," the lady said, "but not too proud to carry
coals as required. No followers, and must be well shaped in
thigh and calf."

"'In . . . in thigh and calf.'" Cordelia's tongue protruded
very slightly from the corner of her mouth as she wrote.
"Very well, ma'am. And would you wish to mention
wages?"

"The right person will be well recompensed," the lady
said airily; and gathering to her angular bosom a little
choked-looking dog, which Fairfax had thought was a fur
muff, she sailed out.

"Well, is it worth my applying, do you think?" Fairfax
said.

"You might. I should warn you, though, that Miss
Harper's last footman ran away to sea."

"As fast as his shapely legs could carry him, no doubt . . .
Mrs. Linton, I wanted to thank you again for all your help
yesterday."

"Liar!" She gave him the bare smile. "You thanked me
amply yesterday. What you are here for is to ask me for
more information. And I am insulted to think you need a
pretext, when you know well I am quite as absorbed as you
in this mysterious matter, and like nothing better than dig-
ging around after secrets."

"Ah. Well, if you will forgive the lie and insult—"

"Very easily."

"Then let me toss another name at you: Mr. Samson
Rowe."

"Keeps the lunatic asylum at Ryhall. North Country born,
physician, once married, soon to be married again, rather
well apparently. Oh, common knowledge enough. Something I can tell you, because my maid is sister-in-law to the
coach-maker at St. Martin's is that Mr. Rowe is having a
new private carriage built. Very smart and fashionable,

japanned sides and mahogany shutters, leather lining inside—eighty guineas cost at least."

"I wonder that he can live so high," Fairfax said. "He cannot charge a great deal for his patients' care: it is within the means of Mr. Griggs, who is not a rich man, and there are not many of them."

"Perhaps he's already spending his new bride's dowry."

"Perhaps so . . ."

"You have a doubtful look. Do you suspect something discreditable in Mr. Rowe? I do hope so; I like to learn discreditable things of people, it puts me on an equality with them."

"No. Well, I am wondering about his asylum. The inmate who escaped, and who lost his life on the *Flyer*, said that there had been a death there lately. Mr. Rowe says there has not."

"Curious. One hears only good reports of the asylum at Ryhall; quite a model institution, it seems." She looked devilish. "But then, if something pernicious *were* going on behind those walls, Mr. Rowe would make sure that no one got to hear of it."

"My thought exactly."

She smiled. "You are quite a frightening person, Mr. Fairfax. To think that whenever you meet someone, you suspect them of not being what they seem."

He smiled too, though this pricked him. "You make me sound quite a misanthrope."

"No, no. Just a man who has been disappointed—which is as much to say, a man who has lived."

"And a woman?"

She drooped a moment, bending her pen in her fingers until it seemed it must snap. "Oh, we trust, you know; it is different . . . But the asylum: that's what we were talking of. And a death that may have occurred, and may not. Well, well. I was about to say that if there has been a death in the district recent, we at the *Mercury* would have heard of it. People like to read columns of deaths, you know, and so we gather coroners' reports and registers of burials . . . But Ryhall is actually over the county boundary, which makes a difficulty." She held up an inky finger. "Not a great one, though. We keep copies of the *Leicestership Post-Boy* somewhere. And I have spies everywhere besides, who bring me news or gossip, which are the same thing. If there *is* anything to be discovered about a death at Mr. Rowe's house, then I am the one to discover it." She stuck up her chin. "Well, a woman should know her own worth."

"And others too, I hope."

"A woman's worth," came a voice from the door at the rear, "is, in the lands of the Turk and the Tartar, reckoned at three sheep, I believe. It makes one wonder whether we undervalue sheep, or overvalue women."

A fair, thickset man in waistcoat and shirtsleeves, of craggy good looks save where his complexion was marred by broken veins, stood with a sardonic smile in the doorway, then came in with a kind of heavy briskness and began looking through the sheets and proofs on the counter.

"But how little we know of these things. Turk and Tartar, we say, barbarians; but they had libraries and cities when we were unwashed wretches in hovels. Is that the galleys you have there? Let me see."

"Mr. Fairfax, this is my husband, Mr. George Linton. George, Mr. Fairfax is acting as secretary to Sir Edward Nugent, and they are on the hunt for the highwayman who—"

"Mr. Fairfax will disoblige me greatly if he catches him," George Linton said, breathing hard as he peered at proofs. "He is the best news we have in this benighted spot . . . Damn the man, he has printed 'Saxe-Coburg' with three different spellings in as many lines . . . And after all, Mr. Fairfax, what is a highwayman but another tradesman? What does he do amiss? Demand money with menaces? But that is only what my creditors do. Instance, this one," Linton said, snatching a letter from a heap on the counter. "A bill from that wretch of a coalman—Cordelia, why didn't you tell me of this?"

"George, you have been ill. I didn't want to worry you."

"Didn't want to worry you." Linton mimicked her, not in a shrill falsetto, but in an accurate echo of her own low tones—and somehow the effect was even more unpleasant. "When was that ever a consideration with a wife? Well, I am not ill now, for a mercy . . . No, Mr. Fairfax, you must not persecute a man for carrying on his trade, that's my belief."

"A stimulating one. Unfortunately this highwayman has switched trades, and turned murderer. Though I know that that too sells newspapers."

"You know that, do you?" Linton said, with a cool look. "You have been a newspaper proprietor yourself?"

"No, but I buy them. Well, I must be on my way—"

"A secretary. What does Sir Edward Nugent want with a secretary? Count his horses and dogs, perhaps?" Linton gave a throaty laugh. "One, two, three . . ."

"Mr. Fairfax is engaged to catalogue the collections of the late Sir Jemmy," said Cordelia, going to trim a candle. She had become slow and deliberate in her movements, as in the presence of a large nervous dog. "The finest in the county, they say, worthy of Oxford."

"Worthy of Oxford." Again the horrible accurate echo. "Well, you know all about it, obviously, my dear. A temporary engagement, then, Mr. Fairfax. And in the meantime you run your master's errands. It is temporary?"

"It is."

"Which explains, then, I should think, your presence here," Linton said, producing a pleasant smile. "You think to advertise in my paper for your next situation? A very good notion."

"No, I do not stand in such need, I thank you, sir."

"Not in such need? Well, I am mistaken, then. But perhaps the *Mercury* would not suit any case. Perhaps a larger organ would be better. There's much to be said for a larger organ, eh, my dear?"

"George, it's a crude jest," Cordelia said, smiling very faintly.

"*Is* it?" Linton made a face of exaggerated wonder. "What has become of us, Mr. Fairfax? Rabelais was full of such jests."

"They are better in the original French," Fairfax said. "I'll bid you good day."

The look she gave him as he left might have meant: *Don't worry: I will still find out all I can,* or *You are not seeing him as he truly is; and I love him.* Or anything. He was tired of trying to interpret looks. He wanted someone with whom he could be honest, without forever probing for meaning like a surgeon at a dissection. But that person was not Cordelia Linton, at any rate, and if he felt lonely and dry and useless the remedy did not lie there—not ever.

Dark thoughts prompted an appropriate reminder: Tom Honeyman's funeral this morning. Fairfax recrossed the river, and when he came to the churchyard of St. Martin's found the burying just completed. An undernourished curate was just putting up his prayer book at the graveside, or one of them. The coachman, Charles Crabbe, had also been buried this morning, he found. Mr. Quigley had borne the expense, and was there as sole mourner.

" 'Twas the least I could do," he said. "He always served me well, and when he got too old for driving, I meant to find him some other work about the inn, as I did with old Jacob. A big hale man he was, but what a little hole he goes into." Blowing his nose, the innkeeper went away.

A handful of people had come to mourn Tom Honeyman, and Fairfax watched them as they spoke in turn to Barbara, pale and splendid in black at the graveside. Words, of course, were always hopeless at such a time; but she seemed, he thought, to make her comforters feel more than usually inadequate. *You insult me by even approaching such grief as mine . . .* Joseph Fox, handsome and glowingly alive, did the hand-shaking and thanking, and greeted Fairfax like a long-lost friend.

"Good of you to come, sir. No news, eh? Well, well. We can't bring poor Tom back, that's for sure. He was a good fellow, a fine fellow; we shan't see his like again. There'll be baked meat and ale at the house, sir, for such as want to come back."

"Thank you. I won't intrude. Mrs. Honeyman, you bear up bravely, ma'am."

She nodded with closed eyes at him. "And now," she said, "we must go and eat baked meat, and all will be well." she took Fox's proffered arm limply, it seemed with distaste.

Fairfax had entertained a faint hope that Bennett Cornwell, whether innocent or guilty, might have turned up at the funeral of a man whom he had apparently been friendly with . . . but Fox was the only young man there, and Fairfax admitted it was faint hope indeed. He did see Henry Griggs there, however, standing a little back, his head bowed and his hands folded in plain, unostentatious respect.

"I laid Jonathan in a parish plot last night," he said, when Fairfax went over, "and it was late, I thought I would stay here one more night, and pay my duty to these poor souls who shared his last journey."

"The souls are not here," Fairfax said. "Only clay."

Griggs glanced at him, as if he feared he were being mocked, but seeing he was not, said, "That is indeed, sir, the only true perception. We do right to make the occasion solemn; but not sad—never sad." He looked at Fairfax again, keenly. "You are a man of education, sir?"

"Well, yes—whatever that means."

"I take it to mean book learning," said Griggs, who gave every remark a serious attention. "Which is, certainly, a good thing. But there is the education of the soul too; a different matter. Do you ever feel the stirrings of the spirit within you, sir?"

"I cannot pretend that I do."

"Good. There can be nothing worse than pretending; better the clean slate. But you do not scoff, sir—that I observe. Well, you may know I am for Huntingdon next. I depart directly to do a field preaching there, at the Mill Common. I hope to begin at dusk. I ask you to come and witness it, and see what effect the workings of the Lord can have. I speak in no boastful spirit—I am only the vessel for what passes. Think on it, sir."

Fairfax hesitated. "I hope I do not scoff, indeed; and I thank you for the invitation. I am much occupied at present—but if I am able to get there . . ."

"Surely. I leave it to you. There is yet no sign, then, of the woman missing from the coach?"

"None." They left the churchyard together to walk up to the George. "It is a mystery, and not the only one. I went to see Mr. Rowe at the asylum yesterday. According to him, there were no deaths there lately, as Jonathan claimed."

"Ah? Well, well; it must be so, then."

"You think Mr. Rowe's word more probably than your bother's?"

"I always trusted Mr. Rowe entirely. Jonathan was never a liar, but he was mind-sick. He must have been mistook."

"I see . . . Mr. Rowe was good enough to show me Jonathan's room. I could not help but notice something he had written on the wall. 'Sweet Nell' were the words. Was Nell, I wonder, the name of the girl he loved?"

"Nell. Aye, so she used to be called . . . Nor a bad creature, but she did not know her own mind. It's a long time ago; I know not where she may be now."

"What happened? Was he jilted?"

"He . . . I would say he was robbed of her, by another. But Jonathan's was perhaps not a temper framed for love in that way, sir. 'Twas too fragile and high-strung. He needed settled peace and content, and hen he would do well. Alas, he did not get it, but he has it now."

In the archway of the George a drunkard was lying half conscious in a pool of his own vomit. A lady lifted her skirts by the loops at her wrists and stepped deftly over him. Henry Griggs, shaking his head, bend down and took the man's arm, trying to urge him to his feet. "Come, friend, come. You'll take hurt there."

The drunkard gave him a thorough cursing for his pains,

hitting out with palsied hands, and turned over in his foul bed.

"Do you not get discouraged?" Fairfax said in genuine puzzlement. "These snubs and repulses—"

"I glory in them," Griggs replied with an eager look. "I rejoice in each one, sir. It is hard to understand, perhaps. Well, I have a long ride ahead of me. I leave you, but I have hopes of seeing you later."

An extraordinary man, Fairfax thought, watching him go; but for the first time, inconsistent. Why should he so swiftly accept that Mr. Rowe was in the right, and his brother mistaken? It made no sense, unless the key lay in his intense religion—such worldly matters being beneath him, and now literally beneath Jonathan, enthroned in heaven.

It was such an alien way of thinking to Robert Fairfax that it fascinated him. He had half a mind to try to get to that field preaching after all. But first there was the chance—slim, admittedly—that Esther Fryatt might meet him as he had suggested. It was getting on for noon now. He went into the coffee room, sat down in a booth with brandy-and-water, and had just reached out his hand for a copy of the *Mercury* lying there, alongside one of their handbills, when he felt a timid touch on his shoulder.

"Esther. This is good of you. Sit down, please, and take something to warm you."

The girl shook her head. "Thank you, sir, but—I'm not come to talk to you. Not myself." Her naked eyes darted nervously about. "There is someone else . . . I met her, and spoke of you to her and—I said you could be trusted. Which—beg pardon, sir—you can be, can't you? Only—it must be just you, and she won't come if she don't feel quite safe . . ."

Fairfax's pulse quickened. He nodded. "It will be in strict confidence."

Esther disappeared. He pretended to look at the *Mercury* while a couple of minutes passed. At last he saw from the corner of his eye a cloaked woman, her face half hidden by a deep calash, enter the coffee room and glide over to his booth. He made to rise, but she stopped him with a trembling gesture and sat down opposite him.

The miniature painter had been skillful: Fairfax recognized at once the large-eyed soulful face with the slightly indrawn mouth.

"I'm glad to meet you, ma'am. I'm Robert Fairfax. And you, I think . . ." Seeing her eyes widen, he said in a softer voice, "I think you are the person sought here," and laid a finger on the handbill, gently tapping the words *mrs. parry*.

"I entrust myself completely to you, sir," she said in a low earnest voice. "Esther said that you were . . . kind."

"I hope so."

"But can you give me your word that you will not betray me? I have done nothing wrong; I don't mean that. But I have the truest and most powerful reasons for keeping myself out of sight—for cutting myself off from those who have known me. Those reasons remain, and will remain, and they are not trivial." The dark silk of the calash, framing her pale face, gave her the look of Renaissance madonnas he had seen on his Tour in Italy: glowing yet unapproachable. "If I cannot talk to you on those terms, then I shall go."

"You know why you are sought? Sought, that is, by the authorities?"

"Yes. Because of what happened to the coach I traveled on."

"And because it was not known whether you were alive or dead. That, at least, is most happily resolved. But we are desperate to find and bring to justice the killer of those passengers, and hoped you might be able to help us. If you can tell me what you know, ma'am, then—then I need never have seen you."

She breathed deeply, then folded her hands on the table. "Very well. That is a simple matter, because I can tell you very little. You may know I left Stamford on the *Flyer*, having booked an inside place to St. Neots, where my home is." Her fingers tightened, delicate knuckles white. "For reasons of my own I left the coach earlier—when it stopped at Stilton. I got down there with my bag, and told the coachman I would not be going on, and so it continued without me. That is why I was not on board when the coach met its—terrible fate, though it must have seemed from the booking records that I was. So you see, there is nothing I can tell you, I think, that will help your inquiries, beyond settling this question." She made a motion to rise.

"Please, wait—that question has puzzled us, certainly. But there are others. The other passengers, for example. Can you tell me anything about them?"

Clenching her hands, she took another deep breath. "There were only two. One outside—a quiet gentle sort of man, plainly dressed; I remember he handed me down at Stilton, and I thought he looked rather—lost and grieving . . . as I was."

"And the other—inside? Did you not know him?"

"He said his name was Twelvetree—the banker. But he did not speak much, and mostly fretted about the box he was carrying, and seemed preoccupied. Again, as I was. It suited me; I did not wish to talk."

"Your late father was Nicholas Twelvetree's partner, was he not?" Fairfax said, keeping his voice low. "Did you not know him?"

"I never saw him that I remember. Our house was not the bank. I never knew too much of my father's business affairs. He liked to keep them quite separate. At the time he took a partner, and then had to sell out to him, I was away at school. My father was a great believer in schooling. When he brought me home, he said he was finished with banking, and we must live modest and quiet. It suited me—and I think my father was rather glad to be out of it, though he did not live long to enjoy the change." Such a limpid, otherworldly look; was it possible to lie with that look? "I did not think to speak to this Mr. Twelvetree of any of this. It was all past and gone, and I had—other thoughts."

"You have perhaps heard that the man traveling as Mr.

Twelvetree was an imposter. He was a tradesman of this town, Mr. Thomas Honeyman. The name means nothing to you?"

"No. I know few people in Stamford, beyond my sister-in-law and her circle. Truly, sir, that is all there is to tell you."

"Your sister-in-law—Mrs. Bland. You had been on a visit to her. And I understand there had been some quarrel between you during that week."

She hesitated. "Yes. We do not—we do not generally get along well together. But this time we quarreled very badly and there were things said between us that . . . should not be said. She said she would write my husband; she said that I could not stay any longer—but we made it up, after a fashion, and I remained there the full week. I did my duty."

Esther had appeared beside them. "I'm sorry—the carter says he's going back any minute, mistress, and we must make haste if we want to ride."

Margaret Parry started to get up. Fairfax reached out, not roughly, to take her hand. Her bare white arm came out of the folds of the cloak. His eye fell on the soft skin inside the crook of her arm, made out the shape of three impressions, faded now, like dints in the skin of a ripe fruit. Hastily she pulled her arm back out of sight.

"I must go, sir. You know that I—I rely on you."

"I will say nothing." He left a tiny pause. "Not even to your husband."

Tears started momentarily to her great eyes, but did not fall. Indeed, it seemed to him that she had not blinked once throughout their interview.

Esther had gone to the door, and was gesturing urgently. "He's going any moment, mistress—quick now."

What would Sir Edward say? Surely, keep her here: don't let her go. But it was a matter of trust . . .

"I may not contact you, at some address?" he said.

"No—no, please, I cannot tell you . . ."

My God, he thought, she fears even me. Of course.

"Then Godspeed," he said, bowing, and Mrs. Parry slipped away like a ghost.

Husbands and wives. Let no man put asunder . . . A strange part he was playing today—and a meddlesome, dangerous one? Those whom God hath joined . . .

Yet surely those whom God had joined should not live like this. Women creeping about with haunted eyes . . . Certainly there was much amiss behind the respectable facade of the Parrys. That was a woman in fear—perhaps fear for her very life.

A rattle of wheels; Fairfax got up and went to the window. Was this breaking their agreement? But he couldn't help it. A light-built farmer's cart, unloaded, was just trundling out of the yard. He caught a glimpse of the two women sitting in the back: Esther Fryatt's carroty hair; the hooded shape, head bowed, of Margaret Parry. There was a painted sign on the backboard; he read CHAS. OAKES, HAY AND FEED, before it was lost to sight.

He sat down again, drained the brandy, then called for a dish of cold meat and capers.

Whether she had a lover or not, Margaret Parry had fled from her husband—truly fled; the desperate flight of a prisoner or victim. What sort of man, then, was William Parry? A paragon, according to Mrs. Bland—but that in itself was odd. Distasteful, he would call it.

Had Margaret dared to speak the unspeakable to her sister-in-law? To suggest that the closeness between brother and sister went beyond normal bounds? And suppose it were true? Suppose Selina Bland had written her brother to tell him that exposure threatened . . . a letter alarming enough to send William Parry out to await the coach containing his wife at a lonely spot, with—literally—murder in his heart?

A wild speculation. And why, then, kill the others? Unless it was too late: unless, having stopped the coach, Parry had been recognized by Tom Honeyman, who certainly knew him. Perhaps even fear of recognition had been enough to make him kill, wildly and desperately. For in such a case, Parry would indeed be a desperate man. He was a promising young lawyer who did good business—witness his work for Mr. Twelvetree—and here was the most ruinous exposure staring him in the face.

Bolting his food, Fairfax imagined what Sir Edward would say: fanciful flights of heated imagination! But Fairfax was a little tired of Sir Edward's lofty assurance; he felt the chafing of the leash. The frightened eyes of women, cringing before that lord of creation, man—these weighed more heavily with him just now. Haunted by the haunted . . . Margaret Parry was still the key, he was sure. Let those oafish lackeys of Twelvetree's roam the woods all they liked.

With something like a palpable *snap* of decision within him, Fairfax jumped to his feet.

Outside he found an ostler and quizzed him about the cart that had just left. Oakes, the feed merchant? Aye, the George always dealt with him, for the stabling. Where from? Huntington; he had been established there for years.

Huntingdon. A long ride for his mare, but then she was used to hard days in the hunting field. He might even be able to keep the cart in sight—though that might be difficult without Margaret and Esther recognizing him. Follow at any rate, follow the trail to where she was hiding out—he could surely do it without betraying or endangering her. And a short distance from Huntingdon, he knew, was the town of St. Neots. It was high time he paid William Parry a visit at home—and investigated the fragile alibi of his too. And he might even get to see Henry Griggs's preaching after all.

It would mean staying in Huntingdon overnight—he could hardly expect the mare to make the return journey in darkness. Very well then; he had *carte blanche*, did he not? Fairfax went to the stables and found Sir Edward's coachman, tipping him and asking him to give Sir Edward a message: Vital inquiries taken him to Huntingdon, returning tomorrow so as to spare the mare, Mr. Fairfax's respectful compliments . . .

He set out with a feeling of freedom. The mare seemed, he thought, pleased to trotting out with him on the open road. The day was cool and breezy. The few rain clouds in the sky were hustled about by the wind and did not break; and the road surface was fair, muddy only in the deepest ruts. All, in fact, too good to last. Just outside Stilton the mare cast a shoe. Luckily the village was a main posting stage, and Fairfax had no trouble in finding a blacksmith; but the cart would probably outpace him now.

"Come from Stamford, sir? Another one," the blacksmith said. Steam hissed upward as he quenched the glowing C of the new shoe. "Had a whole boiling of great haynish fellows coming through the village this morning. All making a mighty noise and wagging pistols about like a parcel of buccaneers. Thinking to catch theirselves a highway robber in the woods past Holme. Any such rogues about will hear you coming for miles, thinks I. They want to be careful they don't shoot theirselves in the foot."

Exactly his sentiments. Mildly cursing the delay, Fairfax went on in an afternoon growing swiftly chilly, and was soon at Stangate Hole, with Alconbury Hill rising ahead in the distance: the place where the *Flyer* had met its end. To his surprise, he could not recognize the exact spot, but the general scene looked much as it had on that memorable day, the bleak straight line of the road, the scutterings of decaying leaves, the masses of woods stretching away in smoky folds on all sides to a cold blue horizon.

A little farther on, at the foot of the hill, he saw the first evidence of Twelvetree's buccaneers. At the opening of a track going into the woods one of the men was sitting on a pile of leaves, a blunderbuss propped beside him, and nursing a strapped ankle: the first casualty. To keep himself warm he had made a sort of fire of dry sticks, which was making more smoke than heat. Another splendid signal to anyone hiding out in the woods.

The sun was well down over the clay-ridged uplands to the west when at last the mare's weary hoofbeats rang out on

the road dipping into Huntingdon. Fairfax was exceedingly
saddle sore—a condition he had always thought of as no
more than a painful tingle; instead, he felt as if his whole
nether regions had been brutally pummeled. He put up at the
Falcon in the marketplace, looking in vain among the gigs
and wagons for Oakes's cart. Of course, the town was full of
inns. But it was not a large place: a modest market town
huddled on one side of the river in the midst of great meadows. Margaret Parry must be here somewhere, perhaps not
alone . . .

"Mr. Fairfax! Sir! You have come after all!"

Henry Griggs hailed him from across the inn yard, came
fairly bustling over. Fairfax had never seen the somber man
so animated.

"I am delighted—more delighted than I can say. To gratify your curiosity—of course. But that is how many come. I
do not think you will be disappointed."

Fairfax chose not to say that he had other business besides. "Mr. Griggs. When do you begin? I fear I must refresh
my body before my spirit."

"Soon—not yet. I usually wait until the day's work of the
laboring people is done." Griggs introduced the man with
him, who was even more sober and flinty-looking. "My
friend Neavis, who keeps the mill here, is class leader for the
Methodist folk of the town. He has been spreading the word,
and I hope there will be many who will gather to drink at the
fount of salvation."

"I hope so, Mr. Griggs," the miller said devoutly. "But
there will be others come to fleer and sneer, I am afraid."

"Excellent! They are the very fish to catch," Griggs said,
rubbing his square hands, and coming as near to chuckling
as Fairfax had ever seen in him. "Well, sir, we gather at Mill
Common, which you see yonder. Come when you are refreshed. You lie here the night?"

"Yes, if I can get a bed."

"There are quite a number of folk come to town for the
races," Neavis said, pronouncing the last word with distaste.

"If you should find difficulty in getting a bed, sir, come to me. I am putting up my good friend Mr. Griggs, as well as another of the brotherhood, who has walked all the way from Molesworth—the millhouse beyond the common—I have room."

A kind thought: charity in action, indeed, Fairfax thought, thanking him. Still he was glad, on going into the Falcon, to find that he could get a bed for the night there. Curiosity—sympathy, even—was one thing, but spending the night under the same roof as three fervent Methodists was another.

After a meal, he asked the innkeeper where he could find Mr. Oakes the feed merchant. Not far, in an old waterside house down by the bridge at the end of the High Street. The merchant, brushing down the cart horses in his yard, was testy. The two women had paid him for a ride into Stamford and back, that was all; he didn't know who they were or where they had gone when he set them down. Here? Yes, here. It was something.

Oliver Cromwell had been born in this town; and though it was far from being in a state of civil war, Fairfax sensed in it the continuing duality in society—in man, perhaps—as he made his way toward the great common on the edge of the town. Groups of soberly dressed, quiet-spoken people were going that way. Others were repairing to inns and taverns, laughing and swearing, pausing here and there to stare at the sedate exodus passing by. There were one or two ribald comments, and Fairfax saw a lump of thrown mud hit the broad back of a smocked laborer tramping stolidly ahead of him. A smartly dressed clergyman stepping up into his carriage gave the files of trudging people a sharp stare. But the two elements did not clash, at least not yet.

At a spot of rising ground at the edge of the common, near the mill, an old cart had been pitched, shafts to the ground. Here Henry Griggs had already mounted up and was standing very still, hands folded and, as Fairfax saw as he drew near, eyes closed. He had no Bible or prayer book.

A couple of lighted oil lamps hung from the cart—evening was coming down fast—and there were some hay bales for the infirm to sit on, and a brazier to spread a little warmth. The appointments of the field preaching were no more luxurious than that. People stood or sat or squatted about in a rough circle, faces lamplit, talking in a murmur. Many more women than men, Fairfax noticed; and they tended to gather nearer to the cart. Some were already softly crooning snatches of hymns, and one or two had their heads deeply bowed in private devotion.

A few people were here, he noticed, only to gape and mock. They passed a jug from hand to hand, shouted for Mr. Punch to come on, sniggered. But they were in a minority, and got no response. Doing a rough count of heads, Fairfax reckoned there were about a hundred and fifty men, women, and children gathered on the common, and more making their way across. Most were of poor-to-middling sort—field laborers, tradesmen, artisans, servants. No powder or lace to be seen. But a few comfortably dressed people, merchants and their wives, hung around the edges, and some well-setup farmers had come on horseback and looked on with puckered skeptical eyes.

Griggs began, quite abruptly, by singing a hymn. It was only faintly familiar to Fairfax; one of Charles Wesley's, he supposed.

> *Jesu, Lover of my soul,*
> *Let me to Thy Bosom fly,*
> *While the gathering waters roll,*
> *While the tempest still is high.*
> *Hide me. O my Savior, hide,*
> *Till the storm of life is past;*
> *Safe into the haven guide,*
> *O receive my soul at last.*

The deep rich voice floated out on the evening air. The melancholy tune, the supplicating words, seemed to hold people in a kind of soothed suspense. Gradually other voices, chiefly those of the women gathered tightly at the front, joined in. The effect, Fairfax felt, was of sadness and poignancy. He could not imagine the hysterical antics that were reputed to go on at field preachings following this gentle introduction. "Other refuge have I none:" they sang, "Hangs my helpless soul on Thee;" a sigh of resignation, an acknowledgment that the world was too hard for mortal flesh, too cruel and vast.

The hymn ended, and Henry Griggs at once began speaking, quite naturally and informally, his hands clasped before him.

"Friends, it gladdens me to see you tonight. I spoke here once before, half a year ago I think, and I am sure there were not so many present that night; and I am joyfully convinced that the blessed spirit of Christ is growing and spreading, as it must do, as it will do. But that previous time, there were several who were saved. They found their heart wrestling sorely with the conviction of sin, and they confessed it. They were plucked as a brand from the burning that night, and I know have lived since then that godly life open to anyone who embraces salvation, and joins the connection in good fellowship and true piety. Brother Neavis here has led the class in this town and the country round, and tells me good things of the spirit that has prevailed here.

"And others, perhaps, carried away something of that saving fire, and kept it within them for a time. But it's hard to keep it forever alight: I know it. For life is hard, and the working day is long, and surely the flesh cannot always be mortified. It is all very well, you might think, for preachers to stand there and say we must be saved—but why is salvation so hard on us? Drink is the road to damnation, they say. But why can't a man have his pot of beer or his nip of gin? Few enough pleasures in the world. And after all, you may say, there are rich folk who drink their fill every day. They sit down to the choicest meats and the finest wines, and dress in silk, and gratify their every appetite. Are they not greater sinners, you might think? Is not this salvation like another tax, that presses most cruelly on the poor?"

"I'll drink to that," cried a man at the back, lifting high a jug, and there was a mutter of laughter from his neighbors.

"Aye, aye," Griggs went on, nodding pleasantly, "so it may seem. It is a mighty convincing argument, for the devil has some very good ones. Oh, yes, perhaps I seem to speak mild. I am not mild. The devil speaks when he urges you to drink, and curse, and root about in the cesspits of sin. And when you say it don't signify, because the high folk and the rich folk are no better, then the devil speaks loudest of all.

"Because in the eyes of our Lord there are no silks and no homespuns. We are all weighed in the same balance, friends. And those who are found wanting are lost for ever. Their souls will howl for the absence of the dear Christ through eternity, be they dukes or plowmen. Be sure of this, friends—greed and intemperance, the love of gain and wealth and dominion over men, are hateful in God's eyes, and the salvation of men who pursue them pitilessly will be dearly bought." Griggs jabbed a forefinger in the air, the first gesture he had made. " 'Woe unto them that join house to house, that lay field to field, till there be no place, that they may be placed alone in the midst of the earth.' So says our book. The promises of God are kept, my friends; you may count on it, and no high estate will save you."

There was a satisfied murmur. This, at least, was the sort of inflammatory stuff that Sir Edward deplored, Fairfax thought, the stuff to send men of property calling for the militia.

"Oh, but please, friends, don't get comfortable in your minds. I don't bring you comfort, not of that kind. There are no 'perhaps' and 'maybes' on the way to salvation. What, after all, is wrong with your pot of beer? I'll tell you: it is the ugly leer of a bad child in the face of his sorrowing father. It is dirt hurled at your Savior, who would see your souls joined with Him in everlasting glory, who gave His blood in pain and travail for that purpose, and instead sees His beloved children turn against Him, and slouch down the path to ruination. That soul comes from the hand of God, who can make nothing that is not beautiful; yet would you befoul and spoil and ruin it? There are only two roads in this life, friends, and I vow it to you most desperately; only two. There is the road that leads to the rock of salvation; and there is the devil's highway, mighty broad and fair in looks, and leading to nowhere but torment. Look into yourself—do it truly!—look, and ask, where am I going? Think on your life, and examine your heart; be still in the silence of your mind, and listen. Do you not feel something—it is a nagging, a shadow, an itch, a weight—it is something beyond words, but there, oh, so definitely there—you know it. That is the knowledge of sin, friends, that sin which causes the wounds of our dear Christ to bleed afresh. It is there all the time, and sometimes when you have been drunken, or idle, or untruthful, you feel its presence so closely. And yet it is so hard to confess it! So hard to let the spirit in, and cry, I have sinned. Jesus, help me, help me . . ."

"Help me . . ." The echo came, in soft fluttering voices, from several of the women near the cart. Fairfax saw one hold her head in her hands, and sway mournfully.

"It is the hardest thing in the world. And it is the easiest thing in the world. It means breaking open your breast, and dashing yourself upon rocks, and weeping with the anguished tears of the newborn. And this new birth means joy, joy such as you have never known. It is letting Christ in. Does he knock at your heart, and yet you are afraid to answer? Don't be afraid! The light and the glory will dazzle you and numb you, surely, for they will be great, very great. But you will know you are redeemed, and no earthly joy you have ever known can compare to it! That is not my promise, my friends. That is the promise that Jesus made when He came to us—us, yes, we humble people gathered in this field, He came to us, as to all mankind; and He is here now. I feel His spirit move: I feel the yearning of hearts for His grace."

Several women were openly weeping. One had thrown back her bonnet and was holding her face up to the sky in what looked like ecstasy, murmuring to herself. Here and there people were muttering, a little self-consciously, fragments of remembered prayers and psalms; other had sat down on the grass and folded their hands and closed their eyes.

How was Griggs feeling? Fairfax wondered. Like Christ on the Mount of Olives? No, a prideful thought, surely. For himself he felt both fascinated and uncomfortable. The religious throb in the air, muted though it was, the pent-up earnestness, was so foreign to his way of thinking that he felt quite an intruder.

Suddenly a big man near the front got to his feet, half stumbling, and raised his hand. He wore a leather waistcoat and his bare forearm was roughened and discolored. A brickmaker or quarrier, Fairfax thought; some grinding and hard-drinking trade.

"I want to say something . . ." Wrestling with oneself, the Methodists called it when these stirrings of conscience, or spiritual feeling, came on. In this big man it was almost a physical reality. He shuffled and wriggled his brawny frame, he wrapped one great arm about his neck with a clawing movement. He gasped out as if for quarter, "I want to . . . I want to be saved."

"Say it louder, friend," Griggs said, with a tremendous tenderness.

"I want to be saved. I'm a sinner, I am, I know it—oh, God, I want to be saved . . ."

"Hear him, my friends. That is the most pleasing sound to Christ. It gladdens Him to hear that, more than the greatest anthem swelling from a cathedral. Speak again, friend, make confession, and be washed in the blood of the Lamb. You will be new-made if you can do it!"

"I've been a sinner—a terrible sinner." The big man turned awkwardly about, hugging himself. His face was crimson and wet in the lamplight, as if truly bathed in blood.

"It's been naught but the bottle with me for many a year—drunk as an ape night after night—and when I'm drunken, I'm black, oh, so black in my heart . . . My wife knows it, because I hit her." He suddenly sobbed like a boy. "I hit her, and then I'm so sorry for it, and then I take a drink and I hit her again . . ."

"Ah, the devil is in that stuff, my friend, and you know it, don't you?" Griggs said. "Speak out, friend, you do well. there are others here, I think, who have done the same. Is it not the truth? Men who grope in the filthy pit of drunkenness—wives dragged down there with them, afraid when he takes a drop: afraid of the curses and the blows . . . Confess it, friends, for you can't hide from your Lord. He sees every tear . . ."

A woman near the front stood up and threw back her shawl. "I'm his wife!" she cried out. "It's true, every word. I've been so frightened of him for so long . . . I've prayed and prayed for you to stop, Jack. I've never stopped loving you like a wife should, but I've been so afraid." She went over to the man, who was hunched over and sobbing into his hands. "I'm not afraid now, Jack. Lift up your face, dear."

Now many were weeping, rocking themselves to and fro, and clasping their hands in prayer. Fairfax could hear a deep mutter running through the crowd, the sum of fragmented utterances: "Praise God." "Jesus." "Save me, save me." At the front another woman leaped up, old and haggard and trembling.

"My man died of it," she cried. "I buried him last winter. God forgive me, God have mercy on me, but I was glad that he had gone because I couldn't bear the beating anymore. God forgive me—God have mercy on his soul . . ." Her voice rose hysterically. A woman beside her, dressed in a dark cloak and hood, reached out comforting arms and held the old woman tightly to her.

Fairfax tensed. The view of her face had been only momentary, but he was sure that the cloaked woman was Margaret Parry. He tried to keep his eye fixed on her figure. It was hard with the flickering light, the people swaying and pressing forward.

"Are you convinced of sin, friend?" Griggs was addressing the big man. "Do you feel the spirit move within you? Are you afraid of it? It is mighty, friend, mightier than all of us. Be convinced of sin, open your breast to the Savior, let Him in! 'The Lord shall preserve they going out, and thy coming in: from this time forth for evermore.' "

The big man had fallen to his knees groaning, as if he had been struck on the neck. His wife knelt beside him, murmuring rapturously.

" 'Joy shall be in heaven over one sinner that repenteth, more than over ninety and nine and nine just persons, which need no repentance.' See, friends, how beautiful the new birth is . . ."

Well, Fairfax was not disappointed. Griggs was an effective preacher, and the weeping, groaning, and fervent prayer going on all around him was just as he had heard described, and had rather doubted. There was no questioning, either, its sincerity. If he felt any disappointment it was in himself. For his spirit held firmly aloof. Here was Enthusiasm, the bugbear of the rational thinker; its abandonment, its passionate singleness of view, its mysticism, made him recoil. Perhaps he simply feared these deep dark waters—feared them closing over his head as he had feared the thought of madness when he had approached Mr. Rowe's asylum.

But he had found Margaret Parry again, at any rate. Her face had come into view once more among the urgently gathering silhouettes around the cart, uplifted, and seeming to hang on the preacher's every word. There was no doubt that she had found something here that she desperately wanted.

Griggs had begun leading them in the twenty-third psalm. The unison was ragged. Fairfax thought at first it was because some people were still chanting their own private prayers and invocations. Then he became aware of noises to

the rear, harsh and raucous, quite unlike the emotional hubbub of the prayer meeting.

It all happened very quickly. Suddenly men of a very different stamp were among them. They were drunk, and full
of themselves, and had come streaming across the common
in a loud-mouthed pack to see the prayerfest and laugh at it.
So much was obvious; and Fairfax guessed they were of the
sporting fraternity who gathered at the races and boxing
matches. They wore broad-brimmed hats and gaiters or riding boots, carried sticks and led dogs, and beer and hilarity
had instilled something of a dog-pack mentality in them.
They moved among the crowd, elbowing people aside and
calling loudly for a song with a bit of go in it. Some flung
their arms round women, inviting them to take a drink from
bottles in exchange for a kiss. One put his hat on a stick and
strutted his way to the front intoning, "Bless you, my children, bless you." The transition to ugliness was swift, perhaps inevitable; but Fairfax had his suspicions about several
smartly dressed young blades, racing fanciers probably,
whom he saw trotting about on horseback and waving their
hats in ironical huzzahs on the edge of the crowd. He
thought it likely they had been treating the men to drinks,
and urging them to go stir up the Methodies for sport.

The turning point was when one of the men tried to climb
up on to the cart beside Griggs. "Let me have a turn," he was
shouting. "I can preach—I can preach you a proper ser-
mon—warm your cockles, it will." He was very drunk, and
kept slipping and stumbling down. Griggs looked on him
with stern, melancholy tolerance. "No, no, my friend," he
said, "don't do it to yourself, 'tis too bad."

Then one of his cronies pushed him aside and leaped up
onto the cart. His drunkenness was more belligerent.
"You're naught but a parcel of ranting, creeping, soft-bellied
rogues! Call yourselves Englishmen? No better'n papists!
You should be raising your voices to Church and King—
Church and King! And women flinging theirselves about—

they should be at home by their fires! Church and King, and
be damned to the lot of you!"

That was enough. Two men who had a minute ago been
at prayer plucked him angrily down from his perch. Repentance had not after all made them saints, and their devotion
was being mocked. The Church-and-King man struggled
with them, hit out, and was hit in return. It was all the signal
his cronies needed. There was a surge forward: raised fists
in the lamplight, the sound of heavy boots scuffing and kicking. Fairfax saw Neavis the miller made into the brawl, but
Griggs stayed on the cart, shaking his head. Women
screamed and then screamed again, scattering, as the brazier
was kicked over and flames flew up. The hay bales took fire
at once; the scene became a horrible melee of black smoke,
firelight, thrashing bodies, people running and tumbling
over one another, while horsemen circled them with yells of
delight.

Suddenly a girl of no more than twelve was running
straight at Fairfax. Her skirts were on fire and she was
screaming. Without time to think he put out his arms to stop
her, pushed her on the grass, beat at the flames with his
hands, and then smothered them with his body. Her screams
subsided to panicked gasps. There was a thunder of hoofbeats close by, and he stayed for a moment with his arms
tented over her, shielding her. Looking up, he felt his face
stung by a sharp flick from the hem of a billowing riding
cloak. He recognized the face of the rider, briefly illumi-
nated in profile, as that of William Parry. No brute hilarity
there, though: Parry's eyes seemed to scan the milling crowd
carefully before he cantered away.

Fairfax found the girl's mother, checked that she had
come to no serious harm, then surveyed the scene. The fire
had broken up the pitched battle around the cart. Griggs had
got down and was nowhere to be seen. He was perhaps behind the circle of Methodists who had linked arms and were
trying to sing a psalm. Other men were still trading blows,
cursing, and spitting. One of the sportsmen was on the

ground being kicked. People were scattering in all directions. He could not see Margaret Parry anywhere.

Something was needed to break this up. Fairfax doubted the handful of parish constables, who came marching across the common with their staves and lanterns, were the ones to do it. These unpaid ragtag officials were notoriously ineffectual. But theses were led by a very stout fearless old man with a stentorian voice, who directed his fellows in beating out the fire and at last mounted on the cart and called firmly on them all to disperse.

"Get to your homes, everybody. I give you five minutes to get off the common. After that I rouse the magistrate and he'll clap you in the jail, innocent or guilty. Now then—you know it's true: when there's an affray like this they don't stop for explanations. Get home to your beds, all on you, I've no patience." He seemed to mutter something about "damn Methodies" as he got down.

There was nothing for it but to join the crowd of people making their way back across the common to the town. A few still stoutly sang hymns as they went, but most looked chastened and sad. Fairfax looked in vain for the hooded figure of Margaret Parry; and the riders had left the field as soon as the constables arrived.

Eleven

They were both here, in Huntingdon. He could not doubt it; and he could not doubt that William Parry was looking very single-mindedly for his errant wife.

His earlier suspicions, the suspicions that had brought him here, had not yet hardened into certainty. But Fairfax was racked with uneasiness as he laid himself in the cold musty bed in his room at the Falcon that night, with little expectation of sleep. There was the itchiness of the gray sheets that were probably full of bugs; there was the pain in the palms of his hands where he had scorched them beating out the young girl's blazing dress; there was the phantasmagoric images of the field preaching, with its mingling of exultation and violence; but most of all there was this unease, and the feeling that though he was on the right track, he was slow and far behind. He had nightmares, but his most vivid dream was a reproduction of the scene at the preaching, which took on the shades of a religious painting: Margaret Parry at the front among the sorrowing women, face uplifted to the figure of Henry Griggs, like an adoring Mary Magdalene . . .

He was up at five, and waiting for his horse in the yard while the sky was still slate-colored and the stable boy swilled his heavy head at the pump. The mare grunted in welcome, nervous after a night spent in a strange stable. Fairfax, after asking the boy for directions, left the town and crossed the bridge into Godmanchester, striking the road southward to St. Neots.

A bright copper sun was up when he came into the town, firing the tower of the great church and fretting the broad marketplace with molten shadows. A handsome prosperous place, its town houses well appointed with new sash windows and carriage gates—it was just the place for a thriving young attorney.

A few inquiries brought him to the house of the late Mr. Poole, a narrow shuttered place of red bricks. It had the look of a miser's retreat. He pulled at an old cracked bell for some time before a hideous old woman in a mob-cap thrust her toothless face out at him.

"Nothing wanted," she mumbled, breathing gin, "master's dead. Put him in his grave yesterday. Nothing wanted."

He had to grease her palm, or claw, with several coins before he could get her to listen to his questions, and then her understanding seemed doubtful.

"Mr. Poole died on Tuesday night, is that correct?"

"Dead as mutton. Put him in his grave yesterday."

"You are his only servant?"

"Not now I ain't. Dead he is, dead as mutton."

"Were you here, with him, when he died on Tuesday? He had no family, I understand, and wanted no clergyman by him. Were you here?"

"I ain't no family of his. Served him twenty year, but there was never any hint of *that*, I should hope not." She tittered, hopefully holding out her hand again. "What's to come of me? I don't know. D'ye want a servant? I don't know as I could shift now. Money goes to a great-nevvy somewhere. He's got one, somewhere. Never came to see him, mind."

"Did anyone come to him on the day he died? What about Mr. Parry, the lawyer?"

"Aye, he was here. And the parson. Lawyer, parson."

"I thought Mr. Poole wouldn't have a parson—didn't hold with them."

"Oh, he hated parsons, didn't he just. Wicked old man. I don't know what's to become of me." She snuffled and jingled the coins.

"Mr. Parry, the lawyer. Was he here on Tuesday?"

"Oh, he came, aye. Came, and went away. The parson."

"The young lawyer—Mr. Parry."

"Him too," she said merrily.

He gave it up.

The Parry house was on the south side of the square, neat and well groomed and pleasant-looking as Mr. Parry himself. Fairfax was unsure of what he was going to say even as he knocked. Have you any real witness to your whereabouts on Tuesday? Why has your wife really fled from you? Who made those bruises on her arm? What were you doing in Huntingdon last night? All these questions were as good as accusations. And that was assuming he had not found her . . .

The door opened.

"My God," he said, and again, "my God."

"I'm sorry, sir, no one's home," the maid said, as best she could through her split and swollen lip. Her blackened eye twitched and watered in the shaft of sunlight.

"You—you must be Mary Fryatt. My God."

She said she couldn't let him in but he brushed that aside and brushed aside to her protests as he hunted about the ground-floor rooms, at last finding a bottle of brandy in a parlor at the back overlooking a neat garden. He poured her a glass and mixed it with a little water and then made her sit down in an armchair while he laid a fire.

"I can't sit there, sir, that's Mr. Parry's chair, and—and no one—"

"No one's allowed to sit in it but him. I can guess. Sit down, Mary. Is that flint and tinder there? Excellent." He lit some kindling and plied the bellows, while the maid sat with gingerly wonder.

"What if Mr. Parry comes back, sir?"

"I"ll answer for it if he does." He looked at her. "I was going to say what more can he possibly do . . . but that's better not said."

She turned her face, trying to keep the eye out of sight. The way she kept her hand pressed to her side suggested there were bruises there too—Fairfax hoped no cracked ribs. She was very like her sister Esther, the resemblance nearly as strong as that of twins, but plumper and altogether more solid-looking. Perhaps that was how William Parry justified it to himself when he beat her.

"How do you know my name, sir?"

"I know your sister, Esther. Mine is Robert Fairfax. I have been looking for Mrs. Parry, on behalf of the magistrates, though we have not been looking for her in the way her husband has. I'm sure you understand what I mean."

She hung her head and would not answer. Firmly he took the hand holding the brandy and water and guided it to her lips.

"I have met Esther, and I have met your mistress. I understand now why she did not come home from her visit; why she took the opportunity to run away. I am on the side of justice, Mary. No hiding the truth, now: it must come out." Deliberately he replaced the bellows on the other side of the fireplace, and saw her watching. She made a nervous movement. "Let me guess. The master wouldn't like this either. Everything in its place." He glanced around the parlor, which had the regimented neatness he had seen at Mrs. Bland's house. Oh, yes, a chill little domestic tyrant who *must* have his way; whom no one understood aright except, of course, his adoring sister . . ."He beat you, didn't he? Mr. Parry did this to you."

She sipped the brandy, made a face, and shuddered. "'Twas last night. He wanted to know where the mistress was and he—he said he'd thrash it out of me if I wouldn't tell. And so . . . I did tell. God help me, I did tell. He got so wild, I thought he'd kill me . . ."

"Hush, hush. You're not to blame. So you knew where Mrs. Parry had gone?"

"Yes. She went to my mother's in Huntingdon. It was Tuesday, when she was supposed to be coming home. She got down from the coach at Stilton, and she walked across country to Huntingdon, and turned up at Mother's door. Mother had been the master's old nurse, and my mistress had always been kind to her, and used to visit her sometimes and take her fruit and sweetmeats when she was poorly. She just couldn't think of anywhere else to go. All she knew was that she couldn't bear to come back home here, to—to him. I know this because Mother wrote me. Poor Mother, she was in such a taking with the mistress turning up like that, though she was more than willing to shelter her as best she could, and so she wrote to tell me."

"I think your sister will have gone there too. I saw her yesterday with your mistress. I'm afraid she lost her position at Mrs. Bland's on Wednesday."

"Oh, no!"

"For speaking up for your mistress, I think, which I gather Mrs. Bland did not like."

Mary sniffed. "That's likely enough. Her and him—I think they're, well, God forgive me for saying it, but I think they'd be more than brother and sister if she had her way. Mrs. Bland was always against my mistress, though she's the kindest young lady, and Mrs. Bland would believe any good of her precious brother and none of her." She sipped brandy, not shuddering this time. "My guess is, Esther must have helped my mistress with her dressing, perhaps, and seen the bruises. She couldn't always hide 'em, poor lady."

"Was Mr. Parry often violent to his wife?"

"It wasn't what you'd call regular. That was what made it so frightening. Sometime he'd be as sweet as honey, and then something she'd do or say would displease him, and you'd see this look come into his eyes . . . I shouldn't be saying this."

"I think it is high time, Mary. You have never spoken of this before?"

"Well, I'd lay hints with Esther about what was going on, so she had an idea . . . but 'tis hard. We're only servants, and afraid—afraid like my mistress was. She must have screwed up a deal of courage to get off that coach."

"And so Mr. Parry beat it out of you? Where you mistress was?"

She nodded, hanging her head. The shame of the victim. "He'd been from home much of yesterday. There was the funeral of that old miser. He'd maybe been hoping for a legacy; he didn't get one, judging from his black looks when he came home late in the afternoon. He didn't touch dinner, just sat mooching and drinking. And watching me. And then he comes out with it, quite quiet like. 'Where is she, Mary?' " She gripped the glass to still the trembling of her hands. " 'Come on,' he says, 'you must have some notion, you were always very thick with her.' He made it sound nasty. I said I didn't know, but he wouldn't leave it— and when I tried to get out of the room, he stopped me. And that's when he started hitting, until—until I told. Then, says he, who is her lover? She must have someone that she's meeting there. I don't know naught of that, says I—and I don't, I never heard of any such thing. I was shocked at what he was thinking . . . though I wouldn't blame her one bit if she did find someone else, someone to value her at her true worth. He started calling her all sorts of names—slut and whatnot; it was horrible. He said she must have been betraying him for ages, and what a fool she'd made of him . . . and then he takes up his riding cloak and saddles up and rides off like the wind."

"To Huntingdon," Fairfax said. "Where I saw him last night, I'll swear . . . And he didn't come home all night?"

"No. I waited up . . . I've had all sorts of things going through my head."

"Mary, where does your mother live? You must trust me.

I mean to help—protect if I can." *If it's not too late:* he seemed to see the words reflected in her look.

"Orchard Lane. 'Tis off the High Street, by the jail. She has rooms above a silversmith's shop."

"Very well. Now, is your pain easing a little? You can sit my horse in front of me, and we can jog along steady . . ."

She was shaking her head. "You'll reckon me mad, maybe; but I want to stay here. What's to come in the long term I don't know. But I want to stay here just in case my mistress comes back. I want to be here if she does."

"Whatever she has suffered," Fairfax said, pressing her hand, "she has been lucky in her friends. Mary, one thing more: where was your master on Tuesday, when your mistress was supposed to come home?"

She shrugged. "He was from home all day, and didn't get back till late. When I said she hadn't come back, he was just—quiet." She got up from the forbidden chair, and he saw her resist an impulse to smooth the cushion. "I think I was more afraid of his quiet than anything."

He rode at speed back to Huntingdon, buoyed by vindication, pricked by alarm.

It was Esther Fryatt who opened the door to him at Orchard Lane, a spot made dark by the barred and grated presence of the county jail. It had taken Fairfax some time to find the little shell-hooded entrance behind the silversmith's premises.

"It's all right, Esther. Your sister told me Mrs. Parry was here. I mean no harm, no dangerous exposure. I know what's been going on. I just—"

"She ain't here," Esther said. "She didn't come home last night."

Fairfax followed her up the wormy stairs, puzzled to hear a voice that he recognized. In a plain shabby-decent room made fusty by a copper suspended over a wood fire he found an old woman in company with Henry Griggs.

"Here's Mr. Fairfax, Mother," Esther said. "The one I was telling you of."

A straight-backed, trim, dignified old body, Mrs. Fryatt looked bewildered but courteous. "Sir—I'm not used to so many visitors, but if you would care to move those things, and take that chair . . ."

Plainly Mrs. Fryatt kept body and soul together by taking in washing. Most of the surfaces in the room were covered with neat piles of linen, and frocks and bodices and shirts hung all round it, giving it an oppressive feeling as if crowded with people.

"Thank you, Mrs. Fryatt, I do very well." He looked at Griggs. "I did not expect to see you here."

"This gentleman just arrived to see—well, to see Margaret," Mrs. Fryatt said. "And I'm sorry I can't oblige, and the same goes for you, sir, if that's your errand—but I believe all will be well, you know, Esther. I do believe it still . . ."

"She asked me last night to call on her here," Griggs said. He was stony and imperturbable as ever. Only the light in those compelling pale eyes suggested the transfigured and impassioned man Fairfax had seen last night. "She was at the preaching, and spoke to me when it broke up. Sore at heart she seemed, yet mightily moved with the spirit. Truly a soul in travail, who needed to lay hold of salvation. I said I would be happy to come to her, and pray with her: I thought we might wreak great things with God's grace today. But I find something is amiss."

"You knew who she was, when she spoke to you?"

"Yes. That is, she told me her name. I suppose she trusted to my discretion as a man of God. As was quite right. I knew that this was the Mrs. Parry who was being sought. But the condition of her soul was all that concerned me." Griggs blinked at him solemnly.

"Always a godly creature," Mrs. Fryatt said. "That was why she wanted to go to the field preaching last night, though she'd kept herself so quiet and hid away. I must go, says she: I simply must go. And so she did ... and never came back all night. I didn't know what to do," she said, pulling out a scrap of handkerchief, in strong contrast to the huge snowy cambric and lace ones about the room, which she was only allowed to wash. "I just didn't know ..."

"The last I saw of her," Griggs said, "was when the preaching broke up—or was broken up. She spoke to me, and then made her way off the common, with the other wronged and abused women." He put a strong emphasis on the words, jerking his chin up.

"I just didn't know," said Mrs. Fryatt, dabbing her eyes, "what to do for the best. You see, sir, Margaret's husband came here last night, when she was out at the preaching. Asking if she was here."

Esther nodded at Fairfax's look. "I kept out of sight. But I heard him. Very mild like, he was." Her lips twisted.

"I said I hadn't seen her, and I didn't know where she was," old Mrs. Fryatt said. "And so off he went. I hope I won't suffer for the lie, but when the poor child came to me she was so anxious to keep secret and retired, even—even from her husband." Her eyes darted to Esther. "And I have been hearing such things about Mr. Parry—things I can hardly believe ..."

"I have just come from St. Neots," Fairfax said, thinking: This is bad ... very bad. "Mr. Parry was not there, and hadn't come home all night. I saw your other daughter there, Mrs. Fryatt. I fear she too has suffered at Mr. Parry's hands. He forced her to tell him where her mistress was. No, no, she will be all right. I pressed her to come away with me, but she wanted to stay, in case her mistress came home."

"Mary ..." Mrs. Fryatt wept again in bewilderment. "I can't believe it ... Perhaps all will be well yet, though, sir— eh? Perhaps Margaret has met with her husband, and they've settled things ..."

Griggs was shaking his head grimly. "When she spoke to me last night," he said at Fairfax's look, "she indicated that other poor woman who was beaten by her husband—you were there, sir, and saw? And she asked me, 'Should we forgive?' Just that."

"What was your answer?"

"I had no answer."

Fairfax met Esther's burning eyes. "We must look for her," he said. "See if anyone has seen her, has news of her. There is nowhere else she could go, think you, Mrs. Fryatt?"

"I misdoubt it, sir. If there were, she wouldn't have sought shelter with me, in a poor moiling place like this, surely. But I was glad to take her in, and do what I could for her. She was always kind to me, and my daughters had given me a notion that—that all wasn't as it should be in that quarter. But 'tis so hard to take it in still—Mr. Parry was very good as a boy, a little willful perhaps, and had to have things just so—but I never thought . . ."

"Hush, ma'am," Henry Griggs said. "'Tis as you say—all will be well. Come, sir. We will go look for her."

Outside Fairfax said, "Did you see William Parry last night, on the common?"

"I did not. You suspicion he was there? There were so many people, including low and brutal types, I fear. I hope she may not have been waylaid by any such. The constables could not watch everybody . . ."

It was of one brutal type in particular that Fairfax was thinking: remembering the flick of a cloak in his face and the smell of a hard-driven horse's sweat. Where to look? And where was Parry? They had come out into the market-place, and he still had no answer to these questions, when a shrill voice broke in on him.

He thought at first it was a woman screaming. Instead he saw a boy—a shepherd's boy, hallooing and wailing both together, and running full pelt into the square with a hammering of nailed boots. He looked as if he would have just run on and on till he collapsed, if a man had not caught him by the arms and held him still.

"Why, what's amiss with the younker?" The man gave

him a shake, making him more breathless. "Turned in his
wits, I reckon."

"In the copsewood yonder," the boy got out as Fairfax
came up. "Lying there—on the ground—all dead, she is, all
dead!"

In life Margaret Parry had seemed ethereal, insubstantial, as
if hardly made of flesh and blood. But in death there: was a
horrible solidity and weight about her slumped body, face-
down on the leaves. Dead weight, indeed. As for blood,
there was plenty of that, from the wound on her head. It
looked dark and oily in the shadows of the copsewood. She
still wore the cloak and calash, but the latter had been half-
clawed off her head by her attacker.

The place was typical of the many fragments of wood-
land that dotted this country. It did not extend far—more of
a stand of trees than a copse—and it was almost within sight
of the mill. But inside it was dense with hardy ferns and with
fallen autumn leaves, and the body might have lain in there
some time if the boy, who was minding a few sheep on the
common, had not slipped in among the trees to relieve himself.

Fairfax, Griggs, and numerous others had followed the
boy to the spot, and they were soon joined by the same stout
and strong-voiced constable who had taken charge of things
last night. He was trying to keep people away, but without
success this time. Again death, the great drawer of crowds.

"Stand back there. I want more light. Ugh, here's a pretty
mess." He knelt down by her head, sucking in breath; then
his eye fell on a fallen branch a few feet away. He picked it
up carefully by one end. The other end was splintered, darkened, oily. "Vile," he said. "Anyone know her?"

"Yes. Her name is Mrs. Margaret Parry. Of St. Neots,"
Fairfax said.

"She was at my preaching last night," Griggs said softly.
The sight seemed to have had a powerful effect on him. He
was shaking with emotion: looked almost about to swoon.

Fairfax remembered how phlegmatic he had been when viewing the bodies from the *Flyer*. "I was to see her and pray with her this morning. God have mercy on her soul. Oh, gentle Jesus, give us strength. She suffered, and suffered." He leaned heavily against a tree, wiping his mouth. His face shone with sweat. "Let her sufferings be at an end, Lord. Oh, God, 'tis an evil world. Too much to bear . . ." There was no holy calm in these utterances. The man was powerfully affected: he looked sick. Fairfax, having conquered with difficulty the urge to be sick, looked away.

"On the common last night, eh? What a ruckus that was. For myself, I wouldn't allow it, but it ain't up to me," the constable said, gently turning the body.

"We were only spreading the word of our God," Griggs said, weakly combative.

"Maybe . . . but what comes out of it, sir, is trouble and mischief, and I fear this is the result. Dear, dear, a sweet face." The constable lifted the edge of her cloak to cover it, then paused. "What's this? I wonder."

This was a weight in the pocket of the cloak, which turned out to be, to the murmuring surprise of the onlookers, a pistol. The other pocket yielded the second of the pair. "Queer . . . and a pity she didn't use them," the constable said, looking at them curiously. "Was the lady in the habit of carrying such things?" he said, looking at Griggs.

"I—I hardly knew her. Except . . ." He swallowed. "Except as a suffering creature, turning to God for succor. Suffering at the hands of the one who should be her protector. I see many such at my preachings. The signs are plain." As he spoke he beat his fist mournfully against the tree trunk.

"She was a fugitive from a cruel and violent husband," Fairfax said. "That much is known. And I saw that husband on the common last night." The pistols, though, were a mystery. Plain, dulled, cannon-barreled, they were breechloaders that needed no rammer. Guns for use.

"Wherever he is, he's a widower now." The constable rose to his feet and began sharply dispatching spectators to fetch the other constables, to find a surgeon, to get some sturdy men with a hurdle or something to carry her on . . . "And you two gentlemen," he said to Fairfax and Griggs, "you come along with me and the boy, if you'll be so good; I must report this to the magistrate."

They went with him to a handsome timber-framed house on Castle Hill, where they were set to wait in a little ante-room next to the kitchens, and were periodically stared at by servants passing by the door with trays and pails. The boy was all in a tremble at going before the magistrate, and it was all Fairfax could do to reassure him that he wasn't going to jail. Griggs seemed in a trance, staring at the floor with slow blinks of his blue eyes; and sometimes he put up his hand to wipe them.

That horror among the ferns and leaves was hard to forget. Fairfax concentrated his thoughts upon Griggs—specifically, his powerful reaction to that horror. Was there more to his relationship with Margaret than that of a preacher with an ardently religious woman who had found some comfort for her sufferings in his words? Eaton Socon, where Griggs lived, was a neighboring village of St. Neots: Fairfax remembered seeing a milepost there this morning. Was it possible that William Parry's suspicions about his wife having a lover were correct, and that this was the man? He was personable—magnetic, even—especially to a woman as otherworldly as Margaret had seemed. Or perhaps not a lover in fact, but the focus of her yearning. He imagined Griggs tempted, and then repenting, wishing to shake her off yet unable to do so . . . He was thinking of this because it was a fact that Griggs had been here in Huntingdon last night too; he had seen her at the preaching. Suppose he was her lover, or had been; and felt his position as a pillar of the Methodist connection threatened by what she might do or say, his ministry thrown into disgrace . . . Yet to kill for it—a man so little concerned with surface, with respectability? Surely not. A man too of great power and persuasion with the spiritually inclined—gently disengaging himself from any such entanglement would have been the easiest course for him. Whatever Henry Griggs was, he was not slinking and underhand. It was easy enough to make him a suspect—but after that, everything fell apart. The other suspect, of course, was a different matter . . . but where was William Parry?

Fairfax was roused by the voice of a servant. Mr. Hawkins would see them now.

Plainly a man of taste, if not tempter, Mr. Hawkins the magistrate was found in a morning room full of chinaware and bibelots, and dressed in a silk banyan and cap beneath which a small irascible face peered at the newcomers. He was not alone. The constable was with him, standing by like a sentry; and in a chair close by him, a glass of mountain in his hand, sat William Parry. His fine eyes lit momentarily on Fairfax, and on Griggs; then he returned to dreary contemplation of his wine.

Incongruous among the gewgaws, the pair of pistols lay on the table in front of the magistrate.

At the magistrate's impatient urging, they told their stories. The boy was in such a funk that Mr. Hawkins sent him away as soon as he was done, perhaps fearful of a puddle on his fine Turkey rug.

"A shocking business . . . shocking. Mr. Parry, will you take another drop? No? You see before you, I am sorry to say, the husband of the late Mrs. Parry. Bear up, my dear sir; I am excessively sorry for you. But you see there can be no doubt."

Parry had risen to his feet and gone to the window, where he stood leaning his head on his arm, gazing out. He looked disheveled, grubby even. Fairfax wondered where he had spent the night.

"Mr. Parry had just lately arrived in the town, having come from his excellent sister, Mrs. Bland, at Stamford," Mr. Hawkins said. "Coming into the town he heard a lot of talk about a woman found in the woods. His heart misgave him for his missing wife, and so he came to inquire of me, as justice of the borough, and an old friend. It cuts me, my dear sir, that you should hear this melancholy news under my roof. But we shall have the culprit, never fear."

"I beg your pardon," Fairfax said, "but there must be some mistake. I saw Mr. Parry at the preaching last night."

"A mistake indeed," drawled Parry, turning heavy eyes on Fairfax. "As my friend here says, I was at my sister's last night, and came here only this morning. I was on my way home. Home," he repeated hollowly, and chuckled.

"Your pardon again," Fairfax said, "but I have just been there, and the maid said—"

"Said what?" Parry was cool.

"That you had gone away last evening."

"So I did. I was wretched, and sought the company of my sister."

Fairfax turned to the magistrate. "The maid at Mr. Parry's house, sir, Mary Fryatt by name—she had received a severe beating from her master, who had forced her to tell him where his wife was. She had fled from him in fear of his violence—"

"Sir, do you realize what you are saying?" the magistrate hissed, outraged. "You speak of a man horribly bereaved, a man of unimpeachable character personally is known to me for several years—"

"Sir, Mr. Fairfax has perhaps been misled by his own zeal in attempting to solve the mystery of my missing wife. It is no great mystery. She left me because, I must regretfully believe, she was betraying me. I don't know what tales the servant you mention may have spun you, sir, but you may know she is sister to a troublesome young chit whom my sister was obliged to discharge from her service. It is very likely she would conjure these lies."

"Their mother, Mrs. Fryatt, at Orchard Lane—she says you came to her last night, asking for your wife—"

"Their mother," Parry said, "as you say. My childhood nurse, Mr. Hawkins, now a washerwoman, and somewhat infirm. Family feeling is strong, no doubt, and they have taken against us, and cooked up a poisonous stew out of gossip and half-truths, as servants do. Forgive me, Mr. Hawkins, but if it is the tattle of servants you wish to hear, then really I had better hold my peace. My sister will, of course, corroborate my story; but then she is only a respectable clergyman's widow, and of course not to be believed."

Fairfax stared at the young lawyer, who looked coolly back. A lawyer, of course; and astute enough for ten such encounters as this. It is not proven that he is a murderer, Fairfax thought, and probably he has taken care that it cannot be proven, but he is definitely a brute and a liar.

"My dear sir," Hawkins said to his friend, "pray do not distress yourself further. We will, of course, make all the necessary inquiries, but they will not be swayed by rumor and slander."

"Oh, I fear nothing, Mr. Hawkins. I fear nothing; I have lost everything. But I wonder a little at you, Mr. Fairfax. You were seeking my missing wife, on behalf of the Stamford Bench who were anxious to trace her—very good; but did your remit include meeting her secretly, as you have just said you did, and keeping her whereabouts a secret not only from the authorities, but from me? From her husband who was half mad for the loss of her?"

"Half mad?" Griggs burst out. "You unholy liar, sir—you made that creature's life a burden to her! In my ministry I come across many such, but they are usually the wives of ignorant and drunken men sunk in poverty. But you—"

"I do not, I think, have to listen to such stuff," Parry said.

"Indeed—indeed," put in Mr. Hawkins, very red. "You should know better than to throw such unfounded accusations about, Mr. Griggs. I am far from pleased to see you in my jurisdiction at all. There was a good deal of trouble and tumult in the town last night, as a direct result of your pitching here to make your—your field preaching, as you call it. If I had my way you and your sort would not be permitted to sow these disturbances. I have had several men before me this morning on charges of disorder—"

"Not of the Methodist connection," Griggs said.

"That is immaterial. The trouble would not have started but for you. And it is my tentative conclusion—pending further inquiries—that it was a result of these disturbances that poor Mrs. Parry met her death. Disorder, enthusiasm, dispute, bad characters about—little short of riot, the constable tells me; and I am forced to say, women encouraged to be abroad late at night, thereby making themselves most vulnerable—it is a recipe for the direst consequences."

He has made up his mind, Fairfax thought grimly. He is not going to consider Parry as the killer, let alone commit him.

"What about the pistols?" he found himself saying—really his own puzzlement breaking out. "Was your wife in the habit of carrying them, Mr. Parry?"

"My wife's habits," he said grayly staring out of the window, "have long been a mystery to me."

"If there are questions to be asked, I will ask them," the magistrate snapped. "And all I ask of you now, Mr. Fairfax, is that you tell me where I may find you if needed. The same goes for you, Mr. Griggs. I may want a full deposition in time. Constable, we must carefully examine all the men who made an affray last night. Now where has the—the deceased been taken, pray?"

"I told 'em to bear her to the Bridge for now, sir."

"Very well. Mr. Parry, my dear sir, you may perhaps wish to—to see her. If so, let me accompany you; it will take me but a moment to dress . . ." The magistrate rang the bell and, having made a note of where they were to be found, waved Fairfax and Griggs away sharply.

Outside Griggs surprised Fairfax by spitting forcefully on the ground.

"Hypocrisy," he said.

Fairfax could only nod. William Parry the respectable wife-beater; and respectability would save him from being tried as a wife-murderer. That was, of course, if the Fryatt sisters were to be believed, as well as the evidence of his own eyes. Of course they were.

And perhaps, as Margaret's murder came to be properly investigated, the authorities would see such things to. But meanwhile William Parry would be further strengthening his defense . . .

"Gentlemen. Pray excuse me." It was Parry, who had come out of the magistrate's house after them. His face was sour, and he tipped his hat ironically. "I have to go and perform an unpleasant duty. I'm not entirely sure why it should be me. She was my next of kin in name only, after all, having chosen to forsake me."

"In the name of God, man, have some compassion," Griggs said through gritted teeth.

"Hm, in the name of God. Just to be secular a moment, sir, you seem to know a good deal about my wife."

"I know a soul in torment when I see one," Griggs said. "Thank God she is free now, and happy."

Parry put his head on one side, a deliberating look. "Well," he said, "she lived a whore, and died like one. A curious mistake you made, Mr. Fairfax. I assure you, a field preaching, with a lot of ragged fanatics, is the last place you would find me. Doubtless the heady emotions of the occasion spoiled your judgment." He walked away.

Fairfax was surprised to find Griggs's hand on his shoulder. " 'God is the judge: he putteth down one, and setteth up another,' " he said. "Well, I must go too. Say good-bye to Neavis and the brethren, and then for home. Justice in this world is no great matter, Mr. Fairfax, no great matter. God is the judge."

Twelve

The journey back from Huntingdon to Cheyney Hall was a wearisome one. The mare was tired, and Fairfax was aching and unrested from his night at the inn, and he was saddened and disappointed. A young woman who had lived unhappily had died wretchedly, and he was no nearer solving the mystery; it seemed that four deaths would go unpunished now instead of three. Near Alconbury, as afternoon came down, he saw a group of men trudging a field path between fox coverts, and recognized Twelvetree's armed servants. Still searching, then: another futile pursuit.

And his mind still nagged at the events of Tuesday—the attack on the *Flyer*. Pistols, pistols. A pair in Margaret Parry's pockets; and she had certainly been on that coach, part of the time. But a woman carrying a brace of pistols . . . ? Surely her murderer must have put them there, for some reason.

The alternative was to think of her using them—perhaps in concert with someone else. A freakish notion.

Unless her fear of her violent husband had been so great—and her determination to live likewise—that she had procured the pistols and carried them with her. Or someone had got them for her: a lover, perhaps? A useless precaution, as it turned out. Perhaps her killer had stolen on her swiftly, on the darkened common.

Fairfax kept thinking again of the three shots that had been needed to kill Charles Crabbe, Tom Honeyman, and

Jonathan Griggs. Two shots were all you got from a pair of pistols before they had to be primed and loaded again, with ball and powder. Easier perhaps with that good practical pair that he had seen on Mr. Hawkins's table, but still not a swift business. He had been thinking till now of the attacker shooting first the coachman, then Jonathan Griggs exposed on top, then Tom Honeyman inside . . . Yet if there were only one attacker, then he would have had to reload after shooting the coachman and Griggs, meanwhile giving Tom Honeyman, inside, ample time to present his own pocket pistols and fire at the assailant, probably indeed with a good chance of success. So it could hardly have been that order. Honeyman first, then, as soon as the coach was stilled. Which would leave poor Jonathan on the roof, or more likely tipped off it into the ditch, and surely presenting no threat requiring a reloading and a third shot. Odd.

Two assailants, then; or assailant and accomplice. An accomplice on the coach, in fact? None other than Margaret Parry? Yet that made no sense—for, after all, an accomplice in what? As far as he had learned, she was simply an unhappy, lonely woman who had made what seemed a good marriage, had found her husband a monster—and had fled from him. Even if she had found solace in someone else's arms—say, the charismatic preacher Henry Griggs—the essence of her plan had been simply to get away.

Again Fairfax came back to William Parry as the likeliest suspect. Parry stopping the coach, expecting his wife to be on it; systematically killing the passengers in a violent rage when he found she was not, and finding himself looking at the corpse of a man who knew him; Parry finally finishing the job last night, in the copsewood.

The best he could come up with. It did not satisfy him as before, because of something Mary Fryatt had said. Something about Parry and Selina Bland being more than brother and sister—or would be if Mrs. Bland had her way. Somehow that had the ring of conviction, more than his previous rash imaginings of something unspeakable going on be-

tween them. An unhealthily, uncomfortably close relationship, yes, with the sister's intense devotion bolstering the
man's self-important and dictatorial nature, and further cor-
roding his marriage. A faintly sickly and twisted setup: yes.
But nothing more. Servants saw much—everything, really;
and if there had been more, then Mary Fryatt would have
come out with it.

Too much imagination, as Sir Edward would say. But
without that, Fairfax could not find a reason for Parry to
have stopped the coach with the intention of killing his wife.
At that point he knew nothing of her deserting him; she was
apparently on her way back home. Later, when she was a
fugitive from him, his jealous rage might well be enough—
enough for what happened in the copse last night, for example. But on Tuesday . . .

Yet in his very first interview with Fairfax, Parry has spoken of his suspicions that his wife had a lover. Perhaps that
was the key. Perhaps during her absence at his sister's, he
had come upon some clue, arrived at some definite conclusion about Margaret's betrayal, and so had set out to meet
the coach and kill her. That at least fitted. But if that was the
case, what was the clue, and who was the lover? Was it
Griggs? Had Parry supposed that whoever the lover was, he
must be on that coach with her, and so slaughtered indis-
criminately? But that was more the behavior of a man of
passionate and undisciplined mind. Parry was nothing if not
tidy.

If someone stepped forward and said they were Margaret
Parry's lover, he might get somewhere. But short of that he
could not see how to convert his suspicions of William Parry
into certainty. He was stuck.

A few miles short of Stilton he needed to relieve himself.
Tethering the mare to a fence, he went into some trees by the
roadside, with a sympathetic thought for the poor shepherd
boy who had done the same with such horrifying results. He
went a good way in before he found a spot private enough

for his taste. He was just wending his way back when a shot rang out.

It was some distance away—but not so far that he didn't feel the disturbance of the air near his face, and hear the crack of the ball hitting a tree close by. It had come from behind him, so he hadn't been able to see the flash of the powder; and whirling round, he looked in vain for a figure in the direction the shot seemed to have come from—a long overgrown bridle path winding through stands of beech and disappearing into deeper woods beyond. Was that a flicker of movement?

Unarmed as he was, he didn't care to wait about. He hurried back to the mare and rode on, his glance darting among the roadside trees. A stray shot from a sportsman? Or had he just had a brush with the highwayman himself? The only other people abroad with guns would be—of course—Twelvetree's menservants on their fruitless quest. They had certainly looked a motley enough band to start taking pot shots at anything in the woods that moved. Not a comfortable thought . . . though better than the alternative that now occurred to him: someone following him, with elimination in mind. He urged the mare on. Four people had been killed ruthlessly; there was no reason to think he inspired any more pity than they had.

Sir Edward was furious with him.

At first, when Fairfax arrived at Cheyney Hall, the baronet was merely short with him: called his absence overnight a pretty trick, sarcastically hoped that great things had come of it, and begged him to consider his employer worthy of his confidence, next time he went a-jaunting . . . Then Fairfax told what had happened from beginning to end, and Sir Edward towered in his wrath.

If Fairfax had not liked and respected Sir Edward, he would not have minded. But he did, so he did. Probably there was a paternal element lurking somewhere. Though only a dozen years his senior, Sir Edward was so massively established and at home in the world, in a way Fairfax felt he never would be. He could not help but feel immature, gauche, and disappointing, and catch echoes of his flighty younger self, who had ignored his father's distresses of mind until they brought old Mr. Fairfax to the grave. Also he felt that some, at least, of Sir Edward's strictures were true.

"I trusted you to act as my agent, and gave you a good measure of freedom. But I expected you to remember that you *were* my agent, and not engaged upon a private quest that you could pick up and let go as the fancy took you. I would call you a Don Quixote, but at least he only charged flocks of sheep and tilted at windmills, while you have played with human lives."

"Believe me, sir, there was no though of *play* in my mind. I pursued my inquiries in the most earnest spirit, knowing full well—"

"Knowing full well that you were keeping me in the dark. I suspect a little vanity here, Fairfax. You thought to strike out on your own, and solve the case, and present the old fellow with the solution like a wrapped posy—hey? What a feather in your cap it would be. Good God, man, don't you realize I don't care how this business is settled, as long as it is, and no more lives are lost? No more lives, Fairfax—that was the main thing."

Fairfax could not speak.

"I don't say you could have prevented what happened to that poor woman. But damn it all, you could have stopped her going to Huntingdon in the first place. What was our one missing piece, eh? Margaret Parry. We'd plastered half the country with handbills about her. Then up she pops at the George, agrees to talk to you, sits at the same table with you. At last! And you let her go, without giving a proper account of herself—"

"She told me all she could, and I believe all there is to know."

"You let her go! Not even an address where she could be found—"

"Sir," Fairfax said, risking another interruption, "she was not a woman upon whom any man with a conscience could exert any kind of compulsion. If you had seen her, you would agree."

"Would I now? You add clairvoyance to your other talents? Damn it, man, I'm not talking of holding the woman down like a wrestler. Firmness was all that was needed: a firm declaration that the officers of the law needed to talk to her and that she must not skip off again. Assurances of safety, secrecy if needed, but she was to stay there and not go disappearing."

"It was only on a promise of confidence that she agreed to speak to me at all."

"Promise! We promise a child that it will not hurt when the splinter is pulled from its finger. We know it is not true, but it calms the child's mind. Mrs. Parry could soon have been brought to see that her best interest lay in cooperating with our investigation. Pander to her fears, yes, but never lose sight of the true goal."

About to speak, Fairfax held his peace. Liberal-minded as Sir Edward was in many respects, he still could not help equating a woman's mind and emotions with those of a child. Probably he would hotly deny it: he was not that sort of boor; but the tone of patronage crept in. And if it was a long way from there to the domineering violence of a William Parry, the two points were on the same road—so Fairfax couldn't help thinking.

And yet the fact remained that if he had pressed or persuaded Margaret Parry not to slip away again, when she met him at the George, then she might very well be alive now.

"Well, 'tis done now," Sir Edward grumbled. "At least a door is closed on that part of the business. I'll admit that her tale sounds probable—leaving the coach at Stilton, and so not being on board when it was attacked. Poor creature: she was not long spared. 'Twas unlikely at any rate that she could lead us to our rogue."

"Unless his name is William Parry."

Sir Edward gnawed his lip. "I don't know. I'll believe the man could be a brute to her—there's often a bully behind those spaniel-eyed types—even to the point of doing away with her. Suspicion will fall on him, even if this Hawkins is less than zealous in examining him; but it will be devilish hard to pin it on him. One cannot wholly rely on the testimony of servants—no, don't go all boiling and republican, Fairfax, I mean as a matter before the law, because they may not be seen as impartial: grudges and so on. And if his wife had strayed, as it were, then there will be prejudice against her on that account. You'll find men, of whom I am not one, by the way, who'll call her a whore just for going off like that. Well, if he did kill that poor creature, then I hope the evidence is found to hang him for it. But Parry as our man for the other crimes . . . ? I don't know. My money is on this Bennett Cornwell, or else some freebooting rascal of his type. Not that Twelvetree's men have had any success out in the woods, as yet anyway . . . And so you have made promises in my name to these browbeaten maidservants as well, have you, sir?"

"To Esther Fryatt. I—I counted on that generous nature for which you are renowned, Sir Edward."

"You needn't try and butter me up. Well, I will see what I can do for her. The other one, too; she'll no doubt be out of Parry's service now. This does not mean I am less displeased, Fairfax. Taking off on secret jaunts, and associating with ranting preachers . . . no, no, it won't do. Perhaps I was wrong to entrust you with this matter. At any rate, from now on you will be directed by me, sir. You will follow only my instructions, and if you should come across independent information, I shall look very poorly on any attempt to withhold it from me—very poorly, sir."

As a kind of penance, Fairfax spent the evening in the library, finding his way about old Sir Jemmy's collections. There were worse punishments. The books were an invitation to woolgathering, so he began making notes for his catalogue with the part of the collection he found least fascinating, the maps. Old Sir Jemmy had collected every-thing from beautiful specimens of Dutch and Portuguese cartography to the old town maps of John Speed to plans of neighboring estates and drainage systems drawn up by local surveyors. On one of these, about twenty years old, he no-ticed, as his eye ranged over numerous smaller farms, Mr. Devereaux's seat, Skellerby, among the scattered Lin-colnshire hamlets and ruler-straight dikes. That at least would be out-of-date, he thought, since Nicholas Twelvetree had bought up and enclosed the neighboring land. He won-dered what Twelvetree was doing now. Lurking in his pastille-scented apartments, probably, and gnawing over the failure of his men to bring back a fresh-caught highwayman from the woods.

At least he was not alone in his failure, then. He went to bed gloomy and chastened, yet with a tantalizing feeling that something crucially important had lately touched his mind, like breath condensing on glass, and then evaporated.

Thirteen

Early next morning, as he was finishing his dressing, Fairfax heard an insistent knocking at the front door of the house. It was Saturday, and tonight was the Stamford Assembly for which the Misses Nugent had been longing. Perhaps the knocking announced the delivery of some anxiously awaited piece of finery, he thought, going down.

Barbara Honeyman stood in the hall. She was in a riding habit, her skin glowing, out of breath. The footman was hovering near her, indecisive. It was no hour for calling, but knowing Mrs. Honeyman, Fairfax thought, she had refused to take no for an answer.

"I must speak with you," she said; and then, as if finding that inadequately dramatic, "I must speak out! I cannot contain it—it will burn me up inside!"

Sir Edward had appeared. "Mrs. Honeyman, I believe," he said, very urbane. "A surprise. Have you ridden over alone from Stamford? And on a cold morning."

"I would have ridden a hundred miles. Sir, I must speak out—"

"Certainly. Cardew, bring some chocolate to the parlor and have the ladies' breakfast served. Fairfax, come in, if you please."

He was not to be excluded then. In the parlor Barbara Honeyman sat down but refused the chocolate impatiently.

"I cannot eat or drink. I have such a frightful burden upon

my heart and there is no relief . . . I believe I know the man who is responsible for the death of my husband." She looked at their faces in turn, then made them both jump by clawing off her bonnet and seizing her tousled head in her hands. "God curse me for a fool! I should have know it—I should have spoken out sooner—but I have been half mad with grief . . ."

"Please ma'am, calm yourself. Take a moment, now," Sir Edward said. "You know we will do all we can on your behalf. Now, what is it you have to tell us?"

"I swear the man is Joseph Fox." She closed her eyes, drew herself up straight, a tragic statue. "I feel—positively degraded to speak of this; but I have long known that Joseph Fox has entertained an unmanageable regard—a passionate affection toward me. God knows I always did everything in my power to repulse it—to nip such a foul and illicit growth in the bud. But his partiality went beyond reason, and sometimes he would use the most unconscionable expressions, and attempt the most improper avowals . . . I never knew whether to speak to my husband of it. But Mr. Fox was an invaluable partner to him, and it was my husband's regrettable habit never to—to see what was under his very nose, nor to believe ill of anyone he liked. And as my own part was blameless, I resolved to bear the inconvenience and indignity, as a sacrifice to my husband's interests. I think I should not have done so, now; for the most horrible suspicion has grown and grown upon me . . ."

"You suspect that it was Mr. Fox who made the assault on the *Flyer*?" Sir Edward said.

"I wish I did not. But my heart screams out what my mind would deny."

"Yet Mr. Fox, by his own account, spent the whole of Tuesday at the timber yard adjoining your house," Fairfax said. "And you, Mrs. Honeyman, confirm that account."

"Yes. Oh, yes. And I hardly knew what I was doing. I was suddenly alone—and afraid. Never believe a woman when she says she is flattered by such attentions, sir. Those of Mr.

Fox have alarmed and disturbed me. A man who could entertain such a passion, while at the same time professing
friendship and regard for my husband . . . When he said that
he had been at the yard all day, I went along with it, out of
that same perturbation and fear. Perhaps also I did not wish
to believe real evil of the man who had been my husband's
closest friend. So I agreed with what Mr. Fox said. My Tom
was gone, and nothing much mattered; and also I did not
want Mr. Fox to know that I had been observing him, again
out of fear of him. But I did observe him that day. He was
not at the yard the whole time. Quite early in the morning,
when I had not long been astir, I saw him go to the stable,
and saddle up the one horse we keep, and ride off on it. And
he did not return until the afternoon." She paused, looked at
them both again. "He knew well, of course, that my husband
was taking coach to Huntingdon that day. And now that my
husband is dead, he has become—No, I was going to say
more particular in his attentions, but that is not so. He
seems—satisfied. As if he can bide his time." She gave a
broken laugh. "Bide his time! He may wait till eternity . . . I
would rather put a gun to my own head than . . . Well." She
abruptly stood up. "I had to speak out. If I am not believed,
no matter."

"Pray, Mrs. Honeyman, wait a moment," Sir Edward
said. "This is startling intelligence, and a serious charge to
lay against Mr. Fox. But don't assume that means we disbe-
lieve." He glanced at Fairfax. "Certainly Mr. Fox has some
explaining to do, as he stated so definitely that he did not
leave the yard all day. This must be looked into. Now, will
you not take a little chocolate to sustain you, while we consider what is to be done?"

He motioned Fairfax out of the room.

"Well, what think you of this, Fairfax?"

Fairfax was mature enough not to reply that it didn't matter what he thought . . . "A tissue of lies," he said.

Sir Edward's plumy eyebrows shot up. "She came all this
way so early, in some plain distress, to spin a yarn?"

"There is truth there somewhere, and something we don't know. I hold no brief for Joseph Fox: he has always been altogether too pat for my liking. But I can't swallow Mrs. Honeyman primly holding her peace while Fox rolls his lustful eyes at her across the yard, can you?"

Sir Edward smiled in spite of himself.

"And as for speaking out *now*—why?" Fairfax went on. "Mrs. Honeyman is a woman of sensibility; makes rather a cult of her spontaneous emotions. If she had suspected Fox, she would have said so from the start, surely, in no uncertain terms."

Sir Edward considered. "'Tis rum, though. Fox is hiding something, to lie like that. And he did make a point of collecting all those reports of our highwayman . . . Damn it, we'll go see Fox straightaway. We'll descend on him, the two of us, and frighten him a little. Grab a cold slice from the kitchen, Fairfax, and be ready to ride. Perhaps we'll get to the bottom of this today, and if we can, I'll dance a hornpipe with Mrs. Graveairs at the Assembly tonight, and sleep easy."

Presently they were riding out of the gates of Cheyney Hall alongside Barbara Honeyman. She sat a horse very well, Fairfax noticed: her country-genteel background, no doubt. She pronounced herself satisfied that they were going to interview Fox, but begged that she be excused accompanying them. They would find him at his lodging; she had forbidden him to come to Water Street. "I did not give the true reason. I said that in my grief I needed seclusion," she said.

"And how did he take that?" Fairfax said.

"He behaved in an unseemly and turbulent manner . . . I never wish harm to a fellow creature; yet in my heart I feel I would rejoice if he were put away—quite put away."

Coming into Stamford they parted at High Street St. Martin's. Sir Edward expressed a polite hope that Mrs. Honeyman would not be alone in the house.

"No, not alone."

"Your servant girl is there?"

"Yes: I didn't mean her." She gave a mysterious smile. "I am not alone, sir: not alone." She rode gracefully onto the turning of Water Street.

Shrugging, Sir Edward led the way into the George Inn to stable their horses. In the yard, they were greeted by a high-pitched shout.

It was Mr. Quigley, who came puffing over in high excitement. "I was just going to send a boy over to Cheyney, sir. There's news—at least, it's something new. Step into my parlor, sirs, if you will . . ."

In his private room the innkeeper unwrapped a linen bundle that lay on his desk. "These, sir, were found by a hedger last evening. He'd seen the handbills here, so he brought them in to me first thing this morning: honest fellow. They had been thrust into a hedge by the road—the Great North Road, sir, just past Stangate Hole, very near where the *Flyer* foundered. He was just thinking of packing up to go home when his sickle struck these."

A pair of pistols, a little scratched and dirty, but not very: they could not have lain in the hedge long. Pocket pistols, quite new, and very similar to the pair owned by Tom Honeyman. Almost identical, in fact. Fairfax picked one up, and read the mark on the barrel: *Whitaker & Son, Stamford*.

Sir Edward breathed heavily. "Fairfax, didn't you say—"

"That Fox had bought a brace of pistols of the same type, at the same time as his friend Tom Honeyman. Yes. Yes indeed."

"They're his, for a thousand pounds." Sir Edward clapped his hands. "Mrs. Honeyman may have spoken more truth than she knew. By God, we'll have him. If Mr. Fox don't explain himself, we'll have him, Fairfax, and I'll dance that hornpipe yet."

Joseph Fox's lodgings were a set of upstairs rooms in a narrow old slit called Red Lion Street. They found Fox only just risen, and rather seedy in shirt and breeches. He looked blearily at his visitors, scratching and scratching at the knot of hair at the base of his columnar throat, and then when Sir Edward wordlessly produced the pistols he sat down heavily on a wooden settle.

"I doubt you will be foolish enough to deny they are yours," Sir Edward said. With a flick of his coattails he sat down on another settle opposite the first. With these, and the old wormy paneling, and a smell of tobacco smoke, and several empty bottles and tankards among the tin candlesticks and old newspapers, the place was more like a bar-parlor than a private dwelling.

"No, they're mine." Fox rubbed his face with both hands, producing a loud rasp. He was one of those men who can never be really close-shaven.

"And you know where they were found, I suppose?" Sir Edward said. "Come, sir, we are not playing a game here. This is a very serious matter. It is not just these, but a grave accusation that has come our way. From Mrs. Honeyman."

The whites, or rather yellows, of Fox's eyes flashed. "What—what did she say?"

"Perhaps we should hear you first."

Fox shook his heavy head, seemingly with profound weariness. "Oh, Barbara, Barbara . . ."

Fairfax raised his eyebrows at Sir Edward, and said, "You use a familiar name, Mr. Fox."

"Of course I do," he said dully. "We—oh, well, Tom is dead now, and it can't hurt him. Barbara and me—we've been lovers for some time. I'm not ashamed—but then I'm not proud of it neither. It should never have happened, I know. But there it is. It started about six months ago, perhaps a little less. These things don't run according to reason: that's their nature. She hasn't told you any of this, I suppose?"

"Her account is quite otherwise," Fairfax said. "She accuses you of unwanted attentions; and also claims that you were not at the yard all day on Tuesday— that you rode away for much of the day."

Fox nodded. "Yes. Yes, well, that follows. I daresay I should have expected this, after yesterday." He began to hunt among the bottles, found one that was half full, and poured a glass; then wagged the bottle at them, with a shade of his old earthy cordiality. "No? Wise, sirs, wise. Never mind. I need a little strengthening, because I have a terrible thing to say. It is not that I killed my friend Tom Honeyman—which doubtless you are thinking now. No. But Mrs. Honeyman is right in one regard. I did leave the yard on Tuesday. And I did throw those pistols into the hedge." He drank deeply, gasping. "You see, the terrible thing I have to say is that I did ride out on Tuesday, with the intention of stopping the Stamford coach, and shooting my friend Tom dead."

"This is very interesting, my friend," breathed Sir Edward.

"No, it isn't. It's a very old story, and it ain't a nice one. I don't know how to explain it. Barbara—she is an entrancing woman. A woman of great spirit also, which perhaps was not very suitable for Tom, who was more of a reflective soul. Oh, he doted on her, no doubt of it. But sometimes I think a woman wants more than to be doted on. Perhaps sometimes it's more of an irritation . . ." He rubbed his hand across his eyes. " 'Twas easy enough for us, with me so near at hand at the yard. Tom would go off on business sometimes, and—well, you don't want to hear about that. I've no excuse, sirs, don't think I look for one. All I can say is I'm a warm man, with a man's desires and needs. And yes, I envied Tom—but not in a nasty jealous way, if that makes sense. I always thought what he had looked wonderful—home and wife, and children maybe to follow. And that thought was still part of it, even while I was—betraying him. And that was how I came to think—along with Barbara—that if he wasn't there, then it might be mine."

"So you planned to kill him," Fairfax said. "And what better plan than that you should waylay him traveling in a coach, and shoot him there, so that it would seem like the crime of a highwayman. After all, you had long studied our highwayman's activities, when you and Tom hatched that scheme of yours; and you still had the brace of pistols you had bought then. You did not, as you told me, dispose of them to a tinker."

"Aye. That was the way of it. Except it was Barbara who came up with the notion, at the end of last week, when Tom said he planned to travel to Huntingdon on Tuesday. Back when me and Tom had had that little scheme in mind, to lure the highwayman and get the bounty, Tom had kept it secret from Barbara. Didn't want to worry her, maybe. Well, I did mention it to her—after we'd abandoned it—and she was curious, and then she laughed. I think she thought Tom could never have gone through with a scheme like that. She could be a little . . . down on him. Well, last week when Tom said he was going to Huntingdon, she came to me and said this was a chance—a chance to get rid of him. Oh, she didn't use those words. That ain't her way of talking, she's more poetical, she carries you along . . ."

"Indeed," Fairfax said dryly. He could well imagine Barbara Honeyman making the proposed killing of her husband sound like an urgent necessity to free her throbbing spirit.

"And it would be easy, she said. I had only to mask my face, and wait at a place where the highwayman was known, and do the deed . . . and no one would ever know. She would say I was at the yard all day, if anyone suspected; but it wouldn't come to that. The crime would just be blamed on the highwayman. It sounds as if I'm blaming her. I'm not. I agreed to do it, that's the terrible thing. It was me who was going to put the plan into—execution." He winced at the word. "And then we would be together, always: with no hiding. She would sell up, and move away from here, and I'd go with her . . . I had the vision of it in my head. And somehow I convinced myself that—that it was *better* like that than going on as we were, betraying Tom, sneaking behind his back . . ."

"Oh, yes," Sir Edward said with a snort. He was pale and

trembling. "Better to put a bullet in your friend's head, kinder altogether, oh, yes, I see that."

"I don't expect you to see, sir," Fox said, mildly and deferentially, "because it doesn't make sense. I know that. I'm just saying how it was. I'm not much of a thinker; I'm driven more by my blood. And my blood took over. Do it, says she: I will do it, says I, and as soon as Tom had left on Tuesday morning, I took horse and rode swift as may be down the North Road. I went round by the Peterborough road at first, and then joined the main road at Stilton. I knew I was ahead of the *Flyer*. I went on to a quiet spot near Stangate Hole, and there I got among some trees, and primed my pistols, and tied a handkerchief about my face, and settled to wait." He refilled his glass and gave a chuckle. "Funny thing. Neither of us—Barbara and me, I mean—had any notion that Tom had decided to try that old scheme on his own, and that he was going after the highwayman that day, while I was going to play the highwayman's part. Strange doings, eh? But perhaps I should have had an inkling that Tom was up to something like that . . ."

Fairfax said, "Why?"

"Well, here we come to it. Tom had told me something just the day before, when we were down at the wharf. Barbara, he said, is going to have a child." Fox held up the bottle, then began to search, grim-faced, for another. "He was delighted. Couldn't get over it. He'd longed for this. But Barbara, he said, was—well, less than delighted, it seemed to him. 'I think perhaps it's the ticklish question of our finances, old friend,' he says to me, in that way he had. And of course, the business was no gold mine, and he wasn't really best suited to it; and here was another mouth to feed on the way. So maybe that was what set him to thinking about going after the reward for the highwayman. A hundred pounds would come in mighty useful. And I think besides he—he maybe wanted to show what he was made of. Well, anyhow, Barbara told me about the baby later that day, when we got on our own for a space . . . You're going to ask whose the child is. I couldn't say." He gave a smile of dreadful pain. "All I know is Tom said to me how delighted and—and surprised he was; because, says he quietly, 'Barbara doesn't like me to bother her too often.'"

There was a silence. Outside there was a clatter of horses on the cobbles, and the sound of someone shouting.

"And so you were prepared to kill your friend," Sir Edward said.

"Yes, sir. That's what I said." Fox set his jaw. "And there my shame ends, though it's shame enough. I waited among the trees by the road, and I got to thinking more and more, especially about what Tom had told me the day before. I thought and thought, until my head seemed like it would burst. And the next thing I know I was riding out of there, and I threw those damn pistols into a hedge, never wanting to see 'em again; and I rode back to Stamford via the by-roads, and I had three or maybe four drinks along the way. Call it six.

"I was pretty well weary and—empty like, when I got back to Water Street. She was waiting. I just said, 'I didn't do it,' and I laid my head down in the warehouse on some sacks, and slept. She tried to rouse me; I didn't want to talk to her again. Unfair maybe. Well, when I woke come evening, it was to the news that Tom hadn't come home, and that the *Flyer* had been attacked. And Barbara says to me, quite calmly, 'We must go up to the George, and see what's going on.' And she looked at me, deeplike, and kissed me, and went to put on her bonnet. And that's when it began to dawn on me that she thought I had gone through with it after all, and that I just couldn't abide to speak of it. As we left to come over to the George, I says to her again, 'Barbara, I didn't do it—I didn't kill Tom,' and she just looked at me, in that melting way of hers, and says, 'Of course you didn't, Joseph. Hush. Don't speak of it.' And that's how she carried on.

We met you for the first time then, sirs, and we went to see the bodies—and there was Tom shot to death. My God.

That was how it would have been if I had gone through with it. I don't know what I was feeling. A million things. Shame, yes, of course shame—I'd been living with shame. Shame was the fool I ate and the air I breathed . . . but I think I felt the greatest shame then. Because here was the object achieved: here was Tom gone, and I didn't even have to bear the slightest weight of responsibility for it. What a gift . . . And then I felt more dirty and foul than if it had been me who had pointed the pistol at my friend. I even felt that I should have been the one to do it after all, if he was doomed to die anyway, because I know that if I had done it, and seen that blood come red from his throat as I saw it all dried and black in the morgue, then I'd have turned the other pistol on myself there and then. Oh, yes, and at least then there'd have been one less worthless wretch in the world."

He began to cry, a noisy explosion that settled into deep, retching sobs. His sturdy body shook with them. For minutes he could not speak. Sir Edward looked at the floor.

"Well," Fox said at last, wiping his eyes with his fist, boylike, "that was pretty much it. Still she took no notice when I said I hadn't done it. She thought it was shame and fear, I suppose; perhaps even thought I was doing a mighty good job of acting out my innocent part. She's a pretty actress herself . . . At last when I tried to get it into her head that I hadn't done it, she stopped saying, 'Don't talk of it' and started to listen. Last night it was. I sat her down, and made her listen. I kept talking of the others who had been killed. Did she really think I had done that too? Shot a couple of innocent people to death while I was about it?"

"Well, after one innocent person, why not two more?" Sir Edward said heavily.

Fox looked at him, then nodded. "So she may have thought. Yes, that I had done the job that thoroughly, left no one alive to tell the tale, I suppose. And all for her. She seemed—almost thrilled by it. And then, when she began to believe the truth, she was strangely angry. If I had not done it after all, then that showed that I had balked at it—that I

had not loved her enough to do it. I said yes: yes, that's right.
And that's when truth came shouldering in between us, for
the first time, I think, in all the fantasy we had had together.
Then she rallied a bit. Said it was providence, or some such,
and we must look to the future: sell up, go away, just as we
had planned . . . I couldn't believe that she really couldn't
see. I let her talk on, and then I said to her that it was all
over; she must know that. It was impossible—perhaps from
the moment I threw away the pistols and came back, perhaps
even from the moment poor Tom confided to me that he was
going to be a father. But it was certainly impossible now.
There has to be . . . respect. Perhaps that sounds absurd. But
as I stood looking at her, I knew there was none, none at all.
I couldn't respect myself, ever; she certainly didn't respect
me. And I couldn't respect her, though I still felt a kind of
tormenting love for her.

"Well, she went wild. She raged at me. She said I was in
her power. She said she would admit that she had lied about
my being at the yard all day, and point to me as the killer. By
then I was—I was almost bored. I hate the tail end of things;
I like things clean-cut. And I didn't much care what she did
anymore, just so long as we weren't tangled up together. I
said to her: do it. I had no fear. What did it matter? I had no
doubt that she would do it, so I wasn't surprised to see you
here today. She wasted no time. What does it matter?"

Fox gave a great shrug, and in his eyes there seemed to
Fairfax to be a desperate appeal, as if he were begging them
to make sense of it for him. A simple, straightforward man,
of strong and basic appetites, caught in the toils of a situation that was not simple or straightforward at all. And
yet . . .

"And yet you were prepared to kill your best friend, to
have his wife," Fairfax said.

Fox smiled quite gently and wistfully. "You can say it all
you like, sirs, but the nail's already deep in, and you can't
hammer it farther. If you wanted to think up a punishment
for me, I don't think you could invent a worse one than hav-

ing to live with that knowledge, every day, for the rest of my life." He pointed to the pistols. "Perhaps you'd take those away with you."

"We shall certainly take them away," Sir Edward said. "But I am not sure if we are going just yet, sir. You have given us much to think of. There is no one, I suppose, to corroborate this extraordinary story?"

Fox flushed, and his unsteady hand banged his glass back on to the table. "D'you think I'd tell such a lie against myself?"

"Rather than face hanging for murder." Sir Edward beamed pleasantly. "I daresay any man would."

Fox looked suddenly weary. He slumped back in his seat. "You may think what you please, sirs, really. I'm past caring. I've told you the truth of it, and mebbe I should have told it before; but I have been more damnably confused and beset than ever man was in this plaguey world."

A man more sinned against than sinning, Fairfax thought. Well, perhaps it comforted him to think so.

Sir Edward was gesturing him to rise. "Well, sir," the baronet said, "what you've told us must be carefully considered. I think it likely we shall need to talk to you again. You will not think of going away, will you?"

"I'm going nowhere," Fox said dully.

"And I'd advise against your trying to have any communication with Mrs. Honeyman also."

Fox chuckled, reaching out for his glass. "Even less likely, sir. Even less likely . . ."

Outside Sir Edward tapped his lips with his riding crop and stared into Fairfax's eyes. "For two pins," he said after a moment, "I'd commit him here and now."

"Then—pardon me, sir—why don't you?"

"Because we have no corroborative evidence against him. Because it's his word against Mrs. Honeyman's. And then there's these damned pistols . . ."

"Which, if he had done the deed, he would surely take

more trouble to hide rather than tossing them into a hedge on the road."

"Hm . . . What the devil's all that noise?" There was more shouting in Broad Street. "Worse than St. Peter's Fair . . . Aye, that doesn't fit. And on top of that—confound it, I more than half believe him. Yet he's one of these plausible plain-speaking fellows, and I always suspect a touch of the Iago in them. I don't know. I think what is needed is another approach—a very *careful* approach—to Mrs. Honeyman." Sir Edward stared up the street. "Now just what *is* going on there . . . ?"

What was going on was something between a street party, a riot, and the conclusion of a fox hunt. But at the center of the crowd gathered before Twelvetree's bank was not a defenseless animal being torn to pieces, though some of the crowd seemed anxious to do a little tearing nonetheless: it was a man riding a horse. At least, he was sitting on the horse, but his hands were bound behind his back, and one of Twelvetree's servants was leading the horse by the bridle. Twelvetree's servants indeed, were the nucleus of the crowd, some mounted, some forming a kind of foot guard around the bound figure, and they were making the most noise, yelling and cursing and laughing and giving themselves three cheers like boys who had successfully completed a dare. One even lifted the musket he was carrying and was about to fire a shot into the air, before the beefy hand of one of his more temperate fellows stopped him.

And wonder of wonders, Fairfax realized as he and Sir Edward elbowed their way through the crowd, Nicholas Twelvetree was there too. He had actually come out of the bank as far as the steps, supported on each side by his clerks like some heraldic figure of avarice rampant. Or revenge rampant, Fairfax thought, seeing the expression on the banker's face as he looked down at the man on horseback.

"We brought him to your door, sir." One of the menservants, assuming the role of leader—a gamekeeper, judging by his corduroy and gaiters—swept off his hat and presented his musket in a very rough approximation of military style. "Delivered fresh, as you might say." There were laughs and cheers. "He didn't want to come, but we persuaded him!"

Laughing nervously, his eyes alight, Nicholas Twelvetree nodded and nodded. "'Twas well done—well done, men. You shall be rewarded."

No sound or movement from the man on horseback. He was a tall narrow-chested, bony young fellow, dressed in a riding coat that had seen much wear, with a cocked hat pushed back to show a pale hollow-cheeked face. He looked neither wretched nor defiant at being bound and paraded thus. He looked, Fairfax thought, simply patient.

"What goes on here?" Sir Edward had soon thrust himself to the front, glaring at the bound man and then at Twelvetree on his perch. "Sir, will you explain this exhibition?"

"Ah, Sir Edward, the very man I want to see. You have saved me the trouble of sending for you, though one of the other magistrates would have done just as well." Twelvetree in his triumph was taking less care than usual to be agreeable. "As you can see, my men have had a signal success. They have brought in your highwayman. The name"—he raised his voice as there was a bellow from the crowd—"the name of that man is Bennett Cornwell. I have, alas, reason to know it."

Bennett Cornwell, sitting straight in the saddle—straight as a soldier, indeed—looked expressionlessly at the gloating man on the steps, and then looked away. Someone shied mud that hit his shoulder; still there was no expression.

Sir Edward addressed him. "Is that your name, sir?"

The young man inclined his head. "It is."

"Where did you find this man?" Sir Edward said. "And have you a reason for restraining him in this way? I warn you, I won't tolerate the workings of a mob."

"Found him where you'd expect him," the gamekeeper said, sticking out his chest. "Deep into Monks Wood. In an old drover's hut tucked in a clearing—snug a place as you ever saw, shored up with hurdles, and all set about with cut branches and furze. This old nag tethered outside. Turf fire inside, and a straw mattress in front of it. And him a-lying on it! Caught him there like rabbit in a trap!"

Eyes gleaming, Sir Edward said, "Cornwell, is this true? Speak man. There is no room for aught but the truth, now!"

"Yes," Cornwell said, almost with uninterest, "yes, that's where they found me."

"That's not all we found," the gamekeeper shouted over the swelling hubbub. "Pass me that pack, Sam. Now—here's a sample of the wares he had in there." Unfastening a leather satchel, he drew out a pocket watch and chain, flourishing them around like an auctioneer. "And these . . ." A collection of silk handkerchiefs, an embroidered purse. The crowd bayed, though Fairfax heard a different note in their cries now—a touch of admiration. Here at least was the legendary glamour and daring of the highwayman.

Twelvetree seemed to hear it too, and called out, "Some of the spoils of his crimes, Sir Edward, you see. And let us not forget that the other spoils lie in the churchyard. I think now you will concede that my men did right to apprehend this dangerous villain?"

Sir Edward gazed at the impassive face of Bennett Cornwell, then nodded. "It was well done . . . Sir, have you anything to say?"

The young man did not look at him. "Nothing."

"Sir Edward, surely now is the time for you to do your part," Twelvetree said. "As Justice of the Peace you can commit this fellow for trial, and there are surely sufficient grounds—"

"I know the law, damn it," said Sir Edward. "And I'll not have its proceedings bawled out in the public street. Disperse these men of yours, Twelvetree. Their spirits are up, and they're like to cause a nuisance. I'll examine the man privily, if a place can be found. Wait—I have it: Fairfax, step up to Mr. Devereaux's house, by St. John's. Present my compliments, and ask him if we may have the use of a room."

Fairfax did so, and found Mr. Devereaux, in his wry aloof way, quite agreeable. "So, they have caught him at last," he said, shaking his head. "I shall be interested to see this fellow again. Oh, Jane, open up the curtains in the front drawing room. We are to have visitors."

Caught him at last, Fairfax thought. Was it so? Was this to be the end of it? Well and good, if so. It was absurd to resent the fact that Nicholas Twelvetree had succeeded where he had failed . . .

Sir Edward directed that Bennett Cornwell's hands be untied, and bound more loosely in front of him and insisted that only the gamekeeper and one other of Twelvetree's posse enter the house with him to give their evidence. In Mr. Devereaux's elegant drawing room, still half covered with dust sheets, Sir Edward sat and stared at the impassive prisoner while his captors repeated their story. It looked bad for him, Fairfax thought. Suspected poachers had only to be apprehended with a snare in their possession to be convicted. What of a man found in a hideout in the woods, close to a notorious highwayman's haunt, with stolen goods all about him?

"Well, Cornwell, what do you have to say?" Sir Edward said. "You must know why you are brought here before me. The roads hereabout have been plagued by armed robberies of late, culminating in a shocking and murderous attack on the public coach this very week. Mr. Twelvetree's men—your stepfather's men, I should say"—Sir Edward frowned—"have been combing the woods looking for a robber's hideout, and it would seem they have found one. Do you deny that place is as they have described, and that you were in it?"

"No," Bennett Cornwell said, looking about him mildly. "All that is true."

Sir Edward motioned to the gamekeeper. "Lay those goods upon the table here, my man. Now. Here is a pocket watch, silk handkerchiefs—marked, I see, with various initials—and also a purse . . ." He held it up to the light. "Good heavens—it is embroidered here with the initials T. J. D. I believe, Devereaux, this must be yours."

"It is," Mr. Devereaux said, taking the purse lightly in his hand. "Well, you have spent the money that was in it, I suppose, young man. I daresay you thought I could spare it."

Bennett Cornwell faintly smiled.

"How do you explain this, Cornwell?" Sir Edward said, his face mottled with impatience. "How did you come by these goods?"

"I do not deny that I was in the place these men have described," Cornwell said quietly. "Nor that these goods were also in that place. But I did not steal them from their owners."

"You received them, then," Sir Edward said.

"No," Cornwell said, with a slow blink of his gray, heavy-lidded eyes. "I know nothing of them."

Sir Edward blew out a sharp breath. "If you think to make a fool of me, sir, and of the law, then you are mistaken. And you are mistaken if you think this insufficient evidence for me to commit you on suspicion of highway robbery. It is more than sufficient. And your silence suggests nothing to me but the perplexity of guilt."

"I have done nothing wrong, sir," Cornwell said with a slight shrug, "and so I have nothing to tell you."

"You were sent to the House of Correction at the end of last year, were you not? And released after a month's hard labor. Where have you been, and what has been your occupation since then?"

"I joined a coastal ship from Boston for a time, before returning to these parts quite lately."

"And deciding to live in a hideout in Monks Wood, I see."

"I was there because I was looking for someone," Cornwell said with sudden distinctness. "Someone whom I have been searching for, and thought I might find there. I used it as a place to sleep, while I searched. Also, I hoped that the person might come back to it."

Sir Edward stared. "And who is this 'person,' sir?"

"That I cannot tell you, " Cornwell said, quite composed.

"You cannot. Do I take that to mean you will not?"

"As you please, sir: yes. I will not say that person's name, and I daresay I cannot be compelled to."

"Nor will you say why you were looking for this person, I suppose," Sir Edward said, with an expression of sheer disbelief.

Cornwell thought, sucking his tongue. "To help the person, sir."

Sir Edward had heard enough. "Well, man, you had better think about helping yourself. You have given me not a single good reason why I should not commit you."

"I suppose not. I can only protest that I am innocent, sir, quite innocent of any charge. That is enough to support my soul. But, I would add, you spoke of armed robberies and I am not armed. These men searched me; and I do not think there were any firearms found in the hut where I was taken."

Sir Edward glanced at the gamekeeper, who shuffled uneasily. "True enough, sir. We didn't find any such."

"Well . . . it proves nothing. They might have been well hidden. And that is a point that can be determined later, when you come to trial. You know, Cornwell, I have no choice but to commit you to jail, to stand trial at the next quarter sessions, on suspicion of highway robbery and murder."

A constable had been summoned to escort Bennett Cornwell to the "Cage"—the lockup at the south end of High Street St. Martin's. He had gone quietly. Meekly, Fairfax would have said; it was hard to imagine him as the wild ne'er-do-well. But then there was something immutably stubborn about the set of his narrow jaw . . .

"An odd fish," Sir Edward said, gratefully accepting a glass of Mr. Devereaux's claret. "Yet he must be our man. I can see no other explanation. Short of catching him *in flagrante delicto*, we could hardly do better. Far be it form me to want to oblige Nicholas Twelvetree in anything, but I am afraid that stepson of his has much to answer for, and he will answer with his life if the court convicts him. I had no choice. Even you, Fairfax, with your contrary ways, must see that."

Fairfax refrained from pointing out that just a short time ago Sir Edward was favoring Joseph Fox as a chief suspect. "It does indeed look exceeding bad for him," he said. "I'm puzzled about this person he was searching for, though. It's a curious thing to invent."

"An accomplice, d'you think? 'Tis possible. Maybe there was a falling-out between 'em or some such. Though it seemed more as if he was trying to protect the fellow—devil knows why . . . Well, if we've netted one bird, we may easily net its mate."

"Yes . . . Would you be agreeable to my talking to him at the jail? He may be induced to let something more slip, even if inadvertently."

"I've no objection. And don't give me that look, my dear fellow. What I said yesterday still stands. You act as my agent, not on your own account. You my dig all you please, for I'll admit you've a rare talent for it. But don't keep your diggings to yourself, sir: no more secrets. In fact, while you're about it, you might step over and see what Mrs. Honeyman has to say for herself, after our friend Fox's curious revelations. We may clear that up into the bargain."

"Indeed. And I shall see you dance that hornpipe, Sir Edward."

"Impudent pup. In truth I have a very good leg for dancing. But you have reminded me: I've promised Letitia a choker for her outfit this evening. Another glass of that, Devereaux, if you'll be so good, and then I must be about my shopping. I'll see you back at Cheyney, Fairfax, if our paths don't cross before."

Several carriages were making their way up St. Mary's Hill as Fairfax headed for the jail: people coming in for tonight's Assembly, no doubt. It was starting to rain again, hard fat drops from black rafters of cloud. There would be spoiled dancing shoes tonight if it kept up and stirred the mud of the streets.

The Cage was well named, though few animals would have lingered long in such conditions. The jailor who admitted Fairfax to the single grated cell stank of liquor, as well he might in such a pestilential spot. The dingy light revealed Bennett Cornwell sitting on the edge of one of the board bunks, an open book in his hand. The other occupant of the cell was man so far gone in alcoholism his face was more raspberry than flesh, curled up half comatose on a bunk.

Fairfax resisted an impulse to cover his nose with his handkerchief; the smell would wear off . . . He introduced himself.

"I have said all I have to say to the magistrate," Cornwell said, and turned a page of his book. Fairfax saw that it was a pocket Bible, well thumbed.

"You have a resource, I see."

"The only resource man needs."

"You remind me of someone I know." Fairfax sat down on a straw-covered bunk opposite, trying not to think of lice. "Mr. Cornwell, forgive me, but I have learned something of your history, and I believe that you were not always devout."

"I was not." The very young, slightly haggard eyes bored into him. "But I prefer to think of my previous self as—another man. My feet were set on a rock of salvation quite lately, and I date my true life from then." He waved a bony hand at his grim surroundings. "That's why this does not trouble me. I am unjustly placed here, but I put my faith in a higher justice."

"I admire such faith, very sincerely. But I urge you to consider that the earthly court—the court of quarter sessions—is a different matter. It deals with earthly things like evidence and witnesses, and that court is going to try you for a highwayman, and if it finds you guilty, hang you."

Bennett Cornwell closed the Bible, though keeping a finger in his place. "You say you have learned of my history, sir. May I ask what it is you have learned?" He had a rather high-pitched, unsteady voice, a voice suggestive of a strongly emotional nature, despite the stiff-backed composure.

"Well, that you are the son of Mrs. Jane Cornwell, who married Mr. Nicholas Twelvetree. That you conceived a violent disaffection for Mr. Twelvetree, and after your discharge from the army, and your mother's death, your approaches to your stepfather were met with repulses which made you quite hate him, even to the point of vandalizing his property. For which he made sure you were put in the House of Correction."

Cornwell inclined his head, eyes unblinking.

"I also know that you had a friendship with Mr. Twelvetree's former clerk, one Tom Honeyman. You stayed at his house when you were without a lodging, and gave him a snuffbox in lieu of your keep. But this friendship would seem to have lapsed, as when you were seen at his house quite recently, there were high words between you."

Cornwell looked away. "Tom is a good fellow," he said. "But wrong about a lot of things."

"Was. Tom Honeyman was one of the dead in the attack on the coach in which you are accused. Did you not know that?"

"No . . ." Cornwell shook his head. "I . . . no . . . Poor Tom. God rest him . . . Sir, I am not a man to take life. That may sound odd coming from a man who has been a soldier. But, I repeat, that was in my former life, before I was newborn, when I trod the devil's highway instead of the path of righteousness."

"You are a Methodist."

"I found salvation with a member of that connection, yes. It was when I was in the House of Correction. A man came, simply out of charity and goodness, to speak to us there, and pray with us, and urge us to mend. He made a powerful impression upon me—so powerful that at first I resisted it. I wrestled with my soul long and hard, even after I was released, but at last I was convinced of sin, and I knew a joy such as . . . well, my old dissipations, what I called joys, were mere dross beside it."

"Was the man a preacher named Henry Griggs?"

"You know him, sir? He is a wonderful spirit! I feel I truly owe him my life. I heard him preach again just the other day. I heard word that he was to lead a revival at Huntingdon, and so I put aside my . . . my searchings for a day to go and hear him. I longed to speak to him again, but the meeting was broken up most shamefully, and I missed the chance. But I felt the spirit of Christ again, moving in me with renewed strength, and so I have no fears."

"I was there myself. Yes, I know Griggs. It was his brother, sir, who was the other passenger killed on the *Flyer*."

Cornwell went white. "That good man's brother? No, no. Surely he would not . . ."

"Who is *he*? And what wouldn't he do? Come, Mr. Cornwell, you know your case could hardly be worse, and this silence can make it no better. Who is this person you say you are seeking? And why do you seek him?"

"I seek him," Cornwell said very carefully, "because I believe that anyone can be redeemed. Even the greatest sinner. Indeed there is more rejoicing in heaven over one sinner that repenteth—"

"Yes, than ninety and nine just men, I know about all that," Fairfax said impatiently. "But what sins? Bennett, you know everything points to you as the highwayman that the law has been desperate to lay hold of. If you want the authorities to believe that you were only looking for some other person who uses that hideout—if you want *me* to believe it—then you must name that person."

After a long moment the young man shook his head. He stood up, putting his face to the trickle of light at the grating. "I believed I could save him," he said softly. "I still believe it . . . I must believe it . . ." He folded his hands and closed his eyes.

"Prayer will not help you," Fairfax said harshly.

Cornwell gave an enigmatic smile and opened his eyes. "There speaks an ignorant man. Oh, I mean no insult. I was one such. And I am thinking quite seriously of what you've said, sir."

"But still you will not tell me." Fairfax got up. "Is there anyone else you would wish to speak to?"

Cornwell thought. "Only Mr. Griggs. He is a man in whom I could place complete trust. I'd give anything to pray with him, here. We might wreak great things with the spirit, I think. But he has much to do."

"If I can fetch Griggs here," Fairfax said, "would you consider talking to me again?" He saw Cornwell's face light up. "Well, is it a bargain?"

"I must reflect, and ask God what to do. No one could be of more aid than that good man. I cannot promise you anything, sir. But if I could speak with Mr. Griggs it would make a great difference to me."

"Very well. And remember, Bennett, there are three people killed. No earthly or heavenly purpose can be served, surely, by hiding the truth of that."

He had made a promise; now how to fulfill it? Griggs had spoken of going home to Eaton Socon, a good distance way. Well, he must be sent for. A brother of the Methodist connection, languishing in jail and asking for his spiritual ministration, was surely the sort of summons Griggs could not resist. Fairfax found a solution in the jailor's young son, a youth who had had a job as postilion at the Blue Boar before it closed down, the jailor had a serviceable horse, and for two shillings the lad was more than happy to ride to Eaton Socon and give a note to Mr. Griggs the seedsman, which Fairfax hastily wrote and tore from this pocketbook.

"At least the North Road'll be safe to travel on now," the jailor grunted, jerking a thumb at the Cage, "with him safe in there."

Was it? Fairfax still didn't know what to believe. Maybe Bennett Cornwell was the killer, and, in a state of religious mania, simply refused to acknowledge the fact even to himself. Maybe he was hoping to pin all the blame on an accomplice. And maybe he was completely innocent.

The rain was coming down harder as Fairfax turned into Water Street and knocked at the old sunken door of the Honeyman house. For some moments he heard confused noises within, and he was about to knock again when the little serving maid flung open the door, her face a mask of terror.

"Oh, sir, thank God! Help, please, I don't know what to do—the mistress, the mistress, she's half dead . . ."

He found Barbara Honeyman in the hall, lying at the foot of the dark carved staircase. There was a red mark on her face and grazes on her hands, though she seemed otherwise unhurt. She groaned and her eyelids fluttered. Then, as Fairfax bent over her, she flung her arms up in front of her face, screaming out.

"No—no, don't—no more . . ."

"Mrs. Honeyman, it's all right, it's me—be calm, it's all right . . . What happened here?"

"I don't rightly know, sir," the girl said. "I was in the kitchen, and then I heard a dreadful thumping noise, and a screaming—and I come through and here she was . . ."

"Is he still here? Is he gone?" Barbara Honeyman levered herself up, wild-eyed, clutching at her stomach. "I'm so afraid—"

"Who, ma'am?" Fairfax put a supporting arm around her shoulders. "Who was here?"

"Fox. He came in—through the back—like a madman. Assaulted me—struck me most cruelly—I tried to fight him—he ran when I screamed . . . Oh!" She grasped her stomach, shrieking. "Oh—such pain . . ."

"Run for a doctor," Fairfax said to the girl, who scurried off. "Mr. Honeyman, can you stand? Where are you hurt?"

"I don't . . . I don't need a doctor. As long as he's gone—

tell me he's not here—he was terrible, murderous, I swear he meant to kill me . . ."

Fairfax took her through to the parlor, laid her down on the settle by the fire. The rear door, he saw, stood open. He went out, past the outhouses, down to the warehouse and wharf. No sign of anyone. The brick path, he noticed as he came back, was wet and muddy, but there were no traces of footprints in the parlor.

He sat down by her. "There's no one around now," he said. "You're sure it was Fox?"

She gave him an agonized look. "How could I not be? He was—all but on top of me. Why is he free? Did you not go to him this morning, after what I told you? Why is he not in jail?"

Fairfax decided now was not the time to challenge her. "We are still making our inquiries into that matter," he said. "Rest easy, ma'am."

The girl was not long in returning with the doctor. It was Dr. Tuplin of the philosophical manner and the young-old face, who greeted Fairfax with friendly unsurprise and asked him to wait in another room while he made his examination. The servant girl stayed in the parlor with them, as was customary for modesty.

Seated in the kitchen, looking into the eldritch eyes of a ginger cat squatting by the stove, Fairfax listened to the bass murmur of the doctor, the sharp treble replies of Mrs. Honeyman. Suddenly they rose to a squeal, an operatic trill of outrage. There was a slam, and then a series of wails as running feet went up the wooden stairs.

Fairfax looked out. Dr. Tuplin and the girl emerged from the parlor.

"You'd better go attend to your mistress, Molly," Dr. Tuplin said. "I think she is in some distress of mind."

"How is she?" Fairfax said.

"Oh, well enough. A few bruises and abrasions, no bones broke." Dr. Tuplin frowned. "You found no one in the house when you entered, Mr. Fairfax?"

"No. No sign of anyone."

"Hm. I'm afraid Mrs. Honeyman must be suffering from a rather nervous condition—the result of her bereavement, no doubt. I am pretty certain that no one assaulted her. It looked to me as if she had tumbled down the stairs." He raised an eyebrow.

"Deliberately, perhaps?" Fairfax said.

"Hm, well, I can't comment. But there is certain . . . hysteria about her mood. Still, no harm done, that's the main thing."

"Indeed. I felt some concern, knowing that she is with child."

The surgeon frowned. "What's this? You must be misinformed, sir. Mrs. Honeyman is not with child, that I can vouch for after examining her. She is at the end of her normal monthly courses. No question of that."

"Not . . ." Fairfax closed his mouth. "Yes . . . yes, I must have been misinformed."

"A posthumous child would be tragic indeed, though perhaps also some comfort," Dr. Tuplin said. "Well, at least the villain is to be brought to justice, it seems. I heard some commotion in the town. The culprit is found?"

"Yes. That is—a man has been taken in the woods, and committed to the jail. His name is Bennett Cornwell."

The surgeon paused in the act of taking snuff. "Really? Cornwell? You astonish me. Good God, I would not have thought it."

"You know him?"

"I suppose I can say yes, I do. Cornwell was imprisoned in the House of Correction—oh, must be nearly a year ago now. He caught a fever, there, as it not uncommon, and I attended him as jail surgeon. A very bitter and troubled young man at that time—though not, I thought, a bad one at heart. He had the fiercest hatred for his stepfather, Mr. Twelvetree. A degree of hostility was not to be wondered at, as Mr. Twelvetree would have nothing to do with the boy, and had even pressed for his prosecution. But what young Cornwell had got into his head was something far worse, which he admitted to me when he was feverish on his sickbed. He had an idea that Mr. Twelvetree had in some way hastened the death of his wife, Cornwell's mother; that there was something suspicious about her demise so soon after their marriage. A shocking accusation indeed, but he insisted he had good grounds for it. I believe it was fairly eating at him like a poison in the mind; and thankfully, I was able to purge him of it, very easily."

"How so?"

"Why, I was the doctor who attended Mrs. Cornwell—Mrs. Twelvetree as she then was—in her last illness. It was a virulent internal canker, beyond the capacity of medicine to cure or even alleviate. It carried her off swiftly. I opened the lady after death, with the approval of Mr. Twelvetree, and I never saw a worse case. She suffered much. I have nothing to say of Mr. Twelvetree's business methods, or general character, but in my attendance on his dying wife I knew him to be a devoted husband, within his lights. He cherished her apart, and gave her the peace and privacy that was her only comfort. It goes to show, I suppose, that there is a little good in all of us; a little of the divine, some might say." Dr. Tuplin smiled drably. "Well, I was able to convince Cornwell of this. I think it had a powerful effect upon him. Sickness did its work too, as it often does, making a man reflective. There was another man in there sick of the same fever; he had been a soldier too, and Cornwell made something of a friend of him, and was concerned for his recovery as much as his own. All encouraging signs in a young man who had led, by all appearances, a somewhat spoiled and self-willed life till then. I believe also a lay preacher visited the House, and made a strong impression on him, even converting him to some degree. I doubt these things last long. But certainly Cornwell came out a different man from the one who had gone in. He visited me a little after his release, and thanked me very cordially for my services, and for setting his mind at rest: very sober, very chastened. I wished him well, and could have hoped for better prospects for him. He had no money and no connections, at least none who would help him. But he said he would do very well, and spoke of trying his luck with the coastal trade."

"Yes . . . so I have heard." Everything fitted with what Fairfax knew, and some gaps were being filled in. There was no doubting where Bennett Cornwell had got hold of the idea of Twelvetree's being responsible for the death of his mother: his friend Tom Honeyman, a tale spun out of Tom's bitter resentment of his late employer. Perhaps Tom had believed it himself; perhaps he had used it chiefly to fuel Cornwell's enmity and stir up any trouble for Twelvetree that he could contrive. But certainly the passionate young man had taken it to heart, and it was surely what had driven him to making a vandalous attack on his stepfather's house. And those threatening messages that Twelvetree had received? The first were likely enough, given Cornwell's state of mind back then. But what about the one he had received this week? That depended: depended on whether Cornwell was indeed a changed man, and innocent as he claimed. The crux of the mater, in fact.

"Well, I think it a great pity if Cornwell has gone to the bad after all," the surgeon said. "He promised so much better. I remember thinking that the House of Correction had, for the first time in my knowledge, actually done the job of correction, albeit unwittingly. Still, need and poverty may soon undo a reformed character, alas." He put on his hat and picked up his gold-headed doctor's cane.

"Stay, sir—this other man who was his friend in the House, the soldier—do you recollect his name?"

"I'm afraid I do not. I took an especial interest in Cornwell, you see. A surly fellow is all I recall. But he recovered from his fever too. Well, I think I've done all I can here. Good day to you." Dr. Tuplin left.

Fairfax was still standing in the hall, deep in thought, when he heard a footstep on the stairs behind him.

"I am conspired against." Her hair hanging in tendrils,

her red underlip quivering, Barbara Honeyman glared tragically down.

"Not at all. Ma'am, I think you should—"

"You do not believe Fox was here."

Fairfax held her eyes. "No, I do not. Not just now. But from what he has given us to understand, he has been often here—when your husband was not."

Her breathing grew quick as a snared rabbit's. "Dear God," she said. "Dear God. I have no help—no resource. His foulest lies are believed. Where is he now? Think on that, sir. He is capable of any crime, and he walks free. Very well. I don't care anymore. There s nothing left for me. If there is blood, Mr. Fairfax, it shall be on your hands." She turned and went back upstairs, like a queen to execution.

Will, not shall, Fairfax thought as he left; she was always straining for effect. But the irritation covered unease. Fox's story had carried conviction, and hers none, yet whence came this business of a pregnancy? Someone had lied somewhere.

And it would do no harm to see if Fox was at home still. Fairfax walked back up into the town through the plashy rain. Another carriage passed him; plainly tonight was quite an occasion for the gentry of the district. In Red Lion Street he knocked and knocked at Fox's door, and when there was no answer tried it and found it unlocked.

Plenty of empty bottles, but no Fox. Well, there was nothing to prevent him going out. And now that Cornwell was committed to jail, he was officially absolved of suspicion. William Parry too, Fairfax thought—at least as far as the deaths on the *Flyer* went; he was still the prime suspect in Fairfax's mind for the murder of poor unworldly Margaret. So, the case of the *Flyer* solved—except that it was not, or not to his satisfaction.

Coming out into Broad Street he noticed a fine old din from the Nag's Head Inn on the left, and as he passed the door the gamekeeper who had led Twelvetree's posse burst out into his path and threw a great bearish arm round his neck.

"Have a drink with us, sir! Take a drop—in honor of a good day's work! You saw him—brought in like a proper trussed fowl! Wasn't that a pretty piece of work?" The gamekeeper breathed beer all over him.

"Congratulations. It must have been a long cold business. I fear I can't stay—"

"Just for one drop. I'm in the chair—we're all in the chair. Master's given us our reward, flat down, from his own purse, cash on the table—that's not counting the official reward on the rogue's head, sir: a guinea for each of us, and the rest of the day off. Now I call that handsome. There's folk who won't spare a kind word for our master, but I've no quarrel with him, not me. Take a drop, sir . . ."

Fairfax thanked him, managed at last to extricate himself. Loud and tuneless singing came from the inn's taproom. Twelvetree must be relieved indeed to reward his servants so fulsomely. They could drink themselves unconscious before the money ran out. Well, good luck to them.

Fairfax had an idea in his mind, but before he could act on it he found himself hailed in a crisp voice from the other side of the street.

A carriage was there, and a very pretty well-dressed lady had just been handed out of it by the gentleman who had hailed him. It was Mr. Samson Rowe.

"Do go in, my dear. I shall join you in just one moment." Mr. Rowe was very spruce in an embroidered coat and silk breeches and tie-wig. He tucked his hands under his coat-tails and regarded Fairfax with a half smile—a half smile Fairfax did not at all like.

"Mr. Rowe. You are in town for the Assembly tonight?"

Samson Rowe looked at him for perhaps another five seconds. "I am, as it happens. My intended has been greatly looking forward to it, as have I. Dancing is the most civilized of amusements. I say these things because they are, as it were, in the accepted sphere of social exchange. Others are not. I am sure you know what I mean, sir."

Fairfax stared at him. "I am sure I do not."

Mr. Rowe shook his great head, all headmasterly tolerance. "Unworthy in you, sir—unworthy. Once a subterfuge is discovered, it is sheer childishness to persist in it, you know. I would expect better of my own patients, most of whom have a very well developed sense of shame."

"Perhaps they can also interpret riddles," Fairfax said shortly. "If so, they have the advantage of me. I have not the patience, and I am getting wet, Mr. Rowe."

Samson Rowe's face turned hard. "Then I shall be plain, sir, if nothing else will make you acknowledge your duplicity. I admitted you to my establishment, and answered your inquiries in the fullest and frankest manner, not as of right, for I did not have to do anything of the kind, but in a spirit of helpfulness to you and the authorities you claimed to represent. I believed that that concluded the matter, and that if it did not, you would have the grace and honesty to apply to me directly again, though such an application would have been something of a nuisance. What I did not expect was that you would use as a tool a person—a woman, no less— pretending to be something she was not, and making it abundantly plain that she came to my house only in a spirit of meddlesome and mischievous inquiry. That was base, sir, and in its implications, slanderous. I only refrain from taking the matter further, out of pity for a mind so weak and contemptible in its absurd suspicions that it is beneath the tribute of attention."

"I don't know what you mean, Mr. Rowe, except that you mean to be offensive. If you will explain, perhaps I can answer you."

"I don't have to explain, my man. And I don't have to warn you, but I choose to, that I will look very poorly upon any further attempts to cast doubts on the running of my establishment, by you or the agents you so ignobly employ. I will be severe, Mr. Fairfax, and I do not lack connections, sir, high connections."

"That much is plain. And no doubt I shall be accused of slander if I venture to wonder how you came by them, Mr. Rowe."

"You are insolent, sir!"

"No. Insolence implies deference, and I do not owe you deference any more than I owe it to any other free man. I do not understand these accusations, but neither do I like them. And I like threats less."

"I have said all I have to say, Mr. Fairfax. Remember it." Very cold, and just a little ruffled, Samson Rowe stalked up the steps.

Fairfax was ruffled too. He had never liked the air of patronage about the man, and to be spoken to in the street like that . . . but soon his inflamed pride went down, to be replaced by puzzlement. Who had visited Mr. Rowe's asylum on a pretext, asking questions? And a woman . . . ?

He had only to frame the question to come up with an answer. It must be Cordelia Linton. He had asked her, after all, if she could find out about any unrecorded deaths at the asylum. He had not expected her to take on the task so directly. It warmed him that she had done it for him, briefly—before he reminded himself that he was forbidden to feel like that, ever. And the he hoped that that pompous humbug had not treated her as he had just been treated.

Well, well . . . Had she discovered anything? Certainly Samson Rowe was discomfited. Fairfax was glad he had got in that remark about Mr. Rowe's connections; and after all, the incongruity was more glaring than ever. A country asylum-keeper, a physician of no family—yet he seemed to have the wealth of a sugar merchant. Of course questions were going to be asked. Perhaps Cordelia had the answers.

Excited by this—not, he told himself, by the thought of seeing Cordelia—he hurried round to the office of the *Mercury*. But it was closed and unlighted, and no one came to his knock. Telling himself he was not disappointed, he stood looked about the muddy High Street, and thinking over what Dr. Tuplin had told him. Especially the most mysterious, tantalizing, and apparently useless part—the other ex-soldier who had been Bennett Cornwell's friend in the House of Correction. If only Dr. Tuplin had remembered his name . . .

Fairfax found that he was looking at a pair of stocks, at the other end of the street—empty, mercifully. Where there were stocks, the Bridewell or House of Correction was usually nearby.

Here it was—a long dank shed of a building, better lit than the Cage—but that was for a purpose. The Cage was a holding cell before trial. The House of Correction was where petty offenders—vagrants, pilferers, prostitutes, drunken prentices—were set to work. The usual work was beating hemp, heavy labor that involved lifting a huge mallet, often from six in the morning to six at night; and Fairfax found several wretchedly clad women at this work, as well as a boy who looked no more than twelve. A whipping post stood against the unplastered wall as a reminder to the idle. The smell here was even more unsavory than that of the Cage. It had been dedicated indeed of Henry Griggs, though typical of him, to minister to a place like this.

Life was endlessly surprising. The warder, who carried a leather switch over his shoulder and worked in a place that would have made a fair anteroom to purgatory, was a civil softly spoken man who, when Fairfax explained his business, conducted him into a little room where the records were kept and apologized for the lack of a fire.

"So, they've taken one of our old inmates for a highwayman? I'm sorry to hear it," the warder said, sighing. And then with an urbane smile: "Mind, they don't often walk out of here and go on to be mayors and aldermen. I don't know why that should be."

The records of admission were in ledgers, neatly ranged in chronological order. It did not take long to find the name of Bennett Cornwell.

> *Committed, Monday, 1st December 1760, by order of
> the Magistrates of the Borough: for conduct disor-
> derly and liable to disturbance of the public peace,
> willful destruction of property, &c, Bennett Cornwell,
> 20 years, of no fixed abode . . .*

"Twelvetree's boy, or near enough," the warder said, looking over his shoulder. "I remember. Quite the rakehell."

Fairfax ran his eyes across the other names for that
month, and the month before: nothing sprang out. "I don't
suppose," he said, "you recall another man who was in at the
same time as Cornwell, and was friendly with him? He had
been a soldier too. They both caught fever, I think."

The warder ran a neat soft finger along the page. "I do,
sir," he said, "I do indeed. Quite a salt-and-pepper pair they
were. Cornwell was the one who settled down, and t'other
fellow was the one who wouldn't on any account. Here's the
man, I'd swear to it. Troublesome character, he was, though
to do him justice, he's never been back."

> *Committed, by order of the Magistrates of the Bor-
> ough: James Allerton, 26 years, no fixed abode, for ri-
> otous drunkenness and affray, &c.*

"Aye, that's the man," the warder said. "I wonder what became of him."

Fairfax was already on his way out.

Fourteen

"James Allerton."

Fairfax simply spoke the name, loudly and distinctly, as he entered the cell. He could not have hoped for a greater effect. Bennett Cornwell jumped up, and the Bible he had been reading fell from his hands and clumped to the floor.

"I'm sorry, Bennett," Fairfax said, sitting down on the bunk as before. "But you are a hard nut to crack, and I must use what means I can. I only want to help you, if you will allow me."

Bennett Cornwell stooped and picked up the Bible with an unsteady hand. "You said you would fetch Mr. Griggs here."

"So I shall. I have sent for him, and I imagine he is on his way to see you. But for now you must talk to me, Bennett. I am not a godly man, but I do have your interests at heart; for the simple reason that I believe you are not the person who should be in this cell. I believe you are not the person who has been using that hideout in Monks Wood for the past ten months, as a base for highway robberies. I believe that person is James Allerton. I do not share your faith, Bennett, but I hope we share a regard for truth. And the truth must come out."

"We do not share much, I think," Bennett Cornwell said, looking very young and earnest. "To you Allerton is merely a criminal; to me he is a soul to be saved."

"And he is the person you have been searching for."

Slowly the young man sat down, and nodded.

"You were in the House of Correction together," Fairfax prompted.

"Yes . . . I was very dark in my mind then; full of the most terrible bitterness of spirit. I believed dreadful things, and planned dreadful revenges."

"On your stepfather?"

"Yes. He did wrong me. He turned my mother's mind against me, I believe, and saw me only as a plague and a trouble, not an erring soul in need of guidance. But I will admit that as I was then, I must have been a sore trial to my mother's patience, and not a good son. My stepfather might have done better by me, that's all."

"But he did not do what, in your resentment, you began to suspect him of doing."

"No. I came to realize that . . . You have spoken to someone?"

"Dr. Tuplin."

"Ah. Yes, he helped me; and Mr. Griggs. It was a new sensation to me, to find people caring for my welfare quite disinterestedly. It was Tom Honeyman who sowed the seed of that monstrous suspicion in me. I don't blame him; he had his own grudge against my stepfather, well merited perhaps, and it led him beyond reason. But I had to go and see Tom, and set him straight, when I came back to these parts lately. He did not take it kindly. A pity. He was a good fellow at heart."

"You did go to sea, then, after your release?"

"Yes. I wanted to get away, and reflect—and shipmasters have no interest in your past. I urged Allerton to come with me, when we were released. But he refused. I was concerned for him. The anger and darkness that began to leave me, as I was drawn to the life of the spirit, were so deeply fixed in him. When we were imprisoned together, he would speak most bitterly of what he would do when he got out. He owed the world nothing, he said, after the way it had treated him.

It was a sad tale. His father was a poor clergyman who turned to drink, and left him little but debts. He had entered the army, and had been a corporal in a good regiment, and seen action in the German war; he was at Minden. But he was discharged because he would not or could not submit to the disciplines of the camp—quite trifling matters, it seems, would make him rebel. Back home—he was born in Lincolnshire—he could find no steady employment. I believe there was a post with the excise, but his superior accused him of pilfering, and threw him out. Allerton said this was unjust, and that if you gave a dog a bad name he would live up to it. He drank and gambled and could not pay his debts—an old story, I daresay. But it gave him a fierce grievance against the world. I recognized it, because I had had it myself. And Allerton clung to it. In the House he kept saying that when he got out, he would be more careful. 'Not more honest, Bennett—where's the use in that? But more careful. Take care of myself, for upon my soul, no other devil is going to take care of me!' I thought it was just his way of talking. He wanted nothing to do with Mr. Griggs, and was utterly impervious to all urgings of religion. Whenever I talked to him of it, he just shrugged. It was this world he cared about, he said. And then he would say that he had half a mind to take to the road when he got out. Still in that half-jesting way: if it was good enough for Robin Hood it was good enough for him, things like that. Yet I saw that he was in earnest too. He kept returning to this notion. And when we parted, I to go to Boston and take ship, he laughed and said I was not to worry about him. There was a good living to be picked up, he said, without having to pull on ropes and eat ship's biscuit.

"Well, he had an old aunt, his only family, a poor decent body, a seamstress, who lived in a Lincolnshire village. She would lodge him sometimes, try to mother him a little. I wrote him there, several times, when I was first sailing on a coaster between Boston and London, and for a time I got replies. He said he was doing prodigious well; he was his own master, and owed nothing to anyone. It was a fine trade he had taken up, he said, but he would never say what trade. Of course I had my suspicions even then. The tone of those letters was most cheerful, but to me, who had been blessed with the revelation of God's grace, there was a darkness about them. Well, in September I came ashore, having done moderate well with a sober godly master, and put a little money by. I was not due to sail again with my master till November, and I thought I would come back to my old home country, and also look up my friend Allerton. I went to his aunt. She saw him but seldom, she said, and never knew when to expect him. Sometimes he would descend on her quite suddenly, and stay for several days, sleeping and eating a lot and hardly putting his head outside the house. Then she wouldn't see him for weeks at a time. But he was doing very well, she said, in some sort of trade; and he made her some very pretty presents. She showed me them: bits of jewelry and trinkets.

"And at the same time I began to hear tales of the highwayman who had preyed on the road between Stamford and Huntingdon for the past eight or nine months. It has been the constant gossip hereabouts, as you know. And now I was sure in my heart that my fears for him had been realized. My friend had taken to the road, as he had sworn he would. A road to perdition . . . And so I began to search for him. I thought that he must be hiding out somewhere, and I prayed that I could trace him before it was too late."

"Before he ran his neck into a noose."

"Partly that. I thought to save him, physically, before he was caught. Once I found him, I was determined to use every persuasion to make him come away with me, and try the sea. Thieving is a crime, certainly, according to Scripture as well as the laws of the land, but such crimes could be repented of, and put behind him. It could only be a matter of time before he was caught: no man pursues such a career for long. If I could just get to him . . . But it wasn't just his physical safety that concerned me. I desperately wanted him to be redeemed. I wanted to help him save his soul, as Mr. Griggs helped me, before it was too late."

"And so you found his hideout at last."

"Yes. The place was well hidden, but its purpose was plain. And so I stayed there. It seemed my best course. I thought he must come to it sooner or later. It was Tuesday I found it, and I have been there ever since, until those men burst in on me today. He had some stores laid in, and there was wood for a fire. So you see . . . My only regret is that I did not get to see him."

"Tuesday . . . So he did not use his hideout after the attack on the *Flyer*. I wonder where else he went to. And why he hasn't been back since . . . Though certainly the last few days, with Twelvetree's men trampling all over the woods, he must have known to keep away."

"Well." Bennett Cornwell folded his hands and gazed up at the grating with its gray ration of daylight. "I hope he is safe."

"Do you?" Fairfax said sharply. "Think, Bennett. You are the one they have locked in this cell, not Allerton. You are the one they intend to try for his crimes. Do you think he's going to ride suddenly into town and say no, no, I am the one? You are a loyal friend—but from what you have told me of James Allerton, he is not the sort to do such a noble thing. And think of this, Bennett: his crimes now are not of the venial sort. He has killed. He is a murderer." Fairfax studied the young mans' bony intense face. Yes, it was possible to see him as a rakehell. He was one of those all-or-nothing young people, extremely bad, then extremely good, just so long as it was extreme. "Now that you have told me this, you must do more. You must tell everything, in a full statement to the authorities. If necessary, you may have to testify against Allerton. Once they have a name, description, details, they can put out a warrant for his arrest. They can talk to the old aunt, perhaps trace the stolen things he gave her . . ."

"I don't know, I don't know . . ." Jumping up, Cornwell

began pacing the narrow dimensions of the cell. "It is a matter of conscience, and I feel my conscience terribly divided. And besides, sir, you know I may not be believed. I have a powerful advocate against me in my stepfather."

"If Allerton can be found and caught, then you will be believed." But where *was* this elusive man? With the old aunt? Cornwell had been careful not it give away where she lived. Possible, but Fairfax thought it an unlikely hideout after so tremendous a crime as the attack on the *Flyer*. Perhaps he had fled this part of the country altogether . . .

"I must think on it," Cornwell said. "I cannot give you an answer now, sir. I must look deep into my heart, and pray. With Mr. Griggs's help, I will apply to God. I know he will give me an answer. Let me speak with you tomorrow."

Fairfax sighed. These Methodies were estimable people in many ways, but things went exceedingly slow with them. "Very well. I'll leave you to think on it. I'll return tomorrow. Oh—is there anything you need?"

For the first time Bennett Cornwell smiled. "That's Christian of you, sir." He took up his Bible. "But I have all I need."

Oh, no, you don't, Fairfax thought as he walked up to the George to get his horse; you need James Allerton to be found, and quickly. The shipmaster might be able to give Bennett Cornwell an alibi for most of the year, but he had none for the time of the attack of the *Flyer*, and the court would be happy to send him to the gallows for that alone. Come to that, there was no proof that Cornwell had not been responsible for that crime, which had, after all, a rather different pattern from the previous robberies. Fairfax didn't believe it, but he didn't fancy trying to bring Sir Edward round to his point of view again.

In the yard of the George he found Mr. Quigley directing a troop of servants in stripping down the handbills from the walls. "Shan't be needing these now," he said, "all over, thank the Lord. Oh—there's a lady been asking for you, sir.

She stepped into the coffee room to dry her skirts, I fancy. Dismal weather for an Assembly night, ain't it?"

In the coffee room Cordelia Linton turned from the fire. Her eyes flashed nervously.

"Half drowned, and dirty as a cockle-gatherer, it never rains but it pours as they say, a demonstrably untrue saying though, and what about the other one, a sunshine shower ne'er lasts half an hour—sheer contradiction." She gave him her hand, then moved away from him as if to cancel the gesture out.

"I am in no clean state myself," he said, looking down at his boots, which were muddied up to the calf. "But it does not become me so well."

"And so how goes it with you, Mr. Fairfax? I hear they have brought the highwayman in and consigned him to jail, and I seem to be the only person in town who is disappointed, if you take my meaning."

"The man they have taken is under suspicion, no more. I came to see you earlier, Mrs. Linton."

"And found me out. That is, found me not in. What a slippery language we have. Well, sir, I have some news for you, and I plume myself on it. I think no one could have found it so swift, or so cunning."

"It concerns Mr. Rowe's asylum?"

"It does. And there *was* a death there!" She spoke excitedly. "You will want to know how I discovered this. I will tell you. I visited the asylum myself yesterday—direct, eh? But no. I posed as the sister of a poor afflicted man who might have to be committed to such a place. I had heard good reports of Mr. Rowe's house, and had come to see for myself, et cetera. Mr. Rowe showed me round, very full of himself. Then I takes a little sick—long ride, weak constitution, *und so weiter*. Must use the necessary house. But instead, I sneak about, and satisfy myself with a peep into a room that Mr. Rowe had assured me was empty, long unused—not so, I swear. There was no one in it, but it bore marks of a recent occupation, well furnished, a bed still made up and so on. A curious room: it had only a blind window—dark as a cell, it quite gave me the horrors. Alas, further investigation proved difficult as"—she grimaced drolly—"Mr. Rowe unluckily came looking for me. Are you quite well, ma'am, and so on, oh dear me yes I must have taken the wrong turning . . . I fancy his suspicions were aroused then."

"Yes," he said, amused, "I'm very sure they were."

"Well, I am not finished yet. When I left, I found a young man waiting near the gates. He was a laborer from the village, and he was waiting for his sweetheart, who is a day maid at the asylum. It was only four; wasn't he a little early? Well, perhaps not, for last Friday, says he, she was let out, along with the other servants, early in the afternoon. He thought perhaps it was a permanent arrangement. Oh, no, it's not, thinks I. Mr. Rowe wanted them out of the way last Friday. A little more asking around the village, and I find that a cart went up to the asylum that previous Friday, and went away again under cover of darkness. I'll wager it was a box that was being taken away, and I don't mean a clothes box. But that was al I could learn. Never mind." She held up a finger. "There's more than one way to skin a cat—unpleasant proverb, and I don't see how there is more than one way. Anyhow, that same day a woman came into the office, asking about a housekeeper's position. She had heard of it, and wanted to apply—had we carried an advertisement for it? It turned out we had not. The woman had only heard of it through gossip. The gossip was that the housekeeper at Skellerby, the country seat of Mr. Timothy Devereaux, had died lately, and so she assumed a new one was needed. How did she know about this? Why, her cousin was a laborer on the Skellerby estate, and had been called in last week to help open the vault in the grounds, for the housekeeper to be laid there. She didn't know the name . . . Well, I have consulted all the records of death for the county for last week, and I've found nothing about a death at the Skellerby estate. I don't know what conclusion you draw, Mr. Fairfax. Call me a suspicious old harpy if you like—well, don't, it wouldn't be polite—but does it not suggest that there *was* a death at Mr. Rowe's house? And that he, and Mr. Devereaux, have been to some trouble to keep it secret?"

"Mr. Devereaux . . . good God. He is the great friend of my employer. Sir Edward holds him in the highest respect."

"Well, of course, there may be a simple explanation that reflects no discredit on anyone, but I should like to know it." She was full of sparkling, devilish pleasure. "Now you may heap praise on me, sir—as much as you like, within reason."

He smiled, with a little devilment of his own. "I could not have done better myself."

"Oh, conceited man! A tautology, that. Man and conceit go together like—

"Like women and looking glasses."

"I feel I should tap you reprovingly with my fan, but I haven't got a fan. I never did get the hang of a fan, you know: either I made a breeze like a nor'easter, or I poked someone in the eye with it, and my wrist would always ache like the devil."

"You may need a fan at the Assembly tonight, if you are going. It seems half the county will be crammed in there."

"I shall be there, yes. It's the very place for gossip. I do *like* prying into people's secrets . . . And what do you make of this one, Mr. Fairfax?"

"It is mystifying, indeed," he said honestly. Where *did* this new revelation lead? His head swam with it all, as well as with the presence of Cordelia, whom he admitted to himself was the most beautiful and heartbreaking woman he had ever known. (There, it was confessed: let that be an end of it.) "I must get to the bottom of it somehow. I only hope I can do it with your skill and resource."

"That little heap will do very well," she said, laughing. "And now I must go home, and try to make myself presentable for tonight. In an evening gown and feathers, you know, I look like a circus horse. Be prepared for the shock. If—if you are to be there, that is."

"I believe so."

She left him with her quick bare smile.

He looked forward to tonight, and was miserable because he knew he should not; could not.

The rain fell harder as Fairfax rode back to Cheyney Hall, but he was too much preoccupied with his thoughts to notice discomfort. Bennett Cornwell; James Allerton. Surely Cornwell would see sense, and tell all. After that it just remained to track Allerton down. So Sir Edward had been right: their quarry all along had been a professional highwayman, and all the peculiarities of the case had resolved themselves . . . It was certainly disturbing to think of such a man being at large. The killings had been merciless, after all. Allerton was capable of dreadful brutality, and it was a tribute, Fairfax supposed, to Bennett Cornwell's loyalty and faith that he still believed his friend capable of redemption. The killing of the coachman could be seen, at a pinch, as an impulse of self-defense, as he had tried to ride the robber down; the killing of Tom Honeyman likewise, as Tom had been reaching for his own pistols. But then to shoot harmless Jonathan Griggs . . . Still those three shots bothered him. He had to envisage Allerton as the coolest and bloodiest villain, calmly reloading while Jonathan, perhaps, shivered and begged in terror. It was horrible: it was strangely excessive.

Well, in spite of Sir Edward's strictures about not keeping secrets, he decided he would delay talking of Allerton until tomorrow, when with luck Bennett Cornwell would have decided to come clean. It was the peculiar and baffling matter of the burial in Mr. Devereaux's vault that nagged at him as he arrived at Cheyney Hall, and after changing, he sought Sir Edward out in his dressing room.

Sir Edward had just had his wig new-powdered, and the air was thick with it. He invited Fairfax to a seat, while he debated between two silk waistcoats.

"I'm not one for fligging myself up, but you have to make a show, you know, at these affairs, else the county'll be whispering and putting you down for a bankrupt . . .

Well, Fairfax, how was our caged bird? Is he inclined to sing yet?"

"He . . . remains quiet and stubborn. But I think we may learn more from him very soon. As for Mrs. Honeyman, she is as keen to blame Fox for everything as he her . . ."

"A sad state of affairs. There are some folks who just shouldn't marry . . . Well, Fairfax, what's amiss? You look as if you've swallowed a stake."

"Sir Edward, I have learned something more today, which leaves me perplexed. Perhaps you can explain it for me. It concerns Mr. Rowe's asylum—and also, I think, Mr. Devereaux . . ." He told what he had heard.

"Damn you, sir." Silent and still throughout Fairfax's narration, Sir Edward now spoke in a clenched whisper. "Damn you, sir, for your insolence and your meddling disobedience."

"Sir Edward, I—"

"Not a word more. I told you, Fairfax, very explicitly, to drop that business. Why did you choose to defy me?"

"Because it seemed relevant to our inquiry. If something was hidden at Mr. Rowe's house, something underhand and possibly criminal—"

"You know nothing, sir. And that was how it should have stayed. You have stirred up waters where you had no business." Sir Edward sat down heavily. "Poor Devereaux . . . he tried his best. Oh, I'll tell you about it, sir. No doubt you would only go prying further if I did not. Yes, there was a death at Mr. Rowe's house lately. It was last week. It was a woman: a woman who was kept quite solitary there—kindly, and for her own protection. She was Timothy Devereaux's wife. I met her but once, years ago: a charming creature! He adored her. She was his queen. But there was a terrible and secret instability in her character. In short, she constantly betrayed him. She let men take her, all manner of men, wherever and whenever they might. Oh, 'twas beyond a moral question. The poor creature plainly had a mania. Well, she soon caught a condition—oh, why mouth it: she became syphilitic, and descended into madness of the most dreadful and turbulent kind. Devereaux was shattered. He still loved her; I believe he never stopped. And so she was placed with Samson Rowe, and Devereaux paid him very well to look after her, to indulge her and give her gentle treatment even when she was at her worst. He gave it out that he and his wife had separated. To be alone, I believe, he confided the truth, as he confided to me the fact of her death, last week, from the condition that had tormented her. He wanted to keep her memory inviolate, and to lay her in his family vault, without the prying eyes of the world invading her shame and his grief. And so her body was taken privily from the asylum in darkness, and carried to Skellerby. He acted as he did to spare himself pain, and to spare her name injury. He thought, poor man, that he had succeeded."

"Sir—this is a tragic history, indeed, and believe me, I am far from intending ever to reveal it to a soul, now that I understand—"

"Why, damn you, the damage is done, is it not? How did you find these things out?"

"From—Mrs. Linton."

"The newspaper creature? Oh, God in heaven, I don't know whether you are fool or knave, Fairfax—but you have played a very ill part, sir. I had hoped that the sorrow of my dearest friend was at an end. Now I fear it is only beginning."

"Mrs. Linton confided this only to me, Sir Edward: and I am sure you may count upon her—"

"Pah, she's a professional dealer in scandal. After all, she carries that rag of a paper for her drunken sot of a husband. What should you know of Mr. Linton, anyhow? It is a small town, Fairfax, and she is a married woman. Cock's life, I expected discretion from you when I took you on, not the opposite. And it goes hard with me, sir, very hard, that you deliberately flouted my wishes."

"I'm sorry to have displeased you, but upon my honor, I never meant—"

"Well meant, hellbent. I have nothing more to say to you, else we shall fall to a quarrel there is no repairing." Sir Edward took up his stock and cracked it like a whip before winding it round his neck. "I suggest you get to the library, sir, and commence your proper work. You will not be accompanying us this evening, for the simple reason that I fear I shan't keep my temper with you around. I shall have your dinner sent in to you."

Smarting, Fairfax went down to the library. A wretched business! And a wretched occupation this was, where one could fancy oneself on an equality—until the master chose to slap you down. He brooded on his wrongs, for wrongs they seemed, though he knew Sir Edward had been angry only on behalf of his friend.

Well, that was where Mr. Samson Rowe's prosperity came from, at any rate. Impossible not to see it as silence money, whatever the gloss Sir Edward put on it. But the tale was more sad and sordid than revealing. Mrs. Devereaux's, then, had been the "empty" room next to Jonathan Griggs's; and her death had been the one that had disturbed him. He must have picked up what was going on, despite Mr. Rowe's efforts at secrecy.

A maid brought dinner to Fairfax on a tray. Through the open library door he could hear the excited voices of Letitia and Amelia discussing the Assembly tonight, with an occasional damping remark from Mrs. Hargrave.

" . . . And then our names will be announced, you know, as we go in."

"Papa's first!"

"Yes, of course Papa's first." Letitia's voice. "And then mine, as I'm the elder."

"I hope the man will be able to pronounce it, and not turn it to Lettice like that young booby of a curate—"

"Foolish girl, he will not say my Christian name," Letitia said. "I will be Miss Nugent, and you will be Miss Amelia Nugent. That's the correct form."

"Is that right, Mrs. Hargrave?"

"Yes, my dear, it is. The title of the eldest sister or brother does not include the Christian name. The late Mr. Hargrave had a younger brother, whose name was Hubert; and they would be socially introduced as Mr. Hargrave, and Mr. Hubert Hargrave. Now, I must go and take my physic: do not crumple your dresses, my dears . . ."

"Hubert!" came the scandalized giggles of the girls, after she had gone; and then the door was closed. Fairfax ate his solitary dinner among the books and prints and dust, and presently heard the carriage brought round to the drive outside, and the departure of Sir Edward and his daughters—the girls full of talk, Sir Edward very quiet—to the Stamford Assembly.

"Work, my friend, that's all there is to it," Fairfax said to himself. He picked up where he had left off, cataloguing the maps. He spread out the first on the table. It was the old estate map, the one with Skellerby marked on it—that made his cheeks burn again for a moment. Skellerby—a very Norse-sounding name, like many of the place names hereabout. Lincolnshire, of course, had been extensively settled by the Vikings. Perhaps that was where Sir Edward got his temper from, Fairfax thought, his eyes scanning the map. Thurlby—a name straight from Valhalla. The names of farms, he noticed, tended to be more comfortable and domestic. Chestnut House Farm, Sweetnell Farm, Lowbridge Farm.

He sat back heavily as if an invisible hand had slapped him.

Looked again. There it was—or had been: Sweetnell Farm. *Sweet Nell.* He had misread Jonathan Griggs's spiky capitals.

Not a beloved person, but a beloved place. Not a lover, but a lost home. One of those small independent farms that, since this map had been drawn up, had fallen victim to enclosure—diminished, cut off from drainage, burdened with debt, and at last sold off cheaply, as Mr. Devereaux had explained. Bought for a song by the greedy and powerful landowner who had instigated the enclosure—Nicholas Twelvetree.

He sat quite still while thoughts reeled through his brain. At last, when it seemed they were done, he reached out a hand for his wineglass—and there came a final thought: Nicholas Twelvetree's menservants, drinking themselves blind in the taverns of Stamford.

Within minutes he was in the stable, saddling the mare himself with fumbling fingers, and then racing out in the rainy dark, onto the Stamford road.

The town was busy as a market noonday—eveyrwhere lights, wheels, voices. But the house of Mr. Nicholas Twelvetree was silent and in darkness. Fairfax tethered the mare to the gatepost but did not mount the steps to the front door. Instead he went round to the side. An iron gate barred the passage, but it was easy enough for him to climb over, just as it would be for the person he sought. Down the passage, and he came to a flagstoned yard flanked by outhouses. There, the servants' entrance. The door yielded slowly at his push. At first he thought it must be on a chain. Then he felt the obstruction at his feet.

An elderly maid. she stirred as he bent over her. There was a cut on her forehead. She was the only female servant he had ever seen at Twelvetree's establishment—and, he guessed, the only servant in the house. The tin candlestick she must have carried as she answered the door lay on the floor beside her.

No time to make a light. Fairfax found the stairs and sprinted lightly up. First floor, Twelvetree's frugal study and dining room, doors closed and surely locked. In darkness, breath pent, he climbed up another flight, hoping—as his quarry must have hoped—that Twelvetree's bedchamber was above, and was not kept locked. Not a man to keep late hours, obviously. While his servants caroused he had gone to bed. Perhaps he would sleep sound and secure for the first time in an age . . .

A door stood open; a guttering light danced out into the passage. Fairfax crept forward, stole in. One candle was burning, revealing Nicholas Twelvetree on the floor beside the bed, white as his nightgown, moaning and putting up beseeching hands. The first blow from the heavy candlestick grasped in his attacker's upraised hand had squashed the pillow on the bed, splitting it so that it bled feathers. Not a praying man, Robert Fairfax prayed nevertheless, as he launched himself across the room, that he would be in time to stop Henry Griggs raining the second blow on Nicholas Twelvetree's head.

Fifteen

Sir Edward opened the window and let a waft of cool afternoon air into the library.

"I used to tell my father to ventilate this place," he said. "Stop the books getting mildew. He liked the smell of mildew, he'd say . . . Well, I saw Cornwell this morning. He was on his way to Boston; said he'd nothing to keep him here. He said he'd take the news to Allerton's aunt on the way." He turned, looked at Fairfax in a diffident way. "It still confounds me how you worked out that Allerton was dead."

Fairfax put down his pen. "I didn't work it out, really. It just came as the last possibility, from a succession of thoughts. Fundamentally, it was a matter of those three people on the *Flyer* being killed. No matter what hypothesis I applied, it didn't fit all three deaths. I had learned a great deal about the people who were under suspicion, but I couldn't imagine any of them committing those three murders: they lacked either the means, or the need. So I came to think: suppose one of the shots had been fired by a person who was *on* the coach, and then ran away? But that made no sense. There was only Mrs. Parry, and I was pretty sure that she genuinely had left the coach some time before, at Stilton. So that left Tom Honeyman and Jonathan Griggs.

"Tom Honeyman had pistols. He certainly didn't shoot himself. Could he have shot Jonathan, got back inside the coach, and then been shot by a highwayman? That was non-

sense. Yet they were the only people on the coach: the booking records at the George confirmed it. Mr. Twelvetree—as
Tom was calling himself—and Mr. Griggs. I was stuck. And
then your daughters gave me the clue."

"My girls? How so?"

"They were talking of precedence and titles, and how an
elder sister is called. Miss Nugent; Miss Amelia Nugent.
And Mrs. Hargrave pointed out that it's the same with brothers. I thought of Henry and Jonathan Griggs. The person
booked on to the *Flyer* was named simply as Mr. Griggs.
Thus, in theory, it might have been either. But it was more
probable that Henry Griggs, as the elder, would tend to use
the title Mr. Griggs. It was just a notion; but I took it up, and
almost as a mere matter of interest, posed myself the question—suppose Henry Griggs has been lying from the start:
suppose *he* was traveling on the *Flyer* that day, and not his
brother?

"Well, there was some strong evidence in support of that
unlikely theory. when I first went to see Mr. Rowe, he mentioned that Henry Griggs's boots had been wet and muddy
when he came to see him on Monday about Jonathan's escape. I had recently had occasion to notice how dirty one
gets, going on foot in such rain as we had—rain that had
been falling heavily earlier in the week. Which suggested
that Griggs had arrived at the asylum on foot—probably
from Stamford, a couple of miles distant. Yet you know, Sir
Edward, that when we first came across Henry Griggs, on
Tuesday, he was on horseback."

"Aye, aye, and the horse limped from a bad shoeing."

"Just so. And it was Mr. Griggs's claim that he had ridden to Ryhall to see Mr. Rowe, and was riding back when
we first met him. Why, then, arrive at the asylum on foot?
More probable, on that evidence, was that Henry Griggs had
taken the coach up to Stamford, and gone on to the asylum
from there. He stayed overnight at Ryhall, as is attested; and
then on Tuesday, why, how was he to get home—or at least,
to Huntingdon, not far from his home, where he was to do a

preaching—except by taking the coach—the *Stamford Flyer*? Not being a man of great means, of course, it was likely he would take an outside place.

"But this too must be nonsense. Because it was Jonathan Griggs who took that outside place, wasn't it? And then I thought—how do we know this? All we know is that Jonathan escaped from the asylum and went missing. And then, when we found the bodies, and the name Griggs in the booking records, along came Henry Griggs and identified the dead outside passenger as Jonathan. But we had only his word for that. Normally it suffices. But suppose, again, that he had lied?

"So, then, who on earth was the outside passenger, who had been so horribly shot in the face? Well, how easy it is to jump to conclusions. He lay in the ditch by the crashed coach, and so we assumed he was a passenger and proceeded from there—just as Henry Griggs had hoped we would. The dead man in the ditch was not Jonathan Griggs. And here I gathered a clue, begging your pardon, Sir Edward, from the matter of poor Mrs. Devereaux."

"I was rather a bully about that, wasn't I?" Sir Edward said with a faint smile.

"A loyal friend, that's all. But the clue I gathered was rather important. Mrs. Devereaux had died at the asylum the previous Friday: the only death there for a long time. Henry Griggs, when I asked him why Jonathan might have run away, said that Jonathan had spoken of a death there, and been upset by it. Yet Henry had last visited his brother a fortnight ago, well before Mrs. Devereaux's death. How then could Jonathan have told him this—unless he had seen him quite lately? And there was another peculiarity—that Jonathan, having escaped on Saturday, took until Tuesday to board a coach to go to his brother. Unlikely.

"No, the dead man in the ditch was not Jonathan. But Jonathan *was* dead. He had not boarded any coach. He had simply walked, in great weakness and distress, from the asylum to his brother's house at Eaton Socon, sleeping under

hedges, drinking from streams, eating not at all, and hiding
in terror when he saw anyone. It took him until late on Sunday night, when he arrived at Henry's door. He was sick and
perhaps had some hint of his own approaching end, which
had driven him to seek his brother out, for he didn't want to
die in the asylum. This Henry confirmed to me yesterday,
when I talked to him in his cell. Jonathan did not live the
night, and died in his brother's arms. Here, Sir Edward, I
must swear you to confidence. Griggs buried his brother beneath a tree on his own little plot of land, where he lies now.
This meant a great deal to him; but he feared, as he fears
now, that it would be disapproved, as it is not consecrated
ground, and that his brother's remains would be disturbed.
That is why, when he went to see Mr. Rowe, he said that he
would undertake the care of Jonathan, if he should find his
way to his house. He wanted no more disturbing of his
beloved brother's peace—which had been disturbed enough
in his lifetime. Henry wants Jonathan just to be known as
missing, perhaps presumed dead—no matter: as long as he
can remain in that plot of ground. Such things as land, home,
security were sacred to both of them.

"And here I gathered another clue—from one of your father's maps. In Jonathan's asylum room he had scrawled,
among pictures of flowers and trees, the words 'Sweet
Nell'—as I thought. No, it was one word, the name of a
farm—Sweetnell. A small farm neighboring that tract of
land bought up and rather ruthlessly enclosed by Mr. Twelvetree some years ago, as Mr. Devereaux told us. And Mr.
Twelvetree's methods, as Mr. Devereaux also told us, left
many of the small farmers reduced or ruined. I remembered
the text Griggs quoted at his preaching: 'Woe unto them that
join house to house, that lay field to field, till there be no
place . . .' We had come across many people, Sir Edward,
who had reason to dislike or even hate Mr. Twelvetree. But
it turns out that the one who hated him most fiercely, with
all the single-minded passion of his nature, was Henry
Griggs. Sweetnell Farm was the paternal home of Henry and

his brother, the gentle, sensitive Jonathan, with his intense attachment to place and familiar things. There they had worked together, lords of their own little domain, in a quiet and traditional way of life that, I must confess, sounded idyllic. Certainly the impressionable Jonathan seems to have found it so. Then Mr. Twelvetree came along, with his plans for enclosure. Henry, typically, tried to fight him, and lost heavily. Their grazing rights were gone, the cost of enclosure stretched them beyond their limit, even the stream that watered their land was choked at its source. They had to sell up for a song, and leave Sweetnell. Everything was swept away. There was a girl Jonathan liked too, but he had nothing to offer her now. The chief thing, though, was the destruction of that security on which his vulnerable nature depended. Was this small catastrophe—small on the map, though not to him—what turned Jonathan's wits? Certainly his brother thinks so, as he told me yesterday. When Jonathan died in his arms in the small hours of Monday morning, Henry had no doubts where to lay the blame for the slow, sure destruction of his beloved brother.

"This I pieced out with Griggs yesterday, in the cell. He has been wholly frank and truthful, and faces his fate with strength and dignity; his faith does not falter. But on that night when I sat here in the library, what perplexed me as I indulged my speculations was: who, then, was the dead man in the ditch? If he was not a passenger, then who? Well, suppose he was the other party to that bloody transaction—the highwayman himself?

"And then I saw how it might be done. We assume that Tom Honeyman was killed without getting a shot in. Not so. Tom, who was thought by his discontented wife to be—well, really not up to much, showed his mettle that day, though he did not live to glory in it. The coach was held up by a highwayman, as he had dared to hope: James Allerton, the highwayman of Stangate Hole, who had a hideout in the woods; whose attacks were growing fiercer and more desperate, and who had had no pickings for some weeks; and who had plainly got wind of a rich traveler coming his way on board the *Flyer*. Masked and armed, he rides out of his hiding place, calls on the coachman to stop. Stubborn Charles Crabbe will not stop, and tries to drive him down—and is shot through the head for his pains, with one of Allerton's pistols. Allerton had been a soldier, remember. The coach tips into the ditch. Inside, Tom Honeyman is readying himself: his hour has come. Allerton dismounts and approaches the coach window, his other pistol at the ready, calls on whoever's inside to deliver—and Tom promptly shoots him in the face with one of his own pocket pistols. He has done it! Allerton falls back, killed instantly.

"But of course there is another passenger—the outside passenger, Henry Griggs, who has jumped or stumbled into the ditch as the coach tipped. Now he ventures forward to look at the highwayman lying there. Is he dead? says Tom from the coach door, thinking of his hundred pounds. Yes, says Griggs, bending over the body; and with that he takes up Allerton's second pistol, turns, and shoots Tom Honeyman. Not cleanly—the ball goes into Tom's throat—but it is enough to kill him. And now, thinking swiftly, Griggs drags Allerton's body over to the ditch, so that it appears he is the outside passenger. Extricates whatever is in his pockets, if anything, so that there can be no identifying items. He can gamble on a highwayman's being an unknown person—that's the nature of the trade, after all—and besides, the face is much disfigured by the shot. He puts Allerton's pistols into his own pockets. And he pushes Tom back against the seat, placing his hand to his breast pocket with the pistol tucked there. The other pistol, in his hand, he reloads and primes with powder from Tom's flask, so that it shall appear Tom never got a shot off. And he opens the strongbox Tom was carrying, to reinforce the appearance of an attack by a highwayman. Which, of course, it was; but it was the scene of private murder too. And then Griggs mounts Allerton's horse—the badly shod horse we saw him with—and rides on to Huntingdon, and our first meeting with him."

"He thought that the man he had killed, of course, was Twelvetree."

"Of course. Tom had made a great point of identifying himself as the banker. There he was, boarding the coach at Wansford while Griggs looked down on his bewigged head from above, loudly proclaiming his name as Nicholas Twelvetree and fussing over his box. There he was, the man who had only been a distant and unapproachable nemesis to Henry Griggs before now—but a nemesis nonetheless. It was just a couple of days since Henry had held his dying brother in his arms—and now here was the man responsible for all that pain and waste! It must have burned and burned within him as the coach went on. And then, when Allerton held up the coach, and was shot—by Twelvetree, as it seemed to Griggs—then swift possibilities ran through his mind. He was not a man to plan murder. But when he saw a way that he could do it—kill the man who so richly deserved to die, and get away with it—then he was deft, rapid, and sure.

"And when the first repercussions came, he was ready again. We found the name Griggs in the booking records, and summoned him; and immediately he identified the dead outside passenger as his brother Jonathan—who only he knew was buried under a tree in his garden. No one would be any the wiser. In a way it was involving Jonathan in the revenge. And so James Allerton was buried as Jonathan Griggs, and a fruitless hunt began for a highwayman who was already in his grave. But there were two problems for Griggs. One he cannot have thought of as he did the deed, though it surely occurred to him afterward. There had been a woman on the coach as far as Stilton. He did not know her, but he had been courteous to her, handed her down, and so forth. Now it turned out the woman was meant to travel on to her home, and was declared missing, and sought in connection with the investigation. Suppose this woman, hearing about the terrible fate of the *Flyer*, should see him and remember him from the coach? The outside passenger was killed—yet she would be able to identify *him* as the outside passenger. His whole deception would be blown apart. The woman—Margaret Parry—represented a threat to him.

"The other problem must have become apparent when he came to Stamford for the inquest. The man he had killed was not Twelvetree at all! It was an impostor: Tom Honeyman—an innocent man quite unknown to him. God knows what resources Griggs summoned up in himself to meet this blow . . . God knows indeed. I think his faith still sustained him, in some curious way: he had to believe in his own righteousness. Nothing else can have given him the dreadful strength of resolve to kill Margaret Parry in the wood on the edge of Huntingdon. She had come to his preaching, being a woman of religious temperament; and must have recognized the man preaching there so movingly and eloquently as the man from the coach. Strange—what did it mean? He saw her too, drawing close to the cart where he stood. When the meeting broke up he spoke with her. He knew that his preaching had made a profound impression on her, and that he could win her trust, so he simply said that he knew the question that was in her mind, and would explain all, if she would meet him later by the mill. So, innocently, she did; and he killed her. He knew that she was being desperately sought, and must soon come to the authorities' attention, and he could not take the risk. The pistols he had taken from Allerton he now placed in her pockets to further confuse the scent.

"He was lucky again. Margaret was in flight from a violent husband—a man quite capable of killing, though he had successfully concealed his nature behind the mask of respectability. And William Parry was there in Huntingdon that night. He lied, of course, about being in Stamford with his sister—who would always back him up in anything. But though he searched the common, and lingered about Huntingdon all night—watching old Mrs. Fryatt's house, I suspect—he did not find Margaret. And the next time he saw her, she was dead. Terrible irony, that she fled from a cruel man to be killed by a kind one. Yes, fundamentally, Griggs was driven on by a passionate nature. A man of absolutes. Mrs. Parry had no lover, of that I am sure. All that was Parry's viciously jealous nature. If she did not worship him as his sister did, then she must be betraying him; it was as simple as that.

"The other problem for Griggs remained. Twelvetree still lived, and his continued existence made a mock of poor Jonathan's death, and of everything Griggs had been forced to do. The account must be settled . . . but Twelvetree was a very well-guarded man. All Griggs could do was send him a note, threatening vengeance—or justice. Twelvetree, of course, thought it came from Bennett Cornwell, the stepson who hated him, and whose whereabouts were a constant source of fear to him. Bennett had sent threats himself, nearly a year ago—before his reform and conversion to Methodism—he had confessed as much to Griggs—but he would not do such a thing now. Twelvetree, however, didn't know that. He still feared dreadfully what Bennett might do someday. Before being sent to the House of Correction, Bennett had accused him of having something to do with his mother's death, a rumor spread by his resentful ex-clerk, Tom Honeyman, and untrue. But Twelvetree realized how it must look to Bennett, and felt he had an implacable enemy in the young man. And when the *Flyer* was attacked, and a man killed who was *thought* to be Nicholas Twelvetree, he was terrified. It looked like a deliberate deed; it looked as if someone was out to kill him. Was that someone his wild and embittered stepson, returned to the district? So he surrounded himself with armed servants, and sent them out daily to sweep the woods. This included, I think, taking an accidental potshot at me. And when they brought Bennett Cornwell in, and he saw him committed to jail, Twelvetree must have felt the joy of salvation. He even gave his men the rest of the day off. After all, he was safe now.

"And then that night Henry Griggs arrived in Stamford. He had been summoned by Cornwell, who greatly wanted his spiritual services. And in Stamford he found Twelve-tree's menservants everywhere, lurching from inn to inn, standing drinks all round, singing their own praises in the street. Tonight Nicholas Twelvetree, usually so well guarded, was completely unprotected. And so he entered the banker's house, ready to finish what he had started."

"And he had reckoned without meddlesome Mr. Fairfax being there to fight him," Sir Edward said, smiling.

"Well, if it had come to a fight . . . Luckily for me, once I seized him, and he knew the game was up, he surrendered absolutely. It was immediate, as if he was preparing himself, from that moment, for the execution he must face. A man of absolutes, as I said. And he does not fear it, not in the slight-est. Which suggests that he does not fear his judgment on the other side."

Sir Edward nodded soberly. "Who of us can be sure of what he shall meet there . . . Well, you have received the ful-some thanks of Mr. Twelvetree, my dear fellow. How does that feel?"

"Not entirely pleasant," Fairfax laughed. "But—a life is a life."

"By the by, I think I have found a place for your Esther Fryatt, and her sister if she likes. Devereaux is willing to take them into his service, on my recommending. He is a gentle employer, that I can answer for."

"You are very good."

"I don't know . . . I keep thinking about Mrs. Honeyman, and what's to become of her. I suppose she deserves noth-ing, yet she is so very alone."

"Yes . . . yet I doubt she will be for very long." Certainly she had lost Joseph Fox. He had, of course, made no attack on her. He had set off that day to the military camp at Wis-bech, with remorseful thoughts of enlisting as a soldier. In-stead he had got drunk again, had second thoughts, and come back to Stamford the next day. But his association with Barbara Honeyman was over—all the more definitely as there was no pregnancy after all. Fairfax guessed that she had invented it as a means to cleaving Fox to her, and screwing up his courage to kill her husband. That day when she had thrown herself down the stairs, she knew it was all up between them. He had come to the house earlier and pushed through the door the various love notes she had written him. So, she had known then that her vengeful accusation had not worked: Fox had not been arrested. Still she tried one last throw, or fall. If she could not have him she would try and destroy him. It had not worked. Fairfax felt a very small measure of pity. He suspected that she would soon have tired of Fox anyway. She had tired of her older, cerebral, ineffectual husband; to her mind Fox no doubt had promised vitality, romance, a new start. But "new," Fairfax thought, was the crucial word. Once the new became old . . . Well, Barbara was an attractive widow, with a small inheritance. She would be all right. She had a world of novelty before her.

"Well, 'tis a pity you missed the Assembly," Sir Edward said. "Though I didn't dance the hornpipe after all." He looked over Fairfax's shoulder at the catalogue. "You are coming on fast now . . . Not too fast, Fairfax. I hope you will spend Christmas with us."

"Thank you, Sir Edward. I look forward to that."

"But then, come the new year, I suppose you must be off to your new tutoring appointment. Surrey, isn't it? I hope it'll be pleasant for you." Turning over the leaves of a folio, Sir Edward said hesitantly, "An odd sort of life it must be, though, Fairfax, always moving on and never settling in one place."

"Oh, well—it suits me well enough," Fairfax said.

"Hm. Well, I'll leave you. Dinner in half an hour, my friend. And I say again—don't go too fast."

When he had gone Fairfax worked on the catalogue awhile, then laid it aside and drew out the letter he had been looking over for the hundredth time when Sir Edward had walked in.

Dear Mr. Fairfax,

I felt I could not close our Acquaintance without communicating to you—first, my Congratulations on your Success. You found the Truth, and Justice, and for once I have nothing flippant to say: only again, my warmest Admiration. Second, my parting regards. George and I are to leave Stamford. We depart today for Bath, or perhaps Bristol Hotwell—he is undecided—where he hopes for a Cure for his Condition. The Mercury, *and Stamford in general, he says are also deleterious in their Effect upon his Nerves, &c; and he means to sell the Paper and the Dwelling-house attached, to the first Bidder. We will stay away, he says, till the Spring, and then look for new Quarters.*

It means I shall be unable to give you my Regards and good Wishes in Person, and must let this Letter stand for them. I hope you will understand me—at least, I think I hope it—when I say that it is better this way.

Yours in remembrance,
Cordelia Linton

At last Fairfax folded the letter up, and put it in the side pocket of his coat. Then he changed his mind, and put the letter in his breast pocket, where he could feel it, before composing his face to cheerfulness, and going in to dinner.

Visit the notorious gambling dens
of London with Robert Fairfax
in Hannah March's dazzling historical mystery

A Distinction of Blood

Available soon from Signet

Read on for an exciting sneak preview . . .

"I don't know who that fellow is with Lord Mortlock," said a voice in a drawled whisper, "but 'pon my soul, he can no more play whist than I can whistle 'God Save the King' out of my . . ."

The rest of the remark was lost in laughter. Robert Fairfax looked back at the gaming room, but he couldn't tell which of the fops gathered about the green tables had spoken of him thus; and Lord Mortlock was already heading downstairs.

"That was my fault, I fear." Fairfax glanced uneasily at his companion as they came out of White's, the coffeehouse and gambling club in St. James. "The revoke—"

"Aye, that finished us. You played like something of a donkey, Fairfax, but then whist is something of a donkey's game, to my mind. All right as an appetizer to the evening, but the money don't move fast enough for my liking."

The money had certainly moved fast enough for Fairfax, who was still sweating a little at the thought of it. Thirty guineas had disappeared across the green baize in as many minutes. Of course, to the man he had partnered, Lord Mortlock, this was a trifling sum; hundreds and even thousands of pounds were routinely lost by the aristocratic gamblers at White's. Moreover, the money with which Fairfax had played had not been his own. But it still made him shudder to see it go so quickly.

Well, at least that part of his deception called for no pretending. Or perhaps he ought to show more nonchalance. The role that Mr. Appleton had asked him to play tonight was that of a gentleman of ample means with a taste for gaming. If he had a fit of the vapors every time he lost, his companion might suspect he was not all he claimed to be.

But it was a damnably difficult role to carry off. Years ago, before the disgrace of his father and the wreck of his fortune, Fairfax had had a brief taste of being the young man about town: he had diced and drunk and swapped unlikely tales of conquests with other gauche would-be bucks. It was more shadow than substance, however, and even then, when he had been comfortably off and with a gentleman's expectations, Fairfax had known the world in which Lord Mortlock moved only from a wondering distance. Then had come years of impoverishment, ended by the very modest competence he now earned a private tutor. Hardly a preparation for the high life.

And Hugh Mortlock, the fifth Baron Mortlock, lived very high. He had a name for it, although his reputation was not quite as notorious as that of his late father, the fourth baron, known as "Black Peter" because of his vices. Young Lord Mortlock's gambling, wenching, and fighting had kept the town tattle-mongers busy for some years past.

But high living took its toll. Not only on the flesh—and the gaunt gray-eyed man crossing Pall Mall beside Fairfax looked older than his thirty years—but on the purse. The town tattle said that Lord Mortlock was hock deep in debt when, five months ago, he finally took a bride: the daughter of a wealthy merchant who brought to the marriage a pretty face and a settlement of thirty thousand pounds.

A plain enough story of the rake reformed. Or was it?

That was where Fairfax came in. Picking his way across frosted cobbles spattered with refuse, feeling awkward in the unaccustomed finery of gold-laced hat and embroidered coat and red heels, he groaned inwardly at the task his employer had set him. He had never wanted to be an actor or a spy, and here he was a combination of both.

"No, if it's deep play you want, my dear fellow, I'll show you the very place," Lord Mortlock said. He whistled over a linkboy to light their way with his torch; the old London streets east of the squares were dark as tunnels in the March night. "There's not much to be said for the company, and you'll get half a bottle of bad wine if you're lucky, but the play is deep. I've seen men drive up to where we're going in a carriage-and-four, and go away paupers. One fellow memorably gambled away his whole property and ended by asking if anyone would take the value of his children's shoes for wager." He gave a bleak chuckle. "Gaming must be the only occupation in which on can gain fame by utterly losing."

"Well, there is no thrill like risk," Fairfax said. He sounded unconvincing even to himself.

"You've heard of Lady Harriet Froome and her King Street faro bank, I daresay," Lord Mortlock said, striding purposefully after the bare glimmering heels of the linkboy.

"Of course," Fairfax said. "You go often to Lady Harriet Froome's, sir?"

"About as often as I please." Lord Mortlock accompanied the words with a quick doglike exposure of his teeth. Fairfax wondered if that was the closest he ever came to a smile. He wondered also whether his own question had been too obviously inquisitive. Suppose Lord Mortlock guessed that his companion had been sent to spy on him? The man was known to have a short temper—had twice fought duels in his youth, they said. Really, this was a tricky position to be in.

But Fairfax had seen no way out of it. Two days ago he had presented himself as arranged at the London home of Mr. Samuel Appleton, who had engaged him to tutor his two young sons on the recommendation of former employers. The boys, Fairfax had been told, were aged twelve and fourteen, bright and biddable; Mr. Appleton was a man who had risen to wealth, offered a generous salary for a term of at least a year, and had a commodious town house in Leicester Fields as well as a villa in Surrey. All in all a reasonably pleasant prospect for Fairfax, whose life had been fraught with insecurity. But when he arrived, there was no sign of his pupils. They were with an aunt by the sea at Weymouth, Mr. Appleton explained. They had both been rather low with a fever caught at the public school he had sent them to—part of his reason for deciding on a tutor instead—and he preferred to keep them there a further couple of weeks until their health was restored.

So, his presence was not yet required, Fairfax thought with perplexity—and dismay, for his funds were low. But Mr. Appleton, a stocky, soft-spoken, deliberate man in a beautifully curled white wig, did not say that. Mr. Fairfax's room was all prepared, and Mr. Appleton was happy for him to join the household at once. And that first evening at dinner, and after a lot of sober careful talk—measuring him up, Fairfax now realized—Mr. Appleton broached the subject of what he wanted his new employee to do in the interim before his pupils returned. Mr. Appleton put it courteously, considerately, but there was never any question of Fairfax having a choice in the matter, not if he wanted that year's employment and salary.

And now here he was approaching the unsavory purlieus of Covent Garden with Lord Mortlock, whom the gossip sheets had once delighted in calling "one of the wickedest men in England," and about to make a rakish night of it. It was fortunate, in this respect at least, that Robert Fairfax was a congenital insomniac, as Lord Mortlock seldom went home before dawn.

Which was one of the things Mr. Appleton had talked to him about . . .

"The notion I have in mind," Mr. Appleton had said over port on Monday evening, "is to introduce you to Lord Mortlock as an acquaintance of mine, staying with me while you look into possible openings in the West India trade. And that you enjoy gaming and . . . the entertainments of the town.

Yes, that will suffice. From there it should not be difficult to secure an invitation to join Lord Mortlock on one of his . . . nocturnal jaunts."

"And—pardon me, Mr. Appleton—but where am I supposed to have come from?" Fairfax had said, not quite believing what he was hearing.

"Let us say Scotland. Or rather, the north of England."

Well, that was something: at least he was not going to have to prowl the gambling dens of London talking in a broad Scots brogue.

"The deception is but little," Mr. Appleton had gone on. "All you are required to be is a gentleman known to me, who wishes to be acquainted with my son-in-law."

Yes: Mr. Samuel Appleton, with his square hands, soft Bristol speech, and plain snuff brown broadcloth suit, was father-in-law to Lord Mortlock. His pride in the fact was plain. Five months ago his eldest daughter, Charlotte, had stepped up to the altar and united herself—and her family—to the ancient and noble house of Mortlock. She was now mistress of a large estate, Minchin Park, in Gloucestershire, and a West End mansion. Her future children—Mr. Appleton's grandchildren—would bear titles; she herself was Lady Mortlock. Mr. Appleton had pronounced all this with dainty relish, though he seemed to savor the words "Lady Mortlock" most of all.

He saw the picture pretty plainly now. After years of extravagant living, Lord Mortlock needed money. Blood without groats was nothing, as the saying went. Charlotte Appleton had money, and her father would jump at the chance of an alliance with nobility. It was not uncommon for old families to refresh their withered stems in this way. An old story, then.

Whether it was a love match was a different matter. It didn't sound like one, but few people would trouble about that. As long as the couple rubbed along reasonably well together, produced an heir in due time, cut the appropriate social figures, and made no open scandal . . .

Ah. There was the problem.

Pouring more port, folding his clean square hands, and fixing Fairfax with a candid gaze, Mr. Appleton had gone on to explain. All was not well with the marriage which, Fairfax guessed, had been the greatest satisfaction of Samuel Appleton's life.

Of course Mr. Appleton had been aware of his prospective son-in-law's reputation. A rake who mixed with rakes, whose name featured in all the gossip of fashion and vice, who was rumored to have been associated some years back with the infamous Hellfire Club of Sir Francis Dashwood . . . Mr. Appleton waved a hand. These were, after all, authentic credentials of aristocracy. Well-born young blades lived like that, and then they settled down.

The trouble was that Lord Mortlock did not seem to be settling down. He was out every night drinking and gaming. He was scarcely in his new wife's company. He hardly seemed to have altered his conduct at all, except that now there was more money to be spent, and he spent it, with abandon.

And there was worse. Rumor had it that Lord Mortlock preferred to find his amatory pleasures elsewhere . . . and that the new Lady Mortlock, who had taken to her exalted status very readily, was in turn finding consolation for her neglect with someone else.

Fairfax had begun to feel a reluctant admiration for the man who told him this. It must have been hard for Mr. Appleton, having to broach these unpleasant and intimate subjects with someone who was a mere employee.

Of course, as an employee Fairfax could not make the obvious retort: but my dear sir, what did you expect from such a match? Romeo and Juliet?

All the same, the marriage did seem to have run into trouble rather early and rather mysteriously. Mr. Appleton might well feel that the bargain that had cost him so much was not working out as it should. And might want to know why . . .

"Where the devil are you going?" Lord Mortlock said sharply now.

Jolted from his thoughts, Fairfax glanced round. From his younger years as a Grub Street scribbler he knew this district blindfold, and he had just turned almost unconsciously into a narrow court that connected with King Street.

"Er—I have a fancy this is the shortest way."

Lord Mortlock raised his eyebrows. "If you say so. You seem to know London pretty well. Where is it you hail from?"

"Yorkshire. But I've been in London on—several occasions. On business, you know."

"I don't know. I know nothing of business, thank God. And what do you do in Yorkshire? Have you an estate there?"

"I have—property there." Fairfax tried to invent an appropriate name. All he could think of was something like Ramsdyke Grange, which he knew he'd not be able to say with a straight face.

"And very sensibly want to get away from. What a blasted moldering tomb the country is. I haven't been near my place in Gloucestershire for half a year."

"The charming Lady Mortlock has not seen it?"

"How do you know she's charming when you haven't met her? Oh, my precious father-in-law will have said so, of course." Lord Mortlock stepped rangily over a heap of gutter refuse and flashed Fairfax an indecipherable look. "Don't believe everything you hear, Fairfax."

He didn't intend to. But he was going to have to listen carefully, and sift what he heard, if he were to carry out this strange commission from Mr. Appleton.

"It can hardly be my place, of course," Mr. Appleton had said that first evening, "to inquire into my daughter and son-in-law's—affairs. That is why I have need of a confidential agent, who can freely enter their circle, observe, judge, and—

"Report back?" Fairfax had suggested.

"Precisely." Mr. Appleton offered a tortoiseshell snuff-box, took a pinch, and sneezed pleasurably. "I see nothing underhand in this—not really. I am simply concerned that this most auspicious union should fulfill its promise. We live in an age of luxury and temptation, Mr. Fairfax, and one cannot expect old heads on young shoulders. But the wisdom of seniority may perhaps offer the needed guidance and direction, when the time is right."

So. Find out what Lord Mortlock does with his nights. If he gambles, how much, and with whose money. If he's seeing another woman, who. If he is already estranged from his bride, why. Once he had the information Mr. Appleton would presumably do the rest. Sorting out one recalcitrant couple would, Fairfax supposed, be a simple matter for a man who owned a large chunk of Jamaica as well as the hundreds of men who labored on it.

"You are a man of genteel education, Mr. Fairfax, and report speaks of you as a man of delicacy and discretion. I rely on your being so," Mr. Appleton said, and for the first time his forthright gaze wavered. He picked at some crumbs on the tablecloth. "Particularly in the matter of my daughter. If you should learn anything that suggests she has allowed herself to be . . . swayed by the attentions of an unprincipled seducer, then I shall want to know of it, of course. But discretion must be absolute, sir."

He was therefore to find out whether the wife was erring as well as the husband. But why so mealy-mouthed about it? Fairfax thought maliciously; where was this sensitivity when it came to the slave market? Well, never mind. Lord Mortlock, at any rate, was to be his first quarry.

SIGNET

First in the Georgian Mystery Series

By Hannah March

The Complaint of the Dove

It is private tutor Robert Fairfax's mission to see that troublesome Matthew Hemsley matures into a fine, young gentleman and that he comes to no harm during his first season in London. But Matthew is soon smitten with Miss Lucy Dove, the toast of Covent Garden's stage. And when Lucy is found strangled, Matthew is found on her doorstep in a drunken blackout. Now Fairfax must save his young pupil—for, unless the real murderer is caught, Matthew will surely hang.

0-451-20880-3

Available wherever books are sold, or
to order call: 1-800-788-6262

S823

SIGNET

COMING IN DECEMBER 2003
FROM SIGNET MYSTERY

MURDER BETWEEN THE COVERS
A Dead-End Job Mystery
by Elaine Viets   0-451-21081-6

Helen Hawthorne has a new dead-end job "off the books" at a bookstore in Fort Lauderdale...until the owner is murdered. But since the arrogant Page Turner III had so many enemies, Helen will have to read between the lines to uncover the truth about a clever killer.

THE CHOCOLATE FROG FRAME-UP
A Chocoholic Mystery
by JoAnna Carl   0-451-20985-0

Lee McKinney and her aunt debut their latest confections—chocolate frogs—at TenHuis Chocolade. The first customer to buy a croaker is the town crank. But when he later disappears and police suspect foul play, it's a chocolate clue that leads Lee to the killer. Includes delicious chocolate trivia!

**Available wherever books are sold, or
to order call: 1-800-788-6262**

Penguin Group (USA) Inc.
Online

Your Internet gateway to a virtual environment with
hundreds of entertaining and enlightening books
from Penguin Group (USA) Inc.

*While you're there, get the latest buzz on
the best authors and books around—*

Tom Clancy, Patricia Cornwell, W.E.B. Griffin,
Nora Roberts, William Gibson, Robin Cook,
Brian Jacques, Catherine Coulter, Stephen King,
Ken Follett, Terry McMillan, and many more!

**Penguin Group (USA) Inc. Online is located at
http://www.penguin.com**

PENGUIN GROUP (USA)INC. NEWS

Every month you'll get an inside look at our upcom-
ing books and new features on our site. This is an
ongoing effort to provide you with the most
up-to-date information about
our books and authors.

Subscribe to Penguin Group (USA) Inc. News at
http://www.penguin.com/newsletters